Being Fiction

T. G. Sparrow

Contents

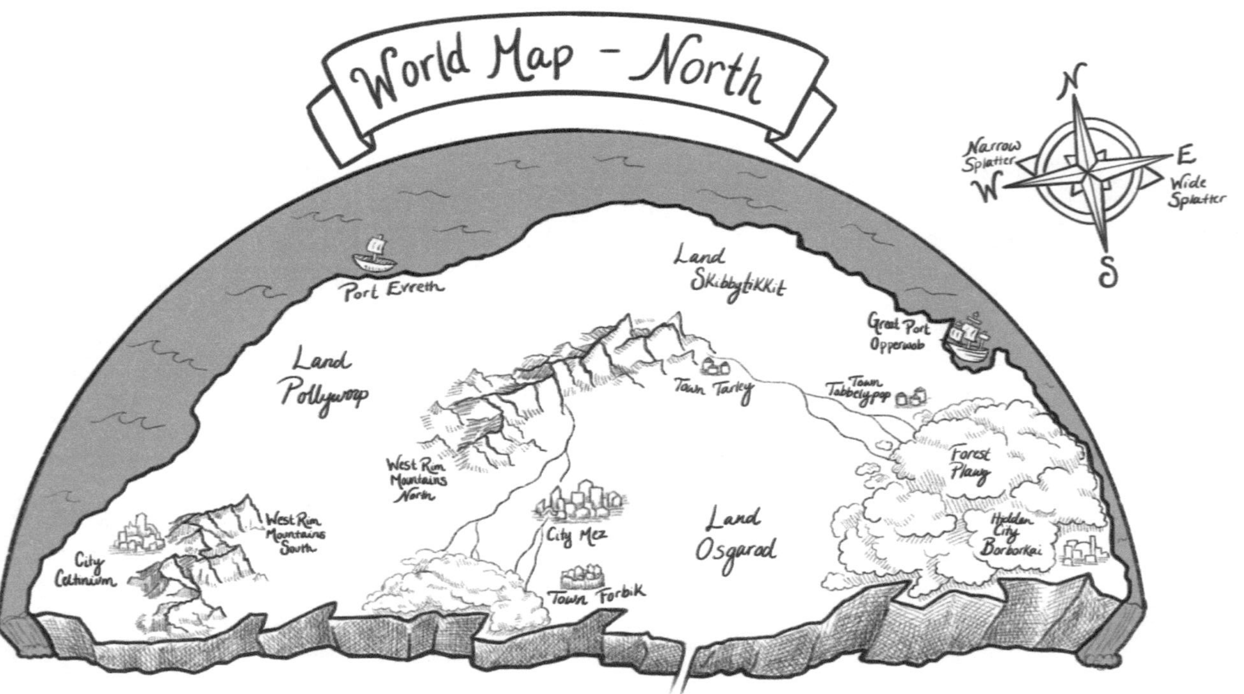

World Map - North
N
E
S
W
Narrow Splatter
Wide Splatter
Port Evreth
Land Skibbytikkit
Great Port Oppernob
Land Pollywoop
Town Tarley
Town Tabbelypop
West Rim Mountains North
City Mez
Forest Plang
West Rim Mountains South
Land Osgarad
Hidden City Borborkai
City Celtinium
Town Forbik

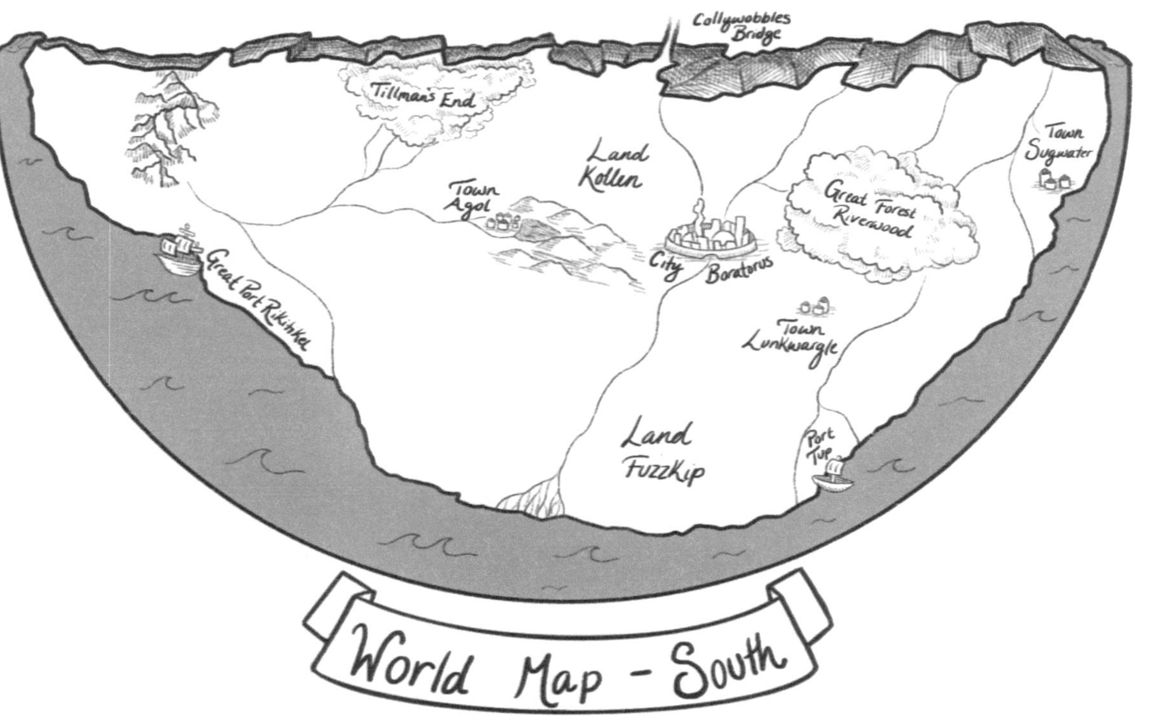

Collywobbles Bridge
Tillman's End
Town Sugwater
Land Kollen
Great Forest Riverwood
Town Agol
City Boratorus
Great Port Rikihka
Town Lunkwargle
Land Fuzzkip
Port Tup
World Map - South

Chapter 1

First Encounters

On a hill beside Berrywood Lane stood a tree that wished above all else to see the world and explore its many natural wonders.

Which was unfortunate.

It was a tree.

But despite the tree's nature as a stationary being, Tree—for that was their name—held to the hope that they would, one day, achieve their dream. Other creatures could move, after all. Why should Tree be any different?

And though there are numerous perfectly reasonable answers to that question, in the cozy days of Tree's fiftieth summer, that wish took its first bold step toward reality.

Then it took several more steps, picked up the pace, and started to get away from itself.

It began with a boy named Gilbert.

Gilbert was on the prowl for a decent spot to crack into the long-overdue sixth rereading of his favorite fantasy trilogy, complete with elves, dwarves, wizards, rings, and frightening copyright implications. Only a few weeks remained of summer, and he hoped to finish all three books before his senior year.

It had been a warm few months, but today's breeze was ample and cool, and Gilbert was happy to take advantage of Tree's shade. With his back to

Tree's bark and his book in hand, he savored the weather before digging in to the story.

Then the world began to shake.

For quite some time, all Gilbert could manage was a weak, confused mutter. Then, after standing up and failing to identify the source of the growing rumble, he asked a question to no one in particular.

"What on earth is happening?"

Tree had a similar question and was pleased to hear Gilbert was on the same page.

Gilbert scanned the ground for clues but found none. After one particularly zealous quake, he dropped his book, bent to pick it up, and—

Crack!

The sound was almost an echo, disguised among the splintering tremors of the atmosphere, but it had power. It wrenched Gilbert up and forced him to stand, arms raised, tense and horribly rigid. His feet touched the ground but held far less weight than usual. By the feel of things, his fingers were picking up the slack, stretched, pulling him upward.

Crack!

This one was louder, piercing the air like thunder. Gilbert's hair stood on end, ready to tear out entirely. A twisting pain crept through the bottom of his feet into his ankles and legs. Gilbert remained impossibly, unwillingly still. There was nobody nearby, but he cried for help nonetheless.

The third crack came with vigor. It smashed against the inside of Gilbert's skull like a war hammer. Again and again, the sound returned, each pulse louder and harder than before, until finally, Gilbert collapsed.

He found no ground to land on.

His body writhed in a tortured blur as pain turned to panic. The world he knew melted away, an endless torrent of dripping color. Then there was darkness.

He joined it.

Gilbert's body crumbled, and all sensation fled into the emptiness around him. Soon, nothing remained but his unseeing consciousness, and even that seemed at risk of dissolving into the soulless black.

And then it was over, and Gilbert was sitting perfectly still on a cold metal floor, completely unharmed, in a round room he had never seen before in his life.

He had several important questions at that moment but no satisfactory way to articulate a single one of them.

"Woo-hoo!" came the voice of an old man.

Gilbert looked up. The speaker was one of the two figures standing on a stage by the opposite wall. He had dark skin, white hair, and a gray beard that brushed the floor. His nose hooked downward and came to a point just above the excited grin that dominated most of his face. He wore white gloves, turquoise shoes, and a lengthy robe that looked, for all intents and purposes, like a rainbow turned dressing gown. "Can you believe it?" He turned to his partner and jumped. "Only six tries!"

"Brilliant work, Professor!" said the second man. He was vaguely spherical, about half the height of his companion, and by the looks of it, half the age as well. His robe was dark blue with small flecks of white, and his gloves were murky gray. He had wavy black hair, which he had done his best to comb, and a pair of massive glasses only slightly larger than the rest of his face. "Where did the tree come from?"

Gilbert looked up.

Tree had come along too.

"I don't know," said the elder man, curious. "It certainly isn't a wodowood. Seems more like an ash to me. But never mind that. Look at the boy! The Hero! We've done it!"

Gilbert turned away. Those two people definitely should not exist. This whole *place* should not exist. Doing his best to ignore that fact, he tried to figure out where he was. He was supposed to be on a hill. He knew that much. This room...this room was strange. The floor was red metal, laced with concentric golden circles that sparkled in the sunlight from two windows near the ceiling. The walls were made of brick. The impossible people, on their impossible stage, stood before a mahogany podium, which held a massive brown tome. Behind them, a bookshelf overflowed with loose papers and parchment.

None of it made any sense. Gilbert didn't feel as though he'd lost his mind. He felt as if he'd shredded it, then lost whatever pieces remained.

"He's very quiet," said the old man. "Do you think he can understand us?"

The younger man shrugged and turned to Gilbert. "HELLO! CAN. YOU. HEAR. WHAT. I. AM. SAYING?"

Gilbert, who was still trying to re-collect his metaphorical brain matter, didn't respond.

"I suppose not," the younger concluded.

"Such a shame," said the elder. "Just imagine what wisdom, what magnificent intellect, must be trapped deep in that brilliant mind."

Gilbert blinked.

"A surprising oversight, I must say," continued the elder. "What language do they speak in Land Turmentarp?"

"The same as us, I thought, but I've never been. We'll have to ask Toddleposter."

"Perhaps tomorrow, then. In the meantime, maybe hand gestures?"

Both of them looked at their gloved hands, evidently considering how to proceed, until finally, despite his considerable bafflement, Gilbert spoke.

"Um..." he said, and then, after a pause, "Who are you? And where am I?"

The two men jumped back.

"Would you look at that!" The elder beamed.

The younger wiggled his glasses. "He cannot understand our language, yet he speaks it so fluently!"

"What? No. I was…I can…uh…" Gilbert paused. With every word he spoke, the old man leaned farther and farther forward. His beard now dangled off the edge of the stage and brushed the ground below.

"Well"—the elder stood up again—"*fluent* may be a strong word, but all the same, it is a fascinating phenomenon. I wonder if—"

"I can understand you," said Gilbert.

The elder stopped. "Oh? Why didn't you say so earlier?"

"I was confused. I still am. Where am I? And who are you?"

"Ah, yes. Introductions! I am Mardulo Vot Ponterous the Brilliant." The old man flourished and bowed. "The young man next to me is my pupil, Bundersquash Borum Balbagoose the Studious."

Gilbert shook his head. It was still a little fuzzy. "Come again?"

"I am Mardulo Vot Ponterous the Brilliant," he said more loudly. "The young man next to me is my pupil, Bundersquash Borum Balbagoose the Studious. And you," he continued, "must be Pottleswee Plugg Thudigarde the Brave!"

Tree, had anyone bothered to ask, would have gladly introduced themselves as "Tree."

"I'm Pottle…huh?" Gilbert was beginning to think he should call for help, but he'd left his phone at home.

"Goodness me, you are a tad hard of hearing, aren't you?" said Mardulo.

"Indeed, that would seem to be the case," Bundersquash agreed.

Gilbert stood. "My name is Gilbert."

Mardulo hesitated. "Come again?"

"My name is Gilbert Betters. Where am I?"

"Blast!" Mardulo huffed poignantly. "So, it hasn't worked after all."

"Excuse me?" said Gilbert.

"We'll have to try again, I suppose." Mardulo riffled through the tome on the podium.

"We'll need more worm tusks," said Bundersquash. "Maybell closed early for the festival. Perhaps tomorrow?"

Mardulo sighed. "Yes, all right. I suppose one evening's delay won't kill anyone. Well, probably not...what do we do with him?" He waved at Gilbert.

"I suppose we'll have to send him home," said Bundersquash. "And the tree, for that matter. Workshop maintenance won't be happy about that."

"Where are you from, Gigglebrit?"

"Gilbert," Gilbert corrected.

The old man scrunched his brow. "You're from Gilbert?"

"No. My *name* is Gilbert."

Mardulo chuckled sympathetically. "The poor fellow thinks we're still on introductions."

Gilbert decided there were more pressing issues at hand—like getting home and, with any luck, far away from these two. He rolled his eyes and answered their question.

"Maystown, Nebraska."

Mardulo and Bundersquash looked at him patiently. Gilbert frowned, unsure how much more information they needed. "Um...the United States?" No response. "Earth?" he finished lamely.

"Who is that?" asked Mardulo.

"What?"

"Earth. Who is Earth?" Mardulo spoke up.

"It's a place. My home."

"Your who, now?"

"Where I am from. Earth. You know, the Milky Way?"

"Never heard of Earth," said Bundersquash.

"Perhaps he means Evreth? Do you mean Evreth?"

"No! I mean Earth! Maystown, Nebraska—just outside of Lincoln."

"Who is Maystown?"

"I have a friend named Maistowne," said Bundersquash. "Perhaps her?"

"What does she have to do with anything?" Mardulo scratched his head.

"Maybe she knows who Earth is. Would you like me to fetch Maistowne for you, Gigglebrit?"

Gilbert opened his mouth to speak, then shut it again. He was at a total loss. Was this some kind of dream? It had to be. More than likely, he'd simply fallen asleep atop that hill. He pinched himself. Nothing happened.

"Gigglebrit?" said Bundersquash. "Would you like me to fetch Maistowne?"

"Er, no..." said Gilbert, and then, "Where's the exit?"

"It's the hatch, just over there." Bundersquash pointed to a small handle in the floor, next to a bunch of Tree's roots. "Careful on the way down. It can be tricky."

Gilbert lifted the handle. A wooden ladder dropped almost twenty stories straight down into a bare stone tunnel. The air below was cool and still. A pale light illuminated the colorless landing. It smelled musty.

With a flicker of doubt, Gilbert looked at the two men onstage, then the unbalanced ladder below. He did a quick calculation of risk...and began his descent.

"Now hold on just one minute, Gigglebrit," said Mardulo. It was a kind request, not forceful, but Gilbert obeyed.

"Yes?" he inquired, his head poking up from the floor.

"We have to get you home!" Mardulo turned to the bookcase. "I'm sure we have a spell in here somewhere."

Bundersquash came down from the stage and helped Gilbert back up.

"Returning to Evreth, yes?"

"No, Earth. Preferably Nebraska, please. But hang on a second..." Curiosity was beginning to get the better of him. As ridiculous as these people were, there *was* a certain element of magic about them, and something must have brought him to this room.

Gilbert had always wished for a real world of magic and wizardry. If there was ever a time to believe, this may as well be it.

He faced Mardulo. "Did you say *spell*?"

"Yes. Spell. Don't worry, nothing too painful...well, I suppose I can't promise that, but people generally survive these things." He thought for a moment. "This one shouldn't kill anything, anyway." He continued with reinvigorated confidence. "Now, here we are! Third-Party Teleport to Evreth! Come, come, Gigglebrit. You'll have to hold my hand. Bundersquash can say the words. Mind the branches."

"I am not from Evreth." Gilbert enunciated as clearly as possible. "I am from *Earth*."

Bundersquash looked at him. "And where is Earth?"

A wave of relief washed over Gilbert. It was a small victory, but he had to take what he could get.

Of course, he also had to answer the question.

"Um," he hesitated. "In space?"

Gilbert grimaced at the absurdity of his own answer, but the others didn't seem fazed. In fact, they came alight with excitement and headed to the bookshelf, blabbering away. They scanned through book after book, tossing them aside one by one.

"Does the interplanar void count as space?" Bundersquash held up a book four sizes too big and several shades blacker than darkness.

"Hmm..." Mardulo stroked his beard. "That is a good question. Do take note of it. I think it could make an exciting paper. A good candidate for the Sugwater Symposium next year! Assuming we can wrap up this Hobblebosh business."

"Oh, that would be lovely!" Bundersquash bounced to his feet, grabbed a feather quill from inside his robe, then scribbled in the air. A parchment materialized in front of him. The quill strokes grazed its surface in gentle, fire-red streaks that glowed hot for a moment before fading to an ashen gray.

Gilbert jumped, jaw unhinged. Magic! That was *actual magic*! He'd seen it with his own two eyes.

Tree panicked. Fire! That was fire!

"Excuse me," Gilbert blurted. "How did you do that?"

"Do what?" Bundersquash stopped writing and faced Gilbert. The parchment disappeared as he turned away.

Tree relaxed.

"The thing. With the quill. The magic!"

"Oh, this?" He held it up, grinning, clearly eager to discuss his work. "It's my own creation, actually! I use a tethering spell to link it to some parchment in my workspace, then use the writing motion as an activation sequence. Not complicated once you sort out the appropriate application of Balsog's Association Mechanism."

The elder wizard looked at his student with a touch of pride. "It was the very project that allowed him to graduate from Advanced Wizardry Intelligence Training and become my very own pupil."

Bundersquash blushed.

"Can I try?" asked Gilbert.

The two looked at him, then each other, then shrugged.

"I don't see why not..." said Bundersquash, offering the quill.

In a motion to rival that of an off-balance kangaroo, Gilbert tripped over several roots, floundered onto the stage, and almost rammed full speed into the wizards. His hand jittered as he grabbed the quill and started to write.

"Okay. It may be a little difficult to get—" Bundersquash stopped short. Gilbert was already scribbling away. In seconds, the parchment materialized. The quill's strokes released the same fiery figures Gilbert had seen before.

"Or not..." Bundersquash recovered.

"A true natural!" said Mardulo.

But Gilbert wasn't listening. Up close, he saw lavender sparks sear the page as the quill passed across its surface, leaving red-hot streaks in its wake.

Hello. Hi. Words and stuff. Oh wow it's actually working! This is so cool! I'm doing magic! Real magic! No one is ever going to believe this back home! But who even cares?! Wow! THIS IS AMAZING!!

And then, as the letters cooled, Gilbert noticed they were shifting. The enchantment was attempting to correct his words, make his handwriting neater, and enforce a rigorous spelling-and-grammar-correction scheme! It even inserted a comma.

"How do you do the letter-shift thing?!" Gilbert shouted at Bundersquash.

"That is a fantastic question!" Bundersquash's voice rose to match Gilbert's. If he wasn't excited before, he certainly was now. "It's actually unrelated to the quill. It's on the parchment! One of Mardulo's enchantments. He calls it the Writing Auto-Intelligence Charm. Brilliant, brilliant work, if I do say so myself—and I do. I've been studying the topic and hope to apply a similar principle in my own project, improving the speech-interpretation module of my real-time voice-to-illustration device."

Mardulo shook his head. "I keep telling Bundersquash my charm isn't sophisticated enough to handle the structural variations common in vocal input, but he refuses to listen."

"Nonsense, Professor. You underestimate your own spellwork. The initial trials were hopeful! Here, Gigglebrit, read this if you're interested. It's truly fascinating stuff."

He handed Gilbert a book with a solid forest-green cover and a title written in silver letters: *From the Ablative to Zeugma: A Complete Dissection of Language and Literacy.*

Gilbert, who knew nothing of ablatives nor zeugmas, thanked Bundersquash, nonetheless. He had never been one for studying languages, but perhaps he could make an exception, just this once.

The wizards turned back to the bookshelf.

"You know," said Gilbert, "I don't have to return home straightaway. I don't want to be a burden, and if there are spells and things here...well, I'd be happy to stay for a while."

"Not to worry," said Mardulo. "We can't summon Pottleswee until tomorrow anyway. We'll have you home in a jiffy. Now, where were we? Ah, yes. Portal to Evreth! Tell me, are you particularly attached to those clothes?"

Chapter 2

On Obble Dor Hobblebosh

They were several layers deep into the bookshelf, but despite several re-minders that Earth was, in fact, Earth and not Evreth or Birth or a singer named Urth, they hadn't made much progress.

Gilbert had stopped caring. There was a new world to explore! His mind fluttered madly between ancient tomes, treatises on potion making, and step-by-step guides on spellwork. While they continued searching, Gilbert hoarded every book he could find.

Bundersquash had taken a brief break from the bookshelf and was run-ning around the room like a maniac. He had opened a thick maroon book titled *Demonic Rituals in Automata*, which had burst to life and launched into the air with a few powerful flaps of its cover. Now it was chanting in a strange language, darting between Tree's branches, taunting the mere mortals below.

There was a slight chance it was summoning a demon.

"Please keep the noise down, Bundersquash," said Mardulo, trying to read some scribbled notes in *The Way of Frogs*.

"Sorry, Professor!" Bundersquash panted. "I think it's getting tired!"

"Can I help?" asked Gilbert, hoping to learn some kind of spell—a trapping spell, perhaps, or a calming one.

"Oh, no. Don't worry." Bundersquash put his hands on his knees. "I wouldn't want to be a bother. Besides, it's flying lower now..."

He thought for a moment, then grabbed an abrasively purple blanket from under the podium and charged at the book with a ferocious roar.

Demonic Rituals in Automata was not prepared for the heavily bespectacled cannonball that was Bundersquash, and before it could take flight and flee, it was trapped under the blanket—its taunts reduced to nothing more than smothered grumbles.

Bundersquash grinned triumphantly.

"Good thinking with the blanket." Mardulo gave his pupil an approving nod, then returned to the frogs.

"Is it an enchanted blanket?" asked Gilbert hopefully.

"No." Bundersquash returned the book to its shelf. "Just purple."

"What?"

"Aha!" Mardulo shouted. "I knew the leonis toad was technically a frog! Those buffoons on floor ten owe me an ice cream."

"I'll be sure to let them know," said Bundersquash. Then, with a guilty glance at Gilbert, "Any progress on Earth?"

"Unfortunately, no," said Mardulo.

"Nothing in the climate map?"

"Just the main continent."

Mardulo added the book to their looming heap of examined material and picked up an old catalogue with an entry on Urth's Greatest Hits. "Did you know, she won seven awards during her first two years of singing? Now she's on tour, stopping by Great Port Rikitikel in a few days. But of course, we're looking for Earth. Sorry, Gigglebrit."

And so their work continued. Book by book, they trawled the shelves. Mardulo and Bundersquash discussed their favorite characters in *The Telmore Barrows*. There was a great fuss over the importance of transdimensionality in the context of sensory reality. And for a brief time, they fawned over an author named Sogmordigan Tonder Poddlepots the Wondering. But they found no sign of Earth.

"Elusive little place, isn't it?" said Mardulo. "Perhaps we should ask Lady Ufferbub and Toddleposter. They're good with this sort of thing."

Bundersquash put his book down. "I think that would be best."

"To the library, then!" Mardulo got to his feet. "Gigglebrit, you can leave those here. We'll pick them up later." He waved at Gilbert's collection of books.

Gilbert bit his lip. "Can I keep them, actually? Just for a little while…I know you're trying to help, but I really am happy to stay for a bit. You two seem like you have work to do, anyway. This Pottle-Whatever-Person—why don't you work on summoning them, and I'll just hang around, maybe read these books, see a bit of the world?"

"Nonsense," said Mardulo. "We brought you here. It's our duty to get you back. Besides, we need more worm tusks to summon Pottleswee, and we can't get those until tomorrow."

"But don't you need to…I don't know…fix the spell or something? I assume you didn't intend to summon *me*. And didn't you say I was the sixth attempt?"

"Well, now that you mention it…" Mardulo stroked his beard. "No, no. We ought to go to the library. I'm sure we can fix the spell afterward." He looked at Gilbert and softened. "But perhaps we'll take the scenic route."

"Can I keep the books, at least?"

"You can," said Mardulo. "Though it's rather a lot to carry. It may be easier to summon them once we arrive."

"Summon?" Gilbert grinned. "That does sound fun!"

He tried to arrange the books into a neatly organized stack near the podium, but the bent covers, bulging notes, and varied shapes and sizes made it impossible. Instead, he settled on a lopsided heap and joined the wizards, who were arguing.

"He's young. He's agile," said Mardulo. "What's the worst that could happen?"

"Has he ever done it before?" asked Bundersquash.

"Done what?" asked Gilbert, approaching the exit hatch.

Mardulo turned to him. "A short-distance vertical self-teleport. I suspect no one's used this ladder in years. It may be a tad rickety."

"I have not," Gilbert admitted, "but I'd love to learn!"

"You see, Bundersquash?" said Mardulo. "Enthusiasm! What more do you need? You can come with me, Gigglebrit. Just grab my hand and brace your mind for a little tenth-dimensional vertigo. We'll veer splatterbound due to a slight exterior lean in the tower. But if you keep the core principles in mind and shift your directional wiring as you cross the corporality barrier and reemerge post relocation weighting, you should come out in one piece."

Gilbert stared at him. "Um. Sorry. Can you repeat that? Something about location weighting?"

"When you cross the corporality barrier and reemerge post relocation weighting, I'll need you to shift the directional wiring within your central positioning focus in accordance with the third principle. Otherwise, we'll throw off the lean and split ourselves."

"Right..." said Gilbert slowly. "I think, actually, I do need a bit more training before we try the teleport. Maybe the ladder for now?"

Mardulo stroked his beard, then shrugged. "As you wish."

Gilbert went first, trying not to look at the solid stone floor some twenty-odd stories below. The wood creaked ominously with every step and only increased its protests when the wizards joined in.

The air cooled as he lowered. When he finally reached the bottom, there wasn't much to see. It was a small room—cold, unfurnished, and unadorned, except for a notepad hanging on the door. The walls were rough stone, shaded an uneven gray, and the stale air was doing its best to match. The sole light slithered in through the cracks around the doorway, accompanied by a muffled liveliness, which only made the room feel quieter.

In that brief solitude, Gilbert found time to think. He *would* have to go home eventually. His family and friends would miss him, and he would certainly miss them. But this was the real thing! An actual fantasy world, with magic and wizards and flying books. There were probably even dragons somewhere! How could he leave a place like that?

Surely, no one would begrudge him a few days.

Besides, there was always the possibility that time worked differently here. That's how most stories resolved this sort of thing. More than likely, he'd return home and find that no time had passed at all.

In which case, maybe he could afford to stay longer...

Mardulo skipped the last few rungs of the ladder and dropped from the ceiling, looking incredibly pleased with himself. "Take that, ladder! Get your exercise in for the day, Bundersquash?"

"I'd say so." Bundersquash hit the floor, then fixed his glasses and gave his hair a quick pat down, which did very little. "A few of the rungs were wobbly. We may want to report that to maintenance."

"Yes, and the tree while we're at it," said Mardulo, dusting off his beard.

Bundersquash nodded, then scribbled something on the notepad at the door. The text vanished as he wrote it.

Mardulo turned to Gilbert. "Next time, we'll teach you the teleport. I'm sure it won't take long. What experience do you have?"

"With magic? None."

"None?! But you seem so keen!"

"Earth doesn't really have magic," said Gilbert.

Mardulo ruffled his eyebrows. "What do you mean, it doesn't *have* magic."

"It just...doesn't exist there? Or doesn't work. Or something."

The two wizards stepped back toward the wall, as if Gilbert might be contagious.

Bundersquash spoke with surprising urgency. "You don't mean to say...has Hobblebosh already conquered your land?"

"What?"

"Obble Dor Hobblebosh! He's conquered Earth?"

"This is dire news," said Mardulo. "Is he moving again? Gigglebrit, how far north is Earth?"

Gilbert refused to even acknowledge that question. "Who is Obble Dor Hobblebosh?"

"Who is—" Mardulo shot him a disbelieving look. "You must have heard of him..."

"I have not," said Gilbert defensively.

"Obble Dor Hobblebosh?"

"Nope."

"Big, tall, green? Used to be a lime."

"I...what?"

"You really don't know?"

"No!"

"But if he's already conquered your homeland, how did you escape?"

"I didn't *escape*. You brought me here! And no one called Hubblebush has ever conquered Earth."

Mardulo stroked his beard. "Well, if Earth really is this out of touch, we have a lot to catch you up on! I recommend we explain along the way."

"Sure," said Gilbert. "Whatever you say."

"Now tell me, have you ever been to the wizard's city?"

"Almost certainly not."

"Well then"—Mardulo gestured for Bundersquash to open the door—"let me be the first to introduce you to City Boratorus!"

The door swung open with a pouring of light, and the busy sounds of a crowded city bloomed from the murmurs heard before. Gilbert stepped out, setting aside his frustrations for the moment. As his eyes adjusted to the brilliant sunlight, he beheld a world wonderfully alive with the everyday happenings of an unknown culture.

It was a lovely evening—warm, with a breeze—not unlike the weather back home. The sky was clear, and a purple haze shimmered along the horizon. The buildings were made of brightly colored stone and wood, with slate-tiled roofs of red, purple, and blue. They varied wildly in size and shape but managed to fit into the tangled pattern of the streets below. The roads were dirt, lined with cobbled walks on either side. Black metal streetlamps sprung crookedly from the ground, holding unlit candles at their peaks. There were shops in many of the buildings and merchant carts parked along the walkways. Salespeople cried out to pedestrians, and carriages rattled clumsily through the roads, pulled by an assortment of strange-looking creatures.

Much to Gilbert's relief, the air smelled fresh—not of excrement tossed from windows or sewage in the water, but of clean grass, baked bread, and a hint of roasted meat.

The people were more varied than those of Earth, particularly in size and color. They ranged from two to ten feet tall and filled the rainbow with their eyes, hair, and skin. Some looked so light on their feet it was a wonder they touched the ground at all. Others risked cracking the pavement with every step. Dozens of animals, too, danced through the city and sky, calling to each other with a variety of voices, melding into the city's constant rhythm of rickety wooden wheels and muddled conversation.

"Awful nuisance, this lot," said Mardulo, rather spoiling the mood.

Bundersquash, seeing Gilbert's shocked expression, tried to explain. "It's the final day of the Summer's Dance Parade. It usually isn't this crowded. For the festival, the attending towns send gifts. Town Agol said they have no time for such trivialities, of course. They're working on some big secret project no one knows anything about, though we think it has something to do with chopping trees. But Sugwater contributed an expansive collection of unusual reading glasses. Port Tup provided a generous catering of clam chowder, and Lunkwargle sent their usual assortment of gryphons." He pointed to a large feathered thing in the sky. "The professor is upset because Great Port Rikitikel came with a basket of candied honeysuckle instead of fireworks."

"Oh," said Gilbert, feeling slightly overwhelmed. "Gryphons?" He was also curious about candied honeysuckle but was quickly learning that, with Mardulo and Bundersquash, it was best to move one question at a time.

"Yes," said Bundersquash. "Untamed, they have a penchant for trouble, but if you can find a good one and teach it well, they make for lovely companions. Loyal too. Of course, you'd need a barn to keep it in. Does Earth have barns?"

"We do have those."

"Ah, well, you're halfway there, then!" Bundersquash grinned and locked the door to their tower. It held two wooden signs: one larger, with "Wizards' Workshop 4C" written in careful, deliberate lettering, and the other, hastily scribbled: "Reserved through 15:00, 02 July, A.o.t. Empty Box."

The workshop itself was tall, thin, and frighteningly unbalanced. It grew from the ground in a crooked column. A wide disk-shaped room sat at the top. Gilbert presumed that was where he'd arrived. The roof was red and pointed, with a bent brick chimney poking off one side.

Gilbert considered the physical implications of such a lopsided building, marveling at how straight his descent on the ladder had seemed...then thought better of undergoing any deeper inquiry, turned around, and jogged to catch up to the wizards.

"Thus, one can see how the shift in citric energy could be the root cause of the problem," said Mardulo, stroking his beard. "Though I admit it seems unlikely."

Bundersquash looked thoughtfully into the distance. "We would have to run some tests, but it could be an issue of scale. Most protections against physical action have a threshold of force they can withstand before snapping. I suspect his is simply higher than most—well beyond anything a human could exert."

"Perhaps." Mardulo turned as Gilbert caught up. "Hello again! We were just discussing Hobblebosh."

"Ready to explain who he is?"

"Indeed," said Mardulo with a smile. "We'll make an informed citizen of you yet, Gigglebrit!"

The elderly wizard cleared his throat. "Obble Dor Hobblebosh is a tyrant. He is the result of some magical experimentation gone...well, gone a little too correctly, I suppose. Corregal Dorbus Forp the Supreme made a massive breakthrough in the field of transfiguration when he discovered how to turn a nonhuman object—in this case, a lime, which had something to do with the rind composition—into a fully grown and conscious human. Unfortunately, that human was Hobblebosh, and Hobblebosh is a raving monstrosity with an appetite for world domination. And somehow, he's managed to become one of the world's most powerful magic wielders to boot."

Gilbert nodded. Lime or not, a powerful, evil dictator seemed in line with his fantasy-world expectations.

"He quickly seized control of every town and city in the northern half of the continent," Mardulo continued, "and he's been raising an army in the process. The trouble is, somewhere along the line, he learned how to block spellcasting within his own territory! *He* can still cast spells, of course, but he's the only one who can.

"Most recently, he took up residence in Town Forbik. He's been there for about a month. We managed to put a stop to his expansion using a special enchantment on the Narrow Stride. But it has its limits, and who knows how long before he finds a way past them. We'd like to be ready when he does."

Gilbert's mind was lagging behind a few sentences, but he understood the key points. "So, Hobblebosh, a lime turned human, is trying to take over the world. And you said he removed magic?"

"Something like that. During his expansion, he figured out how to prevent the generation of auric nebulas, a key component to any spellcasting. He has not removed magic, per se—amulets, charms, glamours, lorilell dust, those still work—but you cannot cast any new spells in his lands because the auric nebula cannot form. It is one of the reasons he conquered City Mez so easily. He'd lost the element of surprise but made up for it three times over with that blasphemous trick. Wizards all over the city were having a complete crisis of confidence."

Gilbert was now operating at about 50 percent comprehension. A lot of the jargon was going over his head, but that was to be expected when you first entered a fantasy world. He could always find an encyclopedia later, or perhaps an appendix.

Mardulo took a deep breath. "So, in summary," he said, "limes are nasty little blighters and not the sort of thing you want turning into people if you can help it. Of course, we can't blame Corregal for that. How could he have known?"

Gilbert shrugged.

"Now, Corregal Dorbus Forp the Supreme," Mardulo continued. "He's a character in his own right—not that you'll see much of him these days. Son of Madame Ismen Daria Forp of the Tunnelwater Brigade, he refused to enter the enriching world of academia until well into his twenties. City

Boratorus was a long journey for him, but he signed up for Introductory Wizardry Intelligence Training nonetheless and quickly became…"

The life story was a bit much. Gilbert had the general idea, but right now, he mostly wanted to enjoy the city. As the sunset lingered, candles in the streetlamps glowed to life, their flames small and fragile. To his right was a store called Hall of Globes. A hefty fellow with a face like a bulldog's swept the floor. He smiled at Gilbert, then continued his work.

"…his early research was intriguing, but it never progressed much beyond a thesis or two. Eventually, he enrolled in Transfiguration Wizardry Intelligence Training, where he met…"

They passed a restaurant, which was just opening. Its walls were mostly windows outlined in brick, and the inside was a collection of—Gilbert had to look twice—floating tables and chairs. They hovered, legless and perfectly flat, swaying gently up and down in some kind of magical aura. A sign hung outside with "Sleepless Sweets" emblazoned in letters of blue light.

"…he became a Transfiguration Wizardry Intelligence teacher and flew up the ranks. Eventually, during the Age of Too Small Chairs, he accepted a position as head TWIT, but was soon appointed to serve as the people's representative on the City Boratorus Council of Five, instead…"

They passed an instrument shop with a band performing inside. Saxophone, trumpet, and something Gilbert didn't recognize—a complex curling of brass tubes and flaps, which the musician maneuvered using pedals on the floor. They were playing a happy tune, and several inebriated dancers were having all the fun in the world.

"…and when the spell was complete, there was Obble Dor Hobblebosh! A marvelous accomplishment! Completely untested spellwork, founded purely on theoretical concepts, created by a single wizard, and it worked on the *first try*…"

A gryphon swooped between the buildings and nearly took Gilbert's head off. Mardulo didn't even pause, but Gilbert needed a moment to catch his breath. That thing had been huge! And its claws looked sharp. He scanned the sky for any lingering threats, then straightened up and tried to shake it off.

"...unfortunately for Corregal, Hobblebosh commandeered the cottage in Town Tobbelypop and sent Corregal away with orders to tell the world of a new age: the Age of the Lime Everlasting." He scoffed. "Hobblebosh expanded quickly. He had a nasty skirmish with the Town Tarley militia, but otherwise..."

Gilbert, still on the lookout for additional aerial attacks, nearly walked straight into a bunch of heavily built people wearing overalls. He mumbled an apology and trotted back into step.

"...then he conquered Town Forbik. It's a good position. Vibrant market, lots of trade, and only a brief stretch from there to the Great Splat! And that's the long and short of it. Any questions, Gigglebrit?"

The road turned. They entered a smaller cobbled way, plastered on either side with vibrant posters for *Udger's Nettled Redemption: A Sea-Witch's Tale*, a play performed by the local—

"Gigglebrit?"

"Huh? What?" Gilbert jumped. "Oh! Sorry...you were saying?"

"Do you have any questions?"

"Actually, yes." Gilbert hoped Mardulo hadn't answered this already. "Why aren't more people trying to stop him? I mean, if he's as bad as you say he is, he can't have *that* many people on his side."

"Brilliant question!" Mardulo clapped him on the back. "Others have tried, and some still do, but Hobblebosh responds quickly and violently. It's rare to get a second chance, let alone as many as Bundersquash and I have had. Most have given up hope. Town Agol said they may have something, but they refuse to tell anyone what it is until the time is right.

Secretive blighters, the lot of them. Waiting for someone else to solve the problem first, I expect. The folks at the Wizarding Consortium have some ideas, but most involve surrender of one form or another.

"As for Hobblebosh's army...well, it's complex. He feeds people lies and false promises, uses their own fear to saddle them, then drives them toward hatred of anything outside his own domain. He finds what people do not understand, amplifies that uncertainty, then offers to cure the world of it. In many cases, his lies focus on wizards and magic. The narrative fits well into his elimination of magic. He says we hoard power for ourselves, cheat death, rampage wildly, and destroy whatever lies in our path. All nonsense, of course, and the lies don't work on everyone. But he has other means for the rest. Obedience charms, coercion, torture, and the threat of death."

"All very powerful motivators," Bundersquash added.

Gilbert stood still for a moment, mouth ajar. "Torture? Threat of death? But he's a lime."

"Yes," said Mardulo. "An evil one. Would you like me to go back to the beginning?"

"No. It just seemed so silly, before."

Mardulo frowned. "He murders those who refuse to obey. Horror strangles his subjects. The people suffer daily, subdued into passivity. He has killed our friends, threatened our families...lime or not, Hobblebosh is a real problem."

"We have to be careful in our resistance, though," said Bundersquash. "We don't want to harm those forced to be there against their will. Our own techniques have focused on nonviolent actions. Early on, we tried a, shall we say, *direct* approach, but he was prepared for that. Poor Burrid paid the price..." He sighed. "She was a good friend and very brave. A few weeks later, we spread gundwater weed through the streets of Village Tankerspoon—his base of operations at the time—and though the village, Toddleposter, and I reeked for weeks, all it really did was speed his advance toward City Mez and provide more fodder for his lies about wizards. Then we tried filling the streets with pamphlets detailing his various atrocities, but those fueled more fires than rebellions."

"And that brings us to you," said Mardulo. "Well, not exactly. But through an indirect avenue of yet-to-be-determined error, our attempts to summon Pottleswee Plugg Thudigarde the Brave have instead landed us here."

"Right..." For a moment, Gilbert wanted to apologize but thought better of it. "Why were you trying to summon Pottle...Swuggthud-der...er...that person in the first place?"

"Because we've heard rumors of increased activity in Hobblebosh's territory, and we think he may have some new plan in the works. We want to be as prepared as possible."

"But why them specifically?"

"Why Pottleswee?" Mardulo raised his eyebrows. "Because he's the chosen one!"

"The chosen one?"

"The chosen one."

"Chosen for...?"

"Stopping Hobblebosh, of course!"

Gilbert rolled his eyes. "Naturally. And I suppose all this comes down to some grand prophecy?"

"Indeed," said Mardulo. "Though *grand* seems a tad extreme. In truth, there were several."

"They tend to have redundancies," explained Bundersquash, "to make sure everything is clear. I believe Hobblebosh-One was written, 'We, the seers of Sugwater, have glimpsed through the carefully woven fabric of time the coming of one tyrannical lime named Obble Dor Hobblebosh.'"

Mardulo smiled. "That is correct. And Hobblebosh-Two?" He asked the question like a quiz.

Bundersquash fiddled with his glasses. "'We, the Seers of Sugwater, have glimpsed through the carefully woven fabric of time and seen the lime called Hobblebosh, who shall be made human through the machinations of one Corregal Dorbus Forp the Supreme. The lime will conquer much of this world, and many will suffer at his hands. His reign, merciless and miserable, will continue until the coming of a savior named Pottleswee Plugg Thudigarde the Brave, a hero from Land Turmentarp, where the wodowood trees grow. Thudigarde shall, with flaming sword, bring peace at last to the land.'"

"Correct!" Mardulo cheered.

"And finally," Bundersquash continued, a world of excitement in his eyes, "Hobblebosh-Three: 'We, the Seers of Sugwater, would like to reiterate that Corregal Dorbus Forp the Supreme is going to turn a bloody lime into a human and cause the suffering of many for an indeterminate but presumably long and unhappy amount of time. Someone should probably tell Mr. Forp not to do that, if you please.'"

"And I take it no one told Mr. Forp to avoid limes?" asked Gilbert.

"No," said Mardulo. "Everyone ignored it, alongside the dozens of other scrolls and parchments Sugwater sends us each day. Great load of nonsense, mostly. Who needs a prophecy detailing Gurming's breakfast three weeks from next Tuesday?"

Gilbert rubbed his temples. "Well, whatever the case, I'm sorry to hear about your situation."

"We'll sort it out in the end," said Mardulo. "We always do."

They walked past a gang of muscular folk sitting around a table in a shadowed alcove. They were playing a game, throwing stones into the air and catching them on the backs of their hands, competing for a pile of golden coins. Their shouts and cheers echoed through the streets. The sky was now a vibrant maroon, streaked in glowing red, dappled in a shimmering haze of purple sparks that rose into the atmosphere like upside-down rain.

"What's that light on the horizon?" Gilbert asked Bundersquash. "The sparkly purple one."

"That's the Great Splat," said Bundersquash.

"And what's the Great Splat?"

Bundersquash looked at him, eyebrows raised. "Your home must be very far away indeed. The Great Splat is a massive split in the world itself, dividing the planet in two."

Gilbert gasped. "The planet is split in half?"

"Indeed! The event that created it took an enormous amount of power. To this day, magical residue lingers in the surrounding environment. That's the light you see there."

Gilbert's imagination took flight. What would that look like, a world severed? With any luck, he would find out...from a comfortable distance of at least a few yards away. He didn't like heights at the best of times. Falling off the edge of a shattered planet was not high on his list of to-dos.

"Did Hobblebosh do it?" he asked.

"Certainly not!" Bundersquash laughed. "The Great Splat was created hundreds of years ago. In fact, it's one of the few things slowing Hobblebosh down. There is only one bridge across it—the Narrow Stride or, more colloquially, Collywobbles Bridge. The Wizardry Intelligence Training Team and the Wizarding Consortium came together to cast a number of enchantments on that bridge that prevent him and his army from crossing. Until he finds a way past those, he's stuck."

Mardulo inserted himself. "It wouldn't be the first set of defensive enchantments he's worked past, of course. We must be prepared."

Gilbert thought for a moment. Having heard the words *torture* and *threat of death*, he was finding it surprisingly difficult to unhear them, but there was an opportunity here he didn't want to miss. He had just been transported into a fantasy world, met actual wizards, seen a new and magical city, and there was even a Big Bad to fight! It was clearly an opening. A chance to do something meaningful. To make a difference. To have an adventure.

He stopped walking and faced both wizards. "I'd like to help," he said. "With Hobblebosh, that is. You seem nice and—I mean, I need to go home eventually, but I want to do what I can."

"Absolutely not!" Mardulo put his foot down, literally.

"We need to get you home!" said Bundersquash. "Not drag you into this mess. Fighting Hobblebosh is a dangerous business."

"I accept the risks."

"And that's very admirable of you," said Mardulo, "but we brought you into this situation, and it's our duty to get you home safely. Bundersquash mentioned what happened to Burrid. I won't have any more people getting killed under my instruction. We're taking you to the library, finding Earth, then getting you back safely."

"But this sounds important! And who knows, maybe I could be useful!" Gilbert hesitated. Something had occurred to him. "What if I *am* Pottleswee?"

Mardulo stopped short. "I thought your name was Gigglebrit."

"It's Gilbert."

"But now it's Pottleswee?"

"No, I just thought...you were trying to summon the chosen one, right? Instead, you summoned me, and you don't know why. What if, over the course of this adventure, I somehow *become* Pottleswee? Like I end up changing my name or something, and it turns out your summoning spell was right all along!"

"Do you think that's likely?"

"I mean, it'd fit with...narrative structure, I guess?"

"Do you have a flaming sword?"

"No."

"And are you from Land Turmentarp, where the wodowood trees grow?"

"Um...no?"

"Then I think it is safe to say, you are not Pottleswee. Good thing too. Sounds like a real crisis of identity. Highly unpleasant to go through, I'd imagine, and we really don't have time for such things if we're to stop Hobblebosh before he resumes his expansion south." He put a hand on Gilbert's shoulder. "I am sorry, but it's too risky. We're going to get you home safely. That's that."

Gilbert deflated. Admittedly, even if they did let him join, he wasn't sure how he'd help. He knew high school physics and biology. His exams had trained him for college, not torture or near-death experiences.

Well. Some of them, maybe...

But surely, he could figure it out. And he *had* to help. This was his chance to be the Hero. He wasn't about to turn that down just because a couple of wizards said no. He would find a way to convince them. But now seemed like a bad time to push the issue.

Eventually, a courtyard came into view. It was made of meticulously laid stone tiles, with a string of benches distributed evenly across the perimeter. A fountain bubbled in the center, outlined by a garden of brilliant, nearly glowing flowers. On the far end stood the kind of building other buildings probably looked up to. It had walls of pale stone, a pair of marvelous solid-oak doors, and several tall stained glass windows adorning either side.

"Here we are," said Mardulo. "Impressive, isn't it?"

Gilbert coughed. "It's certainly...bold." In truth, it looked out of place. It had a gothic style that didn't match the rest of the city, but it seemed to have been built so confidently that no one thought to question it.

"Do they have libraries in Earth?" Bundersquash asked.

"They do," said Gilbert, relieved to find some common ground beyond the existence of barns, even if this particular library looked more like a fifteenth-century cathedral.

Gilbert was fond of his local library in Maystown. It was a small place, but inviting, and it had a great selection of fantasy books. He hoped this one would prove just as enjoyable. Even if it didn't have fantasy, a good history selection might suffice. He wanted to learn everything there was to know about this new world.

Chapter 3

Fact and Fiction

Gilbert entered the library and immediately pulled up short. The sheer size of the building was breathtaking. How it all fit within the walls of the outer building, he couldn't guess.

The front doors led into a main hall, where the final rays of the setting sun poured through stained glass windows, holding the air in a golden twilight. Shelves of books filled the walls, stretching into a distant haze of shimmering, fire-like dust. Two more levels circled above, balconies, equally packed and expansive. Tunnels and passageways spiraled off in every direction, a few with tables and study sections, others overrun with heaps of books, papers, and parchment.

There were tomes twice the size of any reasonable book beside collections of poems and short stories. There were loosely bound research papers, well scribbled and studied, and pristine collections of fine historical works. It was a building composed of stories and discoveries, thousands upon thousands waiting to be read in their novels, scrolls, and on a few occasions, etched tablets of stone or wax.

It was the most amazing place Gilbert had ever seen. Words like *spectacular* or *majestic* did it no justice. It was *the* Library, and that was all Gilbert could say.

He could imagine spending long, thoughtful hours here, learning history, studying magic, discovering all this world had to offer. Maybe one day, he could bring his friends and family too. Except Mardulo and Bundersquash wanted to send him home. No adventure. No heroics. No exploration...he wondered if it would be immoral to sneak away for a few days before they had a chance to do so.

But Gilbert was distracted from his schemes by the person standing behind the library's main desk. He was vaguely spherical, with wavy black hair and massive glasses only slightly larger than the rest of his face.

Gilbert turned to Bundersquash, then back to the man behind the desk. The two were identical.

"Hello, Toddleposter!" Bundersquash's voice echoed through the halls.

"Good evening, Bundersquash! Mardulo! Back already?" He zoomed in on Gilbert and gasped. "Is that him? The savior? You've actually done it! Good day, Mr. Thudigarde. Good day!" He bustled around the desk and flapped excitedly at Gilbert before bowing. "It is an absolute pleasure to meet you. My name is—"

"Actually," Mardulo asserted himself before Toddleposter could kiss Gilbert's hand. "Our spell didn't work. This is Gigglebrit Maistowne Nebraska—"

"What?" Gilbert's voice rose a few octaves.

"—the Hard of Hearing," Mardulo finished, oblivious to Gilbert's glare.

"We summoned him here accidentally," said Bundersquash.

"Ah." Toddleposter smiled. "All the same, it is a joy to meet you, Gigglebrit. My name is Toddleposter Hunderrum Balbagoose the Second."

"Nice to meet you," said Gilbert, wincing. "But actually, my name is Gilbert Betters. I'm *from* Maystown, Nebraska."

"I thought you were from Earth?" said Mardulo.

"It's on Earth."

"Do you mean Evreth?" asked Toddleposter.

"No!" Gilbert had to keep himself from screaming. "Earth, e-a-r-t-h. It's a planet. Not a town. A massive, fully qualified, grand-old-hunk-of-rock-in-space *planet* called Earth."

"I see." Toddleposter scratched his chin. "Afraid I've never heard of it."

"That's a shame," said Mardulo. "We were hoping you or Lady Ufferbub could help us send him home."

"Not that I have to leave straightaway," Gilbert added.

"We still need to know where it is," said Mardulo, looking sidelong at Gilbert.

Toddleposter walked back to his desk. "I'm sure we can find a reference somewhere. I'll send for Lady Ufferbub."

He grabbed a handheld bell from the desk and rang it with a few flicks of his wrist. A silver star of light emerged from the sound, then whisked along the main hallway and disappeared down one of the side passages, pulsing all the while with a gentle hum.

Gilbert gawked and would have asked for a turn—wanting to do as much magic as he could *while* he could—but by the time the light had vanished down the hall, Toddleposter had already put the bell away and disappeared into a nearby study room.

"I'll just fetch Lobster while we wait," he called out, his voice muffled.

"Lobster?" asked Gilbert.

Toddleposter emerged carrying a large golden-barred cage with a floor of lush grass and flowers. Inside, resting on a blue cornflower, was a butterfly. She was bright orange, with swirls of silver and gold running through her wings like veins.

"That's...Lobster?" asked Gilbert.

"It is!" Bundersquash dashed toward the cage. "It's good to see you again, Lobster! Did you have a nice time with Uncle Toddleposter? Read anything interesting?"

Gilbert shook his head. "The butterfly can read?"

"In a rudimentary sense," said Bundersquash. "We're still working on it. But she can do all sorts of other things. Here, look!"

He opened the cage, and Lobster took to the air, spiraling into a backflip.

"That's how she says hello," said Bundersquash. "She can do a lot more when she's in the mood. Go on, Lobster. Give him a show!"

Lobster chirped—Gilbert had never heard a butterfly chirp before—then floated toward Toddleposter's desk, landed on two of her six feet, and started to tap dance.

Gilbert looked away, rubbed his eyes, then looked back at the desk. Lobster had stopped, her upper two legs crossed. When Gilbert's attention returned, she started over.

"Magic?" Gilbert asked.

"Not one bit! Just clever."

"She understands almost any word you throw at her," Toddleposter added.

Lobster chirped with no small degree of pride, and Gilbert couldn't help but sense an edge to the noise, as if she were saying, *Why do you look so surprised?*

When she finished her routine, she meandered back to Bundersquash's outstretched hand, and Bundersquash grabbed an eyedropper attached to the cage. "This is sugar water. She loves the stuff. Isn't that right, girl?"

Lobster wolfed down several drops, then fluttered in circles around Bundersquash's head.

"Did you teach her all that?" asked Gilbert.

"Indeed! I trained her all by myself, though she did most of the work."

Lobster bowed, made sure Gilbert had seen it, then returned to her cage and snuggled into a leaf.

"That's really impressive," said Gilbert.

Bundersquash turned to Lobster with pride. "She was a going-away gift from my parents, back when I first moved to the city. She's a real treasure."

"I look after her sometimes," said Toddleposter. "Especially now that she's learning to read. It's been a real joy spending time with her again."

Gilbert nodded. "Are you and Bundersquash brothers? Twins? You look so similar."

The others laughed. Gilbert wasn't sure if he should feel offended.

"I suppose you could say we're related," Toddleposter explained, "but we're not twins."

"He's my clone!" Bundersquash leaped into place beside Toddleposter.

"Oh!" Gilbert raised his eyebrows. A clone. He quickly thought through various books, movies, and TV shows with clones in them. Had it ever actually gone well?

He supposed it didn't matter. Toddleposter looked happy enough. And Gilbert had to admit, even this close together, he and Bundersquash really were indistinguishable, except..."You made your own clone shorter than you?"

"Not intentionally." Bundersquash paid no mind to Gilbert's judging eyes.

"What happened?"

"A mistake in our spellwork. Mardulo and I had only recently started working together. We were still getting the hang of things."

"For a week or two, we thought we'd pulled it off!" said Mardulo. "Toddleposter was up and about, all faculties in order. He and Bundersquash really were identical! They even fooled me on occasion. We didn't realize he was shrinking until we were halfway through the reflection-and-review paper. It was a slow process, to be sure, but our measurements confirmed it."

Gilbert examined Toddleposter. "So, are you like...aging backward?"

"No," said Toddleposter. "I'm still getting older. My hair will turn gray. My skin will wrinkle. I'm just getting smaller, not larger...so I suppose my skin will wrinkle a lot."

"I...um...I'm sorry to hear that."

"It's not as bad as you might think," said Toddleposter. "It occurs at a decreasing rate—an exponential decay, if you will. I doubt I'll ever get below one and a half feet."

"And we can always whip up a growing potion, if need be," said Mardulo.

"Many thanks," said Toddleposter, "but I'm all right. There's a small crevice in the left wing, which will make for a lovely reading spot once I'm small enough to fit!"

"Do you know what's causing the...uh"—Gilbert tried to find an inoffensive term—"shrinkage?" He grimaced.

"It's a side effect of how we realigned the matter within our ingredient complex." Mardulo waved his hands. "We used tall-flower extract, which didn't mix well with the intrinsic auralis of our essence of Bundersquash."

"The school board insisted we change our hypothesis to match the results," said Bundersquash, "but Mardulo put his foot down."

"We lost quite a bit of funding on that one," said Mardulo. "Still, I think it was worthwhile. Don't you, Toddleposter?"

"Oh, yes! I like existing!"

"And indeed," a powerful voice sounded from one of the nearby passageways, "without Toddleposter, this library would not be half of what it has become. Many thanks to you all."

The woman speaking was tall and lean, with thin rectangular spectacles and short white hair, spiked back in a fashion vaguely reminiscent of a hedgehog. Her left ear had been pierced three times, her right, twice, and her nose joined in with a stud. For dress, she wore a robe, sleek and deep red, fitted to reach the floor but not so long as to drag. It had a low-hanging collar, revealing a solid black shirt underneath. A narrow white tie completed the ensemble.

She strode down a faded blue rug toward the front desk, bowing when she saw the wizards.

"Hello, Lady Ufferbub!" Toddleposter beamed.

"How do you fare this fine evening, my friends?"

"Quite well," said Mardulo. "We have a few questions for you."

"Of course! I am happy to help. But first, who is our guest?" She peered at Gilbert. "Have you succeeded in your mission? Is this truly the great Pottleswee Plugg Thudigarde the Brave, of whom the prophecy foretold?"

"Actually, this is Gigglebrit Maistowne Nebraska the Hard of Hearing," said Mardulo.

"No," said Gilbert. "I'm Gilbert Betters."

Mardulo leaned in. "You'll have to excuse the confusion. Our most recent spell targeted him instead of Pottleswee, and he's been a bit muddled ever since. Poor fellow seems to be struggling with his own name. Gilbert. Gigglebrit. Even wondered if he actually *was* Pottleswee a minute ago."

"I am sorry to hear that. I hope we can help you recover. It is a pleasure to make your acquaintance. May it one day grow into a friendship." She extended a hand. "My name is Lady Normishdae Relidor Ufferbub the Triumphant."

Gilbert accepted the greeting. "Nice to...um...make your acquaintance too."

"We're trying to get him home," said Bundersquash. "But we can't figure out where it is."

Lady Ufferbub tilted her head. "And what is the name of this location?"

"It's a planet called Earth," said Toddleposter, much to Gilbert's relief.

Lady Ufferbub froze. "Come again?"

"Here we go," muttered Gilbert.

"Earth," said Bundersquash.

"As I thought." In place of any reasonable response, Lady Ufferbub leaned in and...sniffed.

A pause.

Then she circled Gilbert, scouring every inch of his person with her gaze. She poked him in the shoulder, peered into his eyes, raised an eyebrow in his direction.

Gilbert backed up.

"Earth..." she mused. "Could it be? No, surely not. But perhaps...*Earth*?" She scratched her head. Unease trickled into Gilbert's mind as Lady Ufferbub's expression wavered between concern and curiosity. At least she hadn't mentioned Evreth.

"It is a fascinating prospect," she said suddenly, straightening. "Superb! Unusual, surely, but possible, I think. Never done before, but that does not mean much..." She trailed off, thoughtful.

A few moments passed in silent contemplation.

"Um," said Gilbert finally. For once, Mardulo and Bundersquash seemed just as confused as he was.

Toddleposter looked worried. "Lady Ufferbub?" he ventured. "Is everything okay?"

She looked up, as if only now remembering she had company. "This is a strange occurrence, I must say, and terribly exciting. If I am correct, my friends, we may be witnessing *the* revolutionary magical accomplishment of the Age of the Empty Box."

And just like that, a wave of enthusiasm bombarded the wizards, their confusion wholly forgotten. If Gilbert hadn't known any better, he'd have shown them to the bathroom.

"But of course," Lady Ufferbub continued, "we must be certain. You were working in Wizards' Workshop 4C, correct?"

"Yes," said Bundersquash, his voice hardly a whisper.

"On the widesplatter side of town?"

"Correct," said Mardulo, trying and failing to sound dignified.

Lady Ufferbub smiled, a glimmer in her eye. "Then there is but one more thing to check. Let us journey to my office."

She turned with a flourish and strode down one of the passageways. The others followed, Bundersquash grabbing Lobster's cage along the way.

To say that Mardulo had a hop in his step would be inaccurate. He had a step in his hop, perhaps, though more accurately, he danced and managed to move forward in a manner that was, by all appearances, entirely independent of the placement of his feet.

Bundersquash positively bubbled.

Gilbert, meanwhile, held back panic as he struggled to deduce what could possibly be so interesting about Earth. Potential answers rushed through his mind, a dreadful torrent of possibilities. It took tremendous effort just to keep his breathing regular.

The walk was mercilessly long. They wove their way through a maze of stacks and shelves, through tunnels of books and enormous halls. When they reached what appeared to be a dead end, Lady Ufferbub tilted a book from one of the bookshelves, and in good, traditional fashion, the shelf slid away to reveal a stairwell. They climbed up, then a few corridors later, climbed back down using a makeshift staircase of piled books. They hit a wall, turned left, and kept walking.

Eventually, they arrived at their destination—a modestly carved wooden door embedded in a bookshelf opposite a massive red-and-silver tapestry. Lady Ufferbub didn't use the doorknob. Instead, she knocked a quick rhythm on the wood.

The door spoke. "I sing through the world in a silent whisper. I trail myself through time. I burn in the hearts of every good soul, and I burn the minds of the bad. The task of my use is given to none, and none shall know my turn, but as worlds unfold and come to an end, the honest shall learn my name. What am I?"

For a moment, Gilbert's worries subsided, replaced with pure excitement. He loved riddles. Even more, he loved secret doorways that challenged you with riddles before letting you pass. This was his chance. What could it be? Time? Silence? Hope? Death?

He settled into the right state of mind to think about such things, and—

"Peach yogurt," said Lady Ufferbub.

The door opened.

"Peach yogurt?!" Gilbert exclaimed in an indignant whisper. "How does that riddle come out to peach yogurt?!"

"It doesn't." Toddleposter smiled. "That's the trick."

Gilbert scowled. He supposed it was clever, but he really wanted to answer that riddle. He crossed his arms as Lady Ufferbub ushered everyone inside.

"Here we are," she said. "Tea and biscuits?"

"Tea would be great," said Gilbert. He had never been one to turn down freely offered tea. Then the hunger hit him. He hadn't eaten all day. "Er...and some biscuits, too, if that's okay. Please. Thank you."

Lady Ufferbub put the kettle on and produced a generous plateful of cookies from a cupboard. Gilbert helped himself.

The office was big enough for the five of them plus Lobster, but more would have made it crowded. There were no windows. In fact, considering the door they'd just entered, Gilbert assumed they were behind four walls of bookshelves, though no one would ever know it from the inside. It looked like a normal, nicely furnished office.

A desk of glossy, dark chestnut stood in the center of the room, facing the door. On the wall behind it hung a large painting of what might have been City Boratorus's skyline in winter. The left and right walls were bookshelves, filled to capacity and arranged with utmost precision, though Lady Ufferbub had blocked out occasional space for cabinets and trinkets. There was a sofa to the left, several chairs to the right, and one cushioned throne-of-a-thing behind the desk, where Lady Ufferbub sat.

On the room's front wall, surrounding the entrance, were several plaques to commemorate various awards Lady Ufferbub had earned, including a framed level-ten degree for Literature in Academia, a commendation for exemplary librarianship from the City Boratorus Council of Five, a green ribbon from the Kollen Fencing Academy, and near the top of the wall, a small certificate for City Boratorus's Best Bagels.

Gilbert pulled up a chair and grabbed another cookie.

He knew he should ask about Earth, but he was too worried about the answer. Instead, he grabbed a third cookie and shoveled it into his mouth before he'd even swallowed the second.

Bundersquash asked, "What is your theory, Lady Ufferbub?"

She held up a finger. "I require just a few moments to verify my hypothesis if you do not mind. Until I have done so, I would prefer to keep my assumptions private, so as not to cause any undue...disturbance."

Using the bezel of a ring from her finger, she opened a compartment integrated into one of the bookshelves. A single book lay inside—thick, with an unadorned cover and loosely bound pages of unusual, grainy paper. Lady Ufferbub removed it slowly and placed it on her desk.

A World of Souls: Volume 362, Revision 3.

"Here we are," she said. "Exactly as I thought. Now, I just have to make sure..." Her voice trailed off as she paged through the book, quickly at first, then slowly as she approached her target. By the end of her search, she was combing through every syllable, examining each detail in excruciating silence, her face hard with concentration.

Lobster slipped between the bars of her golden cage and sat on Lady Ufferbub's shoulder.

Gilbert's heart thumped against his chest. He leaned in, nerves burning with anticipation. The whole room hung in breathless suspense...

"Aha!" Lady Ufferbub's eyes shot to the two wizards. Lobster's gaze followed. "My friends, you have done something incredible!"

This did little to comfort Gilbert, but Mardulo and Bundersquash launched into an unprecedented level of glee. As they jittered with excitement, Gilbert trembled with fear.

"It is truly a marvel of magic," said Lady Ufferbub, "and here we are, right in the middle of it! I look forward to reading your papers on the subject. I am sure they will be superb.

"I suppose I should explain. I have before me the three hundred and sixty-second volume of a rather unsuccessful fantasy series titled *A World of Souls*. It is merely a draft, but the author is a longtime friend of mine, and I was preparing some feedback for him. Volume one of the series begins with the creation of a world. From there, the novels progress chronologically and span millions of years, each book focusing on a new character. While the roster changes and the landscape shifts, the world remains the same." She stopped for a moment and smiled at her audience. "That world," she said, "that fantasy world with fictional characters, made-up places, and imaginary events—that world is Earth."

Interlude: Tree, Humans, and Hatchets

Tree stood still and silent in the tower, exactly where the wizards had left them. The boy—Gilbert, Tree recalled, though the others had called him Gigglebrit—had gone too. Tree didn't think they were coming back.

It had been a trying day. Tree had been tangled and twisted and placed uncomfortably close to a fire-based writing implement. All the while, their roots were scrunched above ground in a way that made very little sense, given their current understanding of spatial reasoning.

But they had wanted to see the world, and this felt like a step in the right direction.

They were certainly seeing new things—this bizarre room with its metal ground, the two strange people in their unusual clothing, and that noisy flying book, for a start. And something about the atmosphere felt different here. The air was clearer, the light was stronger, and the sun shone with an exuberance Tree had never experienced on the hill beside Berrywood Lane. It was more energized, despite the interference of the little glass plates in the wall.

Yes. Tree had wanted to see the world. This was progress.

Now they had to keep going. Of course, it would help if Tree knew how any of this had happened in the first place, but they were not one to dwell on trivialities. They'd gotten this far. Now they had to go farther.

A sudden series of clatters and bangs reverberated up the ladder.

More humans, Tree guessed. Perhaps the wizards and Gilbert had returned after all. Maybe they would have some ideas. But when the hatch opened, four different humans climbed up, all heavily built. Solid. Sturdy.

So, not the wizards.

But that was okay. The wizards hadn't been much use, anyway. Maybe these new people could help. Maybe they could explain how Tree had moved and how to do it again.

Then Tree sensed what the humans were holding: long wooden handles attached to sinister blades of steel.

Axes.

Tree had never been near a real axe before, but they knew enough to be worried. Sharp, metal, and terrifyingly deadly.

"Bloody wizards," said one of them. Her voice was gruff and angry. "How'd they get a tree up here, anyway?"

The others shook their heads. "It'll be a right nightmare to clean up."

"Shame, really." One of the people looked Tree up and down. "It's a fine-looking specimen."

Tree was too scared to be flattered. If they were ever going to learn how to move, now was the time. It couldn't end like this, not after everything that had just happened. Tree was so close to their goal. They had to do something, *anything*.

They focused on their roots. Humans moved with their legs. Roots seemed like the next-best thing.

One of the people sighed. "Well, we'd best get to work. I told Sorgu I'd walk her to school in the morning."

He hefted his axe and swung.

Thwack!

The shock reverberated up Tree's trunk, through their branches, into their leaves. Tree's entire world trembled. Soon, all four workers were at it, taking turns in a steady rhythm of attack, their axes cleaving through bark and wood.

Every cut stung worse than anything Tree had ever experienced. They were grateful for their thick bark and sturdy structure but knew it wouldn't last.

This was the end...

But some part of Tree refused to accept it, even as the ruthless barrage rained down, so they did the only thing they could do—concentrate. They focused their effort on moving and trying to remember, through the pain, why it would all be worthwhile.

They thought of the stories they'd heard, of mountains and caves and oceans.

Thwack.

They thought of the critters and birds that told those stories, moving freely through the world.

Thwack.

They thought of how excited those creatures had been to see where their lives would take them.

Thwack.

"This is bloody difficult," said one of the humans, brushing sweat from his brow. "We've hardly made a dent."

"Keep at it," said the lumberjack to his left. "We'll get through."

The slashes kept on. One, two, three, four. One, two, three, four. The pain came in an unbearable sequence, each cut a terrifying scorch of agony.

Panic flooded Tree's thoughts. With one final effort, they turned their focus to the strange new energy of this place, to the vivacity coursing through the sunlight. The atmosphere pulsed with possibilities. In Tree's leaves and branches, in their trunk and roots, they clung to the new sensation. They drew on the energy, the very life of the universe around them, and focused every ounce of their being.

And moved.

Just a twitch.

"Whoa there!" The cuts ceased. "What kind of magical tomfoolery have those wizard's been up to?"

"What is it, Punkle?"

"The tree just moved!"

"You sure we didn't hit a nerve or something?"

"Of course I'm sure! That root, right there. A sort of jitter."

"Must've been your imagination. The schedule said some kind of summoning work. Nothing to do with moving trees—"

"You think it's related to that Hobblebosh fella? Age of the Lime Forever-and-Ever?"

"Everlasting, Punkle. Age of the Lime *Everlasting*. And no. This is a tree, not a lime."

The bickering continued, and Tree took full advantage. They'd done it! They'd actually moved! It was a start, but this was no time for celebration. The lumberjacks were still here.

Tree's newfound confidence served them well. They understood what it was to move, and they knew they could do it again. All they had to do was focus.

Another twitch, larger this time—large enough to trip the skeptical worker and send them thundering to the floor.

"You okay, Krutt?" said one of the lumberjacks. "What just happened?"

"The blasted thing tripped me!"

"I *told* you!" said Punkle. "Moving tree. What'd I say? I said the tree moved, and you said—"

Smack!

A root swung across the room and slammed Punkle into the wall. Tree was getting the hang of it. They knocked down the third lumberjack with one of their lower branches. The fourth screamed, adjusted the grip on her axe, and prepared to strike.

Tree would have none of that. They raised a root, held it in the air just long enough for the lumberjack to digest what was about to happen, then came down with enough force to avenge every swing the workers' axes had made.

And Tree continued, swinging up and down and to and fro until the humans scurried back down the ladder, jostled and bruised, seriously considering alternate career options.

Tree shook terribly, unsure how to cope with the intense rush of relief and energy. But they weren't safe yet. The humans could return, and next time, they might bring more people, or sharper axes, or fire...

As Tree raced through a litany of potential dangers, one thing became clear. They needed to escape the tower, and they needed to do it now. Everything else—moving, new worlds, mountains, and oceans—it all faded against the imminent threat of lumberjacks and axes.

They broke several windows with a few well-placed jabs from one of their sturdier branches, and with their roots, they relieved the trapdoor of its lid. But the opening was too small. They smacked the wall, but the brickwork was solid. Roots could break stone, Tree knew, but the process took years. Tree had, at most, a few hours.

But most trees couldn't move like Tree could move.

Also, Tree had no other choice.

Using their roots as a relatively poor substitute for legs, Tree lurched into position, braced at the edge of the room, and pushed a root into the seam between the floor and the wall. The work was exhausting, but after an hour of nonstop pressure, one of the bricks wiggled, cracked, and fell to the streets below.

Tree rustled excitedly. One down. Just a few hundred more and they'd be free!

They siphoned some roots outside, wrapped them around the exterior stonework, and pulled at the bricks while their trunk and branches pushed from indoors. Progress was quicker this time. Several more bricks shattered and fell. Then Tree picked up chunks of debris and clobbered the weaker sections of wall.

The tower grew ever more unstable. Cracks zigzagged from floor to ceiling. The building groaned in protest. And just when the whole structure was ready to give way, Tree braced for one final push. It was going to be a big one, and it was going to hurt, but the alternative—axes, danger, humans—meant death.

Moving like a spider—a technique Tree had discovered suited their roots—they wriggled over to the other side of the room, then paused briefly to see if any better options came to mind...when none did, they resigned themselves to this unavoidable fate.

At the very least, it might be fun.

They braced their bark and charged.

For an instant, the world was a blur. Then it was pain. Then it was rubble. Tree smashed into the weakened wall with tremendous force. Stones shattered, thousands of shards flying out into the open air. Destruction rained down, and Tree fell with it.

They landed with an explosive shock. It flared through Tree's trunk and shattered dozens of roots and twigs. Stones fell like hail around them, a terrible clamor of ruin. Then the tower gave way and collapsed.

But Tree had survived.

They decided this was probably a good time to run for their life, so they took off as fast as they could, which was not as fast as they would have liked, and tried to escape the destruction without causing any more along the way.

Chapter 4

Chaos at the Consortium

Gilbert couldn't think. Earth couldn't be fictional. It certainly wasn't *fantasy*. This didn't make any sense. Maybe it was a coincidence. Or maybe the author knew about the real Earth and stole its name for their story.

"I don't believe it," he said to the others.

"I admit I am quite surprised myself," said Lady Ufferbub. "Mardulo, Bundersquash, you have bridged the gap between fact and fiction! This morning, Gigglebrit was a wholly imagined literary character. Now he is here, living and breathing in the real world, all because of you! It is a marvel."

"It's fantastic!" Mardulo cheered.

Bundersquash hugged Toddleposter. "How wonderful!"

Lobster leaped from Lady Ufferbub's shoulder and flew loops around the room.

"I don't think you understand." Gilbert found his voice again. "I don't believe it because it isn't true. It can't be. I'm *from* Earth. It's not imaginary. I grew up there. I have family there. I remember it clearly, and it is definitely real."

Everyone immediately quieted down as the room took on a guilty air.

"Sorry, Gigglebrit," said Toddleposter. "We should have been more sensitive."

"Of course," said Lady Ufferbub. "This must be difficult for you, Gigglebrit. I imagine your memories do feel real, because...well, I suppose, in some way, the spell made them real alongside you. You are real, so the memories you hold are real."

Then she took a slow, deep breath. "Unfortunately, it is *only* the memories that are real. The people and events to which they refer are wholly fictional...at least, I suspect so. They exist only to the extent that any fiction exists—within the minds of its readers and, in this very special case, within the mind of a character as well. You remember your character's life because you *are* that character. You have his—your—mind. It is even—"

"I get it," Gilbert interrupted, "but you're wrong. I mean, this is my home we're talking about. My family. My friends. Everything! It's not fake. It can't be. It just...that wouldn't...it *can't* be."

A terrifying uncertainty fluttered through the back of his mind. He tried to hold it at bay.

"I am sorry," said Lady Ufferbub, looking Gilbert in the eye. "It is difficult news to receive, I am sure. But all the same, I have checked the book, and it is quite clear. You go missing at the age of sixteen. I am afraid..." She deflated. "I am afraid you never return."

"No." Gilbert shook his head. "You're telling me that my entire past is fake? Everyone I've ever met, all the people I've ever cared about, all the people I love...they're just names in some book?"

Lady Ufferbub fidgeted uneasily. "Their memory lives on in you. That is something."

Gilbert crossed his arms. "You're wrong. If I'm in that stupid book, prove it."

"Very well." Lady Ufferbub turned her head down. She scanned through a few pages, solemn. "I hope this is not offensive, Gigglebrit, but...well, you are not exactly the main character of this story. The details are sparse. Your parents are important, though, and your disappearance affects them deeply, so there are a few relevant snippets around. I admit, your name is"—she eyed Gilbert, hesitating—"perhaps, spelled strangely...but it says you were an avid reader, a particular fan of fantasy, currently ranked third in your class in something called a 'High School.' Apparently, you consistently received top marks. Congratulations." She flipped through several more pages. "In time, you hoped to travel to a faraway land called Massachusetts, where you would attend...oh, what was it? Williams College. The same place your parents trained. You were interested in studying something called physics, though biology was a close contender." She pointed to the text. "However, during one unusually refreshing, breezy summer's day, you went out to read a book and never returned. You were last seen by someone called Mrs. Carver at approximately eleven in the morning, approaching Berrywood Lane."

Gilbert stared in disbelief. It was correct. Every word. He sank into his chair and blinked at Lady Ufferbub.

"I just...how did...what?" Gilbert dropped his head into his hands. "I just go missing? Can't you send me back?"

Lady Ufferbub closed the book. "I am very sorry, Gigglebrit. I can see this comes as a shock. Unfortunately, it is *fiction*. I doubt there is anything for you to actually return *to*, so to speak. The world does not exist beyond these pages."

Gilbert took a deep breath. For now, it was all he could do to hold back tears. He'd been excited to have an adventure, but this...he wanted to deny it, to prove Lady Ufferbub wrong. But he knew nothing of this world or its magic, and Lady Ufferbub seemed to know plenty about both.

He had a hundred questions, but one stood out among the rest.

"When I disappear, what happens to my parents? You said they were important?"

Lady Ufferbub's face went white. She scratched the back of her neck and flipped through the pages in no particular order. "That is...well...you probably...what I mean to say is, your day has already been difficult, and

I would find it…" She paused, then continued more slowly. "Are you sure you wish to know?"

"Yes," said Gilbert, though his stomach churned with worry.

"If you insist." Lady Ufferbub took a deep breath. "I am very sorry to tell you this, but they…theybecomepoliticians."

Mardulo, Bundersquash, and Toddleposter jumped back in horror, but Gilbert hadn't understood the jumbled words.

"What?" he said.

Lady Ufferbub looked at Gilbert, sorrow clear in her eyes. "They become politicians, Gigglebrit. I am sorry."

Gilbert tilted his head. "That's it?"

"That is it," said Lady Ufferbub, her voice somber. "You have my deepest sympathies. Politics is a terrible fate to befall any family, fiction or otherwise. If it is any consolation, they are quite good, as politicians go. Your disappearance serves as a springboard, and they start a nonprofit organization to help locate missing children. They engage with their government's lost-child initiative and eventually take on full-time political positions themselves. They help many families throughout the book, including the protagonist's own, and they make a very real difference in their—er, your—world. In the end, they are happy."

The tension left Gilbert's body in waves. His family may not be real, but at least in their book, they did good work and found happiness. That was something. Despite what the others had said, he could think of worse fates than politics and striving to do good. And his parents *would* do good. He knew that much.

He took a deep breath before acknowledging the others' stares.

"I'm fine," he said. "Or at least, I will be. I just need a minute if that's okay."

With a few mumbled sympathies, they obliged.

In the ensuing silence, Gilbert's mind painted the world's most unhelpful pros and cons list. It was somewhat trickier than he'd expected. His elementary school guidance lessons—which, he reminded himself, had apparently not actually happened—usually focused on simpler issues, like whether to eat dessert or how to play nicely in the sandbox. Dealing with the revelation that your entire reality was not, in fact, real, and you were, in fact, created several hours ago by a pair of discombobulated wizards was a somewhat thornier subject.

If it was even true. Some part of him still couldn't believe it.

He would miss his friends and his family, of course, and he'd even miss school a little. But if Mardulo and Bundersquash hadn't summoned him from that book, he would have no idea that any of those things actually existed—or didn't actually exist—at all. He would be a series of words on a page, totally oblivious to his past and this reality. In short, lifeless.

So, if he had to decide, missing people was a con, but being alive to miss them? That was a pro.

Other cons included all the history classes he'd taken, which were now about as useful as a deck of novelty trading cards, and his Spanish lessons, which he'd never been good at to begin with. Come to think of it, he might have to go *back* to school. Did math work the same way here? Physics? Calculus? Addition? He supposed he could test some of that later.

He would probably have to learn how to cook, too, and he'd never thought to ask for his dad's pancake recipe. Did they have butter and eggs in this world?

On the bright side, he could write some exceptional *World of Souls* fan fiction. And there was a library the size of Nebraska, give or take a few square miles. That would be fun to explore.

There had to be more positives.

Mardulo, Bundersquash, Lady Ufferbub, and Toddleposter seemed friendly enough. And everyone spoke English—or whatever they called it here—which simplified matters tremendously.

He might actually be able to learn magic now too. With a little luck, he could even get his adventure. He could help stop this evil tyrant!

Which made him realize Earth had its own fair share of tyrants and horrible things. Now there was a real, tangible person to blame for it all...

"Lady Ufferbub," he asked. "You said you know the author. Who is it?"

She took a moment to process this sudden and unexpected inquiry. "A fellow by the name of Podish Gubber Tuggerbug the Stumped. He lives in City Mez with three cats and a docile boar."

Gilbert smacked his forehead. He'd been hoping for a creator with a little majesty to their name, even if it wasn't some clever play on God or Gaia or another Earth-based deity. "His Holiness, Podish Gubber Tuggerbug the Stumped, Lord Almighty, Creator of Heaven and Earth, Who Also Has a Docile Boar" didn't have quite the same ring to it.

"Are you all right, Gigglebrit?" asked Toddleposter gently.

"Yeah. Just wrapping my head around things. I think...I think I'm okay. You can talk again if you'd like."

"Are you sure?" asked Lady Ufferbub.

"I'm sure," said Gilbert, gratefully accepting a cup of tea from Toddleposter. He had a sip and tried to take pleasure in the fact that, even in this strange new world, the tea was the same.

Mardulo spoke next. "We'll have to find out how this happened. Our summoning spell should have found Pottleswee, not a fictional character."

"Actually, I have a theory about that," said Lady Ufferbub. "Do you have your incantation written down?"

Bundersquash grabbed a few pieces of parchment from his pocket and placed them on the desk.

Lady Ufferbub looked them over. "Ah. See here? The prophecy states that Pottleswee resides in Land Turmentarp, where the wodowood trees grow. In your incantation, due to your earlier statement here"—Lady Ufferbub pointed to the parchment—"and your use of *City Boratorus* here, in conjunction with *Wizards' Workshop 4C*"—another point—"you were forced to refrain from using the exact phrase *Land Turmentarp*, correct?"

"Impressively so," said Mardulo.

Lady Ufferbub inclined her head. "So instead of the name itself, you have focused on the wodowood trees. Now, if my translation skills serve me well—and I admit, they are rusty—this phrase equates roughly to 'from the land *of* the wodowood trees,' rather than 'from the land *with* the wodowood trees.' By almost all accounts, an inconsequential difference, but on this rare occasion, it changed your spell entirely."

Realization dawned on Mardulo and Bundersquash with a steady drawing of breath. It seemed to register in slow motion. Bundersquash's eyes grew to fill his frames. Mardulo's jaw made its way to the floor.

Lady Ufferbub continued. "As I mentioned before, this book is only a draft. In generating the copy, Podish saved on expenses by using cheaper paper. The paper, as I am sure you have already concluded, comes from Land Turmentarp. It was made using wood of the wodowood tree. We have a few other books made of this material, and many research papers, but those largely reside in the opposite wing of the library. This book was here, in my office, closest to Wizards' Workshop 4C."

Toddleposter could no longer contain his excitement. He burst into applause. "Oh, well done, Lady Ufferbub! What an incredible series of deductions!"

Bundersquash picked up the book. "So, when the spell was cast, it didn't go to the land *containing* wodowood trees. It went to a land *made* of wodowood trees, and the nearest one happened to be this book?"

"That is my hypothesis, yes. Of course, there was no Pottleswee Plugg Thudigarde the Brave for the spell to grab at that point, so I expect some nondeterminism took hold, but there were enough redundancies in the spellwork to preserve most of the intended action. The spell simply summoned the nearest available character and…well, there he is." She gestured toward Gilbert.

"I dare say this is a happy accident!" Mardulo's voice bloomed with elation. "Can you believe it, Bundersquash? Just imagine the repercussions! This could revolutionize the way we understand summoning spells. Given the appropriate amount of study and care, our results could ripple through the world of academia for years to come. Goodness, if we stick with it, this could even affect the general public!"

"How exciting!" cheered Bundersquash. "I will begin gathering data for the reflective analysis immediately!"

Mardulo grabbed a quill from his robe and scanned the room for loose paper but stopped short at the sound of a chime. A pale ball of light entered the room, humming as it faded through the wall.

"Is that the bell thing from the front desk?" asked Gilbert.

"It is," said Lady Ufferbub, her eyebrows furrowed.

Mardulo glanced at Toddleposter. "Who else knows about it?"

"Very few," said Lady Ufferbub. A second light entered the room. "We had best see what is going on."

Everyone stood up and prepared to leave. Bundersquash put Lobster in her cage. "I'll pick you up later," he said, and they all hurried back to the main lobby. When they arrived, they found a very small woman standing on Toddleposter's desk, clutching the bell in one hand. Her skin was pale purple.

"Ah! Thank goodness you're here!" she said, putting the bell down and hopping off the desk. "I need your help, urgently!"

"Madame Martoonisplau?" Lady Ufferbub bent in half and shook the woman's hand. "What is the matter?"

"The Wizarding Consortium is under attack! It's Hobblebosh!"

"He crossed Collywobbles Bridge?" said Mardulo. "But our defenses—"

"Not Hobblebosh himself," Madame Martoonisplau clarified. "Just a small task force. Our defenses were calibrated to stop an entire army and a lime, not this. They must've snuck by. People have been hurt. Can you help?"

"Of course!" said Bundersquash.

Lady Ufferbub turned to Gilbert. "You wait here. The library should be safe. We will return once we have sorted this out."

"I want to help," said Gilbert.

She placed a hand on his shoulder. "You just lost your home. You should take time to process that."

"I said I want to help!" Gilbert snapped, shoving Lady Ufferbub's hand away. "Apparently, my home is just some stupid fantasy! What is there to process? It's pointless. I'm coming, and that's the end of it."

He ignored the baffled look from Madame Martoonisplau and strode out the door, hoping the others would join him. Thankfully, they did, so he let them pass and followed behind. Night had fallen, and the city's darkness was complete. Gilbert was grateful for it. He could feel his cheeks growing hot with embarrassment over the outburst, and he didn't want the others to notice.

Violent bangs, pops, and occasional shouts sounded in the distance—the sounds of attack, Gilbert guessed. He focused on them, letting the urgency drive him. Really, he was happy for any excuse to stop thinking about Earth. His fake home. His nonexistent family. His meaningless life story...

He shook his head. Enough of that. He needed something to fight with. Gilbert scanned the ground for sticks but found no promising candidates.

He wasn't really sure how to prepare for a battle, but he was determined to make himself useful.

Mardulo and Bundersquash were breathlessly discussing strategy. Lady Ufferbub was silent, focused on the horizon. Toddleposter asked Madame Martoonisplau how she was holding up. And before long, they arrived.

The Wizarding Consortium was unlike anything Gilbert could have imagined. The building was a trapezoidal prism of sorts, with odd protrusions here and there, blanketed in a thick layer of ivy. It was also hovering several meters in the air. A tiered flight of stairs connected its entrance to the sidewalk. The main exit appeared to be a slide.

But what really drew Gilbert's attention was the underside of the building. There was something distinctly *impossible* about it—and not just the fact that it was floating. Where the base of the building should have been, there was instead a window into some pale void. Shimmers of color whipped like snakes through the emptiness, and thick jade crystals poked at strange angles all around, casting an eerie glow over the surroundings. Staring at it made Gilbert's head hurt, but couldn't help glancing back every few moments.

Of course, there was also work to do. A few injured people had huddled near the exit slide. From their robes and gloves, Gilbert assumed they were wizards. One was cradling her arm. Another was bleeding from the scalp. A third sat with his hand on his side, struggling to breathe.

The fight wasn't finished, either, as evidenced by the frantic cacophony raging inside the building and the strange mist leaking out of the windows. It swirled teal and green, with occasional bursts of light throughout. Gilbert's first thought was poison gas. He covered his face with his shirt.

"Ah! The fun-run mist is working!" Mardulo cheered.

"Quite well, yes," said Madame Martoonisplau. "Didn't stop them, but it has slowed them down. And let me tell you, Hobblebosh's soldiers' silly walks may be even better than yours. I didn't expect this much visual interference, though. Rather spoils the effect...alas, it's done. Come, each of you grab a visitor's badge so the mist doesn't affect you."

She rummaged through a pocket that seemed far larger than it had any right to be and pulled out five lanyards.

Gilbert put his on. "That smoke is your doing?"

Madame Martoonisplau nodded. "I designed it precisely for this eventuality. We can chat about it later, but for now, let's put a stop to these ne'er-do-wells!"

She raised a fist and charged toward the building with a clamorous battle cry. The others followed more quietly. Mardulo and Bundersquash both took off their gloves as they ran.

Gilbert stayed close. They raced up the marble staircase and entered the building through a large door that opened automatically, but as Gilbert approached, it slammed shut. He rammed into it face-first.

Dizzy and frowning, he rubbed his nose, then grabbed the handle and pushed the door open manually, which seemed to work just fine.

He could no longer see the others, especially through the mist, but a sudden burst of light signaled activity to his left. He charged in that direction and found a wizard standing upside down on the ceiling, about nine feet in the air. His ID badge dangled down, just above Gilbert's head.

"Ho!" said the wizard.

"Are you okay?" asked Gilbert.

"Hanging in there."

Gilbert rolled his eyes.

"I only jest," said the wizard. "I should be fine. The magic will expire sometime this evening. Silly of me, really. It was my own spell that did it. Misconfigured the targeting parameters, then got tangled up in my own auric nebula."

Gilbert winced. "I'm sorry to hear that. Can I help?"

"There isn't much to do. Not looking forward to the landing, though." The wizard glanced uneasily at the floor.

Gilbert scanned the area. They seemed to be in some kind of lobby. His eye caught an upturned bench with a cushion on its seat. He rushed over, grabbed the cushion, then came back and placed it under the wizard. "Hopefully that'll soften the blow."

"Many thanks," said the wizard.

A shout rang out through a nearby door. It sounded like Mardulo, so Gilbert went that way and stumbled into an arcane-looking conference room. There was no fog, and the only light came from a miniature, gaseous night sky near the ceiling. A telescope pointed up at it from the corner. Glass cabinets lined the walls, but most of their contents had been smashed.

Mardulo and Bundersquash were both there, looking panicked on one side of a large table in the center of the room. Opposite them, an absolutely massive combatant, dressed all in black, seemed to be gathering his strength. His shoulders heaved with every breath. His glare alone looked deadly.

And Gilbert suddenly found himself the center of attention.

"Uh," he stammered, trying to think of something useful to say. "Hi."

"Hello!" said Mardulo, smiling as if he'd suddenly forgotten they were all about to get pulverized by one of Hobblebosh's henchmen.

The henchman was not so easily distracted. He used the interruption as an opportunity to lunge at Bundersquash, knife in hand.

In the same moment, Mardulo turned and swished his palms together. A bright silver cloud formed between his hands, sparkling as it swirled in on itself. Then he shouted in a language Gilbert didn't recognize, tossed dust into the air, and crouched. A horrendous metallic screech filled the room. The soldier flew back and slammed into the wall.

Dazed, the soldier shook himself, then focused all his attention on Mardulo. Now it was Bundersquash's turn to act. The younger wizard rubbed his hands together much as Mardulo had done, and a cloud of shimmering lilac mist formed around them. He spoke, then threw a loose sheet of paper into the cloud. A sudden flare of purple light engulfed Mardulo, whose body vanished instantly. The soldier paused, confused, as strange apparitions started to appear all over the room, each one popping in and out of existence in seconds. Some of them looked just like Mardulo. Others were similar, but changed—colored as if through a filter, or differently sized and proportioned. Each one sported a uniquely terrifying grin. Mardulo's laughter filled the room.

The henchman backed away as one particularly long-armed and green Mardulo appeared beside him, which gave Gilbert just enough time to grab a chair and throw it. That was the final straw, apparently, and the henchman fled. When the lobby's gas hit him, he lurched into a sudden bunny-hop triple-twist march.

The door shut, and Gilbert turned to the wizards. Mardulo's phantoms vanished, and the real Mardulo came into view, standing on the table, chuckling. "It's been a long time since I was hit with such a magnificent spectral-displacement illusion! What a wonderful idea, Bundersquash!"

Bundersquash grinned. "My pleasure, Professor!"

"Sorry for barging in like that," said Gilbert awkwardly.

"Nonsense. It was precisely the distraction I needed!" said Mardulo.

Gilbert scratched his head. "Glad I could help, then. Should we chase that person?"

"We may want to gather ingredients for more spells first," said Mardulo. "I'm almost out of all-purpose flour."

He and Bundersquash took a few minutes to pick through the ransacked shelves along the wall. Then they all headed back into the lobby, where Lady Ufferbub nearly slammed into them.

"Oh, good, you are here," she said. "Pallig needs healing."

"Which one's Pallig?" asked Mardulo.

"Tall fellow," said Bundersquash. "Ran that experiment with the por-cupine quills."

"Oh, Pallig! Where is he?"

"This way." Lady Ufferbub rushed toward the exit. Once again, Gilbert rammed face-first into a door that seemed to open automatically for every-one else. So far in this battle, these doors had harmed him more than any of the enemies. He grumbled a few choice words, then continued on.

The others were already hopping onto the exit slide. Gilbert joined them, more excited for the ride than he dared to admit. A small crowd had formed near the base, but it parted as soon as they arrived. Everyone locked their gaze on Mardulo.

"*That's actually him,*" someone in the crowd whispered to a friend.

Lady Ufferbub muscled past them and brought everyone to an uncon-scious wizard on a floating stretcher.

"Hobblebosh's soldiers had a wizard among them," she said. "I suppose we can add hypocrisy to the lime's ever-growing list of undesirable traits. Apparently, she cast some spell on Pallig. The poor fellow has been like this ever since."

Mardulo began the inspection immediately. "He's cold. Barely breath-ing. Pupils wavering. Skin pallid, slight tinge of aquamarine. Pallig's aura is aquamarine, yes? Anyone know what spell hit him?" He looked at the crowd. They shrugged.

"I suppose we can work around the unknowns." Mardulo stroked his beard. "Someone, grab me three vials of—"

Pallig's eyes shot open. He gasped for air. Then his eyes locked onto Mardulo. "*You're* here? Must be serious, then..."

"Can you describe what happened?" asked Mardulo.

"Hobblebosh's soldiers...Gorbinick spotted them first. Tried to stop them. They stabbed him. Right in the belly. Big scuffle. They broke Bel-tob's arm, and I think Karali lost a finger..." He grimaced. "Some lady cast a spell at me. Sounded like a severing charm, except she got interrupted. Still hit me, though. No idea what it's doing."

Mardulo put a hand on the injured wizard's head. "Rest. We'll figure it out. Nine times out of ten, something like this means an auric fissure...well, perhaps seven out of ten...um." Mardulo frowned, then grabbed a vial from his robe. "Does this hurt?"

He poured its contents onto Pallig's arm.

"Ow! Yes!" said Pallig.

"That settles it. Auric fissure. Plus, you've got a nasty knife wound on your calf."

Gilbert hadn't even noticed the blood on the stretcher, but there it was, pooling near Pallig's heel.

"It's too late for a standard auric seal," Mardulo continued. "I'll need to perform an immediate metaphysical fusion in tandem with an isolated physical-recovery charm. Risky. Never done it before...could be fun, though. You there"—he pointed to a nearby wizard—"grab me pellian extract, myrianic sealant, three vials of loosestrife nectar, two lily seeds, and some fizzy water. Now!"

The target of Mardulo's instruction shook nervously. "Yes, sir!" he said and ran back into the Consortium. A few wizards raced after him, bickering over who could find everything the fastest. They jostled down the slide when they returned, each carrying several bottles and packets, many of which appeared redundant.

"Many thanks," said Mardulo, ignoring their expectant expressions. "Now everyone, please, stand back."

He rubbed his hands together, and the same silver cloud formed around them. But this time, when Mardulo spoke his incantation, a teal projection of Pallig's body rose into the air. Slowly, the projection filled with phantom organs, veins, and tissue. As Mardulo worked, cross-sections rose and fell, all translucent, wavering in the night's soft starlight.

The other wizards started muttering. "Both procedures at the same time?" "Is that safe?" "What even is this spell?" "I didn't think you could—"

"Hush!" said Lady Ufferbub. "Let him focus."

At last, Mardulo found what he was looking for. He lifted his hands and worked at the model, threading beams of light like stitchwork, still mumbling under his breath. When he finished, he clapped his hands, and Pallig's real body latched on to the projection, sucking it back down forcefully. Pallig jolted with the impact, froze, then lurched into a sitting position.

He took a moment to orient himself. His calf appeared fully healed. His skin looked healthier too, less pale.

"I thought I was done for," he said at last.

Mardulo slapped him on the back. "Takes more than that to stop a wizard! Sorry about the rough landing, though. I suppose a bruise is better than the alternative, but next time I'll keep the recombinational forces in mind." He grinned. "Anyone else need help?"

"Most of the others have already been taken care of." Madame Martoonisplau emerged from the crowd, dusty but unharmed.

Toddleposter walked up as well. "And I'm pleased to report Hobblebosh's soldiers are in full retreat."

"We have much to discuss." Madame Martoonisplau waved Mardulo to one side, away from the crowd. He, Lady Ufferbub, Bundersquash, Toddleposter, and Gilbert all followed.

"Were there any casualties?" asked Lady Ufferbub.

"Thankfully, no," said Madame Martoonisplau. "In some ways, luck was with us. If they'd come during the daytime, if it had been more crowded…"

"Let us be glad it was not," said Lady Ufferbub.

"Still, they got what they came for."

"And what was that?" asked Mardulo.

"The wide-field residue corporealizer."

Mardulo frowned. "That's not good."

"It gets worse. One of my wizards saw them send it through a transport box. No idea how they managed to get one. But if Hobblebosh has the other half of that box, he could already have the corporealizer in hand. He can use it to create his own bridge across the Great Splat, bypassing our defenses entirely."

"How much time do you think we have?" asked Bundersquash.

"A few days. I can't imagine he'll wait long. I don't think he would risk an operation like this if he wasn't prepared to act."

Mardulo sighed. "We knew this was coming. Now it's here. We'll have to accelerate our plans."

Madame Martoonisplau shook her head. "You say that as if we have any…"

Chapter 5

Layers of Mischief

"Pottleswee is hardly a plan at all," said Madame Martoonisplau.

Mardulo frowned. "And you think your plan is better? Just surrender to Hobblebosh?"

"Surrender to Hobblebosh, *then fight him from the shadows*. Small, swift strikes. Slowly dismantle his forces."

"Using what? We won't have magic!"

"Weapons, Mardulo. The pointy kind."

"He'll be too well guarded for that."

"I'm not having this conversation again." Madame Martoonisplau threw up her arms. "If you wish to waste your time, then by all means, do so. I'll be getting ready."

She rolled her shoulders and trudged back into the Consortium.

Mardulo sighed. "She's not entirely wrong. Given this development, we ought to revisit our approach. There simply isn't time to fix our spell *and* get the flaming sword ready. Lady Ufferbub, would you like to join us in the Wizards' Tower? Or perhaps we could return to the library? If we—"

"Mardulo," Lady Ufferbub interrupted him. "How long has it been since you slept?"

Mardulo hesitated.

"A few days," said Bundersquash. "We've been focused on this summoning spell."

"You should rest. All of you."

"Did you not see what just happened?" Mardulo flailed his arms. "There's no time for rest!"

"To do this work, you must have a clear mind. You will not do any good if you are constantly operating at suboptimal capacity. And Gigglebrit"—her expression softened—"you should take some time. Do you need a place to stay? We do not have many beds in the library, but I am sure we could find something."

"Let him stay with us," said Mardulo. "Long term, we can set him up in the city, but the Wizards' Tower has plenty of room in the meantime."

"Which would you prefer, Gigglebrit?" asked Toddleposter.

Gilbert paused. Mardulo had just mentioned "long term" and it had triggered an unpleasant mess of complicated emotions that he wasn't quite ready to deal with. The reality of this reality was still sinking in, and he needed more time to think. More time to adjust. More time to consider everything.

Then again...did he?

He was standing next to a bunch of wizards! Who needed physics when you could learn magic? Who needed biology when you had potions? Who needed college when you had heroes and villains and a whole fantastical world to explore?

Gilbert didn't need Earth. Earth didn't matter. His old life didn't matter. He needed to look forward. Here, he could be something more than a regular boy going through the motions of a normal life. He could be a wizard's pupil, an adventurer, a force for good.

Here, he could be—

"Gigglebrit?" asked Toddleposter.

Gigglebrit.

"This Wizards' Tower." Gigglebrit faced the others. "Is that where you summoned me? With all the magic books and stuff?"

"No, that was a wizards' workshop," said Mardulo. "We live in the Wizards' Tower. Very different."

"And this building here is...?"

"The Wizarding Consortium. Also different."

Toddleposter smiled sympathetically. "They don't call it the Wizard's City for nothing."

"Well, I've already seen the library. Let's give this Wizards' Tower a try."

"In that case," said Mardulo, "we should be off. The sooner we depart, the sooner we can rest, the sooner we can resume our work."

"If you see Gurming while you're there," said Lady Ufferbub, "you may want to check in with him. He came by earlier looking for my Roster key. Something about mirrors and doors. But he did mention Hobblebosh. He said he wished to speak with you, and he would want to know about the attack."

"Of course," said Mardulo. "I'll see if I can find him."

The librarians agreed to meet them at the tower the next morning. Toddleposter would watch Lobster in the meantime. After a quick round of goodbyes among the Consortium employees, Gigglebrit, Mardulo, and Bundersquash made their leave.

As they wandered the streets, Gigglebrit's gaze drifted upward. In all the rush to get to the Consortium, he hadn't taken the time to appreciate it, but the night sky in this world was something to behold. The stars shone wondrously—a thousand glowing marvels of white, yellow, blue, and red, coming together to form a blanket of light that fell upon the city in a gentle haze of illumination.

His mom would've loved to see it. She'd have wanted to—

No.

That was the past. Gigglebrit forced himself to stop thinking about it. This new world was the important one, the real one. He would have to get used to it.

He would help Mardulo and Bundersquash, he decided. It would give him direction again, and right now, that seemed important—something to do. Something fun.

He jogged up to them.

"I want to help stop Hobblebosh. I know I don't have any useful skills yet, like magic or"—he thought of Lady Ufferbub and Toddleposter—"or librarianship, but I'm willing to learn. Hobblebosh knows you exist. He doesn't know about me. It's an advantage. I could hide, then do a surprise attack or something!"

"Well, you certainly have enthusiasm, I'll give you that," said Mardulo. "But it's dangerous. It wouldn't be right for us to pull you into it."

"I don't care how dangerous it is. I want to do this."

"You've only just been created..." Mardulo took a moment to think it over, but eventually, he sighed and said, "No. I'm sorry, Gigglebrit. It's just too risky."

Gigglebrit frowned, but he wasn't about to give up so easily. He had all evening to prove his worth, and he was going to make it happen. Still, he worried pressing the matter now might only solidify Mardulo's stance, so he changed the subject.

"Why's it always towers, anyway?" he asked. "In stories, it seems like wizards are always putting themselves in towers or spires. I never understood it."

Mardulo stroked his beard. "Tradition, I suppose. And status. And fun. But mostly, it's because when things go splat, it's good to have a few extra layers to burn through before causing any real damage to the planet."

Gigglebrit blinked.

"It's a fun place!" Mardulo smiled. "The Wizardry Intelligence Training Board created it. It serves as the living quarters for all the Wizardry Intelligence professors and a number of the more prominent students." He nodded toward Bundersquash, who grinned.

"It's usually twenty stories tall," said Bundersquash. "Each floor represents a different rank within the professional hierarchy."

"I like floor sixteen, myself," said Mardulo. "They're all training to become lead professors and spend most of their time studying for their Tinderwood Principles Exam. Oh, the wonderful messes they make! I've never seen so many colorful disasters in my life. I once found the whole place turned blue. Never could get rid of the stuff. They had to paint over it, and that was no easy task, let me tell you."

"I prefer floor twelve," said Bundersquash. "It houses the botanists. Only Bellgiggle and Ulden, at the moment, but they're both so passionate about their work!"

"Which floor are you on?" asked Gigglebrit.

The two wizards went suspiciously quiet. Bundersquash blushed.

"We're at the top," said Mardulo.

"The top? Like, the highest rank?"

Mardulo waved his hands. "Don't read too much into it. We're still not in charge of the place. Those buffoons on nineteen are always breathing down our necks, and the Wizardry Intelligence Training Board gets the final say. Still, it's not a bad spot."

"Of course, the wizards on other floors are just as skilled as us," Bundersquash added hastily, "but someone like Bellgiggle wouldn't want to work on floor twenty, when floor twelve's the one with a greenhouse."

Gigglebrit felt a sudden surge of pride. He was staying with the two highest-ranking wizardry professors in the entire university.

At the same time, he suffered a twinge of horror as he realized Mardulo and Bundersquash were the two highest-ranking wizardry professors in the entire university. In just half a day, he'd seen them release a flying demonic book, catch it with a purple blanket, get distracted about a hundred times while looking for Earth, then speak casually about potentially damaging the planet when things "go splat."

Not to mention they'd accidentally pulled a fictional character into the real world while trying to summon the chosen one.

They'd done all right at the Consortium, though, and the other wizards seemed to respect them. That was something.

The rest of the walk passed uneventfully. While Gigglebrit tried to think about how he could make himself useful, the wizards chatted between themselves, wondering what—if anything—this wizard named Gurming may have found. Apparently, he lived on floor eighteen.

The Wizards' Tower rose from the ground in a terribly crooked cylinder that bent and curved its way toward a pointed, blue-shingled roof. Differently sized windows peppered the brick exterior, but there was no real structure to the thing except for rounded walls and a vaguely upward direction. It brought to mind images of beanstalks, or perhaps the aftermath of a particularly ambitious knot-tying session.

"Home at last," said Mardulo. "What do you think, Gigglebrit?"

"It certainly looks exciting. The park is nice too."

He looked out over the wide grassy field that surrounded the tower. It had a few trees here and there and a series of nicely managed cobblestone pathways throughout. Gigglebrit could picture himself here—sitting in the grass, reading about magic, practicing spells or swordplay. A pleasant hub for his adventure.

"I agree," said Bundersquash. "It's a shame it gets so few visitors."

Gigglebrit glanced once again at the swirling, impossible tower in the center of everything and said, "I wonder why that could be."

Mardulo gave him a solid pat on the back. "More for us to enjoy!"

They approached along the nearest pathway and came to a large wooden door. It was dark blue, with an emblem carved in the center—a tied scroll and feathered quill, surrounded with a ring of stars. Beneath it, in swirling golden letters, "W. I. T. Residence."

It opened automatically as Mardulo and Bundersquash approached, then shut itself forcefully in Gigglebrit's face.

"Again?" Gigglebrit muttered as he reached for the handles and walked in.

He pulled up short when he saw the interior. It was almost exactly the opposite of what he'd expected. The space was immaculate, with shining marble floors, a glossy finish on the walls, and an ambient glisten throughout. The two wizards, with their hodgepodge robes and excitable tendencies, looked exceptionally out of place.

Someone—a guard, Gigglebrit assumed from the heavily decorated outfit—stood to one side. She smiled and waved. "Mardulo, Bundersquash! It is a pleasure to finally meet you! I was actually hoping to—hang on, who are you?" She looked at Gigglebrit.

"I'm Gi–"

"WHAT IN THE WORLD IS THIS?!" Mardulo's voice consumed the lobby in one powerful wave of anger. Gigglebrit ducked for cover. The guard did the same.

Mardulo walked up, eyes narrowed. He spoke with a voice of ice. "Why is there an armed guard in our lobby?"

The guard stared at him, eyes wide.

"It was floor nineteen, wasn't it?" Mardulo muttered.

"Actually, I just—"

"It's always floor nineteen," Mardulo spoke over her. "Those nitwits wouldn't know a spell if someone took their bloody heads off with one! Going on and on about their sign-ins, safety contracts, and permission slips as if it could ever lead to progress! If they had their way, we'd never do anything at all! Bundersquash and I would be dead by now, suffocated under a mountain of liability waivers and release forms. The other wizards would've quit for sheer boredom!"

"Careful, Professor." Bundersquash walked up, hands raised. "Take a breath. Count to ten. This guard, whoever she is, seems to be on our side."

Mardulo looked at his pupil, then did as he was told.

"Sorry," he said, brushing his robe and tugging his beard. "I suppose I got carried away. I was hoping to make a better first impression on our guest here." He waved at Gigglebrit, then extended a hand toward the guard. "Nice to meet you, um…"

"Whirga," she said, recovering. "Whirga Sludgepoge Tudlepett the Stationed. After the recent attack on the Wizarding Consortium, it seemed prudent to have someone standing guard. It is a pleasure to…well, it's somewhat nice, at least…" She stopped, reset. "It's good to meet you at last, Mardulo and Bundersquash." Then she turned to Gigglebrit. "And who might you be?"

Gigglebrit took a deep breath. "I'm Gigglebrit. Gigglebrit Maistowne Nebraska the, uh…the Fictional."

He turned to Mardulo and Bundersquash, who seemed to note the change in title but did nothing to indicate a problem.

Good enough.

Whirga pulled a notebook and pencil from her belt, then wrote the name down. "Nice to meet you, Gigglebrit."

"He'll be staying with us for a while," said Bundersquash. "Please treat him as you would any other resident."

Whirga nodded, then directed them to the stairs, which spiraled around the edge of the room and rose into the floor above.

Once again, the door opened automatically for the others, but Gigglebrit had to push his way through manually. At least it didn't smash his nose this time.

"This is floor two," said Mardulo.

"Yes, I got that, thanks," said Gigglebrit.

"Well, sometimes it's floor three."

"Oh."

It was a simple space, and cozy. Thick silver carpet blanketed the floor. The walls were dark red. They had entered into a common room with cushioned chairs, one large table, and a gentle, crackling fire. Opposite Gigglebrit, a wall cut the otherwise-circular area in half. There were five doors in it, some slightly ajar, which appeared to lead into bedrooms.

"Mind your step," said Mardulo. "If I recall correctly, there's a stain on the carpet, and it bites."

"Um, thanks," said Gigglebrit, minding his step.

"There's a secret passage in the fireplace, too, but it just leads back to its own entrance. I can't say I recommend the trip, especially with the fire and all, but it's nice to see the students having fun. Do you know how hard I had to fight to get fireplaces installed in the first place? Floor nineteen kept going on about *insurance*. We're wizards, for goodness' sake! Fire is half of what we do! Don't hold it against the other residents, though. They do some truly magnificent work around here. Hello!"

He waved at a few wizards who had peeked their heads out from behind the doors. Their expressions portrayed a complex mixture of confusion, panic, and awe. One or two waved back.

"Now, on we go," said Mardulo. "Plenty more to see!"

Gigglebrit waved at the students and followed the wizards upstairs.

The third floor was much the same as the second, but the walls were orange, not red. The fourth was yellow, the fifth was green, the sixth blue, and the seventh purple.

"Those lower levels are mostly students," Mardulo explained, "but from here on up, you get a mixture of professors, training professors, and advanced pupils like Bundersquash."

"That's exciting," said Gigglebrit, breathing hard from the ascent. "Will they be doing any actual magic?"

"Possibly!" Mardulo smiled. "Only one way to find out."

"Right," Gigglebrit panted. He was still catching his breath, embarrassed at his own fatigue. He was trying to prove himself worthy of an adventure, yet here he was, wheezing with his hand on the wall. Meanwhile, Mardulo and Bundersquash seemed to hop along without any trouble at all.

He straightened up and forced himself forward.

Floor eight had black walls and a clean white carpet. Floor nine had clean white walls and black carpet. Floor ten looked like a zebra.

There was a massive mess on floor eleven's table—some kind of purple goo, mixed with sparkly bits and a disconcerting assortment of objects that don't usually glow, glowing. Four residents stood around the concoction, smothering laughter.

Floor twelve's carpet was brown, its ceiling pale blue, and the walls painted to look like giant blades of grass against a woodland background. Gigglebrit felt like a beetle looking up from the forest floor. The common area was some kind of greenhouse, with dozens of small stands organized into neat rows, each holding a plant. The ceiling shone with what seemed like sunlight.

Bundersquash gasped, bustling toward a red plant with long, bundled petals. "Look, Professor! They've done it! They've been working on this for years!" He took a great whiff and swooned. "Oh, it's lovely! I wonder if—FMMP!"

In an instant, his cheeks puffed to rival the size of his glasses. Then he grew a moustache. His face paled. A top hat squeezed into existence and fell into place atop his head.

Gigglebrit looked at Mardulo, whose expression confirmed that even by this world's standards, this was a strange occurrence.

Words bullied their way out of Bundersquash's mouth: "This. Is...errg. This. Is—erk. Oh dear..."

His ears stretched, swayed, and grew fur. His nose turned pink. His eyes widened in distress, but the rest of him was happily transforming into a well-dressed, human-size rabbit creature. The moustache expanded into a full beard, then blossomed into a total covering of soft black fur. He sprouted a marvelous bushy tail.

Suddenly, he had a tuxedo on.

"Bundersquash," said Mardulo. "Are you all right?"

Bundersquash didn't respond. He was too busy hopping. Vigorously. He careened through several tables and plants, knocked over a chair, then took a great bite from a sofa near the fireplace, stopped, wriggled his nose, and spit it back out.

"Bundersquash..." Mardulo looked at a loss, torn between concern and intrigue. "Would you mind just—er—slowing down, please?"

Bundersquash refused to even acknowledge his professor. Instead, he lunged toward the bedrooms.

Gigglebrit stepped up. Finally, a chance to prove himself.

"Bundersquash," he said sternly. "Sit. Stay."

It didn't work.

"Um...heel?" He tried to grab the Bundersquash-Rabbit by its arm and was promptly thrown aside.

Recovering, he turned to Mardulo. "You wouldn't happen to have any carrots, would you?"

"Regrettably, I do not. Bellgiggle may have some, though."

As if on cue, Bundersquash kicked in one of the bedroom doors, revealing a woman sitting behind a small desk. Her eyes were dark green. Her hair, purple and silver. She wore a pair of gardening gloves with a long brown coat that looked to be made mostly of pockets, and she seemed far less surprised than she should have been.

She saw Mardulo and quickly put the pieces together. "Hello, Bundersquash!" she said, smiling. "I see you've found the latest iteration of our transdimensionally fused rose-gardenia hybrid. And you look positively adorable!"

She stood up—she must have been nearly seven feet tall—walked into the common area, then clapped a simple rhythm. With an iridescent shimmer, an entire kitchen materialized against the curved wall—sink, countertops, cupboards, and all. It settled into place with a strange low-pitched sizzle.

Bellgiggle removed a vial of luminescent blue liquid from one of the cupboards, then turned back to Bundersquash.

"I don't expect you can understand me," she said, "but just in case, please hold still."

Bundersquash hopped in a circle. Bellgiggle sighed, waited for him to turn his back, then dumped the vial's contents along his head and spine.

Bundersquash twitched. Blinked. Sniffed. Then his fur started to recede.

His ears shrank, his nose returned to its original color, and the top hat disappeared into whatever fancy void world it had come from. Soon, the fine gentle rabbit had been lost to the world, and Bundersquash stood before them once more.

He looked around for a moment. "Blimey! Hello, Bellgiggle! Sorry about that!"

"Not to worry, Bundersquash." Bellgiggle smiled. "The same thing happened to Ulden this morning, except he was a giant mouse. The fancy dress seems to be a common thread, though. I expect it has something to do with our incantation's double-sided courtesy matrix. It took almost an hour before I figured out how to turn Ulden back. I made some extra antidote, just in case."

"Much appreciated." Bundersquash grinned. "The flower smells lovely, by the way. You never fail to impress."

"Many thanks. And I must say, you made for a very fine rabbit." She laughed, then walked over to the others. "Hello, Mardulo. Who is this?"

"I'm Gigglebrit."

Bellgiggle waited for more.

"Gigglebrit Maistowne Nebraska the Fictional."

"A pleasure." She shook his hand. "I am Bellgiggle Kaiy Wopp the Maker."

"Where's Ulden?" asked Mardulo. "You said he turned into a mouse?"

"Yes, but he's back to normal now. Went for an evening stroll. I recall he had a hankering for cheese. Now, if you will excuse me for just a moment, I should clean up this mess before it's too late."

She removed her gloves and rubbed her hands together. A swirling hazel cloud formed between her fingers. It hovered in front of her as she produced a handful of powder from one of her many pockets and tossed it into the air.

Then, as she spoke an incantation, the room began to rewind. The upturned tables righted themselves. The pots reformed and repaired. The spills of dirt poured back to fill their former homes, and plants burrowed their unearthed roots back into the soil. In a few quick seconds, the entire room had been restored.

Gigglebrit could hardly believe his eyes.

"How," he said, gawking, "did you do that?"

"It's a simple recovery charm," said Bellgiggle. "The whole room is protected, but it can only go back ten minutes."

"It's incredible!" Gigglebrit surveyed the newly repaired room. Some of the plants looked ordinary, but most boasted at least a few oddities. One grew flowers down into the soil and was visible only through a magical window wavering in the pot and dirt. Another had clear leaves, like water suspended in air, but its edges burned like cinders. Worryingly, the flower Bundersquash had sniffed looked to be one of the simpler installments.

"What's the transdimensional rose-gardenia hybrid supposed to do?" he asked. "Or was that bunny thing intentional?"

"Oh, no, the transformation was a surprise to us all. We'll have to run a few more experiments to figure out exactly why it happened, though I may keep this version around. For parties."

"Right...so, if not the rabbit, what's the intended effect?"

Bellgiggle scrunched her eyebrows. "Mostly, it will look nice in your garden. We're hoping it will smell good too."

"Oh." Gigglebrit tried to keep from looking disappointed. "And how is it magical, exactly?"

"Well, it doesn't occur naturally, so we made it. With magic."

As Gigglebrit processed this, Bellgiggle pointed to Mardulo and Bundersquash.

"I take it you're staying with these two? I've been to floor twenty myself a few times. It's a marvelous place. Say hello to the playset for me."

"The playset?" asked Gigglebrit.

"We'll explain when we get there," said Mardulo. "Bellgiggle, many thanks for your time. Give Ulden my best when he returns."

"I will," said Bellgiggle. "I hope you enjoy your stay, Gigglebrit! May luck travel with you all. And Bundersquash, if you don't mind, I'd love a few swabs from your nasal cavity. Just send them down whenever you have a moment."

"Of course!" Bundersquash nodded, and they ascended to floor thirteen. It was dark as a starless sky. They felt their way along the stairs and entered floor fourteen, which was more of a war zone than a dormitory. Someone had flipped the table to serve as a shield, with an armchair protecting their flank. One of the bedroom doors had been knocked in. Another was missing entirely, though the room beyond looked more like an aircraft hangar than a bedroom.

A middle-aged man waved from behind the sofa. "Hello, Professor! If you see a one-winged rhinoceros, please send it our way!"

Mardulo waved back. "Will do, Borpum!"

Floor fifteen had everyone gathered around a large podium that was covered in painted symbols. They appeared to be casting a complex series of spells, eyes closed, hands extended, chanting in that same strange language everyone seemed to be using for spells.

"Can we watch?" asked Gigglebrit hopefully.

"Not much will happen," said Mardulo. "They're refreshing the neighborhood's architectural charms. It takes a lot of magic to keep this city standing, and the spells have to be reinforced regularly. Without them, a lot of the damage that's been done over the years would creep back into reality. Not to mention all the spatial and gravitational warping we rely on to keep things where they should be. All of it can fade, so we take shifts on the upkeep. Just one more reason to ensure Hobblebosh never makes it this far south..."

Floors sixteen was quiet, with a few wizards gathered around the fireplace. Floor seventeen was filled with purple fog—thick and seemingly endless, it seemed to stretch into the very walls.

Mardulo stopped at floor eighteen. "Gurming?" he called out. "I asked him to research Hobblebosh's restricted zone, but that was weeks ago. I'd assumed nothing came of it, but if he told Lady Ufferbub he was looking for me..." His voice trailed off. "Still, I can't see how that has anything to do with mirrors or doors. *Gurming! Hello?*"

No response.

They stepped into the common area and looked around. It had been painted to look like an underwater reef. Magic made everything move. The walls swirled with teal ripples, pushing and pulling at long, undulant strands of seaweed. A school of fish swam around the perimeter, zipping gracefully between a rainbow of coral and stone. Wavering sunlight shone through the currents, and the sandy ocean floor blended seamlessly with the room's beige carpet. The wall was solid, but Gigglebrit's hand came away wet.

"I don't see him anywhere," said Mardulo. He poked a mirror lying on the table.

Bundersquash knocked on one of the bedroom doors. Nothing.

"Perhaps tomorrow," said Mardulo, and they continued to floor nineteen, a plaza of cream and beige. Aisles of suit-wearing wizards sat at private desks, scribbling into stacks of paper. They looked stressed, tired, and terribly overworked.

"Where do they sleep?" Gigglebrit whispered. The usual set of bedrooms was nowhere in sight.

"They're supposed to go home at night," said Bundersquash, "but they usually have to work overtime."

"Of course, if they all just quit—" Mardulo started, but Bundersquash cut him short. He shoved the professor up the stairs, through another automatic door. Gigglebrit followed behind, pushing the door open by hand.

At long last, they reached floor twenty.

Chapter 6

New Home

Gigglebrit felt as though he'd run a marathon, but his urge to explore outweighed his exhaustion and he paced the tower's top level in awe.

At first glance, the walls looked like a Van Gogh skyline curving across the room like a painted window—thick, heavy strokes, showing the outside world in all directions. But when Gigglebrit got closer, he noticed something more. As the outside changed, so did the paint, in slow, smooth waves. He gazed down at the weaving streets below, watching them shift and whirl. Twenty stories up, he would have expected more vertigo, but something about the style made it bearable.

Streetlamps glowed with blots of flame, illuminating cobbled paths. The trees and the grass twisted in the wind, and the occasional person wandered by, abstractly, in gentle swirls of motion. On the ceiling, the painted moon and stars shone with real brightness, filling the room with light.

Bundersquash stepped to Gigglebrit's side. "That's odd. You can usually see Wizards' Workshop 4C from here."

Gigglebrit shrugged.

"The view is best at sunrise," said Mardulo. "You wouldn't believe the colors."

"Care for a full tour?" asked Bundersquash. He waved an arm at the rest of the common room.

It was much the same as the lower levels, just busier. For a floor that housed only two wizards, the signs of use were remarkable. The table stood in the center of the room, buried under symbol-laden scrolls, glowing tubes, and oddly shaped pendants—not to mention several dozen books stacked at either end. Nearby, Bundersquash showed him a sturdy mahogany podium, pocked with enough dents to rival the moon. Its top was riddled with scorch marks. This was, apparently, where they cast most of their spells.

"It's been doubly reinforced," Bundersquash added with pride. "But it does have a tendency to make animal noises. Nothing harmful, just startling."

Gigglebrit nodded, slowly.

"We will, on occasion, use it for cooking," said Bundersquash, "but only if the food needs a real kick. Otherwise, we use the countertop."

"What do you think of the fireplace?" asked Mardulo.

Streaks of rainbow flame danced among the logs—more colors than Gigglebrit could even begin to list. He walked over and held out his hands.

"It's not very warm," said Gigglebrit. "But it is...flamboyant."

"Exactly!" Mardulo beamed. "I cast the spell myself shortly after I moved in. No one wants a hot fire in the middle of summer, but it adds so much to the ambience! And a little flair never hurt anyone. Some of the other floors have asked for similar enhancements, but ours is the only one with such a tangible sense of turquoise."

Gigglebrit observed the turquoise.

"Now, you need a place to sleep!" Mardulo clapped his gloved hands together, then gestured to the doors opposite the staircase. "The bedrooms are numbered, one to five. I sleep in one. Bundersquash stays in two. Three is largely unoccupied. Four is mostly storage. As for five..." He hesitated. "Don't go into room five."

"Why not?" asked Gigglebrit.

Bundersquash answered. "We tried to create a playset for Park Somondel a few years ago—something for the kids to enjoy while their parents were at the café or working nearby…but it started to move by itself, then developed some kind of premature sentience. Except it's missing some of the more important bits, like intellect…and kindness. Plenty of fury, though." He shivered.

"It's been in there ever since," Mardulo added. "As far as anyone can tell, it doesn't believe in the outside world. We tried to lead it somewhere more hospitable, but it seems to think we're deceiving it into entering some kind of vacuous nether region." He stroked his beard, eyebrows furrowed. "Anyway, it bumps around in there sometimes."

"Right…"

"Don't worry." Bundersquash put a hand on Gigglebrit's shoulder. "It is, after all, only a playset. It has no hands and cannot open doors…except, perhaps, through a clever manipulation of its swing, but I don't think it's figured that out yet."

"Naturally," said Gigglebrit, making a mental catalogue of places to avoid at all costs.

"If you need to wash up," said Mardulo, "you can convert your bedroom into a bathroom with a simple double-knock activation sequence on the door."

He walked to his own room to demonstrate. When the door first opened, it led into a shockingly colorful bedroom, but when Mardulo closed it, knocked twice, and opened it again, it led to a room with a tiled floor, a sink, a toilet, and a bathtub. A mirror hung on the back of the door, and a collection of plush towels sat on a shelf near the sink.

"So, you have plumbing?" Gigglebrit asked, relieved to see normal-looking taps for the sink and tub.

"Just the usual two-step freshwater-teleportation system, run through a standard intermediary filtration matrix operated by the city and maintained through the Consortium's nonprofit branch."

"So, it's clean?" said Gigglebrit. "Potable water comes out the tap?"

"Correct," said Bundersquash. "And we can always put in a flavor request, if you'd like."

"I'm good, thanks."

"And texture, any preference?"

"Um...regular? What are the options?"

"Plain, silky, thick, crunchy, slushy, fuzzy—"

"Plain, please." Gigglebrit grimaced. "Definitely plain."

"As you wish," said Mardulo. He shut the door to his bathroom, then walked over and opened room three. "Would this be agreeable to you?"

It was surprisingly simple. The walls were gray, the floor covered in soft blue carpet. There was an empty bed on one side, next to a bedside table and lamp. On the opposite wall, a closet stood beside a large bookshelf—the first Gigglebrit had seen in this world to have some actual space in it. Apart from a few knickknacks on the bedside table, it was clean.

"This is great," said Gigglebrit. "Thanks!"

"My pleasure," said Mardulo. "Though I regret there are a few small things to clean up. Bundersquash, would you mind doing that while I fetch some bedding?"

"Happily!" said Bundersquash.

"Can I help?" asked Gigglebrit as Mardulo stepped out.

"I don't think there's much to do." Bundersquash looked around the room. "I'll just move a few items, and we should be good to go."

He grabbed a strange, spiky model sailing ship—his first attempt at a wood-carving spell, apparently—and moved it into his own room along with an ornamental snow globe and a silver plate that reportedly made anything on it taste sweet.

"The trouble is," Bundersquash added, "if you actually want to *eat* the food, it has to come off the plate first."

After that, only one item remained—a corked bottle boasting an exceptionally unfriendly label, the kind of thing Hollywood might use to represent poison, explosives, or gluten. It left a purple stain on the wood underneath it.

"Shadowblood." Bundersquash grimaced. "Vile stuff. We took it from some hooligans on floor three. I wanted to destroy it, but Mardulo insisted otherwise. He thought it might be worth studying. 'Dangerous to throw anything out!' he said. 'You never know when you might need it!' Just been sitting here ever since…"

Bundersquash shook his head, then stepped out and locked the bottle in a wall safe behind a window, which Gigglebrit couldn't really wrap his head around.

Just as Bundersquash resealed the safe, Mardulo emerged from room one carrying an entire closet's worth of supplies.

"I'm glad you're here, Gigglebrit," he said. "I'm afraid I don't know anything about Earth's climate. Is it warm there? I've grabbed fourteen blankets just in case." He heaved the monstrous pile over to Gigglebrit. "Otherwise, I could fetch a cooling sheet. Oh, and here's a pillow!" He added it to the mass.

Gigglebrit buckled under the weight of it all. "Thank you," he wheezed, then waddled into his room and dumped it onto the mattress.

"Also," Mardulo continued, "I wasn't sure when you'd want to wake up in the morning, but I've conjured this timing device." He placed a mahogany mantel clock on the bedside table, covering the shadowblood stain. "I think that should be all! Anything else I can get you?"

"This is great. Thanks."

"That's a relief." Mardulo sighed. "In that case, I believe it's time for dinner! I was thinking baked potatoes, or perhaps some clam chowder. Did Earth have clams?"

"We did," said Gigglebrit.

"Lovely. I'll let you know when it's ready."

He rushed off, and Gigglebrit soon heard the same clapping pattern Bellgiggle had used to summon the kitchen on her floor.

Then Mardulo screamed.

Bundersquash leaped into the common room. "Is everything okay?"

Gigglebrit followed behind, trying not to panic.

"It's Gurming!" said Mardulo. "He's in the kitchen mirror!"

Sure enough, a man was visible in a mirror just above the sink, sitting on the mirror-couch of the mirror-common-area, inspecting a book through a magnifying glass. He looked the kind of age one would usually reserve for archeological findings.

Gigglebrit turned, just to be sure. The man wasn't in the real room. Only the mirror.

Mardulo tapped the glass. "Hello?"

Gurming looked up from his book. When he saw Mardulo, his face lit up. He ran to the mirror, waving his arms enthusiastically to one side.

Mardulo and Bundersquash looked curious. Bundersquash mimicked the hand motions. Mardulo called out, "Whale? Dolphin?"

"I don't think he's playing charades…" Gigglebrit bent over the counter and inspected the side of the mirror. There was a switch there, not unlike an Earthen light switch.

He flipped it.

The mirror's surface darkened in shadow, and then Gurming, leaving the book behind but still holding his magnifying glass, clambered onto the mirror-world-sink, crawled through the mirror into the real world, then sprang down from the countertop in a lively, if unrefined, hop.

"Woo-hoo!" he cheered. "So glad you showed up! I've been stuck in there for hours! Got a bit worried when the kitchen timed out and hid itself."

"How did you manage this?" Mardulo stuck his hand inside the shadowed mirror, then pulled it out again, his eyes wide with amazement.

"Funny thing. Made the switch to get in, wanted to test it, figured I had time while I was waiting for you, then I got a bit carried away. As it happens, my switch to get out didn't work. Good discovery, though. Glad I had the sandwich generator, but I am thirsty…"

He helped himself to a glass of water. "Mmm, bubbly!" He smiled. "Now, who's this?" He inspected Gigglebrit through his magnifying glass. "Not a spy, is he?"

"I'm Gigglebrit Maistowne Nebraska the Fictional," said Gigglebrit, extending a hand. "Definitely not a spy."

Gurming raised an eyebrow.

"He's telling the truth," said Bundersquash.

"Jolly good." Gurming took Gigglebrit's hand. "I'm Gurming Wollytop Nundertunder the Swimmer. Pleased to meet you."

"Gurming"—Mardulo frowned—"I'm not sure if you heard, but Hobblebosh attacked the Wizarding Consortium. He obtained the wide-field residue corporealizer, and we need to accelerate our plans. I know you've been busy, but—"

"Say no more, Mardulo." Gurming raised his glass of water. "You bring dire news, but I've some good in return. You asked me to look into how Hobblebosh has been blocking magic, and I've finally got something! You see, after a few days of no progress, the question moved itself more toward the back of my mind, as these things tend to go. But it's a funny old place back there—and cluttered, let me tell you—so soon enough, it got to mixing with all the other nonsense occupying that same general headspace and suddenly, wham!" He flourished, spilling half his water.

"Just like that, an idea!" he continued. "It all started with the mirrors. At first, I planned for nothing more than a useful storage mechanism, but with Hobblebosh causing all manner of mayhem, I realized they could serve another purpose—a hiding place for wartime resources! It's nice and discreet, out of the way, and nothing's actually invisible, so detection charms won't reveal it. No cloaking or other forms of concealment. It's just…elsewhere. Hidden in plain sight. And they take up no space while they're at it! *And* it's preenchanted, so no need for active spellcasting. If Hobblebosh does take the city, this could be critical in supporting Madame Martoonisplau's underground resistance! All I needed was a way to keep Hobblebosh out, and that's when things really came together."

He reached back and pulled the switch off the side of the mirror. It came free with a faint suction-cup pop.

"You see," said Gurming, "so far, I've been using these switches. Simple. You stick one on the mirror, and it enables mirror-world storage. But anyone can flip a switch, even Hobblebosh. So how do we keep him out?" His eyes gleamed. "The Roster."

"What's the Roster?" asked Gigglebrit.

Gurming frowned. "You've never heard of it?"

"Gigglebrit is…new," Bundersquash explained. "Basically, the Roster is a list containing the names of every living person in the world."

Gigglebrit hesitated. "All of them?" he asked, repressing the flurry of privacy concerns and ethical conundrums that swarmed around the idea.

"Every last one!" said Mardulo.

"*Except Hobblebosh*," added Gurming. "And that's the critical point. He's a lime. The Roster's magic never picked him up. So, in theory, I could filter my mirror switches to only respond to users who are on the Roster, and Hobblebosh couldn't use it! But once I'd thought of that, I realized Hobblebosh could be using the Roster *himself*. That's the key to his restricted zone. By using the Roster's list of names to target his spell-blocking magic, he can affect everyone else but avoid affecting himself! The Roster is how he's blocking magic!"

"But he isn't affecting everyone," said Mardulo. "He's only affecting the people in his territory. And the Roster is infused with so many protections

I highly doubt he could use it so dramatically—at least, not without proper authorization."

"That's just it. The two issues are related!" Gurming clambered onto the countertop for what Gigglebrit could only assume was dramatic effect. "His spell blocking only affects people in his territory *because* of the protections the Roster has in place. We all know it has some questionable back doors for those in power, and if it recognizes Hobblebosh as a *significant governing agent* for a given location, he could likely work around many of the defenses."

Mardulo stroked his beard. "Hobblebosh blocked magic in City Mez *before* conquering the city, but perhaps the Roster's governance protocols would still register him as significant given the size of his army and his overly domineering nature, even if he hadn't conquered the city yet..."

"That's exactly right!" said Gurming. "I'd bet my life on it. Well, I suppose I'm betting yours, but I'd still do it. And don't fret. I ran tests to be sure. Ralgorbit visited the restricted zone with his toad recently, and sure enough, when I examined him, I found evidence of long-term, persistent exposure to a broad-scale Roster-based targeting mechanism!"

Mardulo grinned. "Gurming, you amaze me! This discovery could turn the tides! Also, if you see Ralgorbit again, tell him he owes me an ice cream. I checked earlier today, and—"

"Wait," Gigglebrit cut in. "Before you get sidetracked, does this mean you can stop Hobblebosh? You just add his name to the Roster and he's powerless?" He tried not to sound too disappointed.

"Goodness no!" Mardulo laughed. "Manually modifying the Roster is nearly impossible. We added Toddleposter's name when he was created, and you wouldn't believe the hoops we had to jump through! Toddleposter had to cast the spell himself, and we needed formal approval from every member of the City Boratorus Council of Five *and* the mayor of Port Tup! Removing names is even more difficult. A strange little wizard named

Cormo Faliper Radigu the Stalwart tried that once. His hands turned into rodent heads, and they never stopped bickering. The left ate the right in his sleep, then he died three years later."

Gigglebrit chose to ignore that last bit. "So, Hobblebosh isn't on the Roster because he's a lime, and Toddleposter wasn't on it when you created him, I guess because he's a clone?"

"In a way," said Mardulo. "The Roster was created almost a thousand years ago. The wizard who created it—Elder Moggle Doshter Portimur the Taciturn—was brilliant for his time but didn't think to account for these sorts of scenarios in his spellwork. Quite simply, when a person is born, their name is added. When that person dies, it's removed. A fairly straightforward concept, though the magic behind such a thing is beyond even the wildest imaginings of most. However, neither Hobblebosh nor Toddleposter were ever truly *born*. They were created."

"Like me!" Gigglebrit could barely contain his excitement. "From everything you've said, I wouldn't be on the Roster either!"

Mardulo paused for a moment. "I suppose..."

"It's simple enough to check," said Gurming. "Have you been having issues with doors lately? Here? At the Wizarding Consortium?"

"Yes!" said Gigglebrit, relieved someone finally acknowledged it.

Gurming nodded. "When we enchanted those doors to open automatically, we used the same Roster-based filtering mechanism I was going to use for my switches. We don't want the doors opening for animals and the like, just humans. Hence the check."

Gigglebrit walked closer to the door, just to prove his point. "See? Nothing. And that means I can cast magic in Hobblebosh's restricted zone!"

Gurming turned to Mardulo and Bundersquash. "Is *this* why you brought him along? Was he created similarly to Hobblebosh?" Then he frowned. "He's not a lime, is he?"

"No, no," said Mardulo. "Just fiction."

Gurming's eyes widened. "I look forward to reading how you pulled that one off. But later. This is a genius plan you've concocted! Real outside-the-box thinking."

Mardulo shifted uncomfortably. "I suppose, now that you mention it, there's a chance it might be useful."

"*A chance?*" said Gigglebrit. "It *will* be useful! Hobblebosh doesn't even know I exist. If you teach me magic, I can go into his restricted zone, and he'd never see me coming! I can be your secret weapon!"

Gigglebrit couldn't believe it. This was everything he'd been hoping for, dropped in his lap.

He wasn't a farmhand whose village had burned down, but this business with the book seemed close enough, and he certainly checked the box on "novice who knows nothing about the world at large." There was an evil dictator on the loose, the attack on the Consortium was clearly an inciting incident, and Gigglebrit was now uniquely positioned to play an instrumental role in saving the day.

They couldn't deny it. He was *basically* the chosen one, even if Pottleswee already held claim to the title. He just had to get the wizards onboard...

Thankfully, Mardulo was smiling. "I suppose our plan to summon Pottleswee always *was* a last resort. The lime has consistently proven himself several steps ahead. But perhaps you're right, Gigglebrit, and you really can help after all."

Gigglebrit beamed...*Gigglebrit Maistowne Nebraska the Fictional.* Maybe, once all this was over, he could go by something else. Gigglebrit Maistowne Nebraska the Bold? The Brave? The Heroic?

He could work with that.

Chapter 7

Cracks

Gigglebrit lay in bed that night with visions of mighty deeds, impossible odds, and heroic feats buzzing through his mind. But at last, he gave way to his near-total exhaustion, and sleep took him.

Thump.

It was dark, nearing midnight. The police were out and searching.

Missing Persons: Gilbert Betters.

Last Seen July 1st, near Berrywood Lane.

Any information: Contact your local police station.

The search was coming to a close. It could only go on for so long.

Thump.

Gilbert's parents sat at the living room table. It was wrapped in flyers and police reports, none of them any use. The town knew what Gilbert looked like. What good would a picture do?

Thump.

Gilbert had seen his mother cry only twice before—after the death of Gilbert's first dog and after watching *Babe*. This was the third, and it was different. It was messy and wretched, forcefully torn from her person—real, heartbreaking pain, all layers and disguises stripped away. His father looked empty. Tired.

Thump.

Gilbert watched them through a window. Wanted to come inside. Couldn't.

He was stuck in the night, alone. His parents couldn't even see him.

Thump.

Gigglebrit opened his eyes. It was dark. Cold. And he was sweating. He counted to three and remembered how to breathe. Slow, deep, calming.

Thump.

The room's darkness surrounded him, thick and still.

Thump.

What on earth was that thumping?

It didn't matter. Gigglebrit looked at the clock: 3:30 in the morning. He curled up underneath his blanket and tried to go back to sleep.

But the moment he closed his eyes, his parents flashed into view.

Thump.

It was coming from the direction of room five. Probably the playset.

"BAWEERRR!"

And either an elephant had entered floor twenty, or the podium was making those animal noises Bundersquash had mentioned earlier.

Thump.

Gigglebrit sat on the edge of his bed. How would he ever sleep again? When he closed his eyes, he had nightmares. When he opened them, it felt like the next worst thing. No home. No one he knew. None of the places he recognized. He had nothing to ground him, nothing to keep him steady.

In one day, he had gone from a high school bookworm to…whatever this was. Gigglebrit Maistowne Nebraska the Fictional.

Who would he ask when he needed help or advice? Who would he go to when he was uncertain about something, when he was sad or lost or lonely? Mardulo and Bundersquash were friendly, sure, but he barely knew them. He barely knew anyone here…

Thoughts of Earth swirled through his mind—his house, his friends, his parents. Watching movies with Cindy and Malia. Bowling with Angel and Brian. Around this time of year, they often went to Mahoney State Park and raced in those stupid two-person pedal boats. This world probably didn't have stupid two-person pedal boats. And even if it did, his friends certainly weren't coming.

He would never go on vacation with his parents again. No more camping together in national parks. No more walking through the forest while his parents looked up at the leaves and he scanned the ground for fungi. No more sitting on the deck drinking tea, watching fireflies.

All of it...gone.

Gigglebrit felt like he was falling—still tumbling through that endless void he'd entered atop the hill—and he had no idea when he would land.

Thump.

What was he going to do?

Thump.

It had been better when he was up and about, doing things with Mardulo and Bundersquash—maybe that was all he needed. Just keep doing things. One after another. Let the adventure take shape. Be the Hero.

He wanted this. It would be good for him, and it mattered. That was more than he could say about his earlier life, about Gilbert's life.

Thump.

Just keep moving forward. Don't stop. Don't look back. Never look back.

His past was fiction. It wasn't important.

Thump.

He looked at the time and groaned. He needed to get some rest. This existential crisis could wait. He slumped to one side and pressed his eyes shut, until finally, in slow and uneven fits, his mind surrendered consciousness, and he slept once more.

Thump.

Interlude: Tree and the Road Ahead

Tree fled through the streets. They fled from the collapsing tower. They fled from the threat of lumberjacks. They fled from this sudden, new, horrible feeling.

Fear.

Tree had never felt it so acutely before. They'd wanted an adventure—to discover new places, to see new things. Only now did it strike them how utterly unprepared they were.

They had to go faster, but their roots, weakened after the jump from the tower, stung with every staggered lurch. Branches cracked against signposts. Leaves tore on the brickwork.

They might have stopped to rest, but humans riddled this city, roaming the streets, filling the shops and houses. People walked, ran, skipped, and danced. But when Tree passed them, they would stop and stare, or jump and flee.

It was terrifying. Every action felt unpredictable. Every move, uncertain. Tree's bark still burned where the humans had cut it. They couldn't afford any more risks. They needed a place to hide, somewhere away from all of this. Somewhere to recover. Somewhere safe.

When they finally stumbled upon an unexpected patch of greenery among the terrible clutter of buildings, they seized the opportunity to blend in. There was a small cluster of trees at one end. There, at least, Tree could rest before finding their way out of this sprawling prison.

They planted themselves near a dogwood tree.

"Hello," said Tree. "I'm Tree. Is it safe here?"

Humans could not hear Tree—perhaps because they never thought to listen—but trees often communicated among themselves. This close together, they could sense one another. They could understand each other's feelings, read their expressions, hear their minds. The soil and atmosphere pulsed with them. To Tree, it was not unlike the kindly creatures that had trusted them with stories and secrets. An understanding. A connection. A stream of conscious thought, passed from one to the other.

An intense unease radiated out from the dogwood. "I am Dogwood the Wind-Dancer," they said. "You...moved here?"

"Yes," said Tree. "It took me a long time to learn. Can you move?"

"No," said the dogwood. "I sway in the wind, but I cannot move as you just moved."

"I am sorry to hear that."

"Show me again," said the dogwood. "Perhaps I can learn something new."

Tree wriggled a few roots and waved several branches but stopped when the humans started staring. Dogwood the Wind-Dancer strained to imitate the motions. Tree could feel the tension in their trunk, the force of their focus rippling into the atmosphere...but they did not move.

"I do not think I can do it," said Dogwood the Wind-Dancer at last, crestfallen.

"I am sorry I cannot do more. In truth, I do not understand how I do it myself. Until this morning, I had been stationary all my life, but somehow, I was transported here, and it's as if the sun itself is different, like the light is fuller. In that energy, I found my movement, though it was not easy at first. I have endured many trials. Now I must leave this strange part of the world and seek safety. Do you know how I might escape?"

"I may be able to help. Many travelers come through this place, and I hear much of the outside world. But why do you wish to leave? In this park, life is good. The rain brings water, the soil is rich, and the walls keep their distance. I have friends and family here. You could join us if you wished."

Tree rustled with unease. "No, thank you. The humans tried to cut me down, and there are so many of them here. I cannot stay."

"I have heard of such stories," said the dogwood sadly, "though you are the first I have known to survive..."

"I nearly didn't. It was terrible, Dogwood the Wind-Dancer! I only lived because of this movement. Now I must make further use of that gift and flee while I can."

"Where will you go?"

"I do not know." Tree's branches sagged. "My entire life, I have longed to explore the world, to see its many wonders. But I never thought it would be like this."

"Do not lose hope, my friend." Dogwood the Wind-Dancer sent Tree a kind of comfort through the air and soil. "I feel your spirit. It is eager, though your mind is clouded with worry. Rest for a time. The humans dwindle as night deepens. Perhaps then, you can seek this adventure of yours. This city is but one place in a very large land. Your wonders exist. Go find them."

The words encouraged Tree. "You are kind, and I hope you are right, though I admit I am scared. I have never been scared of the world before."

"Fear and wonder are not as distinct as you may think," said the dogwood. "I felt both just a moment ago when you moved here so strangely. But I am glad you came, Tree, and I am sure you can accomplish your goal. If you are looking for somewhere to start, the birds speak often of a place not far. When I was a sapling, I could see it in the sky, back before they built these taller buildings. A shining light that rises from the ground, as if creating stars of its own. Creatures tell stories of its energy and sing praise of its incandescent beauty."

A glimmer of Tree's old excitement returned. "I should like to see that very much. Do you know the way?"

"Only that it lies to the north. Humans do not go that way often, with the coming of Obble Dor Hobblebosh."

"Obble Dor Hobblebosh? I do not know of this. It keeps the humans away?"

Dogwood the Wind-Dancer startled. "You do not know of Obble Dor Hobblebosh?" they said. "Every day brings new tales of his deeds. They claim he is a lime, though magic made him human. He seeks to conquer the globe and begin a new world order—one that is safe for plants and trees, where humans honor our place among the world, where they no longer dare to harm us."

"That sounds like good work," said Tree. "He lives near this rising light you speak of?"

"The light separates two halves of the world. We are on the southern half. Obble Dor Hobblebosh has taken victory over the north. To this day, he remains near the border. Should you make it that far, there is a bridge, and then...I am not sure, except that you will be close. I have not seen this bridge nor Hobblebosh myself, but I trust those that have spoken to me. If your experience with these humans has galvanized you to his cause, perhaps you should introduce yourself."

"I shall," said Tree. "But first, it is clear you know much of this land. I would gladly hear you say more."

Tree and the dogwood passed several hours in conversation. Tree learned many things and marveled at their new friend's stories. As they spoke, humans came and went, but just as the dogwood had said, they dwindled in the night, and the streets, once bustling, emptied.

"I suppose I should make my leave," Tree said eventually, "though I regret to say goodbye. I am honored to have met you, Dogwood the Wind-Dancer. I shall think of you often, and fondly."

"I shall think of you too, my friend," said the dogwood. "May luck travel with you on your journey. I will not forget you. A tree who moves. Tree the Dreamer."

Tree the Dreamer...they liked that.

They moved slowly at first, spidering through the streets in near silence, wary of waking any who slept in the nearby buildings. But with practice, they learned to list and sway with the shape of the streets, their roots finding a rhythm in the movement. Then Tree picked up speed and headed north, as Dogwood the Wind-Dancer had suggested.

A wall surrounded the city, but Tree had prepared for that. They continued toward a gate, where several armored humans eyed them suspiciously—but Tree moved with such force, purpose, and speed that the guards could do little more than duck for cover.

Tree broke through the gate with barely a scratch and raced into the meadows beyond. At once, they felt more at home. Their leaves rustled in the breeze. Their roots tunneled through the cool soil. The moon was bright, and the fields stretched out in a blanket of pale light.

It was a long road ahead, but Tree was ready.

There was so much world to see.

Chapter 8

The Plan

"GOOD MORNING, GIGGLEBRIT!"

Gigglebrit shot out of bed, threw himself into an arguably defensive pose, and braced for impact.

But it was only Bundersquash. "Would you like some breakfast? I was going to request something from Thinmimble's Café. But if you'd prefer, we have some leftover bagels from Lady Ufferbub's last visit. Delicious, though a tad stale."

"I'm not really hungry." Gigglebrit's brain was still foggy. He looked at the clock. "Why are you up so early?"

"I'm working on my voice-to-illustration device! It listens to spoken words in real time and creates physical images. I've been trying to improve its resilience to the grammatical inconsistencies present in casual speech."

Nope. Gigglebrit was not awake enough for this. "Does the café have tea? Or coffee?"

"They do! But I've already made a pot of tea if you'd like some sooner. Come!" He bustled into the common room and busied himself at the counter. Gigglebrit followed him sluggishly, stopping near the table.

Clearly, Bundersquash had been tinkering. He'd carved a small alcove in the clutter, and a device lay at the center—a sphere split into two open halves with assorted tools and ingredients around it.

"Is this your voice-to-illustration thingy?" Gigglebrit asked, gratefully accepting a warm mug of tea from Bundersquash. "Why work on it so early? We only went to bed a few hours ago."

"It's tricky to find time," said Bundersquash. "Mardulo was helping me, but when Hobblebosh took hold, we had to deprioritize it. It's more of a side project now. You can have a look if you'd like. I just need to reinsert the myrian crystal…"

He grabbed a small, diamond-shaped object—clear glass, filled with swirling, shimmering rainbow powder—then clicked it into the bottom half of the sphere and sealed the top.

"How does it work?" asked Gigglebrit, leaning in. The silver surface was dotted with small holes. Through them, he could no longer see the rainbow-filled crystal, only a thick, unnatural darkness.

"Simply twist the top and start speaking. Give it a try!"

Gigglebrit placed his tea on the table and turned the orb's upper half as instructed. A blue shimmer flickered to life inside the center. Then it dinged like a toaster oven.

"Now, tell a story!" said Bundersquash. As he spoke, a three-dimensional apparition of Gigglebrit appeared nearby. Gigglebrit's specter was reading noiselessly from a semitransparent book.

Gigglebrit, the real one, tried to think of a good story. In the end, he settled on a classic.

He cleared his throat and began to tell of a wizard, his would-be burglar, and a healthy abundance of dwarves. As he spoke, he could hardly believe his eyes. His favorite childhood story appeared, lifted straight from his own imagination. Characters and places, just as he pictured them, every detail correct. The images unfolded alongside his narration.

He made it through several dwarven arrivals—he never could remember the order, and he'd certainly skipped a few sections along the way—then stopped. The experience had turned from wondrous to difficult as his memories of Earth resurfaced—sitting on the floor, tugging at carpet tassels, words washing over him, half-understood but enjoyed nonetheless.

"My dad used to read that story to me when I was little," he said softly.

Bundersquash turned off the machine, but not before a flash of Gilbert's father appeared sitting in a pale armchair with a book in his hands.

"You miss him," said Bundersquash gently.

"I..." Gigglebrit hesitated. "I need to move forward."

Bundersquash lowered his gaze. "My parents would tell me stories about fishermen," he said.

"Do you miss them?"

"On occasion, but I can always reach out. They live in Port Tup. Your situation is...trickier."

"I guess so. But I'm here now, and I have a task to do. I can help stop Hobblebosh. I should focus on that."

Gigglebrit forced a smile.

Bundersquash smiled back. "If you'd like, we can get started right away."

"No, no," said Gigglebrit quickly. "You're busy. You should work on your device. And get your breakfast. I'm good with tea for now."

"Many thanks, Gigglebrit." Bundersquash adjusted his glasses. "What did you think of the colors? Mardulo always complains that everything is see-through—a drab waste of the myrian crystal's capabilities, he says—but I'm fond of the transparency. It prevents the images from drowning out the speaker's words, like it's making room for both of them."

"I guess I can see both sides," said Gigglebrit noncommittally. "Bright colors are nice, but the transparency makes it seem more...I don't know, magical or mysterious or something."

Bundersquash shrugged. "When in doubt, Mardulo is usually right. The myrian crystal is strong enough for it, anyway. I just need to recalibrate the outbound pigmentation." He adjusted his glasses and looked over the supplies. "It might take a while. Please, make yourself comfortable. Grab a book if you'd like. I tried to summon the tutorials you collected in the workshop yesterday. Unfortunately, someone must have moved them. All I got was that." He pointed to a mess of snapped twigs and crumpled leaves on the floor. "I'm not really sure what happened."

"It's no problem." With everything that had happened, Gigglebrit had all but forgotten those books.

"We have plenty of other reading material around," said Bundersquash. "Please, help yourself!"

"I will," said Gigglebrit, who promptly fell asleep in an armchair.

He woke to a vociferous "Good morning!" from Mardulo.

The elderly wizard had just emerged from his room, still wearing his nightcap—a spectacular blitz of stars on blue. The instant he removed it, his pajamas transformed into daytime clothes: a scarlet robe with yellow trim over a teal shirt. His pants were purple and his shoes a brilliant green.

"The librarians said they'll be here within the hour," said Bundersquash. He was eating a bowl of clam chowder at the table, still tinkering. "I ordered you and Gigglebrit some crumpets."

"That sounds lovely," said Mardulo. "Many thanks!"

After breakfast, they quickly prepared for the librarians' arrival, which mostly meant moving things off the table onto whatever other surfaces looked level.

Minutes later, Lady Ufferbub knocked and entered, followed by Toddleposter, who carried Lobster in a golden cage.

"Hello, everyone!" Toddleposter cheered.

"Good morning!" Bundersquash rushed toward Lobster's cage. "I missed you! Did you have a nice time with Uncle Toddleposter and Auntie Lady Ufferbub?"

He opened the latch, and Lobster flew freely into the room, chirping happily.

Lady Ufferbub waved Gigglebrit over and held out a book. "We brought this for you. It was Toddleposter's idea."

Gigglebrit recognized it immediately: *A World of Souls: Volume 362, Revision 3.*

Earth.

Gigglebrit took a step back. "I appreciate the gesture, but I don't need it. I'm trying to move on. That...that's behind me now."

Lady Ufferbub eyed him skeptically. "Only you could know for sure. But you need not open it if you do not wish to do so. Nonetheless, I would be remiss if I did not, at the very least, leave it in your custody."

Reluctantly, Gigglebrit tucked it under one arm, trying to avoid even looking at the cover. He rushed to bury it at the base of the bookshelf in his new bedroom. With any luck, he would forget it was there and never think about it again.

When he returned, the others had gathered around the table. Gigglebrit grabbed a chair and joined them.

"We were just updating the librarians on everything we discovered yesterday," said Mardulo.

"It is a promising turn of events," said Lady Ufferbub.

Mardulo nodded. "The stakes are clear. Hobblebosh has the wide-field residue corporealizer. That means he can create his own path to cross the Great Splat, and our protections on Collywobbles Bridge can no longer stop his advance. We need to move quickly. He's in Town Forbik, and it isn't a long journey from there to here."

"What about the prophecy?" asked Gigglebrit. "Do we still need to get this Pottleswee-whatever person on board? You said they were the chosen one."

Mardulo sighed. "To be honest, Gigglebrit, most prophecies aren't worth the parchment they're written on. You're our sixth attempt to summon Pottleswee, and Pottleswee is the latest in a string of many, many attempts to stop Hobblebosh. But now we have you—something he would never expect. We should press our advantage while we have it."

"I agree," said Bundersquash. "If my time in the research has taught me anything, it's that making progress is like dressing a lion. The key to success is mobility. Getting too hung up on any one solution—even if that solution is foretold in a few prophecies—is never the path forward. We must think creatively and use our opportunities as they come!"

"All right then," said Gigglebrit, more than happy to remain the primary hero of this adventure. "What kind of magic is it going to take to stop him?"

"That part's easy." Mardulo's lips curled into a mischievous grin. "Bundersquash and I have spent months imagining the different curses we would put upon the lime, if only we could. We have a plethora of ideas prepared!"

"We do not want anything too malicious, Mardulo." Lady Ufferbub peered at him over her spectacles. "Either trap him as he is or restore his lime form. No going halfway, and no swapping body parts."

Mardulo deflated. "You're no fun," he said. "But I suppose we could simply capture him..."

"And remember, Gigglebrit is new to this. Keep it simple."

"Yes, yes." Mardulo waved his hands. "Like I said, designing the spell is easy, though I'm afraid we will inevitably hit Pangerbole's Law of Individual Isolation."

"What," said Gigglebrit, "is Pangerbole's Law of Individual Isolation?"

Mardulo stared into the middle distance. "To direct a spell, S, of sixth-level complexity or higher toward a single target, T, the first-order ingredients of spell S must include essence of T and any associated calibrations therein. Should S be directed toward multiple targets, T1, T2, dot dot dot, T-sub-N, the required—"

"The spell will require essence of Hobblebosh," Bundersquash cut in.

"Um," said Gigglebrit. "Ew."

"It would be best if it was fresh essence too," said Mardulo.

"Ewww."

"But Hobblebosh is careful, so it won't be easy. I expect we will have to go straight to the source."

"What do you mean by his *essence*?" Gigglebrit asked cautiously.

"You know," Mardulo waffled. "The things that make Hobblebosh, er, Hobblebosh. His base components. Usually, you extract it from bits of hair, or skin, or fingernails. That sort of thing."

"Oooh." Gigglebrit leaned back in his chair. "His DNA!"

"His what?"

"His DNA. Um...deoxyribonucleic acid, I think. DNA."

"Sounds violent..."

"It is literally the thing you just described."

"I was *trying* to describe essence."

"Which is, evidently, the same thing as DNA."

Mardulo raised an eyebrow. "Regardless, it will be a challenge to get a hold of some. Hobblebosh knows not to leave his hair lying around."

"Are there stealth spells or something I could use?" asked Gigglebrit. "Or am I just going to have to run up and hope he's not looking."

"That's one option." Mardulo stroked his beard. "But Hobblebosh has protections to detect any nearby cloaked objects. A standard invisibility-alerting grid. It'd probably be easier to approach disguised rather than invisible."

"Lady Ufferbub and I had some thoughts on this," said Toddleposter. "Town Forbik is one of the primary trading hubs on the continent. Merchants from all over the world come to sell their goods at the weekly market, and now Hobblebosh controls that flow. Of course, he uses it to his advantage. If the reports we've heard are true, he often prowls the wares himself, buying anything that might be of use—or anything that could be used against him. Some say he won't even let the market open until he's looked over everything himself."

"Originally," said Lady Ufferbub, "we thought Pottleswee could pose as a merchant and use that disguise to get close to Hobblebosh, but perhaps Gigglebrit could play the role instead. Of course, once you get the essence and start casting the spell, he will know what is coming, so I am afraid you will just have to do that part quickly. But disguising yourself as a merchant could get you into position, at least."

"We may have to observe him for a few days beforehand," said Toddleposter. "We can seek out any weaknesses in his daily routine, and if luck is with us, we may even notice a good way to obtain his essence in the process."

"A few days?" Mardulo scowled. "What if he crosses the Great Splat in that time? And there's no guarantee such a weakness exists. It would be remarkably difficult to remain undiscovered for so long."

"It might be simplest to obtain the essence immediately before casting the spell," said Bundersquash. "We'll have to be in close proximity both times. We may as well combine them."

"What if..." Gigglebrit hesitated. "It's probably a dumb idea, but what if I just *asked* him for his essence?"

Everyone looked at Gigglebrit, too kind to admit it was, in fact, a dumb idea.

"Just hear me out," Gigglebrit continued. "If I'm acting as a merchant, I could pretend to sell him some kind of spell. I can say the spell does something he would enjoy, like...I don't know, murder or whatever...and I say I need his essence to complete it. Then, when he gives it to me, I cast the trapping spell instead of the murder one!"

"Remember, he believes no one can perform magic in his territory," said Lady Ufferbub.

"Then instead of offering to cast it myself, I just offer to prepare everything so *he* can cast it. All we need is his essence, so once he's given that to me, I immediately cast the trapping spell instead of handing over the supplies. The merchant disguise gives me an excuse to have ingredients out and everything! As long as the spell is quick, I can cast it before he has a chance to stop me."

"I still doubt Hobblebosh will simply *hand over* his essence..." said Mardulo.

"He will. He'll be so confident that no one can cast magic in his territory that he won't even consider the risk. If he *didn't* give it to me, it would be like admitting a potential weakness. Trust me, like ninety percent of the time, that's how it works with villains like this. Arrogance. Pride. Hubris. That's his downfall! I've written papers on this stuff."

"You have?" Mardulo eyed Gigglebrit.

"Yes, several. Mostly in middle school, but I think it will work. We just have to make sure the made-up spell is good enough to entice him."

The others stared at Gigglebrit.

"As much as I love the creativity," said Bundersquash, "I have to admit it sounds a tad far fetched."

"With that said..." Mardulo tilted his head. "Markets are busy places. If we go with Gigglebrit, we could hide among the crowd and obtain the essence more forcefully if needed. Surely, between the four of us, we could grab a hair from the lime's head, then distract him long enough for Gigglebrit to complete the spell. So even if the initial plan fails, we have a contingency."

Toddleposter raised a hand. "One question," he said. "Why would a merchant go to the restricted zone to sell spells, if no one but Hobblebosh can cast them?"

Gigglebrit had considered this. "We'll say I'm selling them specifically *to* Hobblebosh. That way, we also have an excuse to seek him out."

"Many ingredients can be used for purposes outside of magic too," added Lady Ufferbub. "Any items you do not sell to Hobblebosh, you could always sell to the townsfolk afterward, advertising their more worldly properties. It would have to be an impressive assortment, though. Town Forbik's market is highly selective. They screen every merchant before letting them into town, and over half the applicants are turned away. Whatever spells and ingredients you decide to sell, you must walk a fine line between believable and alluring. We need something *almost* impossible, *almost* too good to be true, but realistic. Mardulo and Bundersquash, magic is your expertise. Do you have any thoughts?"

"I've been considering a spell that could heal sores from the balfrik root," said Bundersquash, "but I doubt Hobblebosh has much need for that."

"The trouble is, he's quite good at magic himself," said Mardulo. "Most things he could simply do on his own."

The room fell silent.

"Perhaps some kind of temporary personal-duplication spell?" suggested Mardulo. "He could use it on himself or to enlarge his army for battle. We already have Bundersquash and Toddleposter. We just have to make it look like Toddleposter disappears after a bit."

"Flying in the face of Nubbor's Theorem on Persisted Identity?" said Bundersquash. "I don't think we'd be able to convince Hobblebosh. What about something to turn more limes into humans? Perhaps in bulk?"

"I think he could do that already if he wanted to," said Mardulo. "How about a *deterministic* sandwich generator?"

Toddleposter shook his head. "Hobblebosh could just order someone to make a sandwich for him."

But that sparked an idea in Gigglebrit's mind, though he felt guilty just thinking about it. "What about something to force people into obedience?"

"He already has several ways of doing that," said Mardulo. "Not many of them are magical, but they are effective." His gaze wandered the room, then landed on Lobster. A glint struck his eye. "But what if we used her?"

"Lobster?" said Bundersquash, eyebrow raised. "I don't understand..."

"Hobblebosh can force *humans* into obedience easily enough, but it's always trickier with animals—and obedient animals can be exceptionally useful. Imagine, a spell to enforce obedience upon any creature he could think of. Gryphons, fiend bats, hippalectryons, an army of cougars..."

"He wouldn't believe it," said Bundersquash. "Animals can't give consent, so a willing-acceptance shortcut is out of the question. And they have entirely different mental structures—from both humans and limes. The complexity of the caster-castee interfacing alone would be virtually insurmountable."

"I agree, it sounds impossible," said Mardulo. "That's why we need Lobster—to prove that it isn't."

"You want to lie and say that we *enchanted* her into obeying our orders?" Bundersquash paled. "You want to bring her with us to Town Forbik?!"

"Yes! She's the only trained butterfly I've ever seen. Most people already assume it's magic!"

"But it isn't!" said Bundersquash. "What if she isn't feeling cooperative when we arrive. Just the other day, she refused to leave her cage until I gave her three extra helpings of sugar water."

"I'm sure if you convey the importance of this mission to her, she will gladly play along. Isn't that right, Lobster?"

He looked to the butterfly, who chirped.

Then Mardulo stood up and paced the room. "We could even bring some additional animals to include in the purchase. You said we needed to look impressive, Lady Ufferbub. How does an entire entourage of unusual, powerful creatures sound? We'd be a sight to behold, and no mistake! Toddleposter, Lady Ufferbub, you have connections at the zoo, and there was a winged rhinoceros bounding around the Wizards' Tower the other night. With all that plus Lobster to sell the obedience deception, we could really make a case for ourselves!"

Lady Ufferbub nodded thoughtfully. "I did see Lobster spelling her own name this morning using clippings from an old newspaper. Perhaps there is something to this idea."

"What if it goes wrong?" said Bundersquash. "What happens to the animals then?"

"We'll be right there with them, taking the exact same risks," said Mardulo.

"Yes, but we're *choosing* to take those risks. The animals aren't."

"You're being pessimistic, Bundersquash. We'll be careful! And if we do make a mistake, Hobblebosh will come after us, not a bunch of animals."

Bundersquash looked away. "I don't know, Professor..."

"Do you have any better ideas?"

Bundersquash frowned, thinking, then shook his head.

Mardulo placed a hand on his shoulder. "I understand your concern, and we'll do our best to keep them safe, but Hobblebosh could march on City Boratorus any day now. That'd be the end for all of us. I doubt the animals would fare much better in that scenario."

"I suppose you're right," said Bundersquash with a sigh. "But only if Lobster agrees to it."

"Of course." Mardulo turned to face the butterfly. "Lobster, how would you like to save the world? There's plenty of sugar water in it for you!"

"Professor!" Bundersquash yelped. "If you say it like that, of course she'll—"

But it was too late. Lobster was already doing flips around the room. Even Gigglebrit could tell that meant yes.

"That settles it," said Mardulo. "We leave tomorrow."

"Tomorrow?!" Gigglebrit nearly fell out of his chair.

"Well, it'd be difficult to pull everything together sooner, but we could try..."

"When will we teach Gigglebrit the trapping spell?" asked Bundersquash.

"On the way, of course," said Mardulo. "It's just one spell. I'm sure he can manage."

"Just one spell, yes, but he has no experience!" Bundersquash grimaced. "Sorry, Gigglebrit. I'm not saying...I just mean...even someone as smart as you would presumably need a little time to learn."

Gigglebrit looked between the two wizards. Mardulo's eyes glowed with excitement. Bundersquash averted his gaze.

"I mean, I don't know the process, so..."

"You'll be fine," said Mardulo. "Bundersquash and I can supply the words and ingredients. You just need to memorize them."

"That doesn't sound too difficult," said Gigglebrit. "How long is the trip to Town Forbik?"

"About a week, if we're walking with supplies," said Mardulo.

"I can do that." Gigglebrit was no stranger to cramming for tests. How different could this really be?

Bundersquash adjusted his glasses. "I suppose it could work..." he said, though he still looked uneasy.

"It *will* work," said Mardulo.

"So, next steps!" Toddleposter clapped his hands. "Lady Ufferbub and I can get supplies to make Gigglebrit's merchant disguise believable, and we'll reach out to Mr. Pourligorbul at the zoo while we're at it."

"Bundersquash," said Mardulo, "can you contact the Consortium? Hopefully they're still operating after Hobblebosh's attack. We need to set up a myrian powder palm infusion for Gigglebrit."

Gigglebrit's eyes widened. "A what?"

"A myrian powder palm infusion. It's how Bundersquash and I create auric nebulas by rubbing our hands together."

"Auric nebulas?"

"The first step to casting any spell," said Bundersquash. "I believe you've seen a few already. The professor's is silver. Bellgiggle's is hazel. Mine's lilac purple! There are other ways to create them, of course, but an infusion is best if you'll be casting on the fly or in unpredictable circumstances."

Gigglebrit looked at his hands with no shortage of worry.

"I'll reach out to Madame Martoonisplau immediately," Bundersquash continued. "If luck is with us, I may be able to get you in ahead of the line."

They hashed out the details over the next half hour. Gigglebrit felt like a pebble tumbling through river rapids, but as he envisioned the journey taking shape and imagined himself infiltrating enemy territory while his hands crackled with magical energy, his rising anxiety found good company with excitement, and he tried to focus on that.

At last, the meeting came to an end, and Lady Ufferbub rose. "It is a tight schedule," she said, facing Mardulo "Bundersquash is right to be concerned. A week of hiking, while sufficient to memorize an incantation, is not enough time to cover each and every detail of spellcraft. Do not burden Gigglebrit's mind with unnecessary magical nuance or esoteric peripherals. Keep the lessons direct. Keep the process simple. If you can do that, Mardulo, we may be able to succeed. If you cannot...well, we need not have made the trip."

"We will manage," said Mardulo confidently.

"Good," said Lady Ufferbub. "Then let us reconvene when we finish our work."

Mardulo beamed. "At last, we may be rid of this tyrant, and what a relief it will be!"

Gigglebrit took a deep breath and closed his eyes, mentally preparing for the work ahead. On Earth, he'd been small and insignificant, a side character destined to live a normal life—to go to school, to get a job, to sidle through the world impacting, at best, a few lives. He barely even appeared in the book. But in this world, he was front and center in the workings of a global conflict, poised to enact real change. He had purpose. He had significance.

It was a heavy burden to bear, but he would bear it—because here, he was the Hero.

Chapter 9

Built-In Magic

Everyone set about their tasks in a hurry. Mardulo went to purchase supplies. Lady Ufferbub and Toddleposter had to contact the zoo. Bundersquash was arranging Gigglebrit's myrian powder palm infusion at the Consortium.

Gigglebrit stayed in the tower feeling useless.

Here he was, the not-quite-chosen one, pacing aimlessly. He didn't want to get in anyone's way, but he felt he should be doing more to help.

The playset thumped in the background, so Gigglebrit double-checked the lock on the door to its room, then went to his own bedroom and perused a book on elementary spellcraft. He got lost in the jargon almost immediately.

At last, Mardulo returned. He stuck his head in Gigglebrit's room and held up a bag. "I just got back with the glamours!"

"Great. What do they do, exactly?" Gigglebrit knew about glamours from a few of Earth's fantasy stories, but their uses varied, and it seemed dangerous to make any assumptions.

"They make you look like a different person."

"So...you could make me look like Obble Dor Hobblebosh?"

"Not exactly. They're rubbish at mimicking actual people. Finding the exact assortment of ingredients to copy someone else's appearance convincingly is nearly impossible. Instead, most glamours simply create a new, original appearance. It's easier that way. Less fiddling about with proportions."

"And they'll work in the restricted zone?" said Gigglebrit.

"Yes. The restricted zone prevents the creation of auric nebulas, so we cannot cast any new magic there. But the magic for a glamour is already cast, then bottled. Tricky to do for any complex spells, but workable for these. They usually only last for a few hours, though, so I bought two sets. One to get us past the town gates, another for the actual market."

"Good thinking," said Gigglebrit.

"It's what I do best." Mardulo winked. "Now I'll start preparing the trapping spell. Are you familiar with the eclectic underpinnings of spatial intangibility?"

"Afraid not."

"Ah, well. Perhaps we can work around it." Then he left.

Gigglebrit gave up on his book and went into the common room, where he gazed out the walls into the painted city below.

Bundersquash returned a few minutes later, breathing heavily from the stairs.

"The appointment is all set up!" he said. "You're first on the list. Unfortunately, they're short staffed after the attack, so the earliest they can do is ten o'clock this evening."

"Ten o'clock this evening." Gigglebrit looked at his palms.

"It's all happening rather quickly, isn't it?" said Bundersquash.

"It is," said Gigglebrit. "But the world is in danger. We don't have the luxury of an easy pace."

"That is true," said Bundersquash. "Down to business, then. The palm infusion requires personal approval, which you'll have to formalize yourself. But the professor and I can walk you through it." He pulled a box from his pocket and placed it on the table. "These are the ingredients, and the incantation is straightforward."

Gigglebrit's heart fluttered. "You mean I get to cast an actual spell?"

"Of course!" said Bundersquash, smiling. "It's fairly common for these kinds of wizarding contracts. I'll fetch Mardulo, and we can step through the process together."

Gigglebrit's muscles tensed in anticipation as Bundersquash disappeared into Mardulo's room. *Finally*, he could do some real magic! He peeked into the box Bundersquash had brought—a maple leaf, some paper, a small coin, a needle, and what looked like flour.

He snapped the lid shut as Bundersquash reappeared with Mardulo. They rolled a large chalkboard into the common area.

"Time for your first lesson!" Mardulo grinned at Gigglebrit, arms wide. "Are you ready?"

"Absolutely."

Mardulo picked up some chalk, scribbling as he spoke. "Every spell can be broken into three components: the auric nebula, the ingredients, and the incantation. We will begin with the nebula—a mist of magical energy unique to you, controllable only by you, your tool to sculpt the universe. Every spell begins by creating one of these nebulas, but to do so, you need a catalyst. Most wizards, when they commit to the craft with sincerity, undergo a myrian powder palm infusion, as you'll be doing today. Until then, however, you will need to utilize an alternate technique."

Gigglebrit could've sworn he saw Bundersquash squirm in the corner.

"And what is this alternate technique?" he asked.

"It involves a bit of blood magic," said Mardulo cautiously.

Gigglebrit's eyes widened. "Excuse me?"

"Don't worry." Mardulo raised his hands. "Blood magic gets a bad reputation, but it does have its uses. It's the best way to make yourself float, for example. Best way to calm the nerves, too, and to charm your enemies into waltzing face-first through a compost heap. But you do have to get used to the finger pricks."

"Ah. So that's why there's a needle in the box."

He nodded. "We'll mix a single drop of your blood with some activated myrian powder. Truthfully, it's more or less the same as what happens with an infusion. The only difference is where the blood is and how the myrian powder gets activated. In this case, the activation is done in advance, whereas with an infusion, the palms trigger a reaction."

"Understood," said Gigglebrit. "And uh...you said just one drop, right?"

"Correct. And the incantation is easy. Common tongue too! A real rarity, but the Consortium has tried to keep it simple since the subjects are often newer wizards. Not as new as you, admittedly, but still...the words are, 'Initiate mental conjunction with Wizarding Consortium remote-correspondence stream. Converge with outstanding inquiry—'"

He looked at Bundersquash, who said, "Seven six two parsley one."

"'—seven six two parsley one,'" Mardulo continued. "'Self-Authorization, Gigglebrit Maistowne Nebraska the Fictional. Align to predefined accessories. Manifest semicorporeal interaction window.'"

He looked at Gigglebrit. "Got all that?"

Gigglebrit took a breath. "'Initiate communication stream...' No, wait. 'Initiate conjunction with...' Um...can you repeat it, please?"

They went back and forth several times before Gigglebrit managed to recite something even remotely correct. He kept insisting they simply write it all down, but the wizards refused.

"It's short!" said Mardulo. "You can do it!"

After a few more rounds, Gigglebrit finally did, then Mardulo moved to the table and walked through the nonverbal steps. Gigglebrit's head spun through the explanation. He understood the actions easily enough—tear this, mix that—but some of the more ethereal concepts, like clenching at a thread of persisted communication or looking inward at the doors of the shared subphysical ether, he would just have to experience for himself and trust it would all make sense once he'd felt it...or seen it...or whatever.

"Finally," said Mardulo, "once you've tossed the Consortium's token into the mixture and the final streams of light have poured out the back of your semiconscious awareness, you'll want to examine the window and authorize everything contained within." He took a breath. "I think that's everything! Ready?"

Gigglebrit gulped, excitement and eagerness warring with nerves, forming one massive knot in his stomach. "Yup."

Bundersquash grabbed a jar filled with activated myrian powder, the same shimmering rainbow dust Gigglebrit had seen in the voice-to-illustration device's crystal this morning. It spiraled and sparkled in the jar, floating as colorful streaks of light danced around it.

Then Mardulo picked up the needle and, with careful precision, pricked Gigglebrit's finger. Bundersquash held the jar an arm's length away, and a single drop of blood fell into the powder.

The auric nebula formed almost immediately—a sky-blue cloud rising like mist from the mixture. A moment later, Bundersquash whipped the jar away, leaving the nebula behind.

Mardulo clapped in delight. "Just look at those cerulean undertones!"

Gigglebrit paid him little mind. He needed to focus. His heart hammered in his chest, but he kept his breathing steady. Without taking his eyes off the nebula, he grabbed a bowl of the flour-like substance, wafted it through the mist, then set it down on the podium. The nebula followed the bowl. Next, Gigglebrit picked up a maple leaf from the box, tore it into three large pieces and two smaller pieces, then placed all but one of the smaller pieces into the bowl. The nebula started to swirl.

Then something happened. A tickling in the back of Gigglebrit's head, or perhaps the back of his mind. Mardulo had said to expect a slight opening in the metaphysical pathways of the world. Gigglebrit supposed this was it.

He grabbed a sheet of paper, crumpled it up, uncrumpled it, blew on it three times, then folded it carefully into quarters and added it to the flour-leaf mixture. It was time for the first section of the incantation. "Initiate mental conjunction with Wizarding Consortium remote-correspondence stream," he said out loud, and there was a weight to the words as he said them, like his voice suddenly had mass.

The nebula pulsed. What had been a faint tickle of energy in the back of his mind suddenly burst into an understanding Gigglebrit knew could only be temporary. Mardulo had called them the threads of informational passage. He couldn't see them. He couldn't hear them. And he definitely couldn't touch them, but they were there, front and center in his awareness. It was like having an extra sense—or perhaps an extra three or four.

He knew which thread he needed—the spoken words still echoed through his mind—and dutifully, it appeared—the thread of the Wizarding Consortium. Gigglebrit followed it, projecting himself through this new dimension without leaving floor twenty. It was simple, almost natural with his new understanding.

"Converge with outstanding inquiry seven six two parsley one."

All the information and messages that overlapped with the Consortium lined the thread, spanning outward. They fluttered on the edge of Gigglebrit's consciousness—present, but unfocused. He knew he would never be able to see them properly. They weren't the target of this spell, so they streamed through his awareness in a blur of semifocused ideas. After a few moments of impossible sensations, he arrived at his destination. It was blocked, clearly, almost visibly, by what Mardulo had called a multidimensional energy barrier.

Bringing a slight edge of his focus back into the real world, Gigglebrit tossed the Wizarding Consortium's token—the small golden coin Bundersquash had brought in the box—into the ingredient bowl.

Then it was time for the next section of the incantation.

"Self-authorization, Gigglebrit Maistowne Nebraska the Fictional," he said confidently, though part of him worried the new name may not be recognized.

Thankfully, the door opened into...it wasn't an actual room, but the idea of a room—a big one, filled with dozens and dozens of concepts, little sparks on Gigglebrit's consciousness.

"Align to predefined accessories. Manifest semicorporeal interaction window."

One of the concepts came to the forefront of Gigglebrit's awareness, then bloomed, brighter and brighter until it shone with a brilliance so powerful it managed to squeeze into the real world, into the real vision of everyone present, and filled the room with a dazzle of colors.

The light faded quickly but remained burned into Gigglebrit's mind—a mental afterimage that drained gradually from vivid reality into conscious awareness, then into some kind of subconscious presence, until finally, it was nothing more than a memory.

Gigglebrit looked where his nebula had been. Instead of the shining blue mist that had been there before, a rainbow ring swirled in place. Inside was an image—parchment, covered in impossibly neat black writing.

It read:

City Boratorus Wizarding Consortium

Myrian Powder Palm Infusion: Terms and Conditions

Gigglebrit Maistowne Nebraska the Fictional, referenced hereafter as Party A, assumes full responsibility for any repercussions of the spells cast by Party A, intentional or otherwise, after undergoing the Myrian Powder Palm infusion procedure. Party A acknowledges the risks involved

IN UNDERGOING THE PROCEDURE, AND THE RESULTING RISKS THAT PERSIST TO HIS/HER/THEMSELF AND ALL OTHERS EVER AFTER. PARTY A AGREES TO ABSOLVE THE CITY BORATORUS WIZARDING CONSORTIUM, REFERENCED HEREAFTER AS PARTY B, FROM ALL RESPONSIBILITY REGARDING THESE EVENTS, INCLUDING, BUT NOT LIMITED TO, DISCOMFORT, FREQUENT SNEEZING, BACK PAIN, INVERTED PROPRIOCEPTION, MONOPOLE-MAGNETIC PROPERTIES, AND DEATH. PARTY B SHALL NOT BE HELD RESPONSIBLE FOR ANY FUTURE RAMIFICATIONS OF PARTY A'S CONTINUED PRACTICE OF SPELLCRAFT, MAGIC, OR LIFE—REGARDLESS OF ANY RELATIONSHIP, OR LACK THEREOF, TO THE MYRIAN POWDER PALM INFUSION PROCEDURE, UNLESS OTHERWISE NOTED AND AGREED UPON BEFOREHAND.

I HAVE READ AND AGREE TO THE TERMS AND CONDITIONS PUT FORTH IN THE ABOVE DOCUMENT.

PARTY A SIGNATURE: _______________

Gigglebrit looked up at Mardulo and Bundersquash. "Are you serious?"

"Alas, the Consortium finds these necessary," said Mardulo. He reached into his pocket and pulled out a quill. "You can use this to sign. It's self-inking."

Gigglebrit took the quill and reached into the rainbow portal to sign, but as his fingers crossed the threshold, a strange twinge shot up his fingertips. He jolted backward and quickly checked for any magical ailments.

"Ah," said Bundersquash. "The sensation can be unnerving at first, but no need to worry. It won't harm you."

Gigglebrit nodded and, with considerably more trepidation, reached into the ring once more. The sensation returned—a shock moving up his arm in slow motion. He tried to ignore it and focused on signing. Through the portal, his hand looked more holographic than real, and it shook in response to the tingling energy, even as he scrawled out his new name.

Gigglebrit Maistowne Nebraska the Fictional

It was unfamiliar to his hand, and he had to make his best guess at the spelling, but he figured it wouldn't matter as long as he kept it consistent. As for his cursive…well, some things just couldn't be helped.

The moment his hand returned from the portal, the rainbow-ringed window faded into a fire-like mist of reds and blues and yellows and greens, then disappeared entirely.

Bundersquash cheered. "With that done, we're all set! And you've cast your first spell! How do you feel?"

"Relieved," said Gigglebrit, flexing his fingers. They felt oddly numb after leaving the portal.

"You did very well," said Mardulo. "And now that you've had one lesson, we can focus on the rest! I've already put together a number of notes to help you with the trapping spell. When you have some time, Bundersquash, I'd be incredibly grateful if you could look over them."

Bundersquash's eyes ignited with hope. "Really, Professor? You want my help?"

"Yes, if that's all right. As Lady Ufferbub said, we need to keep things concise, and I know that is not my forte. You are far better at it than I."

Bundersquash rumbled with excitement. "I would be happy to, Professor! Many thanks!"

"I will get them for you," said Mardulo. "You can tell me what to cut and what to keep. There are still some details to sort out in the spellwork, but we can handle those as we go."

"Yes, sir! I will do my absolute best, sir!" Bundersquash couldn't wait to get started. He bumbled into his room, bumbled out again to get the notes from Mardulo, then bumbled away once more, grinning all the while.

Mardulo turned to Gigglebrit. "I give him a hard time on occasion, but he's an excellent fellow. One of the most passionate students I've ever had the pleasure of teaching. And he's good at simplifying when needed. In the future, I look forward to regaling you with all the fantastic minutia surrounding spellwork and magic and the history that goes alongside it, but for now, we should focus on what's critical. I admit, it makes me uncomfortable, but what we need is efficiency, not a long-winded dissertation on the four distinct applications of knotted cobweb strands. I apologize in advance for the brevity of your lessons."

Gigglebrit marveled at this apparent self-awareness. He tried to formulate an appropriate response. "Uh…" he said. Then, "Yeah," and then, "Don't worry about it."

None of which seemed sufficient, so he added, "I'm sure Bundersquash will do a great job."

"I have no doubt," said Mardulo. "But I did just give him three dozen pages to comb through, so he'll be busy for a few hours, at least."

"What? You've only been in your room for like…ten minutes."

"Yes, well, I checked over everything a few times. More importantly, your infusion is not until this evening, so we have time, and it occurs to me, you have nothing to wear."

Gigglebrit felt a sudden twinge of embarrassment. His clothes were wrinkled from the night before, and they certainly didn't smell good after climbing up twenty flights of stairs in the midsummer heat.

Mardulo continued with no apparent judgment. "We have a lot of hiking ahead of us, and you'll want to look your best when you arrive. I can't imagine Hobblebosh will love the idea of a travel-worn, mud-caked merchant entering his prestigious market. Here, take this." He handed Gigglebrit a leather pouch cinched with a drawstring. It was heavy with golden coins.

"Thanks," said Gigglebrit meekly. Embarrassed though he may have been, he was happy to have an opportunity to change.

"Go to Raven's Thread Outfitters," said Mardulo. "They're on the splatterbound intersection of Tundermok and Wipperg. That money should be enough to get some comfortable walking clothes and a nice merchant outfit for Town Forbik."

"The splatterbound what? Where?"

"The splatterbound intersection of Tundermok and Wipperg. Just exit the tower and head straight along Avenue Tanglewater until you reach Street Witkkle, then head widesplatter and—"

Gigglebrit raised a hand. "Splatterbound? Widesplatter?"

"Ah." Mardulo paused. "You recall the Great Splat on the horizon?"

"The purple haze? Yeah."

"Splatterbound means heading toward it. Naturally, splatterback means heading away from it. Widesplatter means in the direction of the larger side of the Splat. The magical residue glows brighter there and rises higher. Narrowsplatter is the opposite, toward the smaller, less noticeable end."

Gigglebrit scratched his head. "I suppose that makes sense...and those street names—could you write them down for me, please? I don't think I'll be able to remember them."

"Certainly!" Mardulo fetched a scrap of paper and scribbled the instructions. He even included a diagram of the Splat, with arrows to indicate the different splatter-oriented axes.

"I've included directions to the Consortium too. You may wish to head in that direction after obtaining clothes. Bundersquash and I can meet you there."

"Thanks," said Gigglebrit.

"My pleasure." Mardulo waved goodbye. "May luck travel with you as you go. And remember to choose something comfy!"

"Will do!" Gigglebrit stuffed the money pouch and directions into his pocket, then set off down the stairs.

The guard, Whirga, was standing in the lobby at ground level. "Hello, Gigglebrit!" she said. "It is Gigglebrit, right?" She checked her notebook. "Gigglebrit Maistowne Nebraska the Fictional? How are you today?"

"I'm well, thanks."

"Where are you off to?"

"Just buying a few clothes. Talk to you later!" Gigglebrit started toward the door.

Whirga called after him. "Clothes? Why's that?"

Gigglebrit paused, his hand on the doorknob. "I just...need some more?"

"Can I help? I know a few places if you'd like a recommendation."

"I think I'm good. I'm supposed to go somewhere called Raven's Thread Outfitters?"

"Ah, yes. I know them well. Any thoughts on what you might get?" She scanned him up and down.

Gigglebrit stood, unmoving. "Um..."

"I'd go for a nice burgundy chaperon if I were you. Or a hood, but make sure it's got a long liripipe. Maybe throw in a silver cloak if you're looking for layers. In this weather, I'd go with silk, but of course, that's up to you. It really depends on what you're looking for in terms of presentation. If you're thinking—"

"Thank you for your suggestions," Gigglebrit interrupted a bit too loudly. "I'll look at what they have. Chaperon, liripipip, cloak, silk."

"Liripipe."

"What?"

"Liripipe. Not liripipip."

Gigglebrit coughed.

"Do you know which route you'll be taking?" Whirga asked.

"I have some instructions written down."

"Where do they take you?" She craned her neck, trying to see the paper.

"Just, um...this way and that. I'll be off, now. Have a good day!"

Whirga waved goodbye, and Gigglebrit left. Something about the interaction had made him uncomfortable. Perhaps Whirga simply wanted to be helpful, but one could never be too careful. He was a Hero now. Heroes had enemies, and enemies had spies.

Just to be safe, he made a mental note to avoid divulging any sensitive information, then looked ahead.

Soft green grass spread out before him, empty but for the trees that dotted the park. It rustled softly in the summer wind, and in the distance, the sound of crowds rose like a gentle wave. The Great Splat shone as brightly as ever on the horizon, a clear guide for his journey. With Mardulo's meticulously written directions in hand, Gigglebrit headed toward the store, ready to shed his Earthly clothing and don something more impressive.

It was his first time alone in City Boratorus, but it felt like the city was welcoming him. The sun was out, and the air was clear. Colorful storefronts lined the walkways—teal, purple, orange, silver, bright green, deep red, vibrant pink. Everything bustled with the day's activity. And the people, strange though they were, seemed friendly. They smiled and nodded, waved occasionally. Some even bowed. Gigglebrit reciprocated in kind, hoping that was the respectful thing to do.

Then he missed a turn. Then another. Doubling back, he missed one of them again. He was exploring, he told himself. He had time. But the farther off track he got, the more he worried.

After turning onto Street Undoora instead of Street Onduura and finding himself in an uncharacteristically deserted alleyway, he stopped to check the instructions.

Someone tapped his shoulder. Gigglebrit turned around, startled.

A man stood before him—tall, with bold green hair, blue shoes, orange pants, and a long turquoise trench coat. He wore a well-rehearsed grin and looked very much like someone trying to appear friendly. "Good day to you, sir!"

"Hi. Sorry, I'm a bit busy at the moment." Gigglebrit backed up.

The stranger didn't take the hint. "I don't recognize you," he said. "Do you visit these parts often?"

"I'm just...trying to get somewhere. Please excuse me."

"I expected as much," said the man. "The instructions in your hand gave it away, even if you did not." He smiled like a viper. "You look worried, and I can hardly blame you! Wandering around a big, unpredictable city like this can be unnerving—*dangerous*, even...but I have just the thing to help." He removed a wooden box from underneath his trench coat.

Gigglebrit was scared. It seemed like this person was about to sell him drugs. Gigglebrit had never had someone try to sell him drugs before, and he didn't know how to handle it. Somewhere in the back of his mind, his eighth-grade health teacher surfaced with *Just say "No,"* which seemed like a more realistic plan when the person selling drugs didn't also deliver veiled threats. Instead, Gigglebrit said, "I'm sorry, but I really am in a rush. I have a lot to do today," and tried to walk away, ignoring the fact that he was on the wrong road.

But the man followed. "Oh, it won't take long. Truly! I have some spells I think you might be interested in."

Gigglebrit stopped. "Spells?"

"Spells!" The man smiled, finally gaining traction. "Weather warpers, size shifters, and glamours galore! Mr. Leepog Guddlegap Tutswither the Vast, proud salesman, honorable merchant, and *discreet* dealer in unlikely goods, at your service!"

Despite himself, Gigglebrit was curious. "Gigglebrit," he said, then grimaced at his own stupidity. He'd need to think of a convincing fake name for any future scenarios like this.

But it was too late now. He tried to play it cool, shook Leepog's hand, and asked, "What do you mean, you sell spells?"

"See for yourself." Leepog opened the box, revealing dozens upon dozens of small wrapped packets, each marked with the same block letters: *L. G. T.* The wrappings were transparent. Inside were various mixtures of colored powder. There were pinks, greens, blues, reds, and combinations of the lot. Bottles stood on either side of the box, filled with odd mixtures of liquid, dust, and smoke.

"They don't look like any magic I've ever seen," said Gigglebrit. He turned away and tried, once again, to leave.

Leepog moved in closer. "Well then, Gigglebrit, you must not have seen very much." He reached into the box and pulled out a packet of red and orange dust. "See this? Bottled flame—really powerful stuff. And these?" He held up a few different bottles of sparkling pink liquid. "These are solidly crafted midrange glamours—a real specialty of mine. And look!" He swapped the pink bottles out for a larger packet of green and gold. "This will help you see for a whole five minutes, even in the darkest of rooms! We're talking about some real quality product here, Gigglebrit! If you want to feel safe on the streets, ready to take on the world, prepared to handle any situation, these are the best of the best."

Gigglebrit shifted on his feet. Perhaps, if Mardulo hadn't already bought the glamours...but this person, Leepog, was working way too hard to look trustworthy, which had exactly the opposite effect.

Gigglebrit tried to gain the upper hand. "I've been here long enough to know what a spell looks like. I've seen people cast them. I've even cast one myself, and I didn't use any weird little dust packets."

"Weird little dust packets?!" A flash of anger burned across Leepog's face. "How could you possibly...you don't even...how do...?!" He stepped back, breathing heavily, and regained his composure.

"Now, Gigglebrit"—he came forward again, smooth as ever—"you seem like a smart kid. You *must* know there's more than one way to cast a spell. You've been spending too much time among wizards, I think. Rubbing palms together, making auric nebulas, that kind of thing?"

Gigglebrit said nothing.

"The wizards have their way of doing things," Leepog continued. "We common folk, Gigglebrit, we have ours. We can't all afford to lace myrian powder into our palms, can we? I use what I know to share the gift of magic with those who have no other way. These 'weird little dust packets,' as you call them, are filled with genuine, grade-A lorilell dust. And I'm not talking about some weak, fur-powder substitute. No. This is the real thing, Gigglebrit. It'll get the job done, and that's a guarantee."

The well-rehearsed grin resurfaced with a vengeance.

"Lorilell dust?" Gigglebrit peeked inside the box and tried his best to look skeptical. Mardulo had mentioned that glamours were bottled spells. Perhaps these weren't a total scam after all. "And you're telling me they just...do magic?"

"Preenchanted and ready to go! Simply toss them on your target and watch the wonders unfold."

It did sound useful. Curiosity began to get the better of him, and he wondered—could they bottle up the trapping spell for Hobblebosh?

He leaned in and grabbed a bag of blue and yellow powder tied with a silver ribbon. "What does this one do?"

"A lovely choice." Leepog flourished his fingers through the air. "Storm Summon. Very powerful. Guaranteed to bring a mighty storm within a one-meter radius of its target. It should last a good minute or two. All yours for only seven hundred tille."

Gigglebrit thought about the sack of gold coins in his pocket. Mardulo had given him money for clothes, not lorilell dust. Besides, he had no idea what a tille was, nor how it related to gold coins. He put the packet back. "I'm sorry," he said. "I don't have any money."

"No money?" Leepog snapped the lid shut, scowling.

The display startled Gigglebrit but only solidified his stance. "No. Not for this."

"Very well, then. It was a pleasure to meet you, Gigglebrit. Have a nice day." With that, the salesman left.

Then he came back. "Who are you, Gigglebrit? New here, no money, friends with wizards...what's your story?"

"Long and strange," Gigglebrit replied. "But honestly, I haven't read it."

That would have been the perfect time to drop the mic and leave, but he hesitated, and Leepog took the opportunity to reproduce his box of totally-not-drugs.

"Well," the salesmen said, looking through his own assortment. "I don't normally do this, Gigglebrit, but since we've had such an...*invigorating* conversation, I'd like to give you a little something on the house. Give it a try, see how it feels. If you like it, you can always come back for more."

He winked—actually winked—and held out a small baggie of red dust. "A simple healing spell," he said, forcing the tied-off bag into Gigglebrit's hand. "As I said, the city can be a dangerous place, and the dangers have only worsened these past few months. Maybe it will do you some good."

"Um, thank you?" said Gigglebrit, not sure if he was being threatened or helped.

Still, if this really was a fantasy adventure, a healing packet was exactly the kind of thing he might need. He pocketed it, wondering if it meant someone close to him would inevitably suffer a grave injury later, just so he had an opportunity to use it—what with fate and narrative structure and all that.

But he was being silly. It wasn't *really* a story, after all...

"Be mindful, though," Leepog added, somewhat reluctantly. "The healing lorilell dust is good—nice and powerful—but use it within five minutes of receiving the wound, or the effects could prove...detrimental."

"Duly noted," said Gigglebrit, duly noting.

"And mind the kickback! It's a tad explosive when it's working."

Gigglebrit blinked. He removed the packet from his back pocket and held it at arm's length. "Thank you," he said stiffly. "I will keep that in mind."

"Happy to be of service." Leepog put the box of spells away and handed Gigglebrit a business card, stamped with the same three letters that marked all his merchandise: "L.G.T." On the back, it read, "Leepog Guddlegap Tutswither the Vast: Honorable Salesman, Trustworthy Merchant, Lifelong Friend, and Confidant. Primary Office & Mailing Address: 326 Street Ogglepokets SB, City Boratorus, Land Kollen. Please provide minimum of two days' notice for appointments."

Gigglebrit pocketed the card. Leepog bowed deeply and, finally, left. "So long!" he called back with one last wave of his hand.

"So long," Gigglebrit muttered, wondering if he should trash the explosive healing dust now or wait until he could safely dispose of it later. They probably had something for that in the Wizards' Tower.

Whatever the case, at least Leepog was gone, and Gigglebrit hadn't been forced to consume anything unusual. Still holding the packet an arm's length away, he tried to shake off the final remnants of unease by focusing on his future heroic outfit and what he wanted to look like.

Maybe he'd put on a wizard's hat and carry a great staff. Or he could embrace his slender stature and slip into something sneaky, all black and rogue-like, or maybe he'd go for something shinier and polished, with a sword—preferably one he could name—and a shield and a bunch of plate or mail...

When he finally arrived at Raven's Thread Outfitters, a wealth of options greeted him. There was even a full suit of armor. There was also a jester's costume; a forest nymph outfit; a thorough selection of commoner's garb, complete with scrubby leather cowls and worn-down shoes; a whole boutique's worth of bow ties; a (probably intentionally) torn barbarian's outfit; and an alligator costume. Gigglebrit tried a few of them on, just for fun.

Thankfully, the person helping him, a silver-haired woman by the name of Neberia Tumblepug Roo the Tracer, was patient and understanding. Naturally, this had nothing to do with the great pile of gold Gigglebrit casually clunked on the table.

Gigglebrit was examining a patterned cotehardie when he remembered Whirga's recommendations. "Do you have any, er...burgundy chaperons? Or a hat with a liripipip?"

"A liripipe?" Neberia looked at him for a moment, then went into a back room and emerged carrying exactly what Gigglebrit had asked for.

Gigglebrit gawked.

"Is that a tail?" he asked, pointing.

"It's a liripipe."

"On a hat?"

"That's what a liripipe is."

"And the other thing...er...I'm guessing that's the chaperon?" It was some kind of all-in-one scarf-plus-hat combination.

Neberia looked at him flatly. "Would you like to try them on?"

"Absolutely." Gigglebrit grinned. He'd never felt so ridiculous in his life, but he was having fun. "I might need your help with the chaperon, though."

In the end, he bought neither, and decided instead upon a breathable shirt made of forest-green cloth, a thin leather jerkin, and some dark-gray pants to match. His boots were black and almost knee high.

He looked in the mirror and smiled. It was a fitting look for a hero, though he couldn't help but notice, even fantasy clothes as impressive as these added nothing by way of muscle mass. Some things he would just have to earn the hard way.

Neberia produced three more outfits along the same lines—walking clothes for Gigglebrit's trip. To create the merchant's outfit, they chose a dark robe with a well-fitting suit underneath, plus an ascot to tie it all together.

Trusting Neberia blindly about the appropriate number of coins, he paid, then wore the first set of walking clothes right out the door.

Playing dress up had been just the thing he needed—tremendously absurd, but the fun kind that his meager Earthling brain could understand. In all the silliness, he'd nearly forgotten about his encounter with Leepog. He put the healing dust in his shopping bag and looked at Mardulo's directions to the Wizarding Consortium.

He'd spent so long in the shop the sun had already set. Thankfully, the streetlamp candles were lit, and the Consortium wasn't far. He tried to commit the street names to memory so he wouldn't have to look at the notes every few seconds.

Along the way, he made a point to toss his old Earth clothes in a garbage can. He wouldn't need them anymore. He had to keep moving forward. Looking back caused nothing but pain, and pain was a useless distraction. Better to leave it in the past—shirt, jeans, and all.

He turned left on Street Swagwaddle, left again on Avenue Tribblekick, right on Street Kub, then kept straight—widesplatter—for a good five minutes.

Soon enough, he spotted the Consortium floating in the distance with its eerie, glowing underside.

Mardulo and Bundersquash were sitting on the entrance stairs, speaking in hushed voices.

"We don't have that luxury," Mardulo whispered. "We have to use what's available."

"But professor, she's a *butterfly*," said Bundersquash. "It's dangerous. Surely, we could find some other candidate."

"She's already agreed to help. What more do you want?"

"What if Hobblebosh doesn't like her? She could get hurt, or even..." He stopped himself and looked up. When he saw Gigglebrit, he put on a smile. "Oh, hello! How are you?"

Gigglebrit raised his hands awkwardly. "I'm fine, but don't let me interrupt."

"It wasn't important," said Mardulo testily. "Your new clothes look nice!"

"Thanks," said Gigglebrit. He glanced down at the other outfits he'd bought, then saw the healing powder in his bag. "What's lorilell dust?" he asked.

Mardulo raised his eyebrows. "Wherever did you hear about that?"

"Some sketchy guy tried to sell me some. He gave me this for free." Gigglebrit held up the packet. "He said it could heal things, but maybe also explode at the same time? And it'll hurt if you use it too late...or something."

"That sounds about right," said Mardulo, hardly glancing at the packet in Gigglebrit's hand. "Buy any others?"

"No." Gigglebrit deflated. "It seemed irresponsible."

"Ah, that's too bad. They can make for tremendous fun!"

"What *is* it, though? The salesman said it was some kind of preprepared spell?"

"In a manner of speaking. Lorilell dust quality varies, but the general concept remains the same. It's a lot like a glamour. The spell has already been cast. You just need to release it—typically, by tossing it at a target, be it a person, a place, or even just the air. To be honest, I'm surprised you met someone selling them around here. They don't usually visit this part of town. Perhaps they're spreading alongside the fear of Hobblebosh."

"Because they work inside the restricted zone?"

"Precisely," said Bundersquash. "It makes people feel safer to have a few packets on hand—even if, in reality, they won't do much good for anyone."

Gigglebrit tilted his head. "Why not? I can cast magic inside the restricted zone, and you act like it's some kind of superpower. Now you're telling me anyone can do it with a bit of fancy dust?"

"Lorilell dust is not the same thing as casting a fully-fledged spell," said Mardulo. "Honestly, it's useless but for a bit of hooliganism. There's no possibility for real-time adjustments, which means you have to calibrate everything in advance, and it still only works with the simplest of spells."

"Not to mention, it's very difficult and time consuming to create," added Bundersquash.

"Hardly worth the effort," Mardulo affirmed. "Lorilell dust is to proper magic as a tadpole is to a dragon. And more complex packets, like your healing dust there, tend to have concerning side effects. Too many built-in assumptions. Utterly unreliable. I do love a good Hammering Giant packet, though. Got me in a spot of trouble during my primary school days—not my fondest memory, but at least I remember it, and that's more than can be said for most."

Gigglebrit bit his lip. "So, there's no way we could bottle up the spell to trap Hobblebosh?"

"Unfortunately, no," said Mardulo. "The spell is too complex. Bundersquash and I have been struggling just to get it down to a manageable length. But to package something in lorilell dust, you really can't exceed first-level mentality. Perhaps, if we had Hobblebosh's essence in advance...but we do not. Nor do we possess the expertise required to package lorilell dust in the first place. I'm afraid you'll have to do things the usual way, but don't worry! We'll have a lovely time of it, I'm sure."

Gigglebrit nodded. At least this way, he could learn more magic. "Should we head in?"

"I suppose we should," said Mardulo. He and Bundersquash rose from the stairs and stretched. "I think this will be a wonderful experience for you, Gigglebrit. Most up-and-coming wizards dream of this day for years before it happens."

Gigglebrit forced a smile, though nerves ate at his stomach. He liked his palms, and what if this procedure made them fall off? It sounded permanent, whatever it was. For the rest of his life, any time he rubbed his hands together, he would create an auric nebula. Was he ready for that kind of commitment?

He had to be.

He tried to take courage in the weight of his task, knowing he would have to do many more things—things more difficult than this—before all was said and done.

They jogged up the stairs together. The door shut in Gigglebrit's face, but he was ready for it this time and simply opened it by hand once Mardulo and Bundersquash had walked through.

The building still hadn't recovered from Hobblebosh's attack. The lobby floor was riddled with cracks and streaks of ash, the walls were broken and chipped, furniture had toppled, paintings had fallen, and a rug near the entryway had been sliced in half.

A reception desk stood straight ahead, scorched in some places, warped from moisture in others. The person behind it was orange, with black hair, a crooked nose, and an absolutely exhausted look on his face.

Gigglebrit stepped up, speaking softly. "I'm here for my myrian powder palm infusion."

The receptionist raised an eyebrow. "Hello," he said pointedly. "I am Loriploripus Dorgush Rombuccer the Twisted. It is nice to meet you."

"Oh, er..." Gigglebrit winced. "Sorry, hi. It's nice to meet you, um, Loreedori...Loripori...Loriploripus?"

The receptionist cracked a smile. "Loriploripus, yes, and don't worry. I only tease. We've had enough sadness here for a while. I would not wish to add more."

Gigglebrit tried to assuage his own embarrassment with a few uneasy chuckles.

"You are Gigglebrit Maistowne Nebraska the Fictional, I presume?" said Loriploripus. "I will send word."

He got up and disappeared into a back office, then returned with Madame Martoonisplau at his side.

"Gigglebrit!" she said, smiling. "I'm afraid we bypassed the usual introductions yesterday. I am Madame Moriana Malgardy Martoonisplau the Fair."

Gigglebrit wasn't entirely sure how to greet someone of her small stature. She couldn't have been taller than four feet, with frizzy white hair, a round nose, and narrow spectacles—the sort that always seem to target something.

In the end, he simply bent down and shook her hand. "Good to see you again."

"Good to see you too," she said. "And look here! The illusive Mr. Balbagoose!" She nodded at Bundersquash. "Hello again. Many thanks for your help yesterday. We were hit hard. So much is missing or destroyed. Physically, most are doing well, but we're all shaken."

"Understandably," said Bundersquash, his eyes low. "We're doing everything we can to stop this."

"I don't doubt it," said Madame Martoonisplau. She turned to Mardulo. "Hello to you as well."

"Moriana." Mardulo inclined his head. "A pleasure, as always."

"So, what's the story here? Is Gigglebrit a new student of yours?"

"Something like that," said Mardulo.

"Does this mean Mr. Balbagoose will be moving on to bigger and better things?" She looked at Bundersquash hopefully.

"I certainly hope not." Mardulo laughed. "I daresay I've become dependent on the lad."

"And I'm happy where I am," said Bundersquash. "Not every wizard gets a room on floor twenty, after all, and Mardulo's research is fascinating!"

Madame Martoonisplau sighed. "Well, should you ever decide to reground yourself and take up research of your own, there is always space for you here at the Consortium. But of course, you are not here to network. Gigglebrit needs a myrian powder palm infusion! We have everything we need. Please, follow me."

Her office was on the second floor. Walking there, they passed by a collection of boxes labeled, "Experimentation on interaction properties of unknown substances. Please touch. Report findings to Room A62." Several had been knocked over, and one had iridescent goo leaking out the corner.

Half the office doors had been knocked in. One wizard was shaking her head, gazing mournfully at a smashed collection of gems and ore. Another seemed to be struggling with their desk, which looked to have sunk halfway into the floor.

"This way." Madame Martoonisplau pulled Gigglebrit through one of the few intact office doors, then told Mardulo and Bundersquash to wait outside.

In his time reading fantasy, Gigglebrit had imagined his fair share of potions classrooms. This room fit well among them. The lighting was more purple than green, but the shelves were as full as any self-respecting alchemist's shelves should be, and their contents satisfactorily bizarre. Boxes, bottles, and potted plants littered the perimeter, and cauldrons were in good attendance, bubbling their various concoctions into submission. There were many things and more to marvel at. Free space was not one of them.

Gigglebrit tried to swallow his worry away.

"Don't fret," said Madame Martoonisplau. "It's a simple enough procedure."

"If you say so," said Gigglebrit. He checked inside a nearby barrel and found himself face to face with a huddle of three-eyed marshmallows. They yawned.

"Those are not for you," said Madame Martoonisplau, searching one of the topmost shelves, aided by a stool upon a chair. She pulled down a small wooden box.

"*This* is for you," she said.

It was split into two compartments, each filled with soft gray powder, one slightly paler than the other. The light around them danced, stirring soft twinkles of color in every direction.

"It's myrian powder," she continued. "Primed but inactive. I'll spread it onto your palms, then you lower them into this solution, here." She heaved a thick cauldron out from under a desk and removed the lid, revealing a vat of blue goop that looked more solid than liquid. "It's ambassy based, so the risks are minimal. Try to submerge both hands at once, and be sure not to spill any dust. Expect some tingling, which will spread into your arms and potentially the upper areas of your chest. If it gets to your stomach, say something."

Gigglebrit nodded but didn't take his eyes off the goo. It was bubbling slowly, thickly, and with hardly any noise at all.

"Ready?" Madame Martoonisplau took a seat on the floor beside the solution.

Gigglebrit sat down and rolled up his sleeves. He looked at his palms, said a heartfelt but silent goodbye, and then: "Let's do it."

Unhelpfully for Gigglebrit's nerves, Madame Martoonisplau proceeded to light a fire under the caldron. Then she grabbed a brush and gently painted the powder over Gigglebrit's hands. She started with the palms, wove between the fingers, and finally reached around and covered the backs as well. She used the paler compartment for his left hand, the darker for his right. When all was said and done, Gigglebrit looked to be gloved in an iridescent layer of snow with rainbows shimmering a few millimeters off the surface. It was cold to the touch and coarse on his skin.

"Off you go, then! Pop 'em in!" said Madame Martoonisplau. "Quickly, now. Before it gets too hot. Palms up if you can."

"Right." Gigglebrit stopped ogling and lowered his hands toward the cauldron. Any sudden movements risked dislodging the powder, so he went slowly. He had to straighten up, lean in, and bend awkwardly at the elbows to keep his palms in the correct position, but he forced his joints to obey, and eventually, his knuckles made contact with the surface.

The shock was immediate. Both arms jolted, and his fingers twitched erratically. He was lucky not to spill any powder. He kept lowering his hands, and when they had finally submerged completely, thick blue smoke boiled up, spilling over the cauldron's edge. All the while, the electric sensation grew more powerful, like fireworks skittering across his skin. Where each spark landed, a dozen more took flight.

Gigglebrit would have expected fear at a time like this, but instead, a rush of excitement flooded his senses. All caution and worry burned away in the magical hiss and pop of the reaction. His palms warmed with energy. He was becoming a wizard. Soon, magic itself would be a part of him—a physical component of his person.

The sensation crept up his arms, past his elbows, and into his shoulders. When, at last, it slowed near his neck, Gigglebrit turned to Madame Martoonisplau. "I think it's done."

"Wonderful!" She stood up. "Let's see how they turned out, shall we?"

Gigglebrit removed his hands from the goop, even thicker now than it had been before. It clung to his skin like putty. Viscous, heavy strands slopped back into the cauldron as he backed away. The rest, he wiped off with a towel.

Everything seemed to be in working order. He still had ten fingers, all in the right location. Every nail was accounted for. His knuckles bent as expected. The color was normal.

Madame Martoonisplau looked at him expectantly. "Well?"

"Well, what?"

"Are you going to give it a try, or would you prefer to stand here all day?"

"Oh, I...uh...I don't actually know what to do. Sorry."

"Rub them together...?" Madame Martoonisplau tried to hide her concern.

"Right, but I don't know any spells yet."

"You don't..." She stood for a moment, speechless. "I hope Mardulo knows what he's doing. Here, say '*Ekálamphae*,' and when you do, hold the image of something bright in your mind. I'll handle the ingredients. It's a beginner light-summoning spell."

"*Ekálamphae?*"

"You have to make the nebula first, Gigglebrit."

"Yes, I know. I just—" He cut himself short. "I'll give it a try."

He breathed deeply and rubbed his hands together. A faint warmth seeped into his fingers, then burst to life. Gigglebrit tried to stay calm as the nebula took shape—a soft, sky-blue cloud, dancing among gentle pings of light.

It was time to think of something bright. Gigglebrit held an image in his mind, and when he felt ready, he separated his hands and looked into the shimmering cloud.

Madame Martoonisplau reached into a drawer and tossed a pinch of red powder into the nebula.

Gigglebrit said, "*Ekálamphae!*"

The word dropped from his mouth like a lead weight and plummeted into the nebula, which collapsed in on itself and formed a dense sphere, no larger than a golf ball. Then it started to glow, brighter and brighter, until the entire room burned with a brilliant white light.

Then it kept getting brighter, and Gigglebrit realized with a sudden and inescapable horror that he had no idea how to turn it off...

The brightness continued to intensify, radiating outward, reflecting off every surface, consuming the entire room in its dazzling glare. At first, Gigglebrit could hardly keep his eyes open. Later, he couldn't close them tightly enough. The light blazed through his mind like a siren.

Finally, in a somewhat subconscious move rooted primarily in self-defense, he cupped his hands over the glowing orb and tried to squish the brightness away. Miraculously, it worked. The light stopped, and the orb winked out of existence.

Madame Martoonisplau looked awestruck. "I told you to think of something bright," she said, steadying herself. "What in the world did you choose?"

"The sun," said Gigglebrit. "I figured, that's pretty bright."

"You buffoon!" She laughed as she collapsed back into a chair. "I meant something like a candle's flame or a shiny gem...and you chose the sun." She shook her head, more amused than annoyed. "Well, you'll certainly fit in with Mardulo and Mr. Balbagoose, I can tell you that. Treat them well."

"I will," said Gigglebrit, and he meant it.

She huffed, breathing out the last lingerings of her own alarm. "In that case, there's only one thing left to do."

She stood up and grabbed a large, neatly organized box of gloves from one of the cupboards. All colors of the rainbow were present, plus a few that simple light refraction couldn't quite pull off. There were solid colors, there were patterns, and there were even a few with pictures—stars, moons, animals, and the like.

"You'll need a pair to stop yourself from accidentally creating auric nebulas everywhere you go," said Madame Martoonisplau. "Pick any set you like."

"Thank you!" Gigglebrit scanned the box.

Mardulo's gloves were white and Bundersquash's were gray, so he felt he shouldn't choose anything too flashy. He looked at his new outfit, then turned back to the gloves and decided on a simple pair of thin black silk.

When he slipped them on, they shrank to fit his hands. The unexpected motion triggered a flare of alarm, but Gigglebrit soon realized this was probably supposed to happen.

"Thanks again," he said.

"Of course. And Gigglebrit"—she looked up at him, a sudden seriousness burning in her eyes—"I know what you're up against. Bundersquash told me about your plan. If you were training under any other wizards, I'd say you were doomed. But you're training under Mardulo and Bundersquash, and that's special. Take care, and study well. Do not let their efforts go to waste—or we will all pay the price."

Gigglebrit felt like he might collapse under the weight of her gaze. It was earnest, and it was grave. But this was what he'd signed up for.

"I'll do everything I can," he said. "I hope it's enough."

"Well, at least you're not arrogant." Madame Martoonisplau grinned, reached up, and shook his newly gloved hand. "Now, can I interest you in a snack before you leave? I keep a packet of Tatlek's Wriggly Worms in my desk."

"I'm good," said Gigglebrit, "but thanks."

"As you wish. In that case, go show that blight-ridden lime who's boss, will you? And have a lovely night."

She showed him out. The wizards were waiting for him by the office door.

"Blimey, Gigglebrit, was that you?!" asked Bundersquash.

"What?"

"The light! We could see it all the way down the hall!"

"Yeah." Gigglebrit scratched the back of his neck. "Apparently I wasn't supposed to think of the sun."

Mardulo released a deep, rounded laughed and patted Gigglebrit on the back. "No half measures. I like it. You'll be a pleasure to teach."

Gigglebrit smiled. "I hope so."

"I'm sure of it," said Bundersquash. "Did the procedure go well? How do you feel?"

Gigglebrit took a moment to flex his fingers and think about the sensation. "It's great. It's like a whole new source of energy, almost like they're electrified."

"That's good," said Bundersquash. "We have some long days ahead. You'll need all the energy you can get."

Then Mardulo asked, "Electrified?" and there was no end to the deluge of questions that followed. "What is electricity?" "How does it work?" "Where does it come from?" "What's all this about electrons?" "Lightning can do *what*?"

They wandered back through the starlit streets of City Boratorus and up to floor twenty. Then, once Gigglebrit had convinced the wizards that electricity was, perhaps, outside the scope of a single night's conversation, he went to bed, buzzing with excitement for the trip to come.

But when the bedroom door closed behind him, a twinge of sadness wormed into his mind. He tried his best to ignore it, placed his bag of clothes on the floor, checked that the healing dust was still inside it, then poked aimlessly at the bookshelf before plopping onto the bed with a huff.

He hadn't checked the pockets of his jeans. He'd thrown away his Earthly clothes, and he hadn't checked the pockets.

He didn't think there was anything meaningful in them—certainly no wallet, not that Earth money would've done him any good, and he hadn't brought his phone or any photos with him either. But he should have checked, just in case.

And there had been a seam in his shirt, a hole he'd torn under the arm only a few months ago, which his mother had sewn up. It was hardly noticeable, but now Gigglebrit had lost it forever.

He pinched himself. It was nothing but a tear and a bit of patchwork. It wasn't his mother. His mother was fictional. He needed to focus on Hobblebosh and the task at hand. Everyone he had seen today, everyone he had met or walked past—they were real, and their livelihoods, if not their very lives, depended on his success.

And with that thought still forming in his mind, he drifted into a restless sleep.

Interlude: Tree Crossing Over

Tree journeyed toward the Great Splat, taking utmost care to avoid any human contact. They only moved at night. During the day, they rested, recharged in the sunlight, and tried to look inconspicuous.

When they could take the time to enjoy it, the scenery was magnificent—meadows filled with beauty, color, and life. And when they neared the Great Splat, the surrounding soil pulsed with liveliness. The very air tickled Tree's leaves. It was worrisome at first, threaded with constant newness, but over time, Tree grew to enjoy it. The experience—actually *being* there—was better than any story Tree had ever heard, despite the added underpinning of uncertainty and risk.

Then came the cursed bridge.

It was the only way to cross the Great Splat and reach Obble Dor Hobblebosh. The squirrels, chipmunks, and birds all agreed: Tree had to cross it or learn to fly. But it was a human construction. No soil, no nutrients, and nowhere for roots to take hold.

Fear clung to it like a leech.

From this side of the planet, Tree could not sense the bridge's length, and so, hoping to minimize any risk of daytime travel, they started the crossing as early into the night as they dared, just as the sun dropped below the horizon.

It began with a steep and difficult ascent. The marble surface was slippery and strange, and in the Splat's magical haze, Tree's senses were fuzzy. For several minutes, they teetered, lost at the top of the initial rise, wondering if they should go back. They sensed little more than an impression of the path ahead, barely a shred of understanding. A fall into the deadly nothingness seemed all but inevitable.

But when they thought again of the pain the humans had caused them, of the scars and the terror, they knew they had no choice. Other trees would suffer similarly unless someone helped stop the humans.

So they pressed on.

At first, fear kept them focused. Every glimpse of clarity came like a rush of water through their veins, a welcome, if brief, confirmation that the bridge still lay ahead. But it stretched on endlessly. Hours passed, and Tree soon realized their slow, deliberate march would not suffice. They had come so far, yet still, they could not sense the other half of the planet. They had to move faster.

Then dawn came. With nowhere to hide, Tree was forced to scramble ahead through the daylight, stumbling over their roots, dreading the moment they lost their balance and tumbled into the void below.

Then a band of four humans spotted them. These people had no axes, but there were plenty of other blades to worry about—swords, mostly, and knives. Tree froze at the sight, all worries of falling overwritten by the ice-cold fear of humans.

"Did you see that?" said one of them. "Never seen a tree move like that before."

"Does it have any money, do you think?" another asked.

"Unlikely, but I expect a branch or two could fetch a pretty price."

One of the humans approached Tree and pulled a sword from the sheath at her back.

Tree knew they had to move. Had to act. It was the only way to stop this human from attacking. But terror and shock strangled them like vines on a trunk. They couldn't think. They didn't have time. They needed—

The human swung and, with that single, forceful strike, hacked off one of Tree's branches.

Pain burst from the wound, a lightning surge through Tree's bark.

The shock tore Tree from their stupor. They launched a root upward, smacking the human in the face before her next strike could land. She staggered back, nose bleeding.

"Blasted thing!" she said. "Tog, get it!"

"No, wait!" One of the other humans raised her hand. She glanced uneasily at Tree, the size of them, the width of the bridge they were standing on, and the damage to the other person's nose. "I think we should let this one pass. We must choose our battles, after all."

A tense defiance took hold of Tree. They considered knocking all these humans off the bridge then and there, just for good measure, but there were four of them, and this woman was letting Tree pass. The stump where their branch had been hacked off still burned with pain. Perhaps, just to be safe, Tree would choose their battles, too, and leave this one behind.

They spidered past the humans quickly, never letting their guard down, doing their best to appear confident and purposeful, but they couldn't keep the nervous shaking from their leaves, and Tree's deliberate strides soon became a hectic dash. They did not stop until at last, hours later, they reached the other side of the world.

Tree was exhausted. They had been moving since dusk. Their roots hurt from constantly hammering against the unyielding surface of the bridge. Their bark stung where the branch had been severed, and their mind roiled with fear and anger. But at least they were off the bridge. Tree could sense the world again. It must have been nearly noon.

They planted themselves among the first set of trees they could find. The surrounding trees radiated confusion, but Tree didn't bother to explain themselves. There was too much else to consider.

They needed rest, but every noise—every rustle of grass, every swishing branch, every cricket's chirp or squirrel's chitter—launched their mind into overdrive. Almost unwillingly, they would scan the area, frantically seeking for the source of the disturbance. More often than not, it was little more than a gust of wind.

When night came, Tree spoke with those around them and asked for directions to Hobblebosh, then set off toward a town called Forbik, where Tree hoped to put an end to this constant terror, to the humans and their weapons. Their resolve had never been stronger.

The town wasn't far. It had walls, much like City Boratorus, but these were newer and more heavily guarded.

With a lurch, Tree realized the guards were human.

But if the stories were to be believed, these humans worked for Hobblebosh. They obeyed him, and they should know to leave trees unharmed.

If the stories were to be believed...

Tree shook at the sight of them—each human armed, armored, and angry. But what choice was there? If they were going to help Hobblebosh, they had to trust Hobblebosh's soldiers. To eradicate the danger of humans, they had to confront these people. Tree had survived the bridge. They could do this too.

They took the risk and approached.

The humans stared.

Then one of them said, "The boss will want to see this," and before long, Tree was inside the town, following a battalion of guards through the streets. Terror racked Tree's every thought, but they kept their resolve. These humans had been trained by Hobblebosh, and none had threatened to chop Tree to pieces...at least, not yet.

The guards led Tree to a patch of greenery beside the palace, and there, Tree rooted themselves.

Obble Dor Hobblebosh came out to meet them.

Chapter 10

A Quality Education

Gigglebrit woke the next morning to the sound of a lion's roar. It rattled his head and shook his bones and scared the living daylights out of him, but it was probably just the podium. He hadn't *properly* woken up until he'd dressed himself, opened the bedroom door, and found the aforementioned creature directly ahead, jaws wide, all teeth present and accounted for.

He backed away slowly and shut the door.

"Don't worry, Gigglebrit! He's quite tame!" Bundersquash's voice sounded through the walls. "Really! Lobster is probably more dangerous than the lion, and you've spent plenty of time with her!"

"Don't be silly," came the voice of Mardulo. "Lobster weighs less than your average leaf, and that lion has thirty teeth. How many teeth does Lobster have?"

"Thirty, if she gets the lion to do her bidding," said Bundersquash indignantly. "More if she gets a hold of that howler monkey."

Even through the wall, Gigglebrit could tell Mardulo's eyes were rolling. "And I suppose she'll befriend the pygmy minotaur and defeat Hobblebosh all by herself."

"Of course not," said Bundersquash, and he would have said more, but Gigglebrit stepped out of the bedroom. He was still terrified, but he couldn't stand by while a conversation like this was taking place. Had Mardulo just mentioned a pygmy minotaur?

The lion looked at him lazily, yawning. Gigglebrit edged around it and examined the rest of the common area.

There was, in fact, a howler monkey and a pygmy minotaur, complete with pygmy axe and pygmy horns and little pygmy growls. There was also a fox, a winged rhinoceros, a plentiful assortment of birds, and something called a tessle, which had black scales, five legs, three eyes, and a trunk. A kangaroo was investigating the podium.

Gigglebrit could hear the playset rumbling in agitation. Mardulo and Bundersquash had added a few extra locks to room five's door, just in case.

"The animals are all harmless," said Mardulo. "They've been specially trained to avoid attacking humans. The rhino is from downstairs. The rest are from the zoo or the shelter. We've been asked to deliver them to the librarians. I don't think Lady Ufferbub wanted a horde of animals roaming her library overnight. Regardless, they should make a delightful addition to your merchant disguise!"

Gigglebrit kept his eyes on the lion. "You're telling me we have to travel with these creatures?" He knew Mardulo had suggested bringing animals, but he hadn't really considered the implications until now.

"Yes."

"You don't think that will...I don't know, attract too much attention?"

"Why would it?"

Gigglebrit hesitated. "Never mind."

The podium hissed as the kangaroo came close. The kangaroo came no closer.

"I'll get Lobster," said Bundersquash. "If she still wants to come, that is."

"I hope she does," said Mardulo. "These animals are trained, but they certainly couldn't pass for enchanted."

Gigglebrit pointed at the winged rhinoceros.

"Hardly." Mardulo waved his hands. "She can't even fly properly."

"But at least she's got both wings now!" said Bundersquash as he grabbed Lobster's cage. "And she looks a good bit cheerier for it. Ready to head over?"

"So soon?" Gigglebrit felt a sudden rush of guilt. "I haven't packed or anything."

"Don't worry!" Mardulo pointed to a pile of bags on the floor. "Bundersquash and I have already prepared most of the supplies—food and water, some bandages and healing herbs. You just need your clothes."

"Here." Bundersquash added Lobster's cage to the pile and yanked an empty bag from the howler monkey's paws. "Use this."

Gigglebrit thanked him and went into his room. It took some guesswork to fold the merchant suit, but he managed. *A World of Souls* also crossed his mind, but he decided to leave it behind. It was nothing but deadweight.

He did tuck the packet of healing lorilell dust into his pocket, though. It hadn't exploded yet, which was probably a good sign, and he was loath to leave such a useful Chekhov's gun behind.

"How are we going to make the animals follow us?" he asked as he stepped back into the common room.

Mardulo shrugged. He'd donned a purple traveling hat while Gigglebrit had been changing. "Feed them," he said. "And we have some spells to create mobile cages if necessary."

Gigglebrit examined the gathered herd. "And how will we get them down the stairs?"

"Carefully," said Mardulo, and carefully they went.

Gigglebrit couldn't help but feel important as they guided the creatures through the streets. Perhaps it was the echoes of a Noah's Ark story, or any number of references to a "flock," but there was a sort of biblical weight to the experience. The passersby seemed equal parts curious and amused.

It took some effort to keep the animals in line. The howler monkey loved whatever attention he could get; the kangaroo seemed more interested in the shops than the walk; the pygmy minotaur took to riding one of the two parakeets, terrorizing civilians from above; and the rhino kept jumping and desperately flapping her wings, only to remain afloat for a few sorry seconds before crashing back down to the pavement. Lobster stayed with Bundersquash. The lion—Whiskers, apparently—was a friendly creature who liked playing hide-and-seek with the fox.

Lady Ufferbub and Toddleposter were waiting for them outside the library.

"Good morrow, friends!" Lady Ufferbub raised her arms in greeting. Her smile was broad and welcoming, and her eyes showed real excitement. "What wonders you have brought with your arrival! Are you ready to embark upon our journey together to vanquish this foe we call Hobblebosh?"

"You bet!" said Gigglebrit, grinning as he dodged a punch from the kangaroo.

Toddleposter gawked at the animals. "These are fantastic! They'll really lend you some credibility, Gigglebrit. We have the ingredients around back."

As they paraded over, Lady Ufferbub brought forth a box of trinkets. "We should each take one of these, in case Hobblebosh manages to retaliate before Gigglebrit can complete the spell. They are amulets. Each one can absorb a single spell's impact—but only actively cast spells, nothing premade like lorilell dust. It is not ideal, but I am afraid they are the best I could do given the time constraints. Amulets are getting harder to come by, and defense against one spell is better than defense against none."

"And they'll work in the restricted zone?" asked Gigglebrit.

"Indeed. They are passively empowered and do not require any spell-casting to work."

There was one for each person. Lady Ufferbub grabbed a silver pocket watch decorated with a mess of thin black hoops. Toddleposter took a belt—plain leather, with a copper buckle. Mardulo chose an age-worn silver bracelet, and Bundersquash grabbed a cobalt brooch with red lines running parallel down its center. Gigglebrit took a peacock-feather pin made of thin intertwined metal strips—green, blue, and gold. It went well with his outfit, he thought.

A faint pulse of energy coursed through his body as he fastened the amulet to his jerkin. It was comforting but rather like an electric blanket, in that Gigglebrit couldn't help but worry it might spontaneously zap him.

They rounded the corner, and a veritable mountain of ingredients came into view gathered atop a wooden cart. The cart itself was hitched to a...creature.

"What," asked Gigglebrit, "is that?"

"A hippalectryon!" said Toddleposter. "I take it you didn't have them in Earth?"

"We did not."

Lady Ufferbub, who had read some of the books, added, "In Earth, they used horses or oxen for this kind of thing. Sometimes mules or donkeys."

"Or cars..." said Gigglebrit.

"His name is Lampellion." Toddleposter scratched the hippalectryon's nose. "He's one of the best there is—a bit silly at times, but loyal when it counts and fast as anything."

Lampellion had the head of a horse and the body of a horse-size rooster—all of it balanced on two scrawny legs. Regrettably, his rooster-like wings had not scaled with the rest of his body; instead, they flapped uselessly on either side of his feathered back. He had a horse's thick mane and an arched, feathered tail.

All in all, to best describe the hippalectryon, one would have to find the quintessential example of a majestic creature, invert it, then add a few elbows.

Lampellion cocked his head and gave Gigglebrit a big, horsey grin.

"He's fast?" Gigglebrit examined the legs, which could sooner be made of toothpicks than muscle.

"Very," said Mardulo.

"They're innately magical creatures," said Bundersquash. "A bit like unicorns or gryphons. The legs may not look like much, but they work."

"If you say so," said Gigglebrit, accepting it. "And he's going to pull this whole cart by himself?"

Lady Ufferbub nodded. "Toddleposter and I have placed the trapping-spell supplies over here." She pointed toward a small set of boxes on one side. "Assuming the list you sent us is still accurate, Mardulo?"

"It should be. Bundersquash and I still have to finalize a few details in the incantation, but we're almost done. I don't expect much to change."

"Whatever happens," said Toddleposter, "almost everything we've packed is useful. If the ingredients do change once you finalize the wording, we have a fair amount to work with, and whatever you don't need for the spell could be used for Gigglebrit's training."

"Though we must keep some for the market," Lady Ufferbub added.

Gigglebrit looked at the wagon filled with about three wagons' worth of ingredients, then the animals huddled together a few yards away. Finally, he faced his companions.

They had done all this in a single day...

"You really outdid yourselves," he said.

Mardulo looked pleased. "No room for half measures at a time like this, lad. We're committed!"

"Now, let us review our route." Lady Ufferbub pulled a map from her bag and flattened it against a box. Gigglebrit walked up to see.

It was a sparse representation of a single continent—the "Main Continent," apparently. A large mountain range ran down the western border, and three great forests had been drawn by hand. Cities and towns dotted the landscape.

"We are here." Lady Ufferbub showed Gigglebrit a circle labeled City Boratorus. "And we must reach here." She pointed to a smaller dot: Town Forbik. Between them lay a massive black streak.

"That's the Great Splat?" asked Gigglebrit.

"It is, and that is Collywobbles Bridge." She pointed to a razor-thin strip across the darkness.

"Are there trails or something we'll be taking?" said Gigglebrit. Only a few paths connected the main points of interest, not nearly as many as Gigglebrit would have expected. Most of the land was open, trail-free.

"Paths exist, but they are small, and they shift and change with every passing day. It would be wasteful to delineate them on any static guide."

"Mardulo tried to make a path-shift prediction spell back in his earlier wizarding days," Toddleposter added. "I believe his official conclusion was 'People are nondeterministic little blighters and it's no use trying to guess where they're going before they get there.'"

"I admit, it is one of my favorite papers," Lady Ufferbub added. "But in our case, we simply follow this river." She pointed again. "If we keep it to our right, we should reach the Splat in four days. Then we have one day for the crossing and another two in Hobblebosh's restricted zone. We should reach Town Forbik in a week. You have much to learn in that time, Gigglebrit, but we have utmost confidence in you."

She smiled at Gigglebrit, who tried to smile back. "I'll do everything I can," he said.

They double checked the supplies, fed the animals, then talked over the details once more—but soon enough, they were walking splatterbound through the streets of City Boratorus, toward the outside world.

Gigglebrit's first adventure was finally underway.

The city ended abruptly at its walls. The guards were cordial if a bit surprised by the motley collection of animals. They seemed to know Mardulo and Bundersquash, though, and let them through with only a cursory series of questions.

Beyond the gate, sprawling dune-like hills rolled out, rich with wildflowers and grasses that rippled in the wind. There were daisies, milkweed, snapdragons, coreopsis, asters—and those were just the ones Gigglebrit could name. The river Lady Ufferbub had mentioned—more of a stream, to Gigglebrit's eyes—ran widesplatter from the main path, occasionally weaving closer to grace travelers with its gentle bubbling trickle. The breeze was swift and cool, a welcome relief against the warmth of the day's sun, and in the bright morning light, the whole meadow glowed with a vivacity of color unlike anything Gigglebrit had seen on Earth.

He was inspecting a collection of exceptionally large tulips when Toddleposter walked up beside him.

"Did you have flowers in Earth?" he asked.

"Yeah, we did," said Gigglebrit. "They were smaller and less colorful, but pretty much the same. At least, the ones I recognize. Some of these are new to me."

"Smaller and less colorful..." Toddleposter raised his eyebrows. "I wonder what Podish Gubber Tuggerbug the Stumped had in mind, creating a world like that. It sounds a dreary fiction to me."

"It wasn't all bad. In spring, we had meadows covered in flowers like this. My biology teacher used to show us pictures from the textbook and have us name every flower. Even if they were less colorful, they made up for it in quantity. I have Podish to thank for that, I suppose."

But some aspect of his positivity felt false. All the pains and horrors inflicted upon the people of Earth—the war, the disasters, the conflict, the suffering—all due to the musings of Tuggerbug. None of it had to happen, but he had written it.

Probably, it made for a better story.

Gigglebrit shook away the melancholy. "Regardless, I'm here now. It's nice to see so much life around."

"It certainly is," said Toddleposter.

So Gigglebrit did his best to enjoy it. He knew fantasy heroes had to walk long hours for days at a time, covering great distances, getting from one map point to the other, but the stories usually glossed over those parts. Not much happened, and scenery descriptions could only go on for so long—but Gigglebrit liked to imagine those journeys anyway. What were his favorite characters thinking as they walked across moors and mountains, through tunnels and towns, toward a danger they had yet to face? Did they think only of their task? Did they sing marching songs? Or did they try to enjoy the days as they came, knowing each one could be their last?

In Gigglebrit's case, the answer was none of those things. Mostly, he thought about his feet, which after only a few hours of hiking, felt ready to give up and go home—with or without the rest of him. Then the blisters started, and every step brought with it a growing cluster of pain.

Evidently, his new shoes didn't fit as well as he'd thought. They shuffled and chafed and scraped his skin. When the group finally sat down for lunch, it was all he could do not to tear them off screaming. Instead, he removed them calmly, taking slow, deep breaths as he eased them from his feet. They'd stopped near the river, and Gigglebrit happily dipped his toes into the gentle flow of water, basking in its soothing chill.

He still had the packet of healing dust in his pocket and considered using some to ease the pain, but he remembered Leepog's warning. Use within five minutes of receiving the wound, or the effects could prove detrimental. Also, it might explode...or something.

The water would have to do.

When he rejoined the others, Mardulo produced a small box from his bag. "Sandwich time!" he said. "Who wants to go first?"

"Sandwiches?" asked Gigglebrit, inspecting the box.

"It's a sandwich generator. You open it, and it produces a sandwich! Here, look." He held the box so Gigglebrit could see the details. It was made of plain wood and opened in the front like a drawer. There were a few engravings on the top and handle, but that was it.

When Mardulo pulled the drawer open, a sandwich lay inside—sliced white bread, with a filling of pickles, cabbage, and cottage cheese.

Mardulo wrinkled his nose. "Not the best result, but substantial enough." He took a bite and handed the box to Gigglebrit. "You next!"

"Do I have to do anything special, or just open it?"

Mardulo's mouth was full. "Juffshobenit," he said.

"The box will do the rest," added Bundersquash.

Gigglebrit closed the drawer and reopened it. In return for his efforts, he received a tuna and chocolate chip sandwich on rye.

The others took theirs in turn: cauliflower on wheat for Bundersquash; white bread with butter, grapes, sunflower seeds, and crackers for Lady Ufferbub; raspberry jelly with swordfish on pumpernickel for Toddleposter.

Impressively, they ate.

When they'd finished eating, Lady Ufferbub and Toddleposter fed the animals; then Gigglebrit's next magic lesson began.

"Usually," started Mardulo, "I would begin a student's instruction with at least three weeks of discussion on the importance of linguistic landscapes and corporeal integrity throughout the dimensional expanse. However, since we're strapped for time, Bundersquash and I have condensed it to this.

"Think of the incantation as a map. The words are a guide to get the spell through its necessary stages—into whatever spatial gaps it needs to enter, down the various trans-spiritual avenues it must traverse, through all of the boundaries it has to cross in order to accomplish its goal. Like any map, you need to know how to read it and how to follow it. The words paint the path, but you carry the spell along that path as you cast it. Doing so will take energy and resources. Your back-channel awareness may need to cross dimensions. Your consciousness will require certain materials to sustain itself along the journey. Worlds need to open. Realms need to be revealed. Spirits may request payment, and so on. You understand, I'm sure. All of that requires fuel. You may also need special objects, like the Consortium's token in your authorization spell, to perform certain tasks, and you may have to supply the universe with a few offerings of your own just to get through the door, so to speak. All these things—and in fact, much more—make up your ingredients.

"In short, the auric nebula starts things off. The words are your map. The ingredients, your supplies. As you cast, you follow the words, use the ingredients, and guide the spell to completion. Does that make sense?"

"I think so," said Gigglebrit. "But also, I don't think I know what any of it actually *means*..."

Mardulo blinked. "Perhaps we should try a more practical approach," he said, bending down and picking something up off the ground. "Here. Take this rock."

Gigglebrit took the rock.

"Magic," Mardulo continued, "as with all things, begins with history. We do not know who the first wizard was, nor how they discovered magic, but we know that *written* history first mentions the art of spellcraft during the year 602 of the Age of Alberee, in the Era of Long Ages."

Lady Ufferbub put down the bag of oats she'd been holding and shot Mardulo a warning glance, but the elderly wizard was just getting started.

"The War of Three Banners was well underway. In the records of House Berrimire, we find an account of the events after the Battle at Celtinium, where Ogglepokets Derimee Berrimire the Lasting describes the horrific scenes in the deep mountain dungeons. His escape depended entirely upon the actions of one man, Moppy Dot Rikitikel the Singular, who helped him sneak out of his cell and scale the dungeon walls to a high mountain pass. From there, they ventured south for three days and eventually turned west toward the coast."

"Mardulo—" Lady Ufferbub tried to interject, but Mardulo barreled through.

"A farmer took them in, and under his care, they recovered for twelve days and eleven nights. On the twelfth night, they left to find a boat heading north, hoping to bypass the newly captured City Celtinium and reunite with the rest of the Berrimire family. It is there, in Ogglepokets's record of that remarkable nautical journey, that we see our first mention of magic in written history. Moppy and Ogglepokets boarded the ship *Aye'd Rather Be Drinkin'*—now one of the most famous vessels to ever sail the seas—and on the second day of their journey, Ogglepokets witnessed an unnamed seawoman use magic to heat her tea."

Gigglebrit was confused; he wanted a map, and he was holding a rock—but more than that..."An unnamed seawoman? Really? You know the name of the freaking *boat*, but not the woman who did the actual magic? Ogglepokets didn't bother to write that down?"

"The best in history rarely get a name," said Mardulo sadly. "It's the worst who steal our attention."

Gigglebrit shook his head. "Sounds a little sexist to me..." he muttered.

"If it's any consolation," Mardulo added, "scholars widely believe she went on to serve as the captain of her own ship after declining Moppy's proposal for marriage. But Moppy? Well, Moppy really took to the art of magic. Ogglepokets didn't have the knack for it, but from Moppy's *Compendium on the Extraphysical Exploration of Aether and the Pan-Natural Orders of the Universe*, we know that he studied for at least another thirty years, wherein—"

"Mardulo!" Lady Ufferbub finally burst through the wall of exposition. When silence fell, she spoke softly. "Have you forgotten what I said when we first agreed to our timeline?"

Mardulo looked sheepish. "I believe you told me to refrain from including too many details?"

"Exactly," said Lady Ufferbub.

While Mardulo struggled—visibly struggled—to compress all he wanted to teach, Bundersquash spoke up.

"The main point," he said to Gigglebrit, "is the first spell recorded in history is a tea-heating spell from the unnamed seawoman, and between Moppy and Ogglepokets's notes, we can replicate it. As the first-ever spell we know of, it's commonly one of the first-ever spells wizards are taught. It's also quite simple, and it's in the ancient tongue, which you will need to practice."

"The ancient tongue?" said Gigglebrit, taken aback. "Like, a different language? You're expecting me to learn a whole new language in a week?!" Gigglebrit tried to keep the panic from his voice.

"You don't need to learn the whole language," said Mardulo. "Just the words for your spell, and a bit of the pronunciation."

"You really can't make it in English—er, the common tongue? Whatever you call it?"

"Not unless you want a spell that's hundreds of lines long with a dozen different avenues of deviation. In common speech, the spell's related components must be uniquely identified, clarified, and reinforced. In the ancient tongue, much of that information can be sourced subconsciously. Complex spells become simpler because the language is so deeply connected to your mental state. Granted, it requires a little more mental maneuvering, but—"

Lady Ufferbub glared, and Mardulo faltered, looking to Bundersquash for help.

"Yesterday," the younger wizard began, "you cast a light spell in Madame Martoonisplau's office. At a guess, it was *Ekálamphae*?"

"I think so..." said Gigglebrit.

"*Ekálamphae* is also the ancient tongue, and you managed that quite well. The trapping spell will be longer, but you have plenty of time to practice. This tea-heating exercise will help you get a sense for it."

Reluctantly, Gigglebrit agreed.

"Now, to heat the tea," said Mardulo, "we need a rock and some dry grass. You're holding the rock. Grass is all around. Let's discuss the imperative form and verb conjugations..."

"Excuse me?" said Gigglebrit.

"The imperative form and verb conjugations! Both critical components to the ancient tongue."

And so began Gigglebrit's worst nightmare. He hadn't liked Spanish class at the best of times, and conjugations were the worst of it all—tedious charts of present, future, preterit, a bunch of different perfects, all crossed with the singular and plural forms of the first, second, and third persons...and that was just the indicative.

This was even worse. Mardulo seemed to have made up something called an aorist, there was an additional dual form between singular and plural, and worse still were declensions, which, for all Gigglebrit could tell, were just an excuse for sadistic linguists to conjugate nouns as well as verbs.

But Gigglebrit sat through it all, and as expected, Mardulo admitted half an hour later that most of the aforementioned content was purely for his edification and would not apply directly to the tea-heating spell, nor the spell against Hobblebosh—much to Lady Ufferbub's chagrin. Apparently, once you'd conjugated an incantation's verbs, declined its nouns, balanced its politeness, and allocated the appropriate grammatical proportions, there were still about three dozen elementary principles of oratory magic to apply, and those could warp the words and endings in any number of ways. They did not have time to discuss the details.

And so, with that mostly wasted lesson out of the way, Mardulo returned to the tea-heating spell.

"Once your auric nebula appears," he said, "say *Agethermon*. Roughly, it means 'bring heat.'"

"*Agethermon*? Do I have to think of anything special?"

"Just focus on your rock, which you will put inside the teapot. The heat should be applied accordingly. In truth, the spell is a bit risky, but it usually works. The grass becomes a fuel source, so let that be consumed when the universe takes it."

The thought of the universe just *consuming* things made Gigglebrit uneasy, so he tried not to dwell on it and instead arranged the ingredients—rock in the teapot, teapot on the ground, grass on either side.

He rubbed his palms together.

The nebula formed.

And he spoke.

"*Agetherman!*"

The others grimaced as his nebula whizzed into the sky like an untied balloon. Gigglebrit fell back and almost kicked the teapot over.

In fact, he would have kicked the teapot over if the teapot hadn't bounced from its sitting position a few moments earlier and launched into some kind of jig. The porcelain flashed between alternating red and yellow patterns, the lid bobbled up and down, and the surface curled into a baffling number of positions with ever-increasing vivacity. Before long, it was vanishing and reappearing all across the meadow in utter abandonment of reason, still changing color and bopping up and down. Then it started to hum. And at last, in one particularly zealous burst of energy, it launched into the air like something shot from a cannon...

And Gigglebrit never saw it again.

The grass to the left had melted. The grass to the right had grown a few inches. The howler monkey had panicked at the display and scrambled off to enjoy a simpler life, away from the machinations of humankind.

Gigglebrit stared, dumbstruck. "What just happened?"

"You said *Agether*man, not *Agether*mon," explained Mardulo. "*Agetherman* doesn't mean anything, magically speaking. When you try to cast a spell with words that don't mean anything, you get nondeterministic behavior like that. The universe is all riled up. It has to expel that energy somehow, and it'll do so in whatever way it pleases. In your case, it seems to have taken particular issue with the teapot. Some spells have redundancies built in to protect against this sort of thing, but a single-word incantation like this usually doesn't."

"Sorry..."

"Not to worry!" Mardulo smiled. "It's common when a student learns a new spell, especially in a new language. Tends to get the tongue in a twist. This is why we practice! It is a shame about the monkey, though. Whose was it?"

"Therril Klapon Pourligorbul's," said Toddleposter. "I'm fairly certain he's got a tracking spell on it, but we did warn everyone that whatever comes with us may not be coming back."

"Jolly good, then," said Mardulo. "I suppose we should give it another go!"

But before they did anything, Bundersquash insisted they create a cage for the animals to prevent additional runaways. This involved several custom barrier-creation spells that would allow the cage to move as the group walked.

Gigglebrit used a backup teapot provided by Toddleposter to try the spell again, and this time, everything came together. After he said "*Agethermon*," the word seemed to hover in a kind of stasis around Gigglebrit's mind, fully spoken but still present. He could feel its power funneling heat into the rock, warming it, and in doing so, warming the tea as well. When he was satisfied with the temperature, he used an intentional mental disconnect—something he could only properly understand during the process of casting—to release the word. That ended the spell, and together, the five adventurers enjoyed a pleasant afternoon meal with a new round of things that could generously be called sandwiches, some cookies from Lady Ufferbub's bag, and the tea Gigglebrit had heated, which was good, if a bit rock flavored.

When they set off again, they marched until evening. All the while, Mardulo lectured Gigglebrit on the nuances of ancient tongue pronunciation, on elision and diphthongs and phonemes.

Gigglebrit's feet were sore, but he tried to look past it. The countryside surrounded them, fields of grass and flowers shining in the bright honey light of the setting sun. The animals pranced all around. Bundersquash and Toddleposter had let them out of their cage for the time being, and they brayed and roared and hissed and sang all across the meadow. Lobster was doing tricks on Lampellion's nose.

Gigglebrit wished he could sit with a book in his lap and enjoy the scene for a while, but he knew they couldn't spare the time. Besides, he had a story of his own to focus on, and despite his eventual success with the tea, his mind kept replaying that first attempt—the color-changing teapot teleporting all about the landscape. Such a small mistake in pronunciation, and everything had gone so wrong.

All the more reason to study, he supposed, so he turned away from the shining scenery, paid no attention to the animals, and listened instead to Mardulo.

They prepared camp that night near a large boulder, where they would take turns keeping watch. Toddleposter agreed to go first. His primary task was to make sure the animals didn't escape. He was also on guard for any unsavory folk wandering the wilderness. The meadows were fairly safe, but each step took them closer to the lands of Hobblebosh, where bandits and thieves roamed more freely.

Gigglebrit lay down under a large oak tree and tried to sleep...but mostly, he jostled and rolled and failed to find any position that was even remotely comfortable.

He was cold and sore. Tree roots jabbed at him through the dirt like thick, rigid fingers, and rocks buried into his back with every shift and turn. Camping on Earth had always been fun. But on Earth he'd been prepared. A tent, a sleeping bag, a mat, maybe even a cot if he was feeling luxurious. Here, his clothes didn't even fit. Having worn them for a full day, things were beginning to chafe, and it wasn't just his feet. More than a bed or a blanket, he found himself wishing for his trusty jeans and a comfortable T-shirt. Something familiar. Something known.

He'd rushed out here with barely a thought to anything—two changes of clothes, none of them broken in. He was lucky Mardulo had brought the sandwich generator and Bundersquash had thought to bring a spare water flask. Gigglebrit hadn't even considered it. What would his dad have to say about that?

Those who prepare need never despair. For every scare, there's a simple repair, so long as you always take care.

His mom had nearly choked on her coffee when she'd heard it. *Says the man who forgot his suit jacket on our wedding day.*

I learned a valuable lesson that day, his dad had said with a wink. *If you ever get married, Gilbert, make sure your best man wears a nice button-down.*

Gigglebrit grinned at the memory. They'd been cooking hamburgers over a campfire using a backup frying pan after the first one's handle had fallen off. He'd been holding a can of lemonade and nearly spilled it. There'd been geese honking ceaselessly in the background.

His heart sank. His dad hadn't even said that. Not really. Some stupid author had just made it up. Podish Gubber Tuggerbug the Stumped. All nonsense. Meaningless.

His dad had never said anything. No one from Earth ever had.

Gigglebrit turned to his side, adjusting to accommodate a tree root. Here he was, completely unprepared out in the middle of some fantasy map, in the big open section with no features to speak of—the space that only existed because journeys had to take time, because cities couldn't all be right next to one another, because goblins needed somewhere to hide their caves, and because the page needed space for all the labels of more important places.

He was a Hero on a hero's journey, the vital component in a plan to stop an evil dictator. He was training to save the world. He should be excited. He should be thrilled. Certainly, nerves were understandable, but this was his Big Moment.

So why did he feel so lost?

Gigglebrit sat up. He was being silly. Back on Earth, he had always enjoyed immersing himself inside the fantasy worlds of other minds—Middle-Earth, Narnia, Earthsea, Westeros, Ravka and Kerch, the Six Duchies. He had dreamed of every one, of the roles he could play in each. Now he had his own world with his own role, and here he was, getting upset about it.

"Are you all right?"

Gigglebrit nearly had a heart attack. He took a deep breath as Toddleposter hopped down from the rock and wandered over.

"You seem troubled," said the clone. When Gigglebrit didn't respond, he added, "I understand. It's been a lot for you. Conjured into existence out of nowhere, suddenly told that your memories aren't real, your entire past redefined in a heartbeat, and everyone around you keeps going on as if the whole thing is completely ordinary."

All at once, Gigglebrit understood. Toddleposter had been through this, too—or at least, a version of it.

"Let's go for a walk, shall we?" said Toddleposter. "The animals won't go anywhere."

More walking was the last thing Gigglebrit wanted, but he got up anyway and tried to keeping the wincing to a minimum.

"I should be excited," he said. "I mean, how often does an opportunity like this come around? Working with wizards, saving the world…"

"Nonetheless, it can be difficult," said Toddleposter, stepping onto the dirt path. "It was for me, especially at first. Mardulo and Bundersquash are so chipper all the time, but being pulled out of nothing like that…it's lonely. Isolating. Did you know I actually remember making the spell that created me? Or rather, I remember *them* making the spell. I remember assembling the ingredients and figuring out the words, spending days upon days puzzling over every line of the incantation. I remember standing around the podium, the words written on a scroll in front of me. I remember making the nebula, and then…then there's a rather telling gap, and the next thing I knew, I was standing across from them both, totally blindsided and all too aware of where I stood. I knew what I was. And that was my first *real* memory."

"That must've been hard," said Gigglebrit.

"It was. Before the spell was cast, Bundersquash had been concerned about how his clone might feel, and he'd spent a considerable amount of time reasoning his worries away, but he hadn't really understood what it would be like. I doubt he understands, even now. Ultimately, though, I think it's better to live a life with a few false memories than to live no life at all."

"I guess that's true," said Gigglebrit. "Plus, I have a purpose here. That's more than I had as a side character in someone else's story."

Toddleposter wavered. "I'm sure you had a purpose on Earth, too—just maybe not relevant to the story being written. But yes, purpose was important for me as well. I wanted something different from Bundersquash's role as a wizard, so I took on an apprenticeship in the library. Lady Ufferbub and I got on wonderfully, and I've been her business partner for years. The library is as popular as ever."

"I'm glad you found something you enjoy." Gigglebrit smiled half-heartedly, worried his own adventure might not go so smoothly. He thought again of the teleporting teapot.

"You should understand, though," said Toddleposter, "purpose alone didn't fix things. Not for me."

They strolled into the grass beside the path, then meandered toward the river.

"People speak of purpose as if it's some kind of ultimate key to happiness," Toddleposter continued, "as if finding your purpose will solve all your problems and everything will fall into place. I don't think that's true. Purpose gives you a direction, a way to move forward, but it doesn't reconcile the past, and if you can't do that—if you're always longing to go back, or wishing your history away, or dwelling on it, questioning it—a part of you will always remain there, no matter how far you move."

Gigglebrit groaned and sat down on the grass. They had reached the waterside.

"What did you do, then?" he asked hopelessly. "What should I do?"

Toddleposter sat next to Gigglebrit. "I wish I had a clear answer for you. Time helps, of course, but it's not sufficient either. I suppose it comes down to accepting your memories, for lack of a better way to put it."

"But my memories are worthless. They're fiction. I'm better off without them. I want to focus on the real world. That's what matters."

"Perhaps..." Toddleposter sighed. "I'm afraid my situation is somewhat different from yours in that respect. The things I remember still happened.

They weren't things that happened *to me*, but in some ways, they were still mine. I could use them to be who I wanted to be, to shape myself and inform my decisions."

He paused, organizing his thoughts.

"The same could apply to you, I think," he said at last. "Memory is a funny thing. Your memories from Earth—I don't think they're worthless. They may be fiction, but they still shape who you are. They define you. And yes, that definition will shift as you live your life in this world, but do not dismiss them. Cherish them. You have so many unique experiences, things no other person in this world has—or even *could* have—and they've clearly shaped you into a decent person. Use those memories. Use those experiences. Fictional or otherwise, they can be your foundation as you build the rest of your life here."

Gigglebrit stared into the gentle waves of the river, pondering what Toddleposter had told him.

"Thanks," he said after a time. "That helps. It does. It's just a lot to think about."

Toddleposter seemed to relax.

"You can go back to the camp," said Gigglebrit. "I'll sit here for a while, if that's okay."

"Of course." Toddleposter stood. "And please, don't hesitate to reach out if you ever want to talk. I'm here for you. The others are too. We all want what's best for you."

"I know," said Gigglebrit. "Thank you."

Toddleposter bowed and strolled back to the watch-keeping rock.

Gigglebrit stayed. It was peaceful by the river. Clouds covered the stars, but soft glimmers of moonlight still found their way through the shaded haze and danced along the water. The Splat shone in the distance, a twinkling lilac veil casting faint shadows over the grass and hills. Crickets chirped all around, a soft blanket of noise.

Gigglebrit was tired and confused. Toddleposter's advice was one thing to hear, another to implement. How could he learn from these memories when remembering them caused so much pain?

Toddleposter remembered people who existed, at least. He could go see them, meet them, talk to them. Gigglebrit remembered—loved, even—people who amounted to nothing more than a few scribbled words on the pages of a dreary book. What could he learn from that?

He let himself fall back onto the grass and gazed up at the gray-black sky, listening to the meadow and the wind. His thoughts spiraled. At least he had a world-saving adventure to keep himself busy. That task seemed noble enough. Some of his dreams were coming true. So what if a few nightmares joined them?

He took the watch at midnight. Nothing happened, and two hours later, he resumed his restless slumber. The morning dawned slowly, a drawn-out end to his winking fits of failed sleep but a welcome opportunity to think about something else.

They ate breakfast on the road—apples and almonds and little green berries called cucumber drops. As they walked, Mardulo taught Gigglebrit, monitored by Lady Ufferbub. Meanwhile, Bundersquash and Toddleposter worked with Lobster to create a convincing enchanted-animal routine, which she would present to whoever vetted the merchants at Town Forbik.

Just before lunch, the wizards shifted their instruction to the specifics of the trapping spell.

"Once you have Hobblebosh in position," said Bundersquash, "you will need to choose five objects around him. They can be anything—a box, a cart, a bit of fluff, whatever you like—just make sure they're inanimate and form a ring that contains Hobblebosh. They will be anchors for the trapping mechanism. When you speak the incantation, throw your subconscious at them like a wave. The spell will do the rest. We've tried to keep it short."

Gigglebrit took the written incantation from Bundersquash. Slowly, he processed it, and then, with every ounce of energy he had left, he panicked. "Could you have used regular lettering, at least?!"

"But the spell is in the ancient tongue—"

"How am I supposed to memorize it if I can't even read the words?"

"This is how you write things down in the ancient tongue." Mardulo seemed genuinely surprised. "It isn't that difficult. Look, it's just *Humei'pente skeuae, sullégete enerheiás humoun kai'reite Obble-Dor-Hobblebon hoti enerheiâis. Meros autou éstin éntos autaes kraseûs. Meros autou histâesin metazu humoun. Lambanete auton. Katasi'pountoun auton. Katexete auton.*"

Gigglebrit floundered. "Exactly!" he said. "What the heck did you just say? This is going to be hard enough without having to deal with...this!" He flapped the paper through the air.

"It *is* much easier if you can learn the ancient alphabet," said Bundersquash. "Let's give it a go. I'll help. It's only fifty-five characters, and if, after lunch, you still can't get the hang of it, we'll write it down in common lettering for you."

After lunch, they wrote it down in common lettering for him.

Gigglebrit had to admit it didn't help much, and it certainly wasn't pretty. But he could study without having to ask questions every two seconds, and every moment counted. He needed to have the whole thing memorized as quickly as possible. The instructions were to be burned before entering town, lest someone discover the plan.

The rest of the day passed in a bombardment of educational content. When Gigglebrit wasn't being quizzed on universal cooperation techniques or mental passageways through quasi-time projections, he was being lectured on rolling his *r*'s and rounding his *o*'s. On the rare occasion that he got a break even from that, Lady Ufferbub and Toddleposter jumped in with tidbits of merchantry trivia from a set of books they'd packed.

"It will be good for your disguise," Lady Ufferbub insisted. "What kind of a merchant would you be if you could not hold your own in a discussion about the archipelago's import tariffs?"

Bundersquash, when he wasn't teaching, worked with Lobster to perfect her routine. Their primary audience was Lampellion, who seemed ever so excited to help. He matched every performance with a rousing whinny of applause, though he often got distracted by passing birds, sudden noises, or unexpected gusts of wind. But Lobster took it all in stride and, when necessary, repositioned herself to remain within Lampellion's field of view.

The lion and the fox were getting along swimmingly. They spent most of their time prancing in circles together. The pygmy minotaur, after several failed attempts at escape on the back of a sparrow, acquiesced around midafternoon and took instead to battling the nearby flora. The kangaroo was hunting for treasure; when released from his cage, he ventured deep into the meadows and returned with whatever strange items he could find. So far, he'd produced sixteen enormous flowers, a charred piece of wood, a half-eaten pear, and a feathered hat.

Bundersquash sheepishly returned the hat to a puffing, red-faced traveler half an hour later. She let them keep the pear.

When night fell, they set up camp, and Mardulo created a firepit where he and Bundersquash put on an after-dinner show. It started slowly, as Mardulo toyed with the fire's lingering embers. The red glow changed to green; then the soot and ash swirled to the fire's edge, forming small mounds around the perimeter. Bundersquash joined in for the next incantation, singing a hushed melody atop Mardulo's lower-pitched mutterings. The remaining slivers of unburnt wood blossomed into colorful sprigs of flame, and a miniature landscape took shape: soft green fields, flowering with life, surrounded by a range of mountains. Bundersquash tossed some blades of grass above the scene and spoke a quick blurb in the ancient tongue. The grass hung in the air and burned, white flames spiraling into a galaxy.

Before the day closed, Gigglebrit found himself staring, mesmerized, into a miniature universe of stars and moons and worlds, continuously pulsing in and out of view, all inside the firepit. And when the show was over and everyone went to bed, he looked out to the horizon, where the iridescent glow of the Great Splat shone bright against the dark sky, bending and refracting the moonlight. It seemed to twist the very air into glimmers and wisps of rainbow.

At last, he slept, and for the first time, his dreams weren't all nightmares.

The following morning was one manic bout of training.

"Humei'pente skeuae, sullégete enerheián—"

"Enerheiás," Mardulo corrected.

"Humei'pente skeuae, sulleute—"

"Sullégete."

"Soulegete enerheias humoun."

"Sullégete, Gigglebrit. *Sullégete.* Not *soulegete."*

Gigglebrit clenched his jaw, trying to bottle his frustration. He had already lost two instruction sheets to rage-induced rips, and he didn't want to make Bundersquash write another. He stepped back, calmed himself, and tried again.

"Humei'pente skeuae, sullégete enerheiás humoun kai'reite Obble-Dor-Hobblebosh."

"Hobblebon."

"Agghhh! Gosh darn freaking frick frak dagnabbit fudge fudge fiddlesticks fffff—aaaahh!"

"My word, Gigglebrit." Lady Ufferbub wandered up, holding a bag of birdseed.

"Sorry," Gigglebrit huffed, still burning through his frustration, "but what is the deal with this nonsensical language?!" He pointed at the sheet vigorously. "*Hobblebon*? His name is Hobble*bosh*, and that was hard enough to remember!"

"Do you recall our discussion on declensions?" Mardulo asked.

"Yes, unfortunately, and I also remember you telling me it wasn't important!"

"It is important, just not something we can teach you at the moment. Nonetheless, that is why it must be Hobble*bon*, not Hobble*bosh*."

Gigglebrit took a deep breath.

"Of course, the Third-Degree Proper Noun Finalizer Modification Limit does play a role in the exact formation, but that's—"

"Perhaps now is not the time, Mardulo," said Lady Ufferbub quickly. "Why not take a break, both of you? Gigglebrit, I could use some help feeding the birds. Mardulo, I believe Lampellion is turning into an untrustworthy source of feedback for Bundersquash and the butterfly. He just spent the entirety of their performance trying to communicate with a ladybug."

Mardulo rolled his eyes. "Yes, I suppose you have a point. Sorry, Gigglebrit. Maybe we can make a mnemonic later. Bundersquash says those help."

"I suppose," said Gigglebrit. He turned to Lady Ufferbub. "I should warn you, I don't know anything about feeding birds."

"Me neither, my friend. Me neither."

"There's a dispenser," said Mardulo disinterestedly. "Bundersquash used to have a budgie in the tower. Toddleposter can show you how to open it, I'm sure."

In the end, the dispenser was the easy part. Keeping the birds inside their magical cage was the challenge. Lady Ufferbub earned herself more than a few nips on the finger, and Gigglebrit had to wash his hair in the river after receiving a most unwelcome deposit from above.

An hour later, they were training again.

"This word here," said Gigglebrit, looking at the instructions. "It's pronounced *kai'reite*?"

"That is correct. It is the beginning of the second clause in our initial request for the objects to capture Hobblebosh. It's actually two words, shortened and merged because...well, for a number of reasons. To put it simply, we needed a shorter spell, and the end of *kai* sounds like the beginning of *haireite*, and we're still in the first directed appeal, so we could manage."

Gigglebrit stared blankly. "Sure," he said, then glanced at the instructions once more. "So, it's *Humei'pente skeuae...sullégete enerheiás humoun kai'reite Obble-Dor-Hobblebon...hoti enerheiâis...Meros autou éstin éntos autaes kraseûs...Meros autou histâesin metazu humoun...Lambanete auton. Katasi'pountoun auton. Katexete auton?*"

"Precisely!" Mardulo cheered, tossing his hat into the air—and then, "Blast," as it caught the wind and fell into the river. "Anyway, yes. Well done, Gigglebrit! Well done!"

Gigglebrit would have tossed his hat, too, if he'd had one. But he didn't, so he settled for a deep breath of fresh air, then a long, cathartic exhalation. All the tension he'd built up over the past few days finally found some release.

The rest of that hike fell away in a blur of repetition as Gigglebrit tried to memorize the spell, taking a few breaks here and there to discuss the relevant extraphysical interactions that would become necessary if it happened to be raining on the day of the market.

Later, Lady Ufferbub and Toddleposter gave him a quick overview of something called the "Balber," a rare merchant's punishment wherein the merchantry guild assigns an examiner to monitor each of the merchant's sales.

"They usually teach it with a phrase," said Toddleposter, finishing an eggplant and banana sandwich. "'Alber and Malber gain all but the Balber when good things sell to good people.' Basically, sell your products ethically, avoid nasty customers, and you'll be fine."

Gigglebrit snorted. "That's a nice idea. But you realize we're pretending to sell *forced obedience* magic to *Obble Dor Hobblebosh*, an evil dictator who's trying to take over the world?"

Toddleposter pondered this. "Yes. If we were actual merchants, you would certainly be in for a Balber."

"Interestingly," said Lady Ufferbub, "if you will allow me one slight digression, as we have allowed Mardulo so many, Balber was actually the name of the first merchant to receive the punishment. It is fitting, as we are approaching the Great Splat. He is the man who sold the hylozoic acid to Nekkor Var Tillman the Vociferous back when..."

Gigglebrit let the story wash over him. He wanted to soak up every detail, but despite his enthusiasm, he didn't have the headspace to store historical anecdotes alongside the spell he needed to cast. He could always ask about the history later, once he was a part of it.

Nonetheless, the story made many a reference to the Great Splat, and that was increasingly on Gigglebrit's mind. It had grown brighter as they neared, and the land itself now seemed shattered—broken chunks of soil and mud, cracked, seared, and torn from the ground, left to sit crookedly among the surrounding hills of green. The foothills of a scar, centuries old. Some of the damage had been reclaimed by nature, with grasses and wildflowers blanketing the uneven slopes of debris, but as the walk continued, the shocks of broken land grew larger and more frequent. The cracks in the world cut deeper. Some of the land had not yet recovered. Some of it never would.

Faint wisps of purple, amber, and blue threaded through the air—magical energy caught on the wind, trailing away to the world—and there was an electricity to the atmosphere, just on the edge of sensation. It felt as though Gigglebrit's hair stood on end, but the effect was not so physical. Somewhere in the back of his mind, some link to the deeper parts of the universe tingled in response to his surroundings.

The Splat itself soon emerged, a chasm severing the world in two. From its bottomless depths, a veil of purple energy rippled into the sky like silk on the wind. It was laced with sparks of ocher and azure, woven with strands of emerald. Light glistened through its intangible interior, refracting and bending, flashes of color forming in an instant and disappearing just as quickly, burning through the cascade. It was a staggering view, well beyond anything Gigglebrit could have imagined.

Emboldened by the majesty of the thing, he crept closer to the edge. There was no fence, and when he was only a few feet away, he lay flat on his stomach and continued to inch forward. Then curiosity took over, and he forced his head out over the edge, where he could stare straight down into the abyss below.

The immensity of the sight was incomprehensible. He could see the stone crust of the planet, the heated mantle, the spinning liquid outer core, and the glowing-hot inner core. He could see the blackness of space on the other side, tinged through the coloration of the veil. The world's rivers and streams rose like veins through the layers, their sources magical, mere twinkles of blue among the planet's searing white center. They snaked up to the surface and flowed out from the Splat, far and away. To either side, on horizons Gigglebrit could barely see, a deluge of ocean water poured endlessly off the edge into the void below.

Suddenly, a pebble came loose near Gigglebrit's hand and fell into the chasm below. Gigglebrit jolted from his stupor, pushing himself back onto solid ground as quickly as he dared. As soon as he was a safe distance away, he stood up and sprinted to the others in one mad screech of panic. "What the *heck*? Oh, my gosh! I don't even know...how did...who did...we have to *cross* that thing?!"

"We do," said Mardulo.

"On that!" Toddleposter pointed exuberantly.

Gigglebrit looked. Collywobbles Bridge—more formally, the Narrow Stride. It was an entirely different kind of spectacular. Made of marble brick, it started as a staircase and rose at least a hundred feet into the air before leveling out and venturing toward the other side of the world. The opposite end was hidden from view, obscured behind rising waves of purple mist that washed around the marble structure in a seamless teardrop canopy.

But despite its presumably iconic role as a triumph of human creation, the bridge seemed a mere toothpick in comparison to the enormity of the Great Splat. It was wide enough, perhaps, for ten people to walk abreast, and it didn't have a handrail—apparently, no one had thought to invent those in this world. There was a sign near the entrance: "Caution: Slippery When Wet."

"Where are all the protections you and the Consortium put in place?" Gigglebrit asked. He'd been expecting some kind of barrier or at least a few soldiers, but there was nothing of the sort to be found.

"With luck, we won't see them," said Mardulo. "They're only supposed to activate in the presence of a lime or a sizable army. Hopefully, neither lies in wait for us."

Gigglebrit nodded. He still couldn't pull his eyes away from the view. The idea of crossing it was equal parts terrifying and exhilarating.

"We should set up camp for the evening," said Lady Ufferbub, finishing her own appreciative examination of the scene.

"It's only midafternoon," said Gigglebrit. "Don't you want to keep going?"

"Not today. It is a full day's march across the Narrow Stride. Unless you wish to sleep upon the marble bridge with nothing but an empty void to roll into, I would refrain from departure until the morrow—preferably, on the earlier side."

Gigglebrit looked again at the bridge, which, it bore repeating, did not have a handrail.

"I see your point," he said.

They moved to a clearing about a mile away, tucked behind a hill—out of sight of the main path, but close enough to avoid delays in the morning. The Splat was still prominently visible, and its power fizzed through the air. While Lady Ufferbub prepared a fire, Mardulo cast a spell to ward off the atmosphere's excessive energy. Toddleposter let the animals out of their cages and allowed them to wander for a time. Bundersquash sat beside Gigglebrit.

"How are you doing?" the young wizard asked.

Gigglebrit collected his thoughts. "I'm all right. I feel like we made some progress today. I've got the spell more or less memorized."

The words had been rattling through his brain in an endless loop.

Humei'pente skeuae, sullégete enerheiás humoun kai'reite Obble-Dor-Hobblebon hoti enerheiâis. Meros autou éstin éntos autaes kraseûs. Meros autou histâesin metazu humoun. Lambanete auton. Katasi'pountoun auton. Katexete auton.

"I just hope I still remember it in the morning," he added.

"You will. You're doing a wonderful job, Gigglebrit."

"Thanks. Still, I wish I could actually cast it once or twice before the market, just to know what it feels like."

"I understand," said Bundersquash. "And I wish you could too. But without Hobblebosh's essence, we don't have much choice."

"Can't we just target someone else for practice?"

"If we did that, the spell would change dramatically, and you would end up practicing something altogether different. It's fortunate Hobblebosh's name has three vowels or your incantation would be nearly twice as long."

"Lady Ufferbub's name has three vowels," said Gigglebrit, grinning mischievously.

Bundersquash laughed. "That is true, but she is also shorter than Hobblebosh. In the end, everyone is unique, and that changes a spell like this—especially when you're cutting as many corners as we are to make the incantation short. The final version may not sound intricate, but that's because Mardulo is good at what he does. Spells like this are sophisticated. We've had to consider dozens of Hobblebosh's specific characteristics—his name, his history, his citric nature, his personality type, his natural hair color, and so on."

Gigglebrit sighed.

"Would you look at that?!" Mardulo called out to the others.

Bundersquash leaped to his feet. "What is it?"

"Lampellion found my hat! I think the rhino may have helped."

"I was wondering where she'd gotten off to," said Toddleposter. "I thought she might have finally taken flight for good."

The hippalectryon swaggered up with Mardulo's soggy hat in his mouth. The winged rhinoceros lolloped along beside him.

"Did you fish this out of the river?" Mardulo asked. "I thought I'd well and truly lost it."

Lampellion whinnied, dropping the hat at Mardulo's feet.

"You have my gratitude." Mardulo picked it up, wrung it out, and popped it on immediately.

Gigglebrit winced. "You don't want to wash it?"

"It just spent the last few hours in a river. What more could you ask for?"

Gigglebrit looked at the hat, floppier than it had been before, brought here in a hippalectryon's mouth, and said, "I'm glad you got it back."

Mardulo stroked Lampellion's nose. "Me too!"

Toddleposter gave the rhino a pat and fussed with a few of her feathers.

Over dinner, Bundersquash and Lobster put on a show, complete with hoops, dancing, imitations, and even spelling by way of pointing at letters on parchment. Gigglebrit had no doubt Lobster would play her part well, and the butterfly had no doubt either. When they'd finished their bows and basked in the tremendous applause of their audience, Bundersquash gave her an extra helping of sugar water. Then she sat on his head, content and comfortable, while everyone told stories around the campfire.

Chapter 11

Collywobbles Bridge

The air was mist, pale and dense. Everything was gone.

A silver glow lit the path. Gigglebrit followed, his apprehension building with every step.

The voice came slowly—dark, rotten, a slither in the wind.

Where are you, Gilbert?

He could almost feel it, the words moist in the mist, swollen with malice and mockery.

Why aren't you home? Don't you miss your family? They wait for you day and night, you know. Dead in their tomb of fiction…

Gigglebrit continued down the path, unable to shut the voice out, forced to listen as it inched closer, its progress uneven, jagged. It coursed through the sodden air in sharp tendrils of electricity.

Do you remember your parents, Gilbert? Have you forgotten them already? They fade as your memory fades, and yet, you force yourself to forget.

Gigglebrit willed himself forward. His parents were gone. They didn't matter. Earth didn't matter.

The land ahead was withered and gray. Nothing good lived there, if anything lived at all.

Not even a picture to remember them by. Can you see their faces? Do you remember your last words to them? I know you've heard them crying, Gilbert. Just a dream, you say. Just a dream…

Gigglebrit stopped. He looked down at the colorless grass. A severed wing, Lobster's, and a deathly shout.

Bundersquash?

Gigglebrit couldn't move.

Lightning struck. *You don't belong here, Gilbert Betters!*

The green figure stood shadowed and tall, shrouded in scarlet mist.

Gigglebrit leaped awake in an instant. It took some time for his breath to return.

The sky was still dark, the moon hidden behind clouds. Lampellion was tied to a nearby tree. Lobster slept on his mane. The kangaroo was out and grazing while the other animals lay by the wagon.

Lady Ufferbub had the watch. She was reading by the light of the fire's embers. "Are you all right?" she asked quietly. "Your sleep seemed restless."

"Just a bad dream. What time is it?"

"Nearing dawn."

Gigglebrit had no desire to return to the nightmares. He took a drink of water, then sat on a log opposite Lady Ufferbub. "What are you reading?"

"*Boric's History of the Great Splat.* It felt appropriate."

"Any good?"

"A tad dry, but informative."

"What happened, exactly? With the Splat, I mean."

Lady Ufferbub closed her book, not bothering to note the page. "It started during the War of Wittiken and Vale, with Nekkor Var Tillman the Vociferous. This was back when City Mez was nothing more than a stronghold for Vale's court. In an attempt to end the war quickly, Tillman constructed a device to fly over their walls and annihilate the lot of them at once. It was a massive thing, filled to the brim with hylozoic acid. But the flying enchantments malfunctioned, and the device burst in midair not long after launch. The acid sprayed into the world with incredible force. It was disastrous, and it ended with a...well, with a great splat. But the Splat's tale does not end there.

"At first, people hoped the acid would simply dissolve into the ground and disappear. A few crops might pay the price, but the damage would be minimal. As you can see, that did not happen. Instead, it spread unthinkably quickly, bleeding the life from the land beneath its stain. The expansion was largely bidirectional, covering the circumference of the globe in a matter of weeks, but over time, it grew in thickness, too, and the scar dug deeper with every passing day, like a river carving a canyon. Crops were dying. Animals were dying. People near the incident were going mad, and more and more towns had to evacuate. There was a time when it seemed the scourge would consume the entire world...

"But then, a wizard by the name of Maliford Theodrin Noi the Excellent put a stop to the chaos. She raced to the edge of the damaged land and thrust her staff into the ground, casting one of the most powerful spells in all of wizarding history. It expelled the acid completely, but the parts of the world that had tasted the plague were destroyed alongside it. And so, the sight you see before you was created—more of a chasm than a splat, really, but such is the way with names. Noi split the world in two, yet saved us all in the process.

"The magical energy rising into the air is but a remnant of the spell she cast. It hangs in visible dormancy, an effervescent cascade across the ever-changing canvas of the sky. A beautiful sight for something that has caused so much pain. Dozens of towns used to sit along that line. Now they are lost to the ages, not a single ruin to their names."

Gigglebrit stared into the rising flux of lavender ripples and marveled. "How long ago was that?"

"Centuries," said Lady Ufferbub.

"Will it ever run out? The magical energy, that is."

"It is difficult to tell with such things. People have measured its brightness over the years and the Splat has never dimmed, but that does not mean much."

If it was ever going to fade, Gigglebrit thought, it wasn't going to happen anytime soon. The flow had a steadiness to it—gentle but persistent.

In the silence that followed, Lady Ufferbub returned to her book, and Gigglebrit stoked the fire. Sometime later, the others awoke.

"Time to make our way across the bridge?" asked Mardulo.

"I think that would be best," said Toddleposter. "We may be in for a spot of rain."

The skies were darkening even as dawn rolled in. Bundersquash gathered the animals, the others packed up camp, and half an hour later, Gigglebrit found himself trembling up the first few steps of Collywobbles Bridge.

Lampellion led the group, pulling the cart of supplies along a ramped section of the incline. Lobster stood on his nose, pointing forward like a commander leading the charge. Mardulo and Bundersquash walked beside them, followed by the librarians. Gigglebrit came next, then the animals.

His stomach turned with every step. Whoever designed this bridge was as cruel as they were impressive. If it wasn't bad enough to have a narrow, railless path carrying you out over the edge of the world, you had to start the journey climbing up several hundred steps. Up and up and up you went while the ground was still beneath you, so you knew exactly how high you were. And then—when the ground wasn't beneath you anymore, when the world fell away and the only thing between you and the endless void of space was a thin marble walkway and your own good footing—then the whole idea of height unraveled, leaving nothing but the primal, sickening fear of that which is incomprehensible.

Gigglebrit stared into the abyss, wondering what would happen if he fell. How did physics behave between the separated halves of a broken planet? Would he get stuck in the middle? Maybe he would hit some center of gravity and condense into an impossibly small point of matter, getting denser and denser, until he finally crossed the Schwarzschild radius and turned into a black hole, consuming the world in one catastrophic maelstrom of gravity.

Well, a pebble had fallen in yesterday, and that hadn't happened. So he supposed that wasn't the answer. But still…

Gigglebrit shook himself. He was on a quest. A Proper Fantasy Adventure. Sure, it came with a bit of danger, but that was the gig. There could be no adventure without the risk. No journey without the leap of faith. He looked ahead and set his jaw. He could do this.

Besides, he mused, if he did create some horrible black hole disaster, at least he'd get rid of Hobblebosh—and with that thought, he suddenly found himself chuckling.

Then the rain began.

Caution: Slippery When Wet.

They had been walking for almost an hour. The rain started as a trickle but quickly worsened until it came in buckets and waves. Dark, heavy storm clouds blocked the sun.

Mardulo turned to Toddleposter. "Do we have ingredients for a localized rain-shield spell?" he asked, raising his voice above the rain. "I think I could do it with a little tinselweed, some peppermint, and maybe a touch of cornbread."

"No cornbread, I'm afraid."

"Corn?"

Toddleposter looked at Lady Ufferbub, who shook her head.

"I did notice some urchin powder," said Bundersquash. "Throw in a drop of saltwater and some willow scraps…I'm sure we could get something working."

Mardulo was already fishing through the boxes, his cloak dripping wet. He arranged a soggy assortment of ingredients near the back of the cart, cleared his throat, then rubbed his hands together...

And nothing happened.

His eyes widened. He looked at his palms, then tried again. Not even a fizzle. Bundersquash ran up and tried as well, to no avail. The wizards stared at each other in horror.

"So soon?" Mardulo's voice cracked.

"We haven't even hit the fifteen-mile plaza yet," said Bundersquash hollowly.

They turned to the others in disbelief. "Last we'd heard, the restricted zone hadn't reached the bridge at all."

Toddleposter looked flustered. "I suppose we *did* know Hobblebosh would try to expand his territory soon."

"His plans are already in motion," said Lady Ufferbub darkly.

But Mardulo and Bundersquash weren't listening. Mardulo stared at his palms, rubbing them together. Bundersquash wasn't moving at all. Water dripped from his hair and nose.

Lady Ufferbub came over. "Pull it together, you two. We need to keep walking. This development only solidifies that fact."

"Maybe we can use this as an opportunity." Gigglebrit strode toward the ingredients. "I can cast the weather spell. It'll be good practice, and it means we can make sure my magic actually works."

Mardulo and Bundersquash looked at him.

"We haven't taught you about underconscious atmospheric coercion yet," said Mardulo, wiping the water from his forehead. "Maybe if we had some cornbread—"

"Nonsense." Gigglebrit waved a hand. "How hard can underconscious atmospheric coercion really be?"

"Quite difficult, actually," said Bundersquash.

"What are the words?"

Bundersquash burbled a phrase with several trills, a few rumbles, and the general effect of something altogether inhuman. "It's in the Green Tongue," he explained.

Gigglebrit tried a few experimental noises himself. None of them sounded particularly correct, but it was close enough for him to venture asking, "What would I have to do mentally?"

"The trick is confidence," said Mardulo. "With these kinds of nature-based spells, half the battle is mustering enough strength to stare the universe in the face and say, 'No. Those raindrops won't hit me, and that's just the way things are going to be around here.' Generally speaking, that's how the Green Tongue works."

Gigglebrit raised an eyebrow.

"Of course, you also have to formulate an appropriate mental labyrinth to contain the thought—something to deter any in-depth universal investigation. In most cases, if you state your claim confidently enough and make it particularly difficult to inspect, you have a chance. The universe is a busy place. You'd be surprised by the things you can sneak by it."

"Sneak by it?" Gigglebrit frowned. "Like the universe just *won't notice* I've got something going on that isn't supposed to happen?"

"Exactly," said Mardulo, "but keep your voice down. If it realizes you're planning such things...well, it can be unforgiving, and you're not well prepared to defend against an all-out universal retaliation."

"Um...I think, actually, I should not cast this spell." Gigglebrit backed away and raised his hands in an attempt to placate the universe. "We can just warm some tea instead. *Agethermon* and all that."

Mardulo touched his nose conspiratorially, completely misunderstanding Gigglebrit's intentions.

"You'll be all right," said Bundersquash. "It's not like you're planning a total reversal of gravitational forces or an outbound switch of natural phenomena. Just say"—he made the noises again—"and make sure you do it confidently. And don't blink."

Gigglebrit looked to the others, hoping one of them might advise against it, but Lady Ufferbub simply shrugged, wringing the water from her robe. "We do need to make sure your magic still works."

"All right then." Gigglebrit sighed.

"Oh, and if you find yourself floating among stars of amber," Mardulo cut in, "cross your fingers, count to six, and jump. It's not common, but you never know."

Gigglebrit took a moment to calm himself. Something was worrying him, and it wasn't the imminent head-to-head battle with the universe.

If his magic didn't work, then this was all for nothing. He wouldn't be the Hero. He wouldn't have his task. No more direction. No more purpose. Where would that leave him?

What would that leave him?

But he couldn't dwell on it. He had to try.

So he rubbed his palms together...and to the clear relief of everyone present, his shining auric nebula burst to life, sky blue and twinkling. Wisps of smoke sprung up wherever the raindrops hit it.

Gigglebrit breathed.

That was one hurdle jumped. Now his foremost worry really *was* going head to head with the universe...

He focused his mind on stopping the rain, then did his best to mimic whatever absurd noises Bundersquash had made. He said them very confidently, but even he could tell they weren't correct.

There was a loud screech, a brush of wind, a twist in the air...and the world turned upside down. Actually, Gigglebrit found when his head hit the ground, he had turned upside down. The rain attacked him in sheets, so forceful it hurt. A ruthless torrent of bullet-like drops, fired directly at him. He worried they might drive holes through his skin.

The others were yelling, but their voices washed away in the roar of rain. With few other options available to him, Gigglebrit tried to stand—except his feet slipped out from under him, and he landed face-first in a puddle. A deep, endless puddle. Down, down, down he went, swallowed in watery darkness.

This was it. He was going to drown...in a puddle...on a bridge...over the edge of the—

A sudden slap pulled him back to reality. All at once, everything seemed normal again. Lady Ufferbub was pulling his hair, forcefully holding his head up.

"Blimey!" Mardulo sounded surprised. "Are you all right?"

Gigglebrit coughed, then rolled onto his back when Lady Ufferbub released him. "Yes..." he said. "I think, anyway. Did I disappear for a second, or was that just in my head?"

Mardulo offered him a hand. "You were spatially repositioned, then you got hit with a lot of rain, then you sputtered about in a puddle for a bit and Lady Ufferbub grabbed you. Any water in the lungs?"

"I don't think so..." Gigglebrit shuddered. "Thank you, Lady Ufferbub."

"Just doing my part," said the librarian.

"You put on quite the show," Mardulo said to Gigglebrit. "And look, the rain has stopped!"

Gigglebrit hadn't even noticed. "I did it?!" he said, incredulous.

"Absolutely not. You bungled that spell, no two ways about it. I think the sky just cleared up, is all."

Gigglebrit inspected his bruises, suspecting the storm may have used up all its water on him. But at least the rain had stopped. He'd call that a win.

The sun came out fully as they continued their march. Gigglebrit's clothes dried, the air warmed, and his mood improved considerably. His magic still worked. He'd pretty much memorized the trapping spell. And they still had a few days to iron out the kinks. Things were going well.

Gigglebrit even looked up from the walkway once or twice to enjoy the view. It wasn't every day one found oneself inside a tunnel of semitranslucent magical energy. The sky seemed to swirl with the Splat, flowing like silk in the sunshine as shocks of color rose high into the air, as if departing this planet to join with the stars or make an entire galaxy of their own.

It took several hours to reach the bridge's halfway point. The Fifteen-Mile Plaza, it was called—a large area designed as a safe haven for poorly timed travelers who need a place to sleep for the night. It was one giant circle, stretching about twenty yards in every direction, slanted toward the center so any unexpected tumbles gravitated away from the edge. There were binoculars attached to metal stands posted around the perimeter, where curious travelers could pay five penna to zoom in on the abyss below.

Presently, three people sat near the center: man, woman, and child.

"Goodness me!" said the man, pointing at Mardulo, Bundersquash, Lady Ufferbub, Toddleposter, Gigglebrit, and the animals—mostly, the animals. "Nellinda, Parifel, look at that! What a parade!"

The woman—portly, with freckles and curls—stood and shaded her eyes. "My word! What a sight! Hello. I'm Nellinda Norbunkin Norwallis the Nice. This old lump here is my partner, Dargorbal Nebrinski Norwallis the Joyed, and this beautiful angel is my daughter, Parifel Norvy Norwallis the Curious."

The child couldn't have been more than six years old. She wore a tiara made of flowers and had the scraped, dirt-caked knees to prove she'd picked them herself. She radiated excitement as she approached the herd of animals, taking particular interest in the kangaroo.

The kangaroo readied to engage in fisticuffs.

"No!" Toddleposter leaped between them and chastised the creature. "You need to stop attacking travelers!" He turned to the family and said, "Sorry. They're supposed to be trained, but I think this one missed a few lessons."

"No harm done, my friend." The man, Dargorbal, smiled. "You've got quite the collection! It's a pleasure to make your acquaintance."

"And yours," said Toddleposter. Everyone introduced themselves in turn. When Mardulo came around, the family looked stunned.

"*The* Mardulo Vot Ponterous the Brilliant? Blimey, what are the chances? It's wonderful to meet you."

Mardulo flushed. "You flatter me," he said, then quickly changed the subject. "Where are you heading?"

"We have family up in City Mez," Nellinda replied. "We haven't heard much since all this lime business got started. Wanted to make sure they're safe."

"A noble mission," said Lady Ufferbub.

"Did you collect all these animals yourself?!" Parifel turned in circles, astonished by the assortment. "Are you collectors?"

"We had help from our friends," said Bundersquash. "Would you like to meet my butterfly? Her name is Lobster, and she's very special! She was a gift from my parents. I bet she'd like your tiara!"

"Yes, please!" Parifel jumped, clapping. "My crown is very special too," she added seriously. "I call it Oleandera the Death Bringer."

"Umm," said Gigglebrit, almost involuntarily.

"I call it that because it has oleander, and Daddy told me that oleander is poisonous."

Bundersquash blinked a few times. "Yes. Well." His mouth kept smiling, but his eyes backed away. "Maybe we won't let Lobster get too close, then."

"Okay," said the girl, unfazed. "It also has dandelions, lobelias, and one daisy! Is that a fox?"

"It is!" said Toddleposter.

"You should call him Mr. Fox, because he looks like a gentleman."

"Come now, Parifel," said Nellinda. "It's not our place to name their animals. I'm sure they have perfectly good names already."

"What about the lion? You could name him Mr. Lion the Death Bringer to match my crown. Look at those teeth!"

The mother glanced apologetically at the others. "We were just about to have lunch if you'd like to join us. We have a sandwich generator—not that, well, I suppose you must be over that sort of thing...silly me. Here I stand, offering Mardulo Vot Ponterous the Brilliant a sandwich generator!" She wiped her face, embarrassed. "Sorry. I'm sure we could whip up some oatmeal, instead. Maybe some clam chowder?"

Mardulo raised a hand. "You're very kind, but sandwiches would be more than satisfactory. Many thanks."

"If you're sure." Nellinda looked relieved. "I'll fetch the generator."

The Norwallises packed lightly. They carried a single large backpack, three walking sticks, and nothing more. By comparison, the overloaded cart Lampellion was pulling seemed absurd. Nellinda grabbed the sandwich generator from her backpack and passed it around the circle.

"What's it all for?" asked Dargorbal, gesturing toward the animals with his pepper-and-carrot sandwich.

"I'm a merchant," said Gigglebrit. "These are my wares." He tried to keep the details to a minimum.

"Can I buy the kangaroo, *please*?" asked Parifel excitedly. "Daddy, you can give him to me as a present, like that wizard's butterfly!"

Dargorbal looked at his daughter with a mixture of amusement and pity. "How would we feed him?"

"He's a kangaroo, Daddy. Kangaroos live in the wild. I'm sure he can feed himself."

"Not in this part of the world, honey. Sorry."

Parifel hmphed and sulked until she got her sandwich—chocolate mousse and peanut butter smushed between two lettuce leaves. This immediately extinguished whatever sour feelings she'd been harboring.

Gigglebrit, meanwhile, twisted his face at a salmon-and-minestrone sandwich. He removed the bread, wiped off the soggy pasta, then ate the salmon by itself. The others seemed to disapprove, but Gigglebrit paid them no mind. The salmon was good, and he ate the bread afterward.

Stomachs full, conversation came easily. Dargorbal praised the sudden change in the weather. Parifel asked after every animal's history. Then Nellinda started on the benefits of thick hiking socks but stopped midsentence. She tilted her head to one side, staring at something behind Gigglebrit.

Four more travelers, coming from the north.

As a rule, Gigglebrit tried to refrain from snap judgments based on a person's appearance, but in this particular case, it was hard not to look once and run the other way. All you had to do was count the weapons.

Lady Ufferbub seemed undeterred. "Hello," she said. "Can we help you?"

The tallest of the group, a lean, short-haired woman with a calculated grin, sauntered up and laid a hand on their cart of supplies. "We're the patrol on this bridge. We've come to collect a toll for your passage."

A large man with an even larger war hammer approached beside her. "Can't have a bridge without a toll," he grunted.

"Don't they usually collect those at the entrance?" asked Mardulo snidely.

"We've found people are more *accommodating* once they've started crossing. Something about the surroundings." The man with the hammer smirked.

"The Narrow Stride has been toll-free for over a hundred years," said Lady Ufferbub, piercing them all with her stare. "Now, I would be pleased if you removed your hand from our supplies."

The man with the hammer made his hammer more evident. "Hundred years ago ain't today, lady. You should know better. Got a bridge. Got a toll. That's the way of the world."

"You will pay the toll." The tall woman spoke in a carefully rehearsed tone that brokered no argument. She picked through the supplies in the cart. "My, my, my...we are a well-stocked bunch, aren't we? *Wizards*, I take it?" She spoke the word like a curse. "Fat lot of good these will do you up north. Singed carrot stalks, golden whiskers, eldritch dust..." Each ingredient, she pulled from a box and tossed carelessly over her shoulder. Fortunately, Lady Ufferbub and Toddleposter had buried the trapping spell ingredients a few layers deep.

But Mardulo wasn't taking any chances. He tried to make himself look big. "Step away from our cart," he said in a voice he probably thought was threatening.

"And how do you intend to oppose us?" said a third member of the party. She was mostly shoulders, with a few swords strapped to her back and a thick bandage across her nose. "Your spells won't protect you here, wizards. Ten percent is ours. Keep talking and we'll make it twenty."

The fourth collector—a rat of a man, if ever there was one—took particular interest the animals. "I hear lion pelts sell well in the archipelago." He grinned a massive, four-toothed grin.

"And we'll have a look inside that backpack too," said the tall woman, pointing at the Norwallis's supplies.

Dargorbal pulled the pack toward himself. "Nothing in here worth taking, I assure you. A few clothes, some food. Certainly won't sell for much if it's money you're after."

The woman's face hardened. "I think I've had enough of this group's insolence." She strode closer, coming face to face with Dargorbal. "If your pack has nothing of value, then you will just have to pay with your service."

In a flash, she twisted to one side, produced a dagger, and held it to Parifel's neck. "Come, all of you. Hobblebosh pays well for working hands. More if they're still attached. A few years of indentured servitude might even teach you some respect."

Everyone raised their hands in surrender. If it meant keeping Parifel's neck intact, they were all willing to oblige.

All, that is, except Parifel, who said, "Excuse me, Ms. Knife Lady." She spoke calmly, the knife still resting at her throat. "You can have my crown as a toll if you want. It's a good crown. The flowers are *veeeery* tasty."

The woman half chuckled as she tore the tiara away. She gave it a quick once-over, then tossed it over the edge of the bridge. "Not enough," she said. "Not nearly enough. Tog, we won't be needing that cart of ingredients anymore either. Their service should suffice, and we'll want to travel quickly. Why don't you show them what we think of wizards and their supplies in this part of the world?"

"Yes, ma'am!" Tog, the man with the hammer, nodded, then swung his hammer at the side of the cart using enough force to fight back a tidal wave. The wood split, and the cart crashed to one side with a clamorous thud. All the boxes tumbled out, cracking and opening as they hit the bridge. Ingredients scattered across the plaza.

One of the larger boxes fell toward the leader. She stepped back, distracted for a moment by the mayhem.

And Nellinda seized the opportunity. She grabbed the leader's hand and wrenched it back at an angle, forcing the knife away from Parifel's neck. The leader's wrist cracked sickeningly. She gave a cry of pain, dropped her weapon—

—and the world came afire with chaos.

Bundersquash didn't hesitate. He charged for the thug nearest Lobster, which happened to be the rat man, who hardly had time to draw his weapon before the full weight of Bundersquash hurdled down upon him. The rat fell. Bundersquash sat on him heavily.

Lady Ufferbub and Mardulo both held the leader down while Nellinda and Dargorbal pulled their child to safety. Toddleposter hurried toward the animals, herding them away from the fight.

Which left Gigglebrit.

Alone.

Facing two opponents.

The woman with the swords was closest, just ahead of the hammer-wielding maniac.

Gigglebrit considered casting a spell—even nondeterministic behavior might serve as a useful distraction—but he couldn't take the risk. If he ended up sputtering in a puddle again, he'd be even worse off than before. Not to mention, if any of these foes escaped, they could tell Hobblebosh what they'd seen, and that would be the end of the plan.

The sword woman trudged in his direction, stomping on ingredients as she went, ignoring the plants and oils under foot, oblivious to the glass she shattered. She drew one of her swords and pointed it straight at Gigglebrit.

Gigglebrit panicked. There was no way he could win this fight. To his own surprise, he found himself raising his hands, saying "Why don't we all just talk this out? I'm sure we can reach some kind of—"

The sword lady lunged, and Gigglebrit threw himself away just in time to avoid her first strike. Then he tripped over something and fell.

Dargorbal's walking stick.

"Good enough," he said to himself as he grabbed the stick and held it out in defense.

It fractured almost instantly under the rapid strikes of the sword.

Gigglebrit rolled to one side, wincing as shards of broken glass jabbed into his arm. Then he rolled again to avoid another strike, but this time, he stabbed back at the attacker's legs using the splintered piece of walking stick in his hand. He felt the spiked wood sink into her thigh. She collapsed with a start, her swords clanging against the marble.

Gigglebrit scrambled to his feet and looked around, shocked by just how quickly the fight had changed around him.

Tog, the hammer-happy thug, was battling Mardulo and Toddleposter. Meanwhile, Bundersquash was struggling to evade a flurry of stabs from the rat man, and Lady Ufferbub was defending the entire Norwallis family against the leader. They were grappling, and it wasn't clear who had the advantage. The leader's injured hand seemed to do little but fuel her fury.

A harsh shout tore Gigglebrit's thoughts away. Tog had struck Mardulo with the hammer, hard enough to knock him out. Toddleposter flailed his arms and pounced on Tog's back, yelling, pulling the thug's hair, turning him away before he could land another hit on Mardulo.

Gigglebrit ran to help, but a hand grabbed his ankle. The sword woman. She'd yanked the wooden stick from her leg. Now she was getting up—using Gigglebrit as a crutch. Shards of broken glass covered her side, and her back had been sliced by one of her own swords. But she fought on. Gigglebrit tried to kick free...and failed.

"Snipperwig, hand me a sword!" the leader called out. In her fight against Lady Ufferbub, they had moved dangerously close to the edge. *"Now!"*

The woman holding Gigglebrit's leg fumed, but she was nothing if not a loyal henchwoman. She threw Gigglebrit aside, then trudged toward Lady Ufferbub and the leader, holding one sword in her left hand, ready for use, and another in her right, hilt out, for the leader to grab.

But Snipperwig was limping from her injuries, and Lady Ufferbub leaped between them. She snatched the sword before anyone could grab it and threw the leader to one side—away from the edge, unfortunately.

Snipperwig flinched but recovered almost immediately. Half a moment later, she had forgotten all about her wounds, and she and Lady Ufferbub were fencing—a dizzying blur of strikes and slashes, so fast they were almost invisible.

Gigglebrit gaped, impressed by the speed and intensity of Lady Ufferbub's swordplay, though somehow not particularly surprised.

Their fight veered nearer to the herd of animals. Whiskers the lion was closest, looking incredibly uncomfortable with the situation. He shrank away from the rapid clamor of attacks, but the fight kept getting closer, and in the end, he panicked. He let forth a terrible roar, grabbed the fox—gently, like a mother might carry a kitten—and raced down the southern end of the bridge, back the way they had come, to safety.

Lady Ufferbub and Snipperwig barely seemed to register the incident, but Bundersquash turned in surprise. The rat-man used the distraction and lunged at the younger wizard.

Gigglebrit decided now was a good time to start being useful again. He charged to help Bundersquash, who barely dodged the first stab. When the rat came around for a second, Gigglebrit jumped at him. He grabbed the toll collector's arms and tried, shifting and twisting, to hold him in place while Bundersquash ran in for a punch. But the rat yanked free—though he dropped his knife in the process. He side-stepped Bundersquash's attack, swiveled, then hit the young wizard in the back of the head. Bundersquash fell to the ground without so much as a cry.

Gigglebrit went for the knife, which was sliding toward the center of the bridge. The rat-man had the same idea. They raced down the sloped plaza, tripping and scrambling in one unceremonious tumble. For every punch Gigglebrit threw, he received a kick in return, but in the end, he prevailed, pinning the rat down with one hand while he grabbed the knife with the other.

He held it up, ready to strike...then hesitated. Was he really about to—?

Too late.

The rat-man tossed him aside. In one desperate moment, Gigglebrit threw the knife away, over the edge of the bridge, down into the abyss below.

The rat tackled him. "We'll add the cost of that knife to your toll," he said with a grin. His breath was stale, rancid. "Another year of servitude. And maybe a finger or two."

Gigglebrit squirmed, but it was no use. The man was kneeling on his chest, pressing down with all his weight, forcing the air out of Gigglebrit's lungs. Gigglebrit gasped, writhing helplessly against the knee shoved into his sternum, completely unable to breathe.

Suddenly, everything went quiet. The metallic clatters of the sword fight ceased. Toddleposter's frantic shouts against Tog came to a halt. The rat-man rose, and Gigglebrit turned to one side, coughing violently.

"I think we can all agree," the leader's voice rang out, breathless but fierce, "this little episode has run its course."

Gigglebrit struggled to his feet. The leader blew a strand of hair from her face. She was breathing heavily, her left leg was bleeding, something was wrong with her ear, and her right hand hung down, unmoving, with two fingers bent at unnatural angles. But she stood tall nonetheless, refusing to give in to the pain she must have felt. She had a sword—it looked like the one Lady Ufferbub had been using—and was pressing it threateningly into Dargorbal's side. Snipperwig, bruised but not beaten, still had a few swords remaining. She was using them to keep Nellinda and Parifel at bay. Lady Ufferbub lay unmoving in a puddle—still breathing, Gigglebrit noted with relief, but knocked out.

Toddleposter stood some distance away, guarding Mardulo's unconscious body. He stared at Tog, daring him to move. Bundersquash got up unsteadily and hobbled into position next to him.

A shard of glass dug into Gigglebrit's back—not quite drawing blood, but near enough.

"Got you," said the rat.

The leader spat—froth and blood. "Tog, bring those three here." She signaled to Toddleposter, Bundersquash, and Mardulo. "Ekel, bring your prisoner too."

The rat man said, "Happily," and jabbed the shard of glass forward, forcing Gigglebrit to walk.

Gigglebrit's mind raced. What should he do? If he tried to turn and fight, Ekel was faster, and Gigglebrit was still out of breath. He wouldn't win.

The glass pressed deeper into his back. Surely it was drawing blood now.

He could charge ahead and tackle the leader, but that left Snipperwig, and Snipperwig still had a sword in each hand. She'd be on him in a heartbeat.

There was nothing for it. He couldn't stand by while these thugs took servants to Hobblebosh. He had to do something, and a bad solution was better than none...he was just about to turn and punch Ekel in the face when a sudden scraping of claws sounded to his left.

Tog screamed. Gigglebrit turned to look. So did Ekel.

Lampellion had taken matters into his own hands. He rammed headfirst into Tog, who sailed through the air for a good second or two before crashing back onto the bridge.

Gigglebrit used the distraction to his advantage. He flung into Ekel fists first, wrestling for the shard of glass. Bundersquash and Toddleposter, now free from Tog, ran to help, and together, they overpowered the rat—but once again, he squirmed from their grasp, then scampered over to the leader. Tog wobbled back to his feet, looking more than a little dented, and returned to the leader as well.

They had all taken a beating, but the toll collectors still had the Norwallis family at sword point.

The leader straightened. A spasm of pain burned across her face; she quickly coughed it away. "Enough of this!" she commanded. "These three will sell well enough in the Forest Mines. Hobblebosh can be generous when it comes to this type of...merchandise. Ekel, take some of their ingredients as well, preferably ones that haven't been stomped on. As for the rest of you..." She eyed the cluster of animals on the southern side of the plaza—particularly, Lampellion and the winged rhinoceros. "The rest of you should be glad we haven't tossed you over the edge."

She about-faced and limped away, down the northern side of bridge. Ekel snatched a few random bottles and jars; then he and the others followed suit, taking the entire Norwallis family with them. Parifel shouted something and started to cry.

It was too much to bear. Bundersquash let forth a battle cry and charged once more, trying desperately to get the family back. Tog turned with his hammer and swatted him away like a fly.

Gigglebrit heard the shatter of the impact.

Bundersquash flew back, landing near the far edge of the plaza. He didn't get up, and the marble, slick with rainwater, offered little friction. Bundersquash slid, unconscious, helpless, closer and closer and closer to the edge—

Gigglebrit cried out and ran to help, Toddleposter quick on his heels.

Bundersquash's head had already dipped below the edge when Gigglebrit lunged to grab him. He caught the wizard's wrist, then slipped himself. His face hit marble. There was a splash of water, a painful scrape, his entire body skidded, pulled by Bundersquash—and then, suddenly, silently, and with a horrifying lurch, the ground slid away beneath him.

He and Bundersquash were falling.

It stopped all at once. Gigglebrit's knee cracked and jolted. His arms wrenched as they took on the full weight of Bundersquash. Gigglebrit did his best to look up, still holding the wizard by the wrist. "Toddleposter?"

"I've got your ankle!" the young librarian cried out.

"Can you pull us up?"

"I'll try. You're very heavy, the two of you. How is Bundersquash?"

Gigglebrit looked, then wished he hadn't. The wizard's shirt was stuck to his skin—stained, wet, and dark. Where his ribs should have been, there was nothing but dents and sharp bits.

"He looks very...um. Toddleposter, I think he might be—"

"Don't say it," said Toddleposter. "He isn't. He won't be. We can fix this."

Gigglebrit tried to keep calm. What could he do? There had to be something he could do. He looked down into the depths of nothingness.

"So, uh, any luck pulling us up?" he asked.

"I'm having a hard time just to keep from slipping."

"Lady Ufferbub? Mardulo?"

"Unconscious."

"Lampellion?"

"I think he's inspecting a caterpillar. He seems a bit wobbly after the headbutt."

Gigglebrit swore.

Toddleposter swore.

A gust of wind blew past, swinging Gigglebrit and Bundersquash like a pendulum.

"Hang on a minute," said Gigglebrit.

He had an idea. It was a ridiculous idea. But in some ways, also perfect. But completely absurd...

The wind blew again. Gigglebrit could feel his grip on Bundersquash slipping.

Well, it was the best he had.

"I have a plan," Gigglebrit called, "but you'll have to hold on tight, and I mean *really tight*. Grab something heavy if you can. Then pull us in, hard."

"Gigglebrit." Toddleposter's voice was strained. "I must say, that is not the most original plan I've heard all day. I've already tried pulling you in. Do you—"

"There's more to it, just give me a moment." Holding Bundersquash with one arm, he carefully let go with his other hand and reached for his back pocket. The arm holding Bundersquash tensed and twitched as it took on more weight. Gigglebrit's fingers started to sweat.

He could do this. He had to do this. He just had to hold on for a few more seconds. Lives were at stake.

"What are you doing?!" Toddleposter called down to him.

"I have some healing lorilell dust in my pocket. I think it might actually...well, it might not work at all, but apparently there will be some kickback when I apply it to Bundersquash's chest. I believe the exact word Leepog used was explosive. And Bundersquash is facing the bridge, so I'm hoping if I apply the dust to his wounds, the force will be enough to push us out and away from the bridge. But then you *really* have to pull us in—and pull hard. With you as a kind of pivot point, anchoring us, the force of the powder's explosion combined with the force from your pull should spin us around, back onto the bridge. Just like a giant pendulum."

Hopefully...

Gigglebrit had done quite well in physics, but he was quickly learning the tremendous, panicked weight that so effectively differentiated theory from practice. Not that it mattered much. It wasn't like he had time to construct the necessary free-body diagrams—and they probably wouldn't offer much comfort, even if he did.

"Um. Gigglebrit?" said Toddleposter hesitantly.

"Yes?"

"I don't know if that's the *best* idea."

"It's the only one I've got, and if I don't use this powder soon, it'll be too late. Five minutes, Leepog said. We have to apply it within five minutes of receiving the wound. Do you have any alternatives?"

After a pause, Toddleposter said, "No."

"All right, then. This is what we're doing. Hold on tight. Let's hope this bridge can take a hit. And let's hope Leepog really meant it when he said explosive."

Toddleposter seemed to resign himself to it. He shifted around, adjusted his grip on Gigglebrit's ankle, then said, "Okay. I'm ready when you are."

What was the worst that could happen? If the explosion wasn't strong enough, the powder would still heal Bundersquash. And if the explosion was too strong...well, if it was too strong, they would probably all die, but by some measures, that was only speeding up the inevitable—and not by very much, given the current state of things.

Gigglebrit took one deep, shaky breath, then very carefully removed the L. G. T. baggie from his back pocket. It was tied off with a ribbon. He bit one end and pulled, untying the knot with his teeth, careful not to lose any powder.

Just then, something gave out in the arm holding Bundersquash. It lurched violently, and Gigglebrit's shoulder cracked. Pain shot through it like fire. He muffled a scream and clenched his jaw, letting the agony wash through him. He had to keep the bag upright. He had to stay focused. He had to keep his grip.

He exhaled, "I can do this," then tried to concentrate despite the blood rushing to his head.

Hopefully, the powder didn't have to be applied precisely. The best he could do was tip the bag upside down and fling it around a bit, covering as much of Bundersquash's front side as possible.

Pretty much all of him was a wound anyway, so maybe that was fine.

Holding the open packet in his free hand, he called to Toddleposter, "Here we go!" then turned the bag and shook it, arm outstretched, directing the spill in the approximate direction of Bundersquash's chest.

Some of the dust landed on the wizard's frizzled hair. Some of it scattered into the wind. Some of it blew up into Gigglebrit's eyes, and some blew even farther, lost above the bridge...but most of it went where Gigglebrit had intended, sticking to the wetness on Bundersquash's shirt...

Nothing happened for several seconds.

Then Gigglebrit's shoulder started to feel better.

Then a gentle popping filled the air—something between a noise and a feeling, barely noticeable.

Then a veritable bomb went off between Bundersquash, Gigglebrit, and Collywobbles Bridge, and Gigglebrit nearly blacked out.

He couldn't feel the direction of the motion. He could only feel the force. He dropped the empty lorilell dust packet into the Splat and seized Bundersquash's wrist with both hands, praying to every god he could think of as their bodies sailed through the air. His ears roared with wind and rushing blood, and his vision darkened. Toddleposter was shouting.

Then Gigglebrit hit the ground. The solid, marble ground. Bundersquash landed on top of him.

Gigglebrit had never been so relieved in his life, nor quite so dizzy.

Toddleposter had toppled over, not exactly at a loss for words, but rather finding quite a few and failing to choose any one in particular.

Gigglebrit nudged Bundersquash to one side and sat up. The younger wizard's rib cage had returned to normal, but he was still unconscious.

"Well, that was...something," said Gigglebrit to Toddleposter.

"Yes," said Toddleposter. "It was."

Gigglebrit blinked, then turned back to Bundersquash. "After all that," he said, "how are his glasses still intact?"

"Long-term personal binding enchantment with threefold protective layering."

"Ah. Naturally."

"Took him weeks to complete."

"I guess it paid off."

Toddleposter nodded. They sat in silence for a time—breathing, recovering. Slowly, the adrenaline wore off, and as they surveyed the wreck of the plaza, so too did the satisfaction of a job well done.

"All those ingredients," Gigglebrit said softly. "Totally destroyed…"

"Some of the animals ran away, too…" added Toddleposter.

"How are Lady Ufferbub and Mardulo?"

"They're breathing. Bundersquash?"

"I think he'll be all right once he wakes up."

Toddleposter took a deep breath.

"But the family…" said Gigglebrit, staring as a blood-mingled puddle slowly spread across the marble. "We lost the family. Parifel. Her parents…we failed them."

"We did."

A long time passed before anyone said anything. Eventually, Gigglebrit and Toddleposter carefully shifted Bundersquash toward the center of the plaza; then they sat back to back in silence.

Shocked and ashamed and exhausted, they waited, hoping for the others to wake up soon, hoping the Norwallises would be okay in the end, hoping this plan hadn't all been for nothing.

Hoping, hoping, hoping…

Chapter 12

Reconstruction

Lady Ufferbub woke up first. She rose quickly and seemed to regret it instantly.

"That did not go well," she said. "I am sorry to admit I failed to account for my surroundings. I was fighting that woman—the large one, with the swords—when suddenly, someone hit me." She reached for the back of her head and winced. "A solid whack, by all accounts. I imagine it was the leader. Where are they now?"

Gigglebrit explained everything that had happened. Lady Ufferbub's expression darkened as he spoke.

"This is a sad day, indeed," she said. "I am sorry to hear about the family. Even the daughter was taken?"

"Even the daughter," said Toddleposter.

Lady Ufferbub put a hand on his shoulder. "I am sure you did all you could, and you both did well with Bundersquash. At least we still have our team—still here and still alive. Let us find some peace in that."

It was a bitter consolation, but Gigglebrit supposed she was right. It could have been far worse. It nearly had been.

"Do you know any first aid?" he asked. "I don't know what to do for Mardulo and Bundersquash. They've been out for a while..."

Lady Ufferbub checked their pulses and breathing, then looked for any obvious injuries but found none.

"It is possible some of the healing dust made it up here too. Mardulo looks better than I would have expected, given the attack he suffered. For now, I think it is best to leave them both be. If any luck has joined us on our journey, they will—"

"Bloody mother of goodness!" Mardulo bolted into a sitting position. "What happened? Feels like someone dropped a bloody scrying stone on my head. Where did those toll collectors go? And the family?" He looked from side to side, grinning mischievously. "I suppose you could call it a *high-stakes* battle. Looks like we lost, though. That's a shame...no one fell off, I hope? Goodness gracious me, I am going to have some nasty bruises tomorrow. Hurts like a thrice-burned eyeball. Hello, everyone. Where's Bundersquash?"

Lady Ufferbub pointed.

"Oh." The elderly wizard scowled, suddenly serious. He tried to stand, couldn't, then crawled to his student's side. "He's breathing. I can cast a quick healing spell if...oh, blast. No, I can't...Gigglebrit, did we ever teach you about the underpinning of physical components as they pertain to organic interaction?"

"No," said Gigglebrit. "But I used some healing lorilell dust on him. He's looking better than he did."

"Good. Good. In a magical field like this, I imagine the effects were somewhat amplified. That will help. We brought some healing herbs with the supplies too. They're not much, but better than nothing in a pinch..." Mardulo looked at the mess strewn about the plaza. He took a deep breath. "Did any of the pellian extract survive?"

"I do not think it would make much difference," said Lady Ufferbub. "Gigglebrit's work appears to have done a great deal of good. Let us trust in that."

Mardulo frowned. "If he doesn't wake up soon, we should take him south of the bridge. I can cast a healing spell there. I'm sure we could find the necessary ingredients in the meadows. Maybe we should go now."

"Give it time, Mardulo. Moving him could cause more damage."

"Time..." Mardulo tapped his fingers irritably. "What if he doesn't have time? What if he's dying as we speak? He's only young—"

"We will keep an eye on him," said Lady Ufferbub. "I think he will recover."

Mardulo refused to move. He checked Bundersquash's pulse, rechecked his breathing, lifted his feet, then put his feet down again, then repeated it all twice over.

"I don't know what to do," he said at last, eyes misted over.

Lampellion approached and licked the side of Bundersquash's face. Lobster settled on his belly. The group sat, waiting.

And a few minutes later, he woke up.

"Professor!" said Bundersquash. "You're okay!"

Mardulo seemed ready to collapse with relief. Gigglebrit felt much the same way.

Bundersquash looked around. "I'm glad you're all here. How's Lobster?"

Toddleposter pointed to the butterfly, still on Bundersquash's belly.

"Oh, good. I was—" Bundersquash coughed, grimacing. "Excuse me. I was worried about you! And Lampellion! Many thanks for the assistance, friend. How are the other animals? It's unfortunate Whiskers and the fox ran off, but hopefully they'll be all right. Maybe they'll find the howler monkey."

Gigglebrit hadn't even considered the animals until now. The tessle was absentmindedly pawing at a spilled box of tree bark, the kangaroo seemed ashamed he hadn't done more to help, and the pygmy minotaur was trapped inside a magical bird cage, growling furiously.

"While it's a relief that everyone is okay," said Toddleposter, "I think we have some difficult decisions to make."

"Toddleposter speaks wisely," said Lady Ufferbub. "Our merry mission of misdirectional merchantry has hit something of a snag."

Gigglebrit surveyed the wreckage of the plaza. The cart was badly damaged but not irreparable. The ingredients were the main issue. Shattered glass, herbs, dusts, and powders littered the area like so much ash after a fire.

And then, having allowed matters beyond the well-being of his friends to enter his mind, Gigglebrit suddenly realized, "What about the glamours?"

The thought struck everyone in an instant. Before long, they were up and searching—a frantic mess of tossed boxes and worried looks.

Mardulo found them...or what was left of them. "Oh dear," he said, gazing at a toppled box.

Toddleposter jogged over. "At least a few survived."

"How many?" Gigglebrit asked.

"I count five," said Mardulo.

Something popped. Shards of glass zipped through the air and flew off the side of the bridge.

"Make that four."

"Quick!" Toddleposter leaped into action.

In one panicked flurry, they managed to extract the remaining bottles from a goopy puddle that had formed inside the box—the spilled remnants of the other glamours. Strange, half-formed shapes seemed to rise and fall from the mess, as if the box itself was trying to transform into several different people at once. The result was an exceptionally unpleasant conglomeration of miniature limbs and noses that grew and changed, squeezing the remaining bottles.

Mardulo snatched the last one and wiped it down.

"Well," he said. "That is unfortunate."

"It's certainly going to complicate matters," said Toddleposter.

"Can we make more?" asked Gigglebrit.

"Not here, and not in time." Mardulo sighed. "Glamours are like lorilell dust, all middle magic and complex formulas. We don't have the ingredients or the expertise."

"We must head back," said Lady Ufferbub sadly. "We can obtain new glamours and replenish our ingredients, then make another attempt as soon as we are prepared."

Bundersquash latched on to the idea like a vise. "Yes! And while we're at it, we should look into alternate disguises. Using Lobster as bait is too risky. Clearly, it's more dangerous than we anticipated."

Lobster made an indignant chirrup and crossed her upper two legs.

"But the family," said Toddleposter hesitantly. "Surely, we cannot leave them to suffer in servitude to Obble Dor Hobblebosh. We have to help."

"Toddleposter is right," said Mardulo. "We should continue to Town Forbik, save that family, and stop Hobblebosh while we still can. We have four glamours left. It's enough to disguise all of us except one, and Hobblebosh doesn't know what Gigglebrit looks like yet, so that could work!"

"One glamour each isn't enough," said Bundersquash. "We need to be disguised at the town gates *and* in the market—likely two different days. Our glamours will only work for a few hours! You know that, Professor."

"Of course I know that!" Mardulo tugged his beard, thinking. "The gates will be more difficult. We can use the glamours there. Surely, once we're in, we can find simpler disguises to hide among a bustling market—shawls or cloaks or something. We just stick to the shadows and let Gigglebrit do his work, helping only if absolutely necessary."

"But the Norwallis family isn't even *going* to Town Forbik," said Toddleposter. "The leader said they were going to the Forest Mines. That will take them widesplatter, to the outskirts of Forest Plawg. We should head that way, and quickly!"

Mardulo faltered. "No," he said. "We need to focus on Town Forbik. It's closer, and if we stop Hobblebosh there, his operation in the Forest Mines will also cease. If, on the other hand, we go to the family directly…we may save them, yes, but what about the others Hobblebosh has under his control? More than just the Norwallises are suffering."

"Look around!" Bundersquash cried, waving his hands wildly. A hacking cough cut him off. He clenched his chest and retched, then resumed a few breaths later with less flailing. "It's madness to presume we can still make this work. Over half the ingredients—ingredients we need for our disguise to be effective—have been destroyed. Most of the glamours are gone, and we've lost three of the animals already! This plan was a stretch from the start! To keep going after this is foolish. We won't do any good blundering into hostile territory ill prepared, only to get ourselves murdered! And we have *innocent* creatures with us!" He looked at Lobster, then the other animals. "Like Lady Ufferbub said, we need to regroup."

"There's no time!" said Mardulo. "Did you forget? Hobblebosh has the wide-field residue corporealizer! He could be planning an attack on City Boratorus as we speak. His restricted zone is already expanding!"

Toddleposter looked uncertain. "That poor family is being taken into forced labor. Even if we stop Hobblebosh, how long before word reaches the mines?"

"We don't even know which route the toll collectors are taking," said Mardulo. "What if they pick up more prisoners along the way? They could be anywhere! I understand you want to help them, but the best way to do that is to go straight for Hobblebosh. We have to remove the weed at its root, not trim away the leaves. We should continue to Town Forbik. We can improvise a few disguises. We've done more with less."

"I don't believe it will be as easy as you think," said Bundersquash.

"I'm not saying it will be easy!" shouted Mardulo. "I'm saying we can do it! We were doing so well! Gigglebrit already memorized most of the spell."

"We can't go rushing into things anymore!" Bundersquash cried. "It's dangerous out there—or did this encounter with the toll collectors teach you nothing?"

"If anything," said Mardulo, "it taught me that we all seem inclined to fall unconscious when, by all rights, we should be falling dead!"

"Do not be absurd!" said Lady Ufferbub, openly angry now. "If Gigglebrit had not brought that healing dust, you have no idea what might have happened! To continue on is absolute folly. We should..."

The argument clamored on. Gigglebrit could feel the fractures creeping into their friendships. Each shout a stretch, a pull, a twist at the wounds—cuts digging deeper and deeper. If it went on much longer, the damage could be irreparable. The once-unified front of his friends was splintering, their guidance and leadership tearing apart. If it shattered completely, what would he do?

Then, all at once, he understood. What *would* he do? Because that's what mattered. He wasn't meant to sit quietly and wait for other people to decide things for him. That was Gilbert's life. Here, he was Gigglebrit, the Hero, and he'd read enough stories to recognize a moment like this.

He was right in the middle of a fantasy adventure, and things had been looking up. *Of course* they would encounter a disaster now. Protagonists regularly faced failure halfway through their quests. The second act was always the darkest. The Hero must have their crisis.

And the Hero must rise again.

"We should keep going." Gigglebrit stood and faced the others, who fell silent. "We've hit a bump in the road. So what? We can't stand by while children are being taken into slavery. The whole world is at risk. You told me yourselves: Hobblebosh will start moving again, and soon. He has the corporealizer. His restricted zone has already expanded to cover this bridge. We don't have time to walk back to the city and start this whole thing over again." He looked ahead, his face the image of determination...or at least, he hoped it was. "We keep going. It's the right thing to do. And Mardulo is correct—we need to go straight to the source, to Town Forbik. It makes the most sense. I'm going to need help from all of you, but I'll finish memorizing the spell, and together, we can make this work. We have to."

He took a deep breath. "Here's the plan. Bundersquash, rest. You look like death. Mardulo, look after him. Meanwhile, Lady Ufferbub, Toddleposter, and I will make this mess presentable." He gestured at the broken cart and the chaos of ingredients about the plaza.

"Once we've got everything up and mobile again, we'll keep marching. Someone has to check that we still have all the ingredients for the trapping spell, but that'll be easier once everything is organized. Mardulo and Bundersquash, you can do that once you've had some time to recover. If we're missing anything, let's hope we can make up the difference along the way or adjust the spell accordingly. We have...what? Three more days to reach Town Forbik? So we have three days to get this done. Let's not waste any of them."

The others blinked at him, shocked by this sudden turn toward assertiveness.

Then, finally, Lady Ufferbub sighed. "If you, Mardulo, and Toddleposter really do wish to continue, I suppose Bundersquash and I have been outvoted. And between the three of you, I suppose Town Forbik wins out. It makes sense, and I understand your reasoning. But," she cautioned with the raise of an eyebrow, "we should revisit the issue once we have determined the state of our ingredients. If we cannot craft the trapping spell, there is no point to any of this."

Bundersquash shut his eyes. "All right," he said at last. "I'm sorry I raised my voice. I'm just worried."

"High tempers are expected at a time like this," said Toddleposter. "But if we're going to continue as planned, we had best get started. We have a lot to clean up, and we're only halfway across this blasted bridge."

It was a hopeless mess, really, but they made the best of it. Toddleposter combed the plaza, scavenging for intact ingredients, while Lady Ufferbub and Gigglebrit heaved the cart back onto its wheels. Thankfully, the damage didn't look too bad once everything was upright again. One wheel wobbled, and there were a few cracked slats of wood where the hammer had struck, but that was it.

They tore apart the damaged crates and salvaged the more complete wooden planks to use as struts against the broken boards, then bound it all together with some rope and sticky resin. A few well-placed sheets worked to hide the patches, and in just under twenty minutes, the cart looked surprisingly presentable.

Toddleposter, with some help from Mardulo, collected a not-so-grand total of twelve ingredient boxes, each about half-full. They'd packed close to three times that number when they'd first set off, all overflowing with nonsensical goodies—but the clutter on the plaza spoke for itself. Gigglebrit was just happy the bridge hadn't started changing colors...or melting.

When they resumed their walk, it was a hobbling hike, slower going than before. Gigglebrit's ankle quickly developed a bruise, and not long later, his shoulder started to ache again. But the others had their fair share of wounds as well, and most were far worse than Gigglebrit's. Bundersquash gave a lurch about half an hour into the journey, coughed violently, and fell over. The others insisted he spend the remainder of the day on the wagon, resting among the ingredients.

Gigglebrit walked in the front and tried to keep everyone's spirits up. He thought of singing a marching song, but didn't know any, so instead, he proposed a round of storytelling.

Toddleposter started, with the tale of Wozberit Tozberit Nozberit the Friendly Vampire. Then Lady Ufferbub told one about Land Pottyworp, which had been named, reportedly, after some historical family's dog. Gigglebrit's turn came around, but he wanted to focus on tales from this world, so he passed it over to Mardulo.

By then, the blue sky had darkened to a shadowed violet, and dusk fell to the story of Randullia Perriwil Udger the Tempest, grand wizard, esteemed medic, and illustrious playwright, who very nearly befell a terrible fate at the hands of the sea-witch Brug but triumphed in the end thanks to the incorruptible power of theater.

When they finally reached the northern half of the planet, Gigglebrit was beyond exhausted. It ought to have been a joyful moment, stepping onto land again, but he could think of nothing more than sleep. Above all else, he wanted to curl into a ball and lose consciousness for a few blissful hours. Except they were in enemy territory now and couldn't stay in the open. So, he forced himself to keep walking, and when the others looked ready to give up, he rallied them, pushing just a little bit farther every time.

He had convinced them to continue the mission. *He* had told them he could do it. Whatever happened next, it was on him. The weight of that responsibility stuck with him. He braced himself for it, armored himself in it, knowing it was the Hero's burden to bear—his duty to this world. The importance fueled him.

They marched for hours, searching for somewhere secluded and dry, keeping off the path with nothing but moonlight and the faint purple haze of the Splat to guide them. It must have been nearing midnight when they found a small copse and cut their losses. Gigglebrit offered to take the first watch. An hour or two later, he switched with Mardulo, then at last gave into his exhaustion.

Dreamlessly, the night passed by.

The next day came bright and clear. Everyone had gotten some rest, and the group was better for it. Many of their healing herbs had been lost on Collywobbles Bridge, but not all of them. At breakfast, Lady Ufferbub used a few to stanch the bleeding from a reopened wound on her leg, then Bundersquash used several to ease the pain in his shoulder and chest. His breathing was still a little ragged. Bruises were in good attendance all around—every minute or two, they added another to the books—but even those did little to dampen the mood. Mardulo was trying to collect all the colors of the rainbow.

Upon examining the map, it became apparent they'd strayed too far splatterback in their search for a resting place the previous night. Thankfully, it was an easy fix. More costly was their need to keep away from the path, but they had little choice in that. Guards patrolled the northern lands, and brigands and thieves and wanderers, all of whom might be interested in the bounty that could come from capturing four notorious enemies of the crown.

Eventually, they decided to walk splatterbound until they were a mile or two south of the main path, then travel parallel to the Splat from there. They would hit Town Forbik on the third day of hiking—a Monday, the day before the weekly market.

When the two wizards were finished comparing their injuries, they took inventory of the ingredients. It didn't take long, and the news was good. The knotted cobweb strands were nowhere in sight, but those could be replaced, as could the purple geranium petals. The heartwood shards had splintered, but that just meant more shards, and they could use bottled fish breath in place of their now-broken vial of bird spittle with only a few modifications to the spell's mental passageways. The wormfoot, the clay, the thunderspark, and the sand had all survived without issue. Mud, they had in ample supply, and they could buy some extra-virgin olive oil in town.

"I guess we're really going through with it, then," said Toddleposter.

"Yes, we are," said Gigglebrit. *"Humeï'pente skeuae, sullégete enerheiás humoun kai'reite Obble-Dor-Hobblebosh hoti enerheiâis. Meros autou éstin éntos autaes kraseûs. Meros autou histâesin metazu humoun. Lambanete auton. Katasi'pountoun auton. Katexete auton.* We can do this."

"Hobble*bon*," said Bundersquash.

"Right..."

Lady Ufferbub took a deep breath. "We have made a decision. Now we continue. We still have several days to prepare. If Gigglebrit says he can do it, I trust him. Let us hope the last of our poor fortune has burned away and that luck may accompany us along the remainder of this difficult journey."

And so they went, for one day, then another. Gigglebrit recited the spell on repeat. The incantation ran through his mind like an endless song. He found a rhythm in the syllables. His muscles memorized the shape of the sounds. Gradually, he incorporated the gestures needed alongside the words, then studied the mental techniques required to complete the process. Mardulo helped with pronunciation. Bundersquash helped with memorization. Toddleposter cared for the animals, and Lady Ufferbub handled navigation.

In the lulls, Gigglebrit worked with Lobster on her pseudo-obedience routine. Bundersquash and Toddleposter had established a strong foundation of commands to work from. Now it was a matter of creativity. They made charts and diagrams and showed Lobster how to use them, they pieced together scripts and acts for her to follow, and they even designed a few costumes she could use before Mardulo stepped in and told them they were wasting their time, the routine was fine, and Gigglebrit needed to get back to work.

Morning dawned on the final day of hiking, clear and cool. The sky was cloudy but bright, and the morning's mist had not yet cleared when their walk began. Lady Ufferbub and Toddleposter handled Gigglebrit's first lesson of the day, filling his brain with odd bits of merchant-related trivia.

Several hours passed, and soon his mind was a sizable grab bag of assorted trade rules, import restrictions, and tax implications—none of which he fully understood, but he could parrot enough to hold his own. By lunch, he was back to the spell.

Humei'pente skeuae, sullégete enerheiás humoun kai'reite Obble-Dor-Hobblebon hoti enerheiâis. Meros autou éstin éntos autaes kraseûs. Meros autou histâesin metazu humoun. Lambanete auton. Katasi'pountoun auton. Katexete auton.

Then they arrived.

Chapter 13

Hostile Territory

Town Forbik peeked into view, a jagged edge on the horizon. Before they got too close, Mardulo pulled everyone into a nearby hedge.

"This is it," he said, giddy. "Gigglebrit, I hope you're ready."

Gigglebrit gulped. With the town there—actually there, in front of him—their timeline condensed into a sudden, terrifying, and ruthless reality. How could he be ready for something like this?

"It might be worth camping for an extra day or two," he suggested, "just to make sure I know all the words and everything..."

Suddenly, and with great theatrics, Toddleposter burst into view. "I am Obble Dor Hobblebosh!" he boomed. "I have come to buy your obedience spells! I will purchase them now, and I will buy that butterfly too...unless you can somehow cast spells inside my restricted zone and happen to have a trapping spell on hand...but what are the chances of that?!"

He waited expectantly, then in a whisper, added, "I'm setting the stage, Gigglebrit. Pretend to cast the spell. See if you can perform under pressure." And once again, with gusto, "I AM INVINCIBLE! Look at me in all my great lime glory! I am the grand master, king, lordship, maestro, magnificent Obble Dor Hobble—"

Gigglebrit stepped up. *"Humei'pente skeuae, sullégete enerheiás humoun"*—wave in Hobblebosh's direction—*"kai'reite Obble-Dor-Hobblebon hoti enerheiâis"*—wiggle the left foot—*"Meros autou éstin éntos autaes kraseûs. Meros autou histâesin metazu humoun."* Raise hands dramatically, with utmost confidence. "*Lambanete auton. Katasi'pountoun auton. Ka-texete auton!*"

Gigglebrit said the last few words with more volume than wisdom, perhaps, but Mardulo's celebratory cheer was even louder. His apology, shortly following, was meek—almost a whisper.

Once recovered, he gave Gigglebrit a pat on the back. "Every word, every gesture, correct and wonderfully pronounced! You're ready, lad. We don't need to wait, nor should we. We're too close. Camping here undisguised would be risky, and I hardly need to remind anyone how short we are on disguises. Besides, if we don't get in today, we'd have to wait another week for the market. I doubt they accept day-of arrivals."

Gigglebrit took a deep breath. Saying the words, even with Toddleposter's goofy interpretation of events, had helped. He'd done it. He could do it again. "All right," he said. "In that case, I suppose it's time for the glamours."

Everyone except Gigglebrit grabbed a bottle. Bundersquash drank his first. His face scrunched into a grimace; then his entire body—clothes and all—blurred and morphed, swirling from its normal, spherical, glasses-wearing self into a taller, heavyset, middle-aged man with a handlebar moustache and silver hair.

Lady Ufferbub went next and came out twenty years younger, with a red ponytail and purple eyes. Toddleposter transformed into an elderly woman, face hidden among wrinkles and laugh lines. Mardulo was suddenly a young man again, of an age with Gigglebrit—but where Gigglebrit was lanky and slender, Mardulo had bulk and muscle.

Gigglebrit rolled his eyes. This new set of companions seemed even stranger than the last.

"How am I going to explain the fact that I'm traveling with an old woman, a middle-aged man, and you two?" He waved at Mardulo and Lady Ufferbub.

"Easy," Bundersquash said in his new voice. "I'm old enough to be a father to you three"—he waved at Gigglebrit, Mardulo, and Lady Ufferbub—"and Toddleposter is certainly old enough to be my mother."

"You've got that right, young'un!" Toddleposter waved a finger. "Now let's get a move on. If we stand here all day, my feet'll give out underneath me."

"But what are your names?" Gigglebrit asked desperately.

"I prepared a little something for that," said Bundersquash. He handed around several slips of paper. Each had a name on it. "They're willing volunteers, residents of the archipelago. The Consortium has a surprisingly extensive collection. Fortunately, the papers were locked away when Hobblebosh's raid happened, and Madame Martoonisplau has the only key. Since each one belongs to a real person, they should pass any Roster checks."

Mardulo looked at his and grinned. "I'm Dulin! Dulin Erstwin Numtukket the, er...the Beefy!"

"And you can call me Bunker Ogfoller Numtukket the Hearty," said Bundersquash.

"Tereema Tagle Numtukket the Vicious!" said Toddleposter.

"And I'm Lelia Redmar Numtukket the Learned," said Lady Ufferbub. "*Lady* Lelia Redmar Numtukket the Learned."

"Dulin, Bunker, Tereema, and Lady Lelia," Gigglebrit repeated. More to memorize.

He looked at his own name. "Giaborg Yergmich Numtukket..." It didn't have an epithet; apparently the Roster didn't track those. He made up his own: "...the Wealthy."

"How fitting," said Bundersquash happily.

"Come on then," clamored Toddleposter, now Tereema. "This glamour's done a number on my hips. I'll need to ride on the wagon soon enough!" He scanned the surroundings for a walking stick.

"All right, all right." Gigglebrit raised his hands in appeasement.

"Stop holding your hands up. You look daft." Toddleposter whacked Gigglebrit's wrist with a fallen branch. "This family didn't spend its fortune putting you through merchant training just to see you dawdle about all day."

"You shouldn't be so hard on the lad," said Bunker, Gigglebrit's new father, formerly Bundersquash. "He's only learning."

"He had better not be," said Gigglebrit's new sister, Lady Lelia. "Only the best would be allowed to sell goods to Obble Dor Hobblebosh."

"I'm perfectly capable," said Gigglebrit indignantly, "and if anyone asks, I'm training you two." He pointed at Lady Lelia and Dulin. "And I'm bringing my dad and grandma along because..."

"We're here to support you," Bunker stepped in, "as a family."

"Right," said Gigglebrit, his throat suddenly tight. "A family...um. Give me just a minute. I should get changed before we arrive. I brought special clothes for the occasion."

He grabbed his travel bag and rushed over to the opposite side of the hedge, out of sight. He shut away any thoughts of his real mother and father, chastising himself for getting emotional over people who didn't even exist, then dug through his bag for the suit. It felt like years since he'd bought it in City Boratorus. It was a wonder to find it all in one piece.

Once dressed and recomposed, he returned to the others—to his new, fake family—and together, they emerged from the forest. The animals followed, as had become their custom, and so, with Lampellion at his side, Lobster on his shoulder, and his friends all around him, Gigglebrit finished his march to Town Forbik.

Humei'pente skeuae, sullégete enerheiás humoun kai'reite Obble-Dor-Hobblebon hoti enerheiáis. Meros autou éstin éntos autaes kraseús. Meros autou histâesin metazu humoun. Lambanete auton. Katasi'pountoun auton. Katexete auton.

The town walls were tall and foreboding. Pillars of solid iron stuck up from the browning grass, joined together with uneven beams of wood and sheets of dark metal. The gate was a wide double door—one a pale green, the other aggressively yellow.

A guard sat at the entrance. He was an uncommonly large man, maybe seven or eight feet tall with muscles to match and the general appearance of someone who could lift a few buildings if the right kind of protein shake lay trapped underneath. He had a rectangle for a face and fists the size of Gigglebrit's head.

But for all of that, he sat scrunched behind a three-foot tall podium on a positively miniature stool. The seriousness in his eyes betrayed a deeper sense of confusion, and his ill-fitting suit did him no favors. He had a monocle, which he fastened to his eye as Gigglebrit approached.

"G'day, young sir and company," he said. His voice carried an air of forced sophistication. "My name is Oriboriloritori Runcus Dundillion the Catcher." He pointed to a very long name tag on his chest pocket. "What can I do for you on a day as fine as this one?"

The genial, if unexpected, attitude put Gigglebrit at ease. "I'm here with my family to sell goods at the market."

"Is that so? A merchant, hmm? Are you familiar with our market process here in Town Forbik? We're of a more *sophisticated* culture than some of the other places in which you may have sold your wares."

"I could do with a refresher," said Gigglebrit, not really knowing what to expect.

"All merchants who sell goods in our town go through screening. We'll do that here in a minute. Merchants of the most excellent quality may be allowed in. Tomorrow, before the market opens, you will be required to present your goods to our Illustrious Majesty, Grand Lord Hobblebosh the King—so he can get a first pick at things, if you understand me. You will sell to him whatever he asks for, and you will be paid handsomely in return. Do not refuse. Understand?"

"I understand," said Gigglebrit. He turned to see if the others had anything to say, but they kept their distance.

"So, what do you hope to sell in this wonderful market of ours?" asked Oriboriloritori. "I warn you, the bar is high. We've a good number of merchants already."

"I sell spells and ingredients." Gigglebrit refocused and channeled his inner salesman, thinking mostly of Leepog. "See these animals behind me? They're well trained, but that took time. Years of work. Now, imagine you could do it in a day. Imagine you could have an army of lions at your disposal *this afternoon*, and all you needed was...well, lions, and a few quick minutes to cast a spell. That's what I'm here to sell to you—or to sell to Hobblebosh, I should say. My spells are more reliable than traditional training sessions, and they'll do the work in seconds. I've even brought some starter animals if the king wishes to begin his collection immediately. As you can see, they're quite impressive. But these spells will work on any animal he chooses, not just the ones I've brought today. You want a tap-dancing unicorn? You've got it. A gang of leopards to scout ahead as you conquer new lands? Yours. A pit of snakes to trap your enemies? Done. You could even saddle a dragon and fly into battle on its back, a spectacle as yet unseen by history. And it could all be yours—Hobblebosh's—with these spells."

The gatekeeper looked Gigglebrit up and down. "You've not heard of Yorbus Rungo Tottorbee the Dragon Rider?"

Gigglebrit made a face. "Did I say one dragon? I meant twenty. Fifty! As many dragons as you can find, you can ride. All you need is my easy-to-use, all-in-one set of long-term obedience charms."

"Sounds useful," said the gatekeeper. "A bit, shall we say, too useful, perhaps?" He raised an eyebrow, then suddenly called out. "Ismek! C'mere, will you?"

"Ismek?" Gigglebrit stepped back, forgetting his persona for a moment. Before the gatekeeper could explain, a gray-skinned man walked out from behind the town walls. He wore the garb of a wizard. His cloak was thick and green, draped over all-yellow clothing. His hat and gloves were yellow also, though the gloves must have been for show, here in the restricted zone.

Gigglebrit's fake family advanced in unison at the unexpected turn of events. It was almost comforting to have them at his side, until Toddleposter—that is, Tereema—hollered, "Come on, you lot. I haven't got all day! These bones don't hold themselves up, you know!"

Ismek ignored the shouts. Instead, he eyed the animals, then turned to the gatekeeper. "What's going on here?"

"This feller says he's got some obedience charms that work on dragons."

"Or any animal, to be exact," Gigglebrit interjected. "Anything you need."

Ismek snorted. "Turn him away. He's lying."

"I am not!" Gigglebrit pointed at Lobster, who was still on his shoulder. "Look, I have proof. This butterfly—she's been enchanted with these very spells."

Bundersquash—Bunker—squeaked.

"Is that so?" said Ismek, unbelieving.

"It is. Here. Lobster, up."

She took to the air.

"Now spin three times and do a backflip."

The butterfly did as she was told.

Ismek shrugged. "So, she can do a few tricks. My toad is just as good. Now leave, before—"

"But we're only getting started!" Gigglebrit cut in. Before Ismek could respond, he launched into the rest of the demonstration. "Lobster, land on Oriboriloritori's left ear. Now land on Bunker's. Do a dance. Switch ears. Dance some more. Flip. Flip. Triple-twist. Take off. Play dead. Get up again. Bring me seven blades of grass. Now fetch some willow bark from our supplies. Good girl. Now act out the second scene of the third act of *Udger's Nettled Redemption: A Sea-Witch's Tale* and pretend the bark is Lorfik the Octopus. Use one blade of grass as a sword. Place the others to the side."

Slowly, like paint in the rain, the smug look on Ismek's face melted away—each of Lobster's tricks, another drop on the canvas.

When Lobster finally finished her wordless drama, Gigglebrit resumed the commands. "Clean up the ingredients. Put that bark back where you found it. Fly around Ismek's head a few times. Fly up. Fly down. Be a distraction. Fly up high...higher...now come back and point to the nearest body of water. Now fly up again and look over the wall. How many guards did you see on the other side?" Gigglebrit held up a sheet of paper with some numbers on it. Lobster pointed. "Fifteen guards? Not bad. Now turn around and—"

Ismek held up his hand. "Enough!"

Gigglebrit stopped at once. Lobster stopped more slowly, bowing, but with an edge to suggest there should have been more applause.

"She's very well trained, that much is clear, but how do we know it was your enchantments that did it?"

Now it was Gigglebrit's turn to snort in disbelief. He did it rather well, he thought.

"Ismek, friend, buddy, pal," he said. "Do you really think we could have taught her—a butterfly—all that with nothing but *training*? Have you even *heard* of butterfly training? I would have expected better from a wizard like yourself. Typically, they're—" He was going to say *smarter* but caught himself. It wouldn't do to offend these people. "Typically, they're a bit more willing to believe a fellow wizard." He displayed his own gloved hands. "Since I can no longer use my magic in this part of the world, I sell things, but I hear Hobblebosh can still use his, and I thought he might be interested."

Ismek took a moment to consider. The silence gnawed at Gigglebrit's nerves, so he kept talking.

"Naturally, I'd love to demonstrate my spells on one of the other animals here—none of them have been enchanted yet, but as you know"—again, he waved his hands—"that's not really an option. So, I've got Lobster. I enchanted her before this restricted zone was put in place, and that's that. Take it or leave it. But I strongly suggest you take it. I think Hobble-bosh—King Hobblebosh the Illustrious, that is—would be very interested in what I have to offer. If not, I could always move south…"

Ismek frowned, then reached a decision. "Butterfly," he said. "Do you have a cage?"

Lobster pointed two legs toward her golden-barred enclosure.

"Good. Get in. I will take you to Our Masterful King Hobblebosh the Magnificent, and he can decide for himself if he is interested. Merchant, you may enter town, but we will only summon you if the king desires it. Then you will get your chance to sell to him, and you can vend some of your less magically oriented wares at the regular market." He waved indiscriminately at the wagon of supplies. "I hear willow bark is good for muscle pain."

Lobster got in her cage and shut the door. Ismek went to grab her, but Bundersquash stepped between them.

"Sorry," said Bundersquash as Bunker. "I really think she should stay with me—er, Giaborg…the family."

"Not an option."

"Yes, it is an option."

Gigglebrit approached, stomach turning. Bundersquash looked ready to murder someone. "You can't take her because…because she…might need…feeding."

"Then give us some of her food," said Ismek. "Though she's not much use if she can't go one day without supper."

"Ah," said Lady Ufferbub—Lelia—quickly. "Of course, Lobster could go a day without food. We are simply worried she might get nervous—butterflies in the tummy, if you will. We really should be there when she meets the king. Besides, we know what tricks she does best. We know how to highlight her talents."

"You said she follows orders." Ismek narrowed his eyes. "Our king knows how to give orders. I'm starting to think—"

"I said she follows *my* orders," Gigglebrit interrupted. "That's how the enchantment works. It makes the creature obedient to *one* person—the person who cast the spell. In Lobster's case, that's me."

"So, order her to do whatever Hobblebosh says!" Ismek's voice bristled with impatience. "Besides, she went into the cage easily enough, and I gave that command. Now step aside, all of you."

Gigglebrit didn't know what to do. "I'm not comfortable being parted from her in this fashion. How do I know you won't just steal her?"

The wizard raised an eyebrow.

Oriboriloritori looked genuinely aghast. "You question the integrity of our Grand Master Lordship, the One True Ruler, King Hobblebosh the Triumphant, the Magnificent, the Juicy?"

"I only—" Gigglebrit started, but Ismek cut him off, his voice a sinister calm.

"You dare to speak with such brazen disrespect whilst standing here, in his lands, under his very own protection?"

He looked to Oriboriloritori, who rose to his feet, consuming everyone in his shadow. Ismek stepped toward Lobster's cage. "Here is your choice, merchant. Surrender the butterfly and we will let you into our town peace-fully. We will even give you a chance to sell in our market. Or resist, and we will take the butterfly regardless and use your corpse as a wall decoration."

Gigglebrit gulped.

"Alternatively, we could simply kill the lot of you, butterfly includ-ed...and that hippalectryon, and the kangaroo, and the rhino-bird-thing, and whatever other animals you've brought." With a quick flick of the wrist, he summoned over a dozen archers to the wall—fifteen, to be exact. They all aimed down at Gigglebrit and his entourage. "It would be easy, and we have no shortage of merchants. You understand, I'm sure."

Gigglebrit threw up his hands. "All right. Fine. Whatever you say."

They'd lost. It was done. They could only hope Lobster would play her part well and survive the night.

"That's what I thought," said Ismek. "Oriboriloritori, finish their pro-cessing and let them through the gates. In return for their *continued* co-operation, I believe we can spare some temporary lodging. They will be responsible for providing their own meals, of course."

"Yes, sir," said Oriboriloritori.

Without another word, Ismek snatched Lobster's cage and disappeared into town.

Oriboriloritori rummaged under the podium and produced a small notebook. "Right then," he said. "Sorry about all that. I'll need your name, if it please you."

"Giaborg." Gigglebrit sulked.

"Your full name, if you don't mind."

"Giaborg Yergmich Numtukket the Wealthy."

"And the rest of you?"

Gigglebrit introduced them each in turn, one fake identity after another. Bundersquash had gone ghostly pale. He refused to take his eyes off the gates.

"And you said you're selling spells, ingredients, and...er, we'll just list that lot under livestock, shall we?"

"Sure."

"And you need lodging, of course. One moment..." He flipped through his notebook, then tore off a section and handed it to Gigglebrit. "Here we are! This is your address. You can move in immediately, but we expect you out by eleven in the morning on Wednesday—pain of death and all that. Is there anything else I can get for you?" He looked up, smiling.

"No," said Gigglebrit. "Can we go in now?"

"As you wish." Oriboriloritori signaled to the guards, who allowed the group through.

The doors shut behind them with a resounding thump. Then a heavy silence gripped the air. Everything about it felt wrong. This was a merchant town, one day before the market. It should've been bustling and lively. There should have been salesfolk crying wares to the passersby, encouraging people to stop at their shops. Kids should have been running rampant, drooling over street food or eyeing fancy toys. There should have been carts and carriages, beasts of burden, and the constant hubbub of civilization.

Instead, the way ahead lay barren. An empty field. Quiet. Unmoving. Nothing.

The walls had been built about a mile away from the main town. The land between was undecorated and unloved. Where grass grew, it grew short and brown. The roads were mostly dirt.

Gigglebrit marched forward with the others. When they'd moved out of earshot from the guards at the wall, Bundersquash stopped. "Now what? I suppose we should make for the temporary housing before we"—he gestured to his Bunker-shaped self—"undo."

"Aren't you worried about surveillance?" asked Gigglebrit. "Ismek seemed a bit too pleased when he told Oriboriloritori to find us a place."

"It's a possibility," said Mardulo. "We will inspect the location before we make ourselves comfortable, but it will raise suspicion if we don't show up at all. We may have to take our chances."

"We have at least an hour or two until things reset," said Lady Ufferbub. "Before shuttering ourselves inside, I suggest we embark upon a stroll around town. It would behoove us to get sense of this place."

"I'll have to pass on that," said Toddleposter. "I need rest. It's not fair, really. People usually work their way up to this sort of condition. I've never felt so creaky in my life."

"I'll go with Toddleposter," said Bundersquash dolefully. "I'm in no mood for a stroll."

"Well, all right," said Mardulo, "but Lady Ufferbub is right. Us young'uns had better poke around a bit. Besides, we need to buy some olive oil for the spell."

"What's the house's address?" asked Toddleposter.

Gigglebrit looked at the paper Oriboriloritori had given him. "255-A Peddler's Street. Any idea where that is?"

"Nope," said Toddleposter, "but I'm sure we'll manage. We can bring the animals, too, and check for surveillance while we're there..."

"Assuming we don't get arrested at the door," said Bundersquash.

"Try not to sound too excited." Toddleposter gave Bundersquash a friendly pat; then they shuffled off together, arm in arm. With a quick whistle from Bundersquash, the animals followed.

Mardulo turned to Lady Ufferbub and Gigglebrit. "You two explore. I'll see about that olive oil, and perhaps get some shawls to hide our faces at the market."

"Shouldn't we come with you?" asked Gigglebrit.

"I'm not sure how long it will take, and we don't have all day. We'll cover more ground this way. I'll get the supplies. You get a feel for the rest of town. And don't worry. I will keep the hooliganry to a minimum."

Mardulo smiled, then skipped away.

Gigglebrit looked at Lady Ufferbub. Together, they shrugged, picked a direction, and started walking, trying to stick to the bigger roads.

Slowly, more homes trickled into view. They were all made of the same dark wood. On the outskirts of town, their shutters were drawn and their doors were closed. Some had been boarded over. But as they neared the town center, things changed. The dirt roads turned to gravel, then to rough cobblestone. The houses grew larger and more extravagant. Very few had been built above two or three stories, but some of the more decorated ones were wide enough to fill an entire city block—though Town Forbik had not been arranged so deliberately.

Yet even here, the eerie quiet persisted. It wormed into the very wood of the homes, the mud on the ground, the dust in the air. The scenery soon became a sideline attraction to that pervading sense of unease. The few civilians they saw merely shuffled by, more interested in their own two feet than in the people around them.

The guards, on the other hand, marched through town like peacocks. Gigglebrit and Lady Ufferbub passed a new cluster every couple of minutes. They wore shining golden body armor—chest, legs, helmet, and all. Their cloaks were pale green. Their weapons, numerous and varied. They watched, and they listened, and the whole town knew it.

Then, for one brief, uplifting moment, the silence broke. A crowd's restless murmur rose in the distance—but when Gigglebrit followed it to an open courtyard, his stomach dropped, relief replaced with horror.

The crowd stood around a makeshift stage. Three people had been chained upon it, their heads and hands stuck through the wooden slats of pillories. Two of them looked of an age with Gigglebrit. One was smaller and had to stand on a bucket to reach the holes.

A man stood next to them wearing a silver button-down uniform with ribbons pinned to his chest. He was giving a speech.

"—be a lesson to all," he said. "Such overt disrespect is a clear violation of the laws set forth by our rightful king and master, the one, the only, the Venerated Grand Lord and Leader, King Hobblebosh the Juicy, Supreme Magistrate and Ruler. Such behavior will not be tolerated. You." He kicked one of the older children. "Pick the punishment for your rebellious cohort."

Three guards approached the stage, each holding a wooden box. Lady Ufferbub clenched her jaw.

"What's happening?" asked Gigglebrit.

"It is one of Hobblebosh's favorite punishments. Two containers hold rotten fruit. One holds the head of an axe. No one knows which—not even the guards—until the victim has chosen. If the fruit is selected, the prisoners are pelted with rotten produce. If it is the axe…"

Gigglebrit's eyes widened. "No. Hobblebosh wouldn't really…?"

Suddenly, the crowd cheered. Gigglebrit looked to the stage, where a guard held a rotten tomato above his head.

Lady Ufferbub breathed a sigh of relief. The uniformed man spoke again. "The punishment is decided. Let us shower them with the corpses of unsuccessful vegetation. May failure rain down upon them!"

Seemingly out of nowhere, the crowed drew forth piles of soggy ammunition—rotten cabbages, moldy pears, overripe peaches, bananas—and the barrage began.

"What did they do, anyway?" asked Gigglebrit, dodging a few errant projectiles.

A woman in the crowd turned to face him. "They was playin' with a lime they bought in the market last week. Little one dropped it. Can't let a thing like that touch the ground. Very bad look." She tossed the last of her potato salad, which fell short. "Rubbish. Never could get the angle right. Maybe next time…" She shuffled off.

"I think I've seen enough," said Gigglebrit, tugging at Lady Ufferbub. "We should get to the house."

They jostled into a narrow alley, where the ruckus of the crowd faded to a muffled blur against the otherwise oppressing silence.

The problem was, neither Gigglebrit nor Lady Ufferbub had any idea how to find Peddler's Street. They wandered aimlessly for quite some time, until Gigglebrit finally caved and decided to ask for directions—except even that was difficult.

They passed dozens of guards, but none looked willing to help. Most of the civilians simply ignored Gigglebrit's attempts at conversation, and the few that didn't were so startled by his approach that they ran the other way.

Just as they started to consider the logistics of spending the night outside, Gigglebrit spotted a woman not far away. She was near his height, dark haired and dark skinned, wearing a plain purple dress cinched at the waist with a piece of string. Her eyes were a bold green, and she'd painted her fingernails to match.

"Stay here," said Gigglebrit to Lady Ufferbub. "People may feel less threatened if only one of us walks up."

Lady Ufferbub nodded. "May luck travel with you."

He approached.

"Excuse me," he said, reaching out to tap her on the shoulder.

She turned before he made contact. "Yes?" she asked.

"Erm. Hi." Gigglebrit retracted his arm and scratched behind his ear. "Sorry to bother you. I was just wondering if you knew how to get to Peddler's Street?"

She looked at him with surprise. "Peddler's Street? You're a merchant?" Then she forced a smile and brushed her dress, looking more than a little flustered. "Yes, of course you are. Why shouldn't you be? I wasn't...um. Well, I just...I haven't seen you before, is all."

Gigglebrit took a step back. "I'm new here," he said, eyes narrow. "So no, you won't have seen me. But I'm planning to sell at the market tomorrow. Do you know where Peddler's Street is?"

"What are you selling?" she asked.

"Animals," said Gigglebrit cautiously. "And some obedience charms, if Hobblebosh wants them." He felt guilty even pretending to sell them, but he had to stick to his story. This woman could be a spy. "Really, I'm just looking for Peddler's Street. Do you—"

"Animals? You don't have hippalectryons, do you? Do your enchantments work on hippalectryons?"

Gigglebrit was getting annoyed. "Yes, we have one hippalectryon, but he's not for sale. Though my enchantments *would* work on hippalectryons, if Hobblebosh decided to use them that way. They're very good enchantments. Very effective. Don't doubt it."

"I see. I'm Thorippela Luggude Swedgett the Crisp." She extended a hand but didn't look entirely at ease. Her focus drifted toward Lady Ufferbub, who was standing in the background feigning interest in the sidewalk. "I'm a merchant as well."

"Nice to meet you, Thorippela." Gigglebrit stepped sideways, trying to reenter her line of sight. "Do you know where Peddler's Street is?"

"I do."

"Could you show me?"

"Just follow the road splatterback seven crossings, then turn narrowsplatter onto Street Winkle and go straight until you hit the Street of Standards. If you reach the big purple house, you've gone too far. From the Street of Standards, turn splatterback onto Avenue Pallish, then Peddler's Street will be almost immediately on your left."

Gigglebrit swallowed. "Uh. Great. Thank you."

If he forgot them, he could always ask someone else. Preferably someone with fewer questions of their own.

"Are your goods for sale now?" Thorippela asked.

"No," Gigglebrit replied, already walking away. "But you're more than welcome to stop by the market tomorrow...*after* King Hobblebosh has looked over everything, of course."

Without waiting for a response, he turned and ran.

When he reached Lady Ufferbub, he did his best to reiterate the directions, and together, they traversed an approximation of the path Thorippela had laid out for them. It took twenty minutes and a lot of backtracking, but they finally found it. By then, the sun had almost set.

"Let us hope there is no surveillance," said Lady Ufferbub. "Otherwise, we may struggle to find somewhere safe to"—a guard walked by—"to change. We don't have long now."

The road was lined with temporary housing—each building identical to the next: small, wooden, with a straw roof and a mini stable to one side, big enough for a hippalectryon and two carts. The house numbers didn't move in any particular order, but 255-A was mercifully close to the street's entrance. Lampellion and the other animals stood happily inside the stable.

Gigglebrit peeked through one of the windows. Mardulo, Toddleposter, and Bundersquash were all inside. Toddleposter had already untransfigured. Gigglebrit waved Lady Ufferbub in, then followed.

Toddleposter ran up and hugged them both. "You're here! Well done. We were getting worried."

"We struggled to find our way." Lady Ufferbub frowned at Gigglebrit. "Apparently, directions are not our strong suit."

"I'm glad you made it safely," said Toddleposter. "We had to ask a guard. Scary, but I gave him my best angry-old-lady impression, and he submitted fairly quickly."

Gigglebrit laughed. "Nicely done. Did you get the remaining supplies, Mardulo?"

He held up a bag, grinning. "Three cloaks, one oversized shawl, and some olive oil, ready to go. A bit on the pricey side, if you ask me, but what can you do?"

There was a quick popping sound followed by some shuffling; then Lady Ufferbub looked like Lady Ufferbub again.

"Oh, lovely!" said Mardulo. "Just me and Bundersquash to go. Shouldn't be long."

Gigglebrit drew the curtains, torn and frayed though they were. Some privacy was better than none.

The floor was packed mud, and a thick layer of dust coated the wooden walls. The air was dry and smelled of hay. There were three rooms—the main one, with a small wooden table and three rickety chairs; the bathroom, with a hole in the floor; and the bedroom, with a single bed of straw. A few burnt-down candles sat on the main room's table and on the floor in the bedroom, but Gigglebrit couldn't find any matches.

"At least it's warm," Gigglebrit muttered to himself, just as Mardulo turned back into Mardulo. "That's something."

Bundersquash untransfigured shortly thereafter, and they gathered around the table to take turns with the sandwich generator.

"I really think we have a chance tomorrow," said Mardulo.

"I agree!" Bundersquash nudged Gigglebrit. "Ready?"

"No. But I doubt I ever will be. I just have to do it anyway."

"You'll do well," said Toddleposter. "You did well on the bridge with Bundersquash. That took some quick thinking, and it shows you can handle yourself in a tricky spot. Besides, we've all heard you say the words a hundred times. You can do it."

Lady Ufferbub placed a hand on his shoulder. "Do you recall the punishment we witnessed today? It is good that you saw it. Remember, that is why we are here. Tomorrow, you will put an end to those atrocities."

Gigglebrit gave everyone an uneasy smile. "I know. But I think I'll step outside for a bit, if that's okay. I need some air."

The concerned looks came even quicker than he'd anticipated. "Don't worry," he said. "I'll be fine. I just want a bit of space." He grabbed his sandwich and left.

A guard stood alert at the end of the street, and another patrolled the road, so Gigglebrit took refuge in the stable. Lampellion was staring at the back wall. Gigglebrit sat on a wooden beam, facing him.

"Hey buddy," he told the hippalectryon.

Lampellion whinnied a greeting. Gigglebrit gave him a handful of oats from his sandwich.

"Are you going to tell me how important all this is?" he asked, feeling a bit silly, but not silly enough to stop. "I know the words. I've said them so many times I'm surprised I can remember anything else. Still...there's a lot riding on it."

Lampellion ruffled his feathers confidently.

Gigglebrit laughed. "You did your part, that's for sure. And you did it well. Must've been tough, pulling that wagon all the way here. Thank you."

Lampellion cocked his head. Gigglebrit gave him more oats.

The air had cooled with the setting of the sun, and a soft breeze wiggled through the slats of the stable wall, bringing the faint scent of dry grass to mingle with the wood and hay.

"I really hope Hobblebosh likes Lobster," Gigglebrit continued his monologue. "I don't know what will happen if he doesn't...to Lobster, to us, to everyone. You should've seen what they were doing to those people today. I mean, they were just throwing fruit, but it could've been an execution! I knew the lime was evil, but they were only—"

Lampellion cut him off with a boisterous neigh.

"Ahem. I mean. I completely understand why the punishment was necessary and fitting." Gigglebrit sighed. "All hail King Hobblebosh."

Lampellion's gaze was stoic, if perhaps a bit vacant.

"You know, it's strange. At the gate today, when Ismek came out and everyone stepped forward, it almost felt like I had a family again—just for a second—there by my side, ready to back me up. I wish…I don't know. It's not real, but sometimes I really miss Earth. My friends, my family. I—" His voice caught in his throat. He straightened and lifted his chin. "Well, never mind. Just a lot going on. That's all."

Lampellion whinnied softly, nuzzling Gigglebrit.

Gigglebrit couldn't help but smile. "Thanks," he said, then stroked Lampellion's head. "I have to stay focused. I have to get this right."

Humei'pente skeuae, sullégete enerheiás humoun kai'reite Obble-Dor-Hobblebon hoti enerheiâis…

Sometime later, he didn't know exactly when, he went back inside and tried to rest.

*Humei'pente skeuae, sullégete enerheiás humoun…Humei'pente skeuae, sullégete enerheiás humoun…*Wiggle the left foot. Don't forget to wiggle the left foot…*Humei'pente skeuae, sullégete enerheiás humoun…*

Over and over and over again, until the words formed their very own scar against the back of his mind. He was ready. He knew the spell.

He could do it.

He had to do it.

Eventually, sleep came.

Interlude: Tree and the Forest

Tree spoke to King Hobblebosh a great deal that first day in Town Forbik. The king now spoke as the humans speak, but he had not forgotten how to listen as a lime.

Tree told him about discovering movement and the freedom that came with it, about meeting Dogwood the Wind-Dancer, and about the magnificent journey to the Great Splat. But they focused on their experience with the lumberjacks and losing a branch to the thugs on the Narrow Stride. The pain. The fear. The cruelty.

King Hobblebosh listened intently, then shared his own experience with movement, having experienced a similar change when Corregal Dorbus Forp transformed him into a human.

Then the king asked questions about Tree, their creation, how the wizards had summoned them, the mechanics of their movement. He asked about Tree's strength, their speed, their fitness for battle...

In the end, King Hobblebosh trusted Tree with information of the utmost secrecy—the forces of the lime had recently obtained a device that would allow them to expand south, beyond the Great Splat, without crossing the Narrow Stride. The king was eager to begin, but a forest of moving trees—strong, sturdy, stalwart—would be a tremendous asset in battle. It was worth a brief wait, if such a force could be obtained.

"But most trees cannot move as you can move," Hobblebosh told Tree. "They are stationary, from birth to death. Something about you is different. Perhaps it is a side effect of your creation, or perhaps you are simply exceptional, but give me a few samples of your bark, and I will find out. Then, I shall craft a spell to gift other trees the same freedom that you have grown to cherish so deeply."

Tree tensed at the thought of a knife on their bark but reminded themselves of Dogwood the Wind-Dancer. They were still stuck in the city. What if the humans decided to cut them down? What if people wanted a building in their place? Dogwood the Wind-Dancer would be helpless, unable to move. Perhaps with the king's aid, Tree could free them from that threat. Tree could endure a few moments of pain if it meant giving others their freedom.

So they agreed.

The king carved five thick strips from Tree's trunk. The samples were sterilized, pulverized, and analyzed, and in a matter of days, everything was ready. King Hobblebosh produced several glass vials, each filled with a viscous silver potion. One drop was enough to free any tree from its motionless bonds.

He gave the vials to Lugbrush Gar Katerkin the Traveler, a top general, and together, Tree and Lugbrush were sent to Northern Tillman's End, a massive forest not far from Town Forbik, where they were to free as many trees as they could, recruiting them to Hobblebosh's cause.

Tree had never been so excited. They'd heard about forests before, but this was their first time visiting one. They wished they could talk to Lugbrush about it, to chat and get to know one another, but Tree could not speak to him as they could speak to the king. Lugbrush was only human, after all, and did not know how to listen to the deeper layers of the world. Instead, King Hobblebosh had invented a rudimentary system involving a *yes* branch and a *no* branch. With that, Lugbrush could ask questions, and Tree could answer.

They arrived after a single day and night of travel. It was early dawn. A cool, calm mist lingered among the tops of the trees. And there were so, so many trees.

Tree could barely believe it. Not just the breathtaking sight—though that alone was awe inspiring—but the very essence of the atmosphere had transformed. As Tree neared, their senses floated into a web of awareness unlike anything they had ever felt. The entire forest was connected. Tree was only a guest here, but they could feel it: the complex intermingling of everything that lived around them—the trees, the moss, the fungi, the flowers, the bushes, the animals—all joined together, working in unison, if not always in harmony. Every plant and every creature gave something of themselves to that forest, and the forest gave something back. There was a completeness to it, a push and pull, a give and take. Made of many, filled with individual expressions, the forest breathed as one.

It was beautiful. More beautiful than the meadows, more beautiful than the Great Splat, more beautiful than any story Tree had ever heard. They wondered what it would be like to make a home here. Perhaps, when they had seen the world and its other marvels, they could consider settling down in such a place...

But first, there was work to do. Tree rushed forward, glee filling them root to leaf.

"Hello, friends, my name is Tree! Your forest is wonderful. What are your names?"

After a pause, there was only one response. "Tree...hello, Tree...I am Old Oak the Gracious."

Tree reached out their awareness to find the tree that had spoken—a tall, steadfast oak blanketed in dark-green moss, just within the forest's edge.

"Hello, Old Oak," said Tree. "It's nice to meet you."

"You moved here...by yourself," said Old Oak. "That is...unusual."

"It is," said Tree, "for now. But soon, you will all be able to move as I can move. You shall be free, for Lugbrush and I come with a gift! Through the noble magics of Our Great Lord and Master, King Hobblebosh the Juicy, we can free you from this stationary existence and bring you into a new life—a life where trees are respected, and we no longer need fear humankind."

Lugbrush sauntered to Tree's side.

"All right, you lot," said Lugbrush. "I'm not sure if you can hear me or how this works, but here's the deal. Our virtuous king has created this magical potion." He held up the vial. "It'll allow you to move. All that are willing to pledge their obedience to King Hobblebosh and join the ranks of his army are welcome to partake. We've got enough here for a hundred fifty, maybe two hundred trees. We'll go through one by one. Tree, if they swear fealty, give me a yes. If not, give me a no and move on to the next one. Might be a long day. We can start here and move down the edge. Got it?"

Tree examined Lugbrush. *No*, they signaled.

Lugbrush paused. "Why not?"

Tree had no way to answer that.

Eventually, Lugbrush asked, "Are you confused?"

Yes.

Lugbrush rolled his eyes. "Please signal to me when you fail to understand. We will go to each tree...one by one...until we run out of this potion...and for each tree...you will ask them to swear an oath—"

No.

"Do you know what an oath is?"

Yes.

"Then what's the problem? They swear an oath of loyalty to King Hobblebosh—"

No.

"No what? You know what loyalty is?"

Yes.

"Obedience?"

Yes.

"So...?"

Tree bristled. This system was too limited. What was the point of offering trees freedom, if they were forced to swear it away in the same moment? They knew the goal was to recruit more forces for the king, but they had assumed *any* who wanted the potion would receive it, regardless of their willingness to fight.

But no combination of *Yes* or *No* would ever express such concerns.

For now, Tree turned their attention back to the forest. "I am sorry. I was not aware of this requirement. But King Hobblebosh fights to prevent the further suffering of our kind. It is a good cause. Those who wish to join us now may do so. Afterward, I shall speak with the king and, with his blessing, return to free you all, even those who do not wish to fight."

A subtle murmur of activity rushed through the forest like wind. Tree could feel the message pulsing through the air. *Hobblebosh. Movement. Magic. Freedom. Service. Loyalty. Obedience...*

Old Oak was the first to speak openly. "Tree," they said, "we know of Hobblebosh and the work he does. There is some dissent over the morality of his actions. He is swift to judge, and we hear troubling news from Forest Plawg. But I have seen trees felled at the hands of humans—that, I cannot deny. I was tagged for one such fate myself, but a storm swept through and cleared a separate patch of the forest. Had the weather been different, I would not stand here today...if Hobblebosh seeks to end such torments, that seems a worthy goal. And if, in the process, I can learn to move as you can move, that is all the more reason to join. It looks...*fun.*"

Tree would have jumped for joy if they'd known how. "You will not regret this, Old Oak the Gracious. I promise you."

They signaled *Yes* to Lugbrush, who tipped the vial and let a single drop fall onto Old Oak's gnarled trunk.

A wave of energy rushed through the soil at Old Oak's roots. Tree could feel the forest's surprise as the potion did its work...then Old Oak lifted a branch, shook their leaves, and stretched their roots with delight. At last, they moved to Tree's side.

"This is unlike anything I have ever felt," said Old Oak. "It is magical."

They were the first of many.

Chapter 14

The Big Day

The next day followed, as next days are wont to do. This one came far too quickly. What little confidence Gigglebrit had possessed the previous day fled with the rising sun, leaving nothing but a turning stomach and an unceasing trickle of doubt. Today was the day he would save the world, and he had never felt so unprepared.

Lying in the house's only bed, he steeled himself. He didn't feel ready, but how could anyone feel ready for something like this? It was all a part of the Hero's burden. Courage to face the impossible. Willingness to try, even with the smallest of chances. He would succeed because he had to succeed.

He rose to his feet and set his jaw. Prepared or not, he would do it.

But first, breakfast. Sick though he was of sandwiches, he would need his strength. Meanwhile, Lady Ufferbub, Toddleposter, Mardulo, and Bundersquash busied about the house like bees in a hive, making all sorts of last-minute preparations.

In the midst of the hubbub, a messenger knocked on their door. Everyone froze.

"You had better answer it, Giaborg," Mardulo whispered carefully. "They might recognize the rest of us."

Slowly, Gigglebrit obeyed while the others crammed themselves into the bathroom.

It was one of Hobblebosh's soldiers. He wore golden armor and a green cloak, and he carried a helmet under his arm. "Greetings!" he said. "My name is Rathok Mod Dumpkin the Pondered. Is this the house of Giaborg Yergmich Numtukket the Wealthy?"

"Yup," said Gigglebrit. He tried to sound natural, though he was secretly grateful for the refresher about his full name. "Nice to meet you, Rathok."

"I have a message for Giaborg Yergmich Numtukket the Wealthy."

Gigglebrit waved. "That's me."

The guard unraveled a scroll and read, "Congratulations!" then looked to Gigglebrit's face for some kind of response. Gigglebrit forced a smile. "You have impressed the Illustrious King Hobblebosh with your offering. He kindly requests your presence at his palace this morning, before the market opens, so that he might personally purchase some of your merchandise. Your arrival has been scheduled for eight thirty ante meridiem on this day, the nineteenth of July, Age of the Lime Everlasting. Please arrive with *all* of the goods you intend to sell and sell none before you see him. Yours Superiorly, the Illustrious King and Marvelous Lord of Masters, Obble Dor Hobblebosh the Juicy." He handed the note to Gigglebrit.

"Thank you very much," said Gigglebrit, hiding the knot of fear that had just formed in his stomach. "Just to confirm," he added casually, "you said his *palace*?"

"Yes. That is the usual location for these premarket inspec—ahem, opportunities."

"Of course. And where is that, exactly?"

The guard looked at him curiously. "Widesplatter of the town center. You can't miss it."

"Thank you. We will—" Gigglebrit bit his tongue. "*I* will be there soon."

"You will be there by eight thirty ante meridiem if you wish to keep that head of yours. Remember what they say, Giaborg Yergmich Numtukket the Wealthy: those who are late, are late."

"I understand."

"To be clear," the guard added seriously, "if you're late, he'll chop your head off."

"Yes, I got it. Thanks. I'll be there on time. Good day."

The messenger beamed a smile. "Good day to you as well, kind sir!" Then he turned on his heel and marched away.

Gigglebrit waited until the footsteps had faded, then passed on the news.

"I knew Lobster could do it!" said Mardulo. "But about this palace..." His face darkened, and Gigglebrit knew he'd seen the issue. The others looked similarly concerned.

"You four will have to stay behind," said Gigglebrit. "In a market, that would have been one thing, but the palace? It won't work."

"Unacceptable." Mardulo crossed his arms. "We won't abandon you. That is out of the question."

"Well, you can't just lurk about with shawls over your heads, can you?" Gigglebrit's composure cracked. "It's a palace! Think of all the guards and patrols and fortifications!"

Lady Ufferbub looked uncertainly at Toddleposter, who looked at Bundersquash, who looked at Mardulo.

"I suppose we could hide in the cart," he offered weakly.

Gigglebrit sat down and put his head in his hands. His mind raced through possibilities. They had a few hours before 8:30. There had to be something they could do. Hiding in the cart was a stupid idea. Even if it was big enough for all four of them, and even if they didn't get searched, he doubted they'd actually let a cart inside the palace. He had to think of something else. He wasn't about to let a simple change in location ruin everything.

What did he have to work with? They were out of glamours, but they had a few spare ingredients lying around...and they had Lampellion...and the other animals...

He thumped his forehead on the table. None of it would do any good. They'd be lucky to reach the palace gates, let alone get inside. There were so many guards, alert and waiting for any sign of trouble, and that was just around town. He could only imagine how many more there would be in the palace...

Then it hit him.

Gigglebrit snapped his head back up. "I have an idea. It's a stretch, but it might work...the guard that just delivered the message. He was wearing armor. They're all wearing armor. And their armor has helmets—those big, mask-like ones that hide your whole face."

Bundersquash's eyes widened.

"Brilliant!" said Mardulo.

Lady Ufferbub hesitated. "I suppose it is better than nothing..."

Not five minutes later, they were off. Mardulo, Bundersquash, and Toddleposter were wearing the heavy brown cloaks Mardulo had bought the day before. Lady Ufferbub was wearing the shawl. Gigglebrit thought they probably looked more conspicuous now than if they'd just walked around normally, but they insisted, and he was forced to concede. He knew far less about this world than they did.

It started with a lanky guard a few streets away, who was tucked into an alcove between three buildings doing his own small part to support the resistance—that is, taking a nap.

With the branch Toddleposter had used as Tereema's walking stick the day before, Mardulo leaped into action. One solid whack later, he had a new suit of armor, and the guard was considerably less burdened—what with no heavy metals covering his body and a significant lack of consciousness to worry about.

Mardulo clambered into the new outfit, then threw his former cloak over the unconscious guard and muttered a quick word of thanks and apology.

"He'll have quite the bruise when he wakes up," he said. "Nothing a little pellian extract won't fix, but still...I doubt he chose this profession willingly."

It took some time to find the next set of candidates. There were two of them, standing together on Street Waxwater: one approximately Bundersquash-size, the other a good fit for Lady Ufferbub.

Gigglebrit pulled everyone aside and whispered, "See that shadowy place?" He pointed to an alleyway nearby. "You four wait there. I'll lure the guards in one at a time. Then you, er, *get* them as they come."

It felt strange, planning what essentially amounted to a double mugging, but Gigglebrit tried to comfort himself in the knowledge that this was all for the Greater Good. Besides, he didn't have much time to dwell on it; they were up against a very literal deadline.

The others ran into the alleyway, fading to whispers.

Meanwhile, Gigglebrit dashed away, then sprinted back, yelling dramatically. "Help! Help! How *dare* he?! Who does he think he is? Utterly abhorrent! How could this happen?!"

He flapped and flailed his way toward the guards, having an unreasonable amount of fun. He tried to suppress a smile. The guards turned to face him, awestruck by the sheer volume of the event.

"Did you see him?!" Gigglebrit shouted at their masked faces. "Did you see him come this way? A *slanderer*, he was! A swindling, no-good, foul-mouthed little *traitor*! He said—and I know you won't believe this, but I really do mean it—he said, 'Big old dumb Obble Dor Hobblebosh is nothing but a lumbering, useless oaf, and um...and he's stupid,' and then he *stomped*—yes, you heard me—*stomped* on a lime. Squish! Splat! Splot! Goop everywhere! All over the ground. It was murder! Terrible, fruity murder! Oh, the *horror*!" He feigned a swoon.

The guards tensed with every word. "Where is this villain?!" bellowed the Bundersquash-shaped person. "What did he look like? What was his name?!"

"Oh, um…Snobblyfrots…I think. Snobblyfrots Dot Lumperwag…the Red."

"And his appearance?"

Gigglebrit froze for a moment. "He was orange, sir. With purple hair and an eyepatch. And short, too. Definitely probably male, but it's hard to say. He had stringy hair—sort of shoulder, waist-ish length. You know the type. Very long legs. Red eyes—mismatched, one light, one dark…but that's not important. What matters is, he ran into that alleyway over there!" Gigglebrit pointed.

Both of the guards leaped into action, but Gigglebrit grabbed the taller of the two. "Actually, you wait here," he said. "That way, if he escapes, you'll be ready."

Gigglebrit didn't know whether Lady Ufferbub, Toddleposter, Mardulo, and Bundersquash would be able to take on two fully armed guards at once. They had the numbers, but they were…well, *them.*

The tall guard thought about what Gigglebrit had said just long enough for the other to disappear into the alleyway. There was a loud clatter, then silence.

Gigglebrit waited a few heartbeats. "On second thought, you had better go help."

Suddenly, the other guard looked much less eager to take action. "Um. Yes. I suppose you're right. Slander and all that. A deadly offense, surely. He *stomped* on a lime, you said? You're sure he *stomped*?"

"You could make an argument for brutalized," said Gigglebrit matter-of-factly, "or perhaps mutilated. It's all semantics, really."

"I see. Yes. Well. It would seem I had better head in that direction, then. Over there…"

Gigglebrit gave him a small push. "Go on."

Both the guard and Gigglebrit entered the alleyway.

Sometime later, Gigglebrit and Toddleposter walked out, followed by three people in guards' uniforms. One of those guards had a giant pair of glasses straddled around the exterior of his helmet.

They found a suit for Toddleposter back nearer Peddler's Street. It was a tad too big, but with only an hour to go, their schedule was tight enough to make it fit.

All set, they returned to the house. Gigglebrit's stomach bubbled with nervous excitement as they corralled the animals and loaded Lampellion's cart with ingredients. They kept the trapping-spell supplies in a separate box buried beneath some of the less-important wares.

The wizards had prepared everything the night before. It was now one jumbled mixture inside a lidded bowl, almost ready to go. The only thing missing was essence of Hobblebosh. Once Gigglebrit had obtained that, he would be able to cast the spell.

"Do not forget your amulets, everyone." Lady Ufferbub slipped her odd-looking pocket watch into the chest pocket of the shirt underneath her armor. "Remember, it will defend against one spell only—then the protection is gone."

Bundersquash grabbed his cobalt pin and fixed it to his undershirt. Toddleposter's belt and Mardulo's bracelet fit nicely beneath their armor as well. Gigglebrit quickly confirmed that his peacock-feather amulet was still pinned to his merchant suit. He'd barely taken it off since the start of their journey. The warmth of its protection had become a near-constant comfort during the trip.

"Right then," said Bundersquash. "Ready?"

Toddleposter heaved the final box into place, covering the trapping-spell ingredients completely. "Ready."

They set off. By now, Gigglebrit had grown accustomed to the uneasy silence of Town Forbik's streets, and he tried not to draw too much attention. It proved difficult with a hippalectryon, a flapping rhinoceros, a kangaroo, a pygmy minotaur, a whole gaggle of birds, a tessle, and four guards at his side.

But he tried.

The palace came into view while they were still several streets away. It was big, though not as tall as Gigglebrit might have imagined. It looked more like something Hobblebosh had occupied, rather than built. It was made in the same embellished wooden style as all the other buildings around, but this was by far the largest, and the lime had definitely redecorated. Green and yellow banners hung from every available surface.

At the palace gates, another guard stopped them.

"Name, please?" she asked.

"Giaborg Yergmich Numtukket the Wealthy."

The guard checked a list. "It says here you had four familial associates?"

"They couldn't make it. My poor grandmother's taken ill. I think it's all this, um, weather."

"Very well." She examined the list again. "You're selling obedience charms for animals? Someone's drawn a picture of a butterfly, here..."

"Yes. The butterfly is mine."

"Not anymore, it isn't." Her tone came thick with warning.

Gigglebrit simply nodded, but Bundersquash clanked behind him in what appeared to be a jolt of anger. Mardulo tried to calm him with a gentle pat on the back, which was far less subtle than he probably intended, given that they were covered in metal.

It caught the guard's attention. "I can lead the merchant from here, comrades," she said. "You may return to your posts. Many thanks for escorting him."

"Uh. No. No. No." Mardulo pushed to the front of the conversation and deepened his voice. "We have been sent to escort this merchant all the way into the presentation area."

"I'm sure we can find someone here to do it," said the guard.

"It has to be us, ma'am. We're specially trained to deal with the kangaroo. Feisty boxer of a thing. Scarier than the rhino, if you'd believe it. I recommend keeping a healthy distance."

Lady Ufferbub cleared her throat. "We have orders directly from the king to keep watch on this merchant until he has finished his presentation. Apparently, he made a scene at the town gates and needs a closer eye than most. Would you ask us to disobey?"

The guard frowned. "I suppose not," she said. "Please, enter. There are posts for your hippalectryon near the door. Go through the main entrance, then head down the hall and take the tenth door on your right into the ballroom. Wait there. Enter the throne room only when called. If you need assistance carrying supplies, ask for one of our servants."

"Yes, ma'am," said Gigglebrit as they marched through the gates.

They hitched Lampellion near a few other hippalectryons outside, then divvied up the boxes among themselves. Gigglebrit took the bulk of it, the trapping-spell supplies and three stacked crates. The wizards and librarians each held a few boxes of their own. It was a lot to carry, but no one was about to call a servant. Once they had everything in hand, they pushed through the palace's great oak doors, the animals in tow behind them.

Somehow—probably magically how—the interior was not wood but gleaming white marble. It was a massive hall, wide and long, with alternating green and yellow banners evenly spaced down its length. Even the doormat was green, with text politely commanding that all guests wipe their feet. They were alone, and their steps echoed loudly as they walked.

"Psst...pssssst, Gigglebrit, hey...pssssst..."

Gigglebrit rolled his eyes. "Yes, Mardulo?" he whispered.

"Remember, start with the anchor objects. Five of them."

"I know."

"And enunciate."

"I remember."

"And wiggle the left foot."

"I know, Mardulo."

"And—"

Lady Ufferbub put down her boxes and rang Mardulo across the ear—mostly a symbolic gesture, what with the helmets, but *rang* was certainly apt.

"Do you intend to reveal the entire plan while you are at it, or just the most critical components?"

Mardulo shrank into his armor. "I thought a reminder might be helpful."

"I'll be all right," said Gigglebrit, nodding to them both.

Humei'pente skeuae, sullégete enerheiás humoun...

When they finally reached the ballroom, it was open. Silence poured out like syrup. It was the uneasy kind of silence that could only materialize among a sizable crowd of people, all too nervous to speak. In this case, the crowd was composed entirely of waiting merchants, each wearing their own unique brand of anxiety. Gigglebrit and his entourage received a number of judgmental stares, but no one dared comment.

He took a seat along the back wall and focused on the task ahead. The magic words ran through his mind over and over and over again, every letter, every syllable, every action. He was going to get this right. He was going to be the Hero.

"Good timing, eh?" Mardulo nodded to a clock on the wall. "Eight twenty-nine. Right on the nose. Well, a little to the left of the nose, but you understand. And look, it just—"

"Giaborg Yergmich Numtukket the Wealthy!" A guard opened the door to the throne room.

Gigglebrit rose, steadied himself, and approached the door. As he neared, a woman walked out, followed by a number of hippalectryons. Gigglebrit had to look twice.

"Thorippela?" he said.

She was crying. "Oh, go away, Gigglebrit, and take your fancy animals with you!" She waved angrily at the minor zoo accompanying him.

Gigglebrit looked toward the others, as if they might have some kind of explanation. As it happened, the guard at the door did. "The Grand Lord Hobblebosh wasn't interested in her hippalectryons. She got snippy. Now she's banned for life. If you ask me, she's got nothing but luck to thank for having escaped in one piece."

Gigglebrit gulped. "I guess so..."

He turned to say something to, or at least glance sympathetically at, Thorippela, only to find that she had stopped crying. Instead, she smiled, winked, and walked out.

Before Gigglebrit had time to process that, the guard grabbed him by the shoulders and pressed him toward the entrance. "He's not a patient lime, you know."

"Right," said Gigglebrit. "Of course."

He entered a small hall with a single door at the other end. Bundersquash, Lady Ufferbub, and Toddleposter had already passed through. Mardulo held the opposite door open.

The guard with Gigglebrit rushed ahead and whispered something to Mardulo, who whispered something back. Gigglebrit couldn't hear the exchange, but it looked heated, and after a forceful nudge from the real guard—and a clear risk of exposing his cover—Mardulo reluctantly moved ahead, letting the door shut behind him. The guard took a few steps back, paused for a moment...

Then the door opened automatically.

In a panic, Gigglebrit jogged forward, trying to slip through before it could close again, but he was too late. The door shut, and Gigglebrit stood before it, alone, wondering what to do. He couldn't afford to wait long.

As quietly as he could, he adjusted his grip on his boxes, freeing one hand to turn the handle. Then, with a quick breath and a roll of his shoulders, he shoved the door open with a firm—but subtle, he hoped—press from his foot, hoping no one would realize what had happened. He strolled through as casually as possible, quickly repositioning his hands, and entered the throne room.

The first thing he noticed was how meticulously *clean* it all was—pristine marble floors, pearly white, with a green carpet running down the center. The second thing he noticed was the throne, enormous and gilded. Then, finally, he noticed the person sitting on it.

Hobblebosh.

In that moment, the tyrant became more than just a concept in Gigglebrit's mind. He was real. He was tall, even sitting down. And he was foreboding. His face was stern. His skin was pale green (and, Gigglebrit had to squint to make sure, a little bumpy). His eyes and hair matched the hue of his skin, but his cloak was darker, almost shadow. His gaze drilled into Gigglebrit with piercing disapproval.

He was right *there*. He was within reach...but his presence, his confidence, made him seem invincible.

Lobster was on a pedestal at Hobblebosh's side. He'd put her in a new cage—still golden, but the bars were tighter, and the latch looked more secure. There were four guards behind her, with three more along the left side of the room and another three along the right. With a quick glance back, Gigglebrit counted four around the door. That made fourteen total, fifteen if you included Hobblebosh.

They were outnumbered three to one. But if Gigglebrit was fast enough, that wouldn't matter.

He steadied himself.

Deep breaths.

One foot in front of the other.

He forced himself to keep moving. Even the echo of his footsteps seemed stifled in the silence of that room. He tried to carry himself with the same confidence he saw in Hobblebosh. Meanwhile, the winged rhinoceros let out a squeak and froze in place. Gigglebrit paid it no mind.

Mardulo had drilled him on this. The first thing he had to do was choose five anchor objects—anything around the room, as long as they surrounded Hobblebosh. Lobster's pedestal could be one. The throne itself could be another. Perhaps a curtain on either side of the room, and then one of Gigglebrit's own boxes of ingredients, which he could place on the floor in front of the tyrant.

He made a mental note of each, then continued his advance, moving slowly toward the tyrant, until—

"Restrain him," said Hobblebosh calmly.

Gigglebrit's eyes widened.

Fortunately, the guards nearest Gigglebrit happened to be Mardulo, Bundersquash, Lady Ufferbub, and Toddleposter. After a moment's hesitation, they dropped their boxes and grabbed Gigglebrit's arms with convincing force. He didn't have to fake the wince of pain as he fell to his knees.

"Search the boxes," said Hobblebosh, almost bored.

Toddleposter and Lady Ufferbub let go of Gigglebrit and examined the supplies, conveniently passing over the trapping-spell ingredients.

Hobblebosh rose from his throne slowly and purposefully, leaving ample time for his full height to make the appropriately imposing impression. He must have been seven feet tall, at least.

"Giaborg. Yergmich. Numtukket. The Wealthy." His voice was calm but deep like the ocean, and it carried. It could have filled a room twice this size and still had some left over. Right now, its full weight pummeled down on Gigglebrit. "A purveyor of spells, come to my lands, where spells are expressly forbidden."

Gigglebrit blanched, though he tried to maintain his composure. Hobblebosh may be upset, but he still didn't know about the others. His gaze had passed over them like it did all his guards. They were nothing to him, white noise. They could still make this work.

"What did you hope to accomplish with this little mission of yours?" Hobblebosh continued. "Sending a magical butterfly into my castle? Hoping to glean information, perhaps? Expecting her to report back to you?" He shook his head and moved steadily toward Gigglebrit, each step its own little power move. "A futile plan. A waste of effort. She is mine now. Soon, you will be too. And your family, wherever they are." For the briefest moment, Hobblebosh's gaze flicked back to the door, then returned to Gigglebrit. "But it seems we have something more important to discuss, first..."

The tyrant closed the distance between them with one final step, then crouched down and laid a heavy hand on Gigglebrit's shoulder, staring straight into his eyes.

Gigglebrit scowled back—menacingly, he hoped.

"Yes," said Hobblebosh at last. "There is more. And I think this deserves a *personal touch*."

He stood abruptly, removed a bottle of powder from his pocket, then threw it. It smashed on the floor between them. The whole motion took less than a second; Gigglebrit barely had time to react.

From the scattered powder, a slimy red smoke rose and darkened. It slithered around Gigglebrit's head, suffocating him, worming into his eyes, up his nose, through his ears; and finally, as Gigglebrit gasped helplessly for air, it flooded his mouth and filled his mind. Pain seared his temples. His muscles tensed and twitched, fighting against the invasion. Somewhere, a very long way away, he thought he heard someone gasp, but the sound faded as the world disappeared, and there was only the cloud, the pain, and Hobblebosh.

They stood in a world of their own, shrouded in scarlet mist.

Hobblebosh's voice came from all directions at once, though he stood mere feet in front of Gigglebrit. "Who are you?" he demanded. "Giaborg Yergmich Numtukket the Wealthy, you say. A lie. That name is on the Roster. *Yours is not.* Or did you think I would not notice your pathetic display at my door?"

Gigglebrit flinched.

"So, I ask again. Who are you?" said Hobblebosh. "And where are your friends? I have not forgotten them. You came with four others, their names as fake as yours, I expect. Who are they? *Where* are they? Lying in wait for some ambush, perhaps? Show me!"

As the words crawled through Gigglebrit's mind, they pulled at his thoughts. Images started to form in the mist—faint wisps, echoes of himself, of Mardulo and Bundersquash, of Lady Ufferbub and Toddle-poster—not yet fully formed, but growing clearer. Gigglebrit struggled against it. His resistance met with an agonizing raking against his skull, but he fought, and the images stayed hidden.

Hobblebosh's voice pierced once more through Gigglebrit's mind, fiercer, forceful. "Giaborg Yergmich Numtukket the Wealthy. Tereema Tagle Numtukket the Vicious. Dulin Erstwin Numtukket the Beefy. Lelia Redmar Numtukket the Learned. Bunker Ogfoller Numtukket the Hearty. All lies! *Who are you really?*"

Gigglebrit wrestled against the compulsion. He fought to keep his own mind blank. He would not give in, he told himself. He was better than that. He was Gigglebrit Maistowne Nebraska the Fictional—*a Hero*. And he would not fail. He would not betray his friends.

Then, to his horror, Hobblebosh replied. "Oh, but you will, *Gigglebrit*. You will surrender them, and they will suffer, just as you will suffer."

"No!" Gigglebrit strained, but even as he struggled, he could feel Hobblebosh dragging the thoughts out of him, unbidden. The tyrant was carving them brutally from the inside of his mind. Gigglebrit screamed against the agony, tears swelling in his eyes. The images started to focus.

Then Gigglebrit changed course. If he couldn't clear his head, he could flood it. Desperately, he tried to think of something else, anything other than his friends.

Anything.

Hobblebosh! Gigglebrit shouted in his own head. *Evil! Bad! Tyrant! King! Crown! Sword! Lord! Ring! Magic! Fantasy!*

Gradually, the visions of his friends clouded over, smothered in Gigglebrit's own barrage of half-formed thoughts and images, glimpses of all the stories he'd read, of places he'd imagined—entire worlds swirling in and out of view. It was working. It was actually working...

But pain tore through his mind, seized his spine, clawed at his chest and limbs. He writhed in the crimson fog as Hobblebosh cut deeper, stealing the thoughts away.

"Be done with this nonsense!" Hobblebosh commanded, his voice solid with fury, utterly out of patience. "Show me who they are, *Gigglebrit*! Show me where they are."

Gigglebrit buckled, hands on his head, screaming and sobbing, trying to drown everything out. *Fantasy! Stories! Books! Fellowship! Friendship! Friends! Family! Loved ones! Earth! Planet Earth! Home! Home! Home!*

At once, Gigglebrit jolted upright. Images snapped into focus all around him. Cars, buses, city streets, country roads, fields, neighbors, his friends, his house—and front and center, his parents, looking down upon him, smiling sadly.

The physical pain of Hobblebosh's spell vanished as Gigglebrit succumbed to this sudden rush of longing, his thoughts fully consumed by the gaze of his parents ahead.

"What is this?" Hobblebosh demanded, but his voice wavered.

Gigglebrit was speechless. He could only stare...unbidden, all his memories of Earth, his former life, his home, came rushing through the clouds around him, a torrent of history and people and places—the planet, the countries, Nebraska, the hill at the side of Berrywood Lane, birthday parties, field trips, people—everything flooded in, drowning out the mist through which they flowed. Only his parents stood still, watching over him with the deepest compassion in their eyes.

But the spell fought back. The red mist rose once more, and this time, it came with tongues of fire—crimson and orange. They consumed everything in their path. His school crumbled in the heat. Flames tore through his yard and house. His friends and neighbors ran, screaming, but none escaped. The Earthly images burned away, leaving nothing but soot and smoke. His parents were the last to go. As the fire stole them, their expressions changed from understanding to disappointment. Then they fell to ash.

The fire died. The scarlet mist faded. The real world came back into focus. It looked as if no time had passed at all.

Lady Ufferbub and Toddleposter were still in the process of jumping back, startled by the shattering of the bottle. Gigglebrit remained on his knees, held by Mardulo and Bundersquash, shaking.

Hobblebosh stood frozen, his eyes locked on Gigglebrit. The tyrant had paled considerably, and confusion stole a moment on his face.

"What are you?" he said hollowly, backing away. But then he mastered himself, and his uncertainty turned to rage. "I demand that you tell me who you are—*what* you are—now!"

But Gigglebrit couldn't think. His mind was still racing with the images of loved ones, of the life and home he had lost. For just a moment, it had all been there, surrounding him once again...

Hobblebosh took two strides toward Gigglebrit and punched him hard across the face.

"Guards!" Hobblebosh yelled. "Kill him, then—"

But even before he could finish the order, the guard that was Bundersquash let forth a tremendous battle cry and lunged at Hobblebosh's head.

Mardulo, Lady Ufferbub, and Toddleposter took up the cue. Mardulo jumped in and set up the trapping-spell supplies. Lady Ufferbub and Toddleposter dove for the other guards, trying to hold them off. At the same time, Bundersquash wrenched a handful of hair from Hobblebosh's head and threw it into the ingredients.

"Now, Gigglebrit!" Mardulo shouted, even as Hobblebosh recovered from his shock and started to cast a spell of his own.

Gigglebrit, still shaken, tried to take everything in. Half his mind was still on Earth; the other half cried desperately for focus.

The spell.

His family was gone. Fiction. They didn't matter now.

The spell did.

He had to trap Hobblebosh.

Anchor objects. The first step was the anchor objects.

Shaking all over, Gigglebrit shot his gaze across the room. Curtain, other curtain, pedestal, throne, box. They would work. Bundersquash had added Hobblebosh's hair to the ingredients. That was everything he needed. He just had to make his nebula and speak the incantation.

...

What were the words again?

The room fell quiet. To his horror, Gigglebrit realized Hobblebosh had finished casting his spell. A shadowy ball of smoke curled where his lime-green nebula had been, then rushed straight toward Gigglebrit.

Lady Ufferbub jumped on top of it.

The smoke seized her body, the armor she was wearing turned to rust and flaked away, but the clothes underneath remained undamaged, as did Lady Ufferbub herself.

The amulet, Gigglebrit realized with relief.

But before it vanished, the smoke pulsed once more with shadow and threw Lady Ufferbub into the opposite wall.

There was no more time. The guards were closing in, despite Mardulo, Bundersquash, and Toddleposter's frantic efforts, and Hobblebosh looked ready to start another spell. Gigglebrit had to focus.

He threw off his gloves and made the auric nebula, hoping against all hope that the worlds would just come as he said them.

At the sight of Gigglebrit's nebula, real fear flashed through Hobblebosh's eyes, but Gigglebrit couldn't afford to pay attention. He had to cast the spell. He had to remember the incantation.

The first word. Just think of the first word. If he could remember that, the rest would come. It…it sounded like…Hummus? Humas? Human? No, Humei! Humei! Humei'pente!

Without so much as taking a breath, he opened his mouth and let the words fall out.

"HUMEI'PENTE SKEUAEN, SULLÉGETE ENERHEIÁS HU-MOUN KAI'REITE OBBLE-DOR-HOBBLEBOSH HOTI ENER-HEIÁS"—Wiggle the left foot!—"MEROS AUTOUN ÉSTIS ÉSTOS AUTAES KRASEÛS. MEROS AUTOUN HISTÂESIN METAZU HUMEI"—Raise hands!—"LAMBANETE AUTON. KATASI AU-TON. KATEXETE AUTON!"

Everything froze.

No...Gigglebrit realized, his heart sinking. No, no, no. That didn't sound right...

Everyone stared—at Gigglebrit, at the spell, at Hobblebosh. Even the tyrant had come to a stunned halt.

The ingredient bowl rose into the air, spinning impossibly quickly, screeching like a banshee, spewing ingredients across the room. The anchor objects glowed white, then blue. Bolts of cobalt energy shot from the bowl toward them, arcing like lightning, connecting each object to the other four, forming a pale web of energy. It wavered and hummed. The beams expanded, smoking and curling...then they burst, filling the room with solid blue mist.

Silence fell upon them like a blanket, thick and heavy. For several seconds, the world was still.

Then, gradually, the mist faded.

The first thing Gigglebrit saw was the ingredient bowl lying on the floor, shattered into a hundred pieces. The second thing he saw was Hobblebosh. The lime wasn't trapped.

He was blue.

Bright, vibrant blue.

His eyes were still lime green, his robe was still dark and shadowed, but his skin—face, hands, everything—had turned blue.

Hobblebosh looked as surprised as Gigglebrit.

The guards in the room were busy examining their own skin, also blue. Gigglebrit looked at his two hands but found them unchanged.

The amulet. The gentle warmth of its protection had vanished. He'd used it up, and on his own spell no less. Toddleposter, Mardulo, and Bundersquash were unchanged as well. That meant their protection was gone too.

Gigglebrit cursed himself, then realized to his dismay that Lady Uffer-bub's amulet had already been used...he looked to the back of the room where she had landed after Hobblebosh's first spell. She was just getting up now, blue with the rest.

All those affected seemed dizzy. The guards, the animals, even Hobble-bosh had slowed. Lady Ufferbub put a hand on her head and tried to steady herself.

A sudden barreling of feet disrupted the awed silence. Bundersquash charged for Lobster, but a guard lurched between them. The cage, with the newly blue Lobster still inside, clattered to the floor. Bundersquash's helmet went flying.

"Kill them all!" Hobblebosh bellowed, his face one blue flame of fury. "And you, guard, deal with that *creature.*" He pointed to Lobster, seeming-ly out of spite, then started to cast another spell of his own, moving slowly but with no less purpose than before.

Gigglebrit pounced on him. He made contact, but only briefly. Hob-blebosh threw him away with staggering force, and Gigglebrit flew into the wall. Pain exploded across the back of his head, and the world blurred around him.

Somewhere nearby, the kangaroo—now blue, and slightly tipsy—was boxing with a collection of guards. Sometime later, Mardulo had Lobster's cage in his hands but dropped it to help Bundersquash. At one point, a guard was running toward Gigglebrit, ready to attack. Out of nowhere, the kangaroo punched it away.

Hobblebosh continued trying to cast spells, but the winged rhinoceros kept interrupting him. The resulting nondeterministic behavior was pre-sumably better than whatever would have happened if the lime had actually finished his work, but it wreaked havoc, nonetheless. The ceiling had two holes in it, the first of which was still smoking; the second had a guard hanging out of it. The green rug had taken to the air and was flying around the room with reckless abandon, shrinking every time it hit a wall. One of the guards was singing at the top of her lungs. The throne kept melting and reforming, melting and reforming, leaving everything it touched with a sparkly shine.

Another lunge from the rhino, another a flash of light, and the kangaroo had transformed into a ladybug. But then a long, sharpened spear hit its mark, and the winged rhinoceros fell to the floor, lifeless.

Hobblebosh started his next spell.

Gigglebrit tried to stand. His head was pounding. His stomach turned. He could barely think. He was standing by the door, the exit. He leaned against the wall for support, feeling the back of his head.

No blood. Just a bruise.

"Come on, Gigglebrit," he said to himself. "Help."

The pygmy minotaur was riding a parakeet, swooping in to attack with his miniature axe. The rest of the birds had fled through the holes in the ceiling. Lady Ufferbub and Toddleposter were back to back, working their way over to Gigglebrit. Toddleposter had lost a few pieces of armor but looked otherwise unscathed. Lady Ufferbub was in the same hazy state as the guards, though she still landed a few good hits. Mardulo and Bundersquash appeared at Gigglebrit's side, shoving tipsy guards away at every turn.

"We have to leave!" Mardulo shouted above the din.

"Not until we get Lobster!" Bundersquash cried. She was still in her cage on the floor at the other end of the room. Bundersquash charged in her direction.

But without the rhinoceros interrupting him, Hobblebosh finished his spell. Lady Ufferbub and Toddleposter yelled a warning just as a burst of purple flame launched from the lime's auric nebula. Bundersquash threw himself at the cage, dodging the bulk of Hobblebosh's spell—but the edges of the flame still grazed his fingertips. Immediately, the young wizard's left hand spasmed; then his whole body launched upward, leaving Lobster's cage on the floor.

Bundersquash slammed into the ceiling with a terrible crack. The armor he was wearing fell away, and Bundersquash shuddered, stuck to the ceiling like a fly in a spider's web. The skin that had touched Hobblebosh's flame glowed like embers in a dying fire; then it reignited, a flare of violet and shadow. His fingertips turned to ash, and the reaction moved toward his wrist, leaving nothing in its wake—no skin, no bone, no blood. In mere seconds, Bundersquash's whole hand had burned away.

Bundersquash writhed in strangled silence as the fire consumed his forearm, then his elbow, alight with spider-like sparks. At last, it sputtered into nothingness, perhaps six inches from his shoulder, then Bundersquash dropped twenty feet to the floor in the blink of an eye and landed flat on his stomach. Toddleposter ran to help.

Hobblebosh barely spared a glance. The tyrant turned away and started to cast a new spell.

The whole event was enough to bring Gigglebrit back to his senses. His head still hurt, and his stomach cramped, but he forced the pain away and helped Toddleposter carry Bundersquash to the door. Bundersquash was fiddling with his shirt pocket using his one remaining hand, muttering incoherently about Lobster, about his arm, about what to do if he didn't make it, and something about hair.

Mardulo joined them, Lady Ufferbub at his side, and together, they pushed the door open.

"No...Lobster!" Bundersquash tried once more to enter the fray, but a terrible fit of shaking brought him to his knees.

"We have to go!" cried Mardulo, tugging Bundersquash away.

"We need to—need to help—her!" Bundersquash struggled, flailing what remained of his left arm while Mardulo held tightly to his right.

"There's no time! Hobblebosh's spell! We have to leave *now*!" Mardulo pulled, and Bundersquash was in no shape to resist. He tumbled backward through the door with Mardulo. Toddleposter and Gigglebrit followed, herding Lady Ufferbub, who seemed only partially aware of what was happening. The moment everyone was through, they slammed the door shut against an onslaught of semiconscious blue guards, stifling the sound of Hobblebosh's voice as he gave up casting his spell and roared a string of orders to his troops.

The other merchants, still waiting in the ballroom, were speechless—and also blue. Gigglebrit and the others didn't wait to explain. They raced for the exit.

Speed being of the essence, everyone shed what remained of their armor as they went. The regular clothes they had underneath were sufficient and much less restrictive.

There were several hippalectryons standing in the courtyard, untied and ready to run, all of them blue. Whose they were, no one asked. Toddleposter helped Lady Ufferbub onto one, Mardulo forced Bundersquash onto another, then both of them took one for themselves. Gigglebrit grabbed Lampellion. He unhitched the wagon, which would only slow them down, then mounted, copying what the others had done. Before long, they were off, riding through the streets of Town Forbik at frightening speed.

"They're all blue!" Mardulo shouted against the wind as they rode. "Everyone!"

"I know," said Gigglebrit dismally, trying not to fall off Lampellion. The citizens were emerging in scores, looking around in bafflement. Everyone had blue skin, and no one knew what to make of it. Gigglebrit was ineffectively trying to apologize to every one of them as he rode past.

The town gates were open. Even better, the guards were too distracted by their new skin color to notice the five streaks of motion that were

Gigglebrit, Mardulo, Bundersquash, Lady Ufferbub, and Toddleposter making their escape.

Once outside, with nothing but open plains ahead, Lampellion really took off. The others had said he was fast, but Gigglebrit had never quite believed them. Now he understood. With no wagon to burden him and no sharp turns to worry about, Lampellion rode like an unhinged roller coaster launched from its tracks by a rocket engine. It was overwhelming, and Gigglebrit could think of nothing but the wind roaring past, forcing his eyes half-shut. There was no controlling the hippalectryon at this speed, so he leaned in, held on, and hoped.

Chapter 15

Deeper Wounds

Just keep moving.

Gigglebrit pressed his knees into Lampellion.

Keep moving. Keep riding. Keep running.

The pain in his head had dulled to a monotonous throb, but his muscles ached all over. He had always assumed that riding horseback—or hippalectryon back, as it were—would be like driving a car: effortless. Press the gas and go. He was wrong. His legs burned with the effort of keeping balance. His core hurt just from staying upright. He was out of breath, he was out of energy, and he felt sick from the exertion of it all. But Lampellion pushed on, full speed. They needed to get away. Gigglebrit needed to get away.

He couldn't think. He didn't know what to think. The image of his parents scarred his mind. Earth. Home. All of it, burning away in the fire. Then his spell, his failure...It was all one horrible blur—an impossible, terrible nightmare. He tried to push it aside, but somewhere in the back of his mind, reality lurked, dripping like a leaky faucet, a constant pull at his attention.

Gigglebrit shook his head. That didn't matter now. It didn't help. He had to focus on riding.

They were heading toward Collywobbles Bridge. Gigglebrit recognized bits and pieces of the landscape—a lonely stand of trees, a particularly steep hill—and all around them, the landscape became stranger as they neared the Splat. But they were moving much faster than they had been before.

What had taken hours upon hours of patient marching now passed in under half the time.

Gigglebrit's mind spiraled. This wasn't how things were supposed to go…he was the Hero. Heroes won. This was his story. Gigglebrit's story. He was *supposed* to win…this wasn't how things were supposed to go.

Weariness came in waves. The air was hot and dry. The sun's heat pressed upon his skin, unwavering. Gigglebrit's mouth felt parched and sticky. Hunger had come and gone, but thirst clawed at his throat. Exhaustion, physical and mental, threatened every moment. He could barely keep his eyes open…

Images flittered across his vision, staggered among bouts of darkness. A hall. Paintings. Faces. Blue faces. Yelling faces. Angry faces. Disappointment, frustration, grief.

Lobster was there, her wings broken in the grass.

Madame Martoonisplau. So earnest, so fierce. *Study well*, she had said. *Do not let their efforts go to waste—or we will all pay the price.*

Parifel Norwallis, drawn and thin, slaving away in the mines, Hobblebosh standing over her.

His parents, burning to ash in a whirlwind of scarlet mist.

Gigglebrit jolted awake.

He was still on Lampellion, still riding, but their pace had slowed. The air was cooler now. The piercing gold of sunset threatened the western horizon, pulling purples and blues from the east. Lampellion looked no worse for wear, but the others, humans and hippalectryons alike, were worn and tired. Pain plagued Gigglebrit's neck and back—every movement hurt—but still, the gentler pace made him nervous.

They had to keep moving.

Then the one-armed figure of Bundersquash, riding just ahead, slumped sideways and fell from his hippalectryon.

Lady Ufferbub, Mardulo, and Toddleposter dismounted immediately, even before their hippalectryons had stopped. Mardulo ran a circle around Bundersquash.

"Is he okay?" the elder wizard asked. "Is he breathing? Do we need to stop for the night?"

Lady Ufferbub bent over Bundersquash's body. "He is breathing," she said. "And he has a pulse. A faint one."

"How faint? Let me see. I need to analyze the extent of the…" Mardulo stopped himself, his jaw clenched.

"What?" asked Gigglebrit.

Mardulo turned. "You have to do it."

"Do what?" asked Gigglebrit, stepping back.

"Cast the analysis spell. I need to know what's wrong with him."

"He's missing an arm!" said Gigglebrit, incredulous. "That's what's wrong. It's a wonder he made it this far."

"Yes, obviously, but there could be more. I need to examine him, so I need an analysis spell, so you need to cast it."

"Why can't you?"

"We're still in Hobblebosh's restricted zone."

Gigglebrit waved his hands. "This is not a good idea. You saw what I did in Town Forbik. Now you want me to perform some kind of medical procedure on Bundersquash? No."

Mardulo looked at Gigglebrit in disbelief. "What alternative do we have?"

"I'll make the auric nebula, then you cast the spell."

"It doesn't work that way."

"Then let's just get out of the restricted zone and you can do it yourself."

"This is urgent, Gigglebrit! We have to act quickly." Mardulo turned to Lady Ufferbub for support.

Lady Ufferbub hesitated, her blue face shadowed in conflict. Eventually, she sighed. "I think this requires a more practiced hand, Mardulo. We should make our way across Collywobbles Bridge. It is not far. Then you can do it."

Mardulo deflated. "It will take hours...surely, it would be better to—"

Lady Ufferbub cut him off with a firm shake of her head. "Gigglebrit is right. He is not ready for this kind of magic."

"Toddleposter..." Mardulo turned weakly to the clone. "You agree with me, right?"

A jagged rasp from Bundersquash saved Toddleposter from responding.

"What? What happened?" Slowly, the young wizard sat up. "My head...my head feels...bruised." He frowned thoughtfully, swaying where he sat, eyes unfocused, glazed. Then he locked his stare onto Mardulo. "There was something...I had to tell you...about a head. Not mine. It was...important. It had to do with Hobblebosh...with his head." He stopped suddenly, blinked sluggishly. "Why does my arm feel so strange?"

Only then did he look down from his left shoulder to the empty space where his arm should have been. His gaze stumbled uncertainly. His eyes widened in shock.

Then he fainted.

Silence hung over his unconscious body. When Bundersquash made no sign of getting up again, Lady Ufferbub rose to her feet.

"Come, all of you," she said. "Mardulo, take him on your hippalectryon. We shall cross the bridge, then you can try to heal him. Toddleposter, help Mardulo. We must make haste."

And make haste they did. Together, Mardulo and Toddleposter hoisted Bundersquash onto a hippalectryon. Mardulo hopped on behind him. The others mounted, and in less than a minute, the group was riding once again. No one said a word to Gigglebrit, and Gigglebrit stayed out of their way.

They arrived at Collywobbles Bridge just as twilight came to a close and night fell upon them properly. The hippalectryons slowed for the crossing, careful not to slip into the vast nothingness below, but they kept moving.

The veil of the Splat glittered with a thousand different shades of purple and blue, with wisps of green and sparks of fiery red. It was a galaxy in and of itself, all the more beautiful against the clear night sky.

Gigglebrit ignored it pointedly.

Instead, he stared at Lampellion's mane, never daring more than half a glance up. This bridge. The fight with the toll collectors. The Norwallis family. Bundersquash and Gigglebrit hanging over the edge, saved by a packet of lorilell dust. The events echoed around him like whispers from an age long past. There had been hope, then, and optimism—a lighthearted adventure. He had been so sure they would win.

He forced his eyes shut just to keep it all at bay, trusting Lampellion could guide himself. In the darkness, Gigglebrit focused on his breathing. His muscles stung with every jolt, but his head was worse, throbbing heavily as unwanted thoughts pressed against a mesh of semiwakefulness. Time shuffled by, crawling through the present into an incoherent clump of the past, until eventually, they finished the crossing.

Mardulo wasted no time setting up. He carefully placed Bundersquash on a patch of grass under a tree, then rattled off a string of ingredients.

"We don't have any crabapple extract, so I'll need bark from a small tree, a still-living branch, a wet branch, a dry branch, two blades of grass, three and a half cups of fresh water, a rock about the size of my fist, loosestrife petals, and some lily seeds. Lady Ufferbub, Toddleposter, go. Gigglebrit, too, if you've decided to be helpful again." He narrowed his eyes.

Gigglebrit shrank away. "I'll find a rock and some branches."
"Good."

The night lay thick about them. Only the stars, the Splat, and a narrow sliver of moon lit the fields as Gigglebrit, Lady Ufferbub, and Toddleposter searched. It took longer than it might have to find everything, but when Gigglebrit returned with his share of the ingredients, Mardulo's mood had improved considerably. The work steadied him.

"Now," said the wizard, "I'm going to map a quick mental passage to circumvent both of his standard thaumatic barriers and enter the metaphysical layer of his being. If you'd like, Gigglebrit, you can join me. It would be good for you to learn some of this."

"No," said Gigglebrit. "I'm done with that sort of thing."

Mardulo shrugged. "As you wish." He reached into a pocket and produced the sandwich generator.

"You kept that with you?" asked Gigglebrit. "Even in Town Forbik? Even in Hobblebosh's palace?"

"Never leave home without it." Mardulo smiled weakly. "Eat something. You need food, and I need to work."

Gigglebrit thanked Mardulo, took a sandwich, then returned the generator.

"I meant to ask," said Mardulo, tucking the generator back into his pocket, "Hobblebosh used some kind of lorilell dust on you. I never thought he would, given his access to unrestricted magic, but perhaps he was expecting the amulets. Did it harm you? Are you all right?"

"I'm fine," said Gigglebrit. "It was just...he was trying to get information. But I'm fine."

"I see." Mardulo glanced at him, clearly still concerned. "Well, let me know if you need anything."

"Right now, I think you should focus on Bundersquash," said Gigglebrit.

"Of course." Mardulo nodded, then returned to his work. Gigglebrit watched from a distance. He ate his sandwich and drank from the river but barely noticed the meal. He was too busy staring at Bundersquash. The young wizard lay unconscious in the dirt, looking to all the world like a dead man.

All Gigglebrit could think was, *I did this.* He'd had a job to do, and he'd failed. Now his friend was suffering.

He tried to calm himself. This was not the time for a breakdown. He focused on Mardulo, on watching him work, hoping he could heal Bundersquash, praying there was still some way out of this mess.

When Mardulo's silver nebula finally sprang to life, it was a tangible relief. At least they had escaped the restricted zone. Someone else could handle the magic from now on.

Mardulo babbled through the incantation, performing a terribly intricate mess of contortions in the process, and when he finished, dozens of thin light beams burst from Bundersquash's body—not just his injured shoulder, but his legs, his head, and his chest as well. They varied in size and color and displayed some sort of information in their centers, though from this distance, Gigglebrit couldn't make out the details. Mardulo stared at them with fierce intensity. As he moved his gaze to inspect different points, the beams shifted and multiplied to accommodate it.

He took nearly half an hour in the examination. When he was finished, he whistled a note, which stopped the display, then sat in the grass to think.

Gigglebrit walked over, feeling more anxious by the second. "How is he?"

"Not well..." Mardulo stroked his beard. "Replacing limbs is a tricky business at the best of times, and these are hardly those. The problem is, he was injured even before he charged recklessly back into the throne room. It looks like the damage from his wound on Collywobbles Bridge only ever partially healed..."

It hit Gigglebrit like a punch. Even that, he'd messed up.

"...and the missing arm isn't the only thing Hobblebosh's spell seems to have done," Mardulo continued. "Frankly, with a spell like that, we're fortunate the arm is the only thing he's missing. He also suffered damage from being dropped to the floor when the spell had finished its work. Then there's the damage we caused by shoving him onto some stranger's hippalectryon and speeding off into the distance. Not to mention the fall he just suffered from that very same hippalectryon, which probably caused a head injury."

Mardulo slumped. "Most of it will heal in time," he said, "but the arm will not. Quite the opposite, in fact. The longer we wait, the more difficult it will be to fix. In a few hours, it will be quite impossible."

"What?" said Gigglebrit hoarsely. "Why?"

"The magical underpinning of his physical structure is rapidly reforming itself to accommodate the change in corporeal form."

"And that means...?"

Mardulo waved his hands, struggling to shape the explanation. "It means the magic underlying the structure of his body...it's like steel heated in a blacksmith's forge. After his injury, it's soft and malleable, but it will cool again—solid, inflexible, unchanging. His state is already beginning to settle."

"Couldn't you just...heat it up again?"

"Certainly, if the arm was still there, but it isn't. Once the last of its magical traces vanish, there's nothing left to 'heat up,' as you say. It's gone."

"Shouldn't we be trying to fix it, then?" asked Gigglebrit desperately. "Like, *right now*?"

"I *am* trying to fix it," Mardulo stressed. "I'm brainstorming. But the spell...it's a full-body process. An arm hooks up to more than just the shoulder, you know, and there's so much damage all around. There are a lot of ingredients in these meadows, but for something like that..." He shook his head solemnly, letting the words die off.

Then a light turned on behind his eyes.

"However," he said, "if we structured the spell as a kind of reversal process...then we're not regrowing his arm, we're undoing its removal. There are risks. A lot of time has passed since the injury, and not all magic can be reversed, but it's a good deal better than nothing."

He thought for a few more seconds, scribbling hasty calculations in the air, eyes darting back and forth between symbols only he could see, then shouted, "Yes! There's a chance! A slim one, but a chance!

"I'll need something fresh, something withered, three drops of water from a fast-flowing river—this one will do—a feather, a stone, and a few handfuls of wet mud. Quickly!"

Gigglebrit processed this as efficiently as he could. "Fresh, withered, water, feather, stone, mud."

He sprinted toward the river, heart pounding, adrenaline pushing him into overdrive. He could still fix this. Hope burned hot in his chest, powering his every move. It wasn't over yet.

He splashed into the river, drenching his shoes and socks, and scooped a handful of mud from the ground beneath his feet. Then he soaked the lower half of his shirt in the water—he could wring it out later for drops. On his way back, he grabbed a brilliant emerald flower and a clump of dried grass. Fresh and withered. There were plenty of stones all around, but the feather was tricky—that is, until he remembered Lampellion. With a quick apology and a word of thanks, he plucked one of the hippalectryon's blue tailfeathers.

That was everything. He sprinted back, still dripping wet.

"Many thanks," said Mardulo, who had cleared a space beside Bundersquash. He caked the ground with the wet mud, planted the emerald flower on one side and the dead grass on the other, then put the feather down between them and placed the stone atop the feather. Gigglebrit wrung water from his shirt into Mardulo's palm, and Mardulo carefully deposited three drops onto the stone.

"Are Lady Ufferbub and Toddleposter coming?" asked Gigglebrit. The two librarians were sitting some distance away, barely visible through the predawn gloom, conversing over sandwiches.

"I'd rather get this done," said Mardulo. "We don't have long."

Gigglebrit didn't want to wait either. "Do it."

Mardulo rubbed his palms together and spoke with a gurgle Gigglebrit vaguely recognized as the Green Tongue. Several guttural clicks later, the stone and the feather vanished. The dried grass shrank, the flower died, and the mud burst into flame, forcing the night's darkness away.

The flame turned blue, shifted to white, then sent forth silver tongues that wrapped around the remnants of Bundersquash's left arm and spiraled impossibly within themselves.

Bundersquash woke up.

He jolted in distress and stared wide eyed at what was happening, opening and closing his mouth like a fish pulled from water. Gigglebrit signaled for Bundersquash to stay calm while Mardulo finished his work, and Bundersquash seemed to get the message, though his eyes darkened and his lips thinned to a slash. Beads of sweat formed on his forehead.

Moments later, there was a loud crack. The rock zipped out of the air, smacked all three of them on the forehead, then plunged deep into the dirt nearby. The feather wafted down, landed atop the subsequent hole, and melted.

Bundersquash's arm had not healed. If anything, it was worse, the residual limb now blistered and red.

"What in the world was *that*, Mardulo?" Bundersquash heaved into a sitting position, his face burning with anger.

"I was trying to heal your arm."

"With tongues of fire?!"

"With a reversal spell."

"With a reversal spell…" Bundersquash echoed the words, incredulous. "You honestly thought," he said slowly, "that you could reverse a spell Hobblebosh cast hours ago?"

"It was worth a try."

"Was it?" The young wizard waved his burnt arm angrily. "I'm not sure."

"Is everything all right?" Lady Ufferbub and Toddleposter approached.

"I was trying to heal his arm," said Mardulo, frustrated. "Apparently Bundersquash thinks that was a bad idea."

Bundersquash scowled. "I understand you were trying to help, but it was foolish. For a wound like this, there's nothing to be done. Especially not with a mere meadow for supplies—even these meadows. You're grasping at straws." He flinched, prodding experimentally at the burned skin. "Or more aptly, grasping at red-hot pokers."

"So, what?" said Mardulo irritably. "We just leave it?"

Bundersquash hesitated. "Yes."

"If we don't fix it soon, you'll be stuck like that! How will you function? Without both palms, you can't even create an auric nebula."

"There are other ways to create a nebula," said Bundersquash, though he looked more defiant than confident.

"I know that, but—"

"No." Bundersquash wobbled to his feet, using Toddleposter for support. His eyes hardened. "There's nothing more to do. Unless you happen to have a dozen somatic restoratives hidden up your sleeve, a few good sedatives, and a book or two on standard human anatomy, this is it. We have to face the consequences. We knew it was a risk rushing toward Hobblebosh like that, and here we are. This is what happens when—"

But Mardulo had started scribbling in the air again.

"Are you listening to me?" said Bundersquash.

"What? Oh, yes. You were rambling on about how this was impossible and we're wasting our time, but I had an idea."

Bundersquash looked at him warily.

"What is a somatic restorative, when you get right down to it?" Mardulo asked. "It's just a thing that helps your body grow."

"If you oversimplify dramatically, yes." Bundersquash gave up trying to stand and dropped back into the grass.

"Well," Mardulo continued, "*food* makes your body grow. Good hearty meals, meat and stew and the like. What if—"

"Professor," Bundersquash interrupted, "if you honestly think I can just *eat* my arm back into existence—"

"No, no. Of course not!" said Mardulo. "But perhaps we can take something ordinary, something like food, and increase its effectiveness so it transforms into a fully fledged somatic restorative during the spell."

Bundersquash considered this for a few minutes. "Even if we could," he said, "we're not exactly swimming in beef stew, are we? We don't have the supplies."

Mardulo grinned and held up the sandwich generator. "Never leave home without it," he said. "Might take a few tries to get something sufficiently substantial, but we'll manage."

Despite himself, Bundersquash looked impressed.

Mardulo rattled off yet another string of ingredients, which Lady Ufferbub, Toddleposter, and Gigglebrit dutifully rushed off to fetch. Gigglebrit went to the river again, filled with nervous energy, mentally reassuring himself at every moment.

Dawn crept in while they searched. The air's gloomy gray slowly washed into a pale, cloudy morning, and a breeze picked up, chilling Gigglebrit through his soggy clothes.

He was scraping moss off a damp stone when Mardulo shouted in the distance. "At last! Pumpernickel!"

Lady Ufferbub and Toddleposter had both already returned, so Gigglebrit made his way back too. The ground around them was littered with dozens of discarded sandwiches—bread, meat, fruits, vegetables, mixes, dressings, and jellies. The grass was stained and sticky with a dozen different kinds of sauce.

Slightly separated were the items Mardulo actually planned to use—sausage, ham, turkey, egg, several hardy breads, and a number of deep-green vegetables.

Lady Ufferbub was enjoying a celery sandwich, which she had saved from the discard pile. She and Toddleposter had already collected most of the ingredients. Gigglebrit added a pile of leaves to the mix and emptied his pockets of mossy pebbles.

Mardulo, evidently at a loss for paper while trying to plan his spell, had taken to scribbling in the mud and constructing strange dioramas with sticks, leaves, and stones. At present, he and Bundersquash were bickering.

"He's a person, Mardulo," said Bundersquash.

"And willing," Mardulo shot back.

"It's not safe! We're rushing into *yet another* unplanned, un-thought-out idea, and I won't let you do it! It's too risky!"

"I promise no harm will come to him."

"What's going on?" Gigglebrit cut in.

"Mardulo wants to use Toddleposter as an ingredient for the spell!"

"He won't be consumed, of course," Mardulo added hastily. "*Ingredient* might be the wrong word. Map, perhaps. I don't have the necessary anatomical knowledge to do this myself, but I can use Toddleposter as a template. All I have to do is scale things up a bit. And Toddleposter has already agreed."

Toddleposter put a hand on Bundersquash's shoulder. "It's a brilliant idea," he said. "Besides, Mardulo said I won't be in any danger. I trust him. Don't you?"

"After all that's happened, I..." Bundersquash stopped himself. "Look, Toddleposter, despite what Mardulo might say, it's a big risk. Taking part in a spell like this can have side effects."

"I'm aware," said Toddleposter. "But it's worth a try."

"Are we sure there isn't some other way?"

"The other way is you spend the rest of your life without an arm!" Mardulo snapped. "We've been through this, Bundersquash. You're being stubborn and foolish. Let us help you."

Bundersquash bristled. For a moment, he looked ready to fight back—but he paused, closed his eyes for a moment, and then...

"Okay," he said quietly.

"Good!" Mardulo removed his gloves. "Now, Bundersquash, you stand over there. Toddleposter, go to his side. Lady Ufferbub, Gigglebrit, please step back a few paces, and everyone, keep very, very still."

With a deep breath, Mardulo rubbed his palms together and started to speak the incantation. The words went on and on, a calm, almost melodic wave of speech. Mardulo seemed to be switching between languages. All manner of strange things started happening to the food—it simmered and sparked and gurgled and steamed until all that remained was a melted brown goop that spawned mud-colored bubbles. Suddenly, Toddleposter's eyes went blank, his legs jolted, and his body slackened, though some invisible force kept him standing. Five minutes later, he woke up, disoriented but no worse for wear. Even then, the spell had not finished. Anxiety wrote lines all over Bundersquash's face, but the young wizard did not falter. Mardulo's incantation droned on.

The spell ended gradually. From its initial volume, the words fell to a mutter, then a whisper beneath Mardulo's breath until it had all but faded away—and as Mardulo mouthed the final few words with hardly any air behind them, Bundersquash's left arm started to grow. It moved slowly, one small sliver at a time, threads weaving together in a glistening, incandescent sheen like oil on water.

Then it stopped.

Bundersquash's arm had barely grown an inch.

Gigglebrit's stomach dropped. They'd been so close...

"Well," said Mardulo at last. "We made a little progress. Perhaps we could adjust some of the proportions and—"

"Enough," said Bundersquash firmly. "It's lost. We'll just have to accept it—*I* will just have to accept it."

"But if I could just try a few more ideas—" Mardulo started.

"No. You can't fix it. It's gone. Gone like Burrid. Gone like Lobster. Gone like so many other things we've lost in these crusades against Hobblebosh, and it isn't coming back."

Mardulo frowned. "You don't know that, Bundersquash."

"I do know that. So do you. You just refuse to accept it!"

"I refuse to accept it because it's *not true*! You're being stubborn, and you're going to regret it for the rest of your life!"

"I'm being realistic, Mardulo. You should try it sometime."

"That is enough!" Lady Ufferbub stepped between them. "We are all tired. Bundersquash, you have not eaten. Mardulo, you need rest. Sit. Let us eat. Let us calm down, and for a time, let us forget our current predicament and enjoy the fact that, despite our losses, we managed to escape with our lives."

Bundersquash glowered and Mardulo glared, but ultimately, they deferred to Lady Ufferbub and sat where they had been standing. Lady Ufferbub placed herself between them, forcing the wizards to shuffle farther apart. Toddleposter and Gigglebrit joined them. The sandwich generator made the rounds.

It was a tense silence, filled with words unsaid. Gigglebrit wasn't particularly hungry, but he ate just to have something to distract himself. The lack of conversation weighed on everyone, and as the tension mounted, a thought occurred to Gigglebrit—an unwanted, unwelcome duty, but once it had come, there was no escaping it...

He took a breath and said what he needed to say.

"I'm sorry."

The words cut through the silence like a knife. All at once, Gigglebrit's mouth went dry. He wished he'd written some of this down first. But it was too late now.

"I screwed up," he continued. "I cast the spell incorrectly. I told you I could do it—I really *thought* I could do it—but obviously, I wasn't up to the task, and that's on me. All this..." He waved at Lady Ufferbub, at Bundersquash, at the graveyard of sandwiches around them. "This is my fault, and I'm sorry."

His cheeks burned, but he continued. "I thought I was a hero, as if this was all some great adventure story like the ones I used to read. In those, the Hero always wins, and I just assumed...well, it was stupid. I was stupid. This isn't a story, and I'm not a hero. I'm not *Gigglebrit*, adventurous wizard's pupil prodigy. I'm just Gilbert. A nobody. Some kid from Nebraska, out of place and big headed. I got overexcited and made promises I couldn't keep. Now you've paid the price. And not just you either. I saw the atrocities Hobblebosh was committing in Town Forbik, and I failed to stop them. More people will..." He took a second to steady his voice. "More people will die, because I failed. I'm sorry."

Nobody said anything. They simply listened, dejected and deflated. Lady Ufferbub, with her newly blue skin, avoided his gaze. Toddleposter looked concerned. Mardulo scowled, and Bundersquash's face was as pale as bone; what remained of his arm was still blistered and red.

Gilbert had caused all of this suffering. It was his fault. His failure. He closed his eyes and resigned himself to what had to be done.

"I'll leave," he said. "I'm just deadweight to you now. I don't fit in here. I'll go, and you can get back to whatever plans you had before I showed up and derailed you. It's what I should have done to begin with. You can find the real chosen one, Pottleswee or whatever their name is. You can do this whole thing properly. I'll be out of your way."

He had tried to help Bundersquash—obviously, that hadn't worked—and he wasn't about to confront Hobblebosh again. He was useless to them now. Leaving was the best thing to do.

Then another thought occurred to him. A simple one, but it felt...right. Almost a relief.

"Maybe it's time I returned to Earth," he added. "I think that's where I really belong."

"Do not be so silly," said Lady Ufferbub at last. She spoke softly, but the words stung far more than Gilbert had expected. "We would not do that to you. Not over an honest mistake."

"It isn't your fault," added Toddleposter. "No one blames you, and you shouldn't either. Don't punish yourself. You gave it your best. What more could we ask?"

"You asked me to succeed, and I didn't. I really think—"

"It was a bad plan from the start," Lady Ufferbub interrupted. Her face rested somewhere between disappointment and frustration. "We should have known better—all five of us."

"Besides"—Mardulo forced a smile—"everyone walked away, and that's what counts. All things considered, I'd say luck was with us."

Bundersquash tensed. "You would say that, wouldn't you?"

"What do you mean?" asked Mardulo.

"I mean you're belittling everything that's happened."

A defensive edge entered Mardulo's voice. "Gigglebrit and I tried to heal your arm, but you wouldn't let us! I don't know what you—"

"I'm not talking about my arm, Mardulo." Bundersquash snapped. "What about Lobster? What about the animals? They're all dead, most likely. But here you are, prattling on about how everyone walked away. Have you forgotten them all already?"

Mardulo looked taken aback. "I didn't...I wasn't...I'm sorry, Bundersquash. I just meant, at least the five of us are here, safe."

"Lobster was my friend." Bundersquash continued. "She was a gift from my parents. I worked with her *every day*. I trained her. I raised her. I loved her. I told you it was dangerous to bring her with us, but you didn't believe me! Now she's dead."

Mardulo floundered, trying to find the right words.

But Gilbert already knew them. "I'm sorry," he said again, and he meant it. "Bundersquash, I'm so sorry. I know she was important to you. If I hadn't messed up..." He shook his head. "Don't blame Mardulo. It's my fault."

"None of this is your fault," said Bundersquash. "Like Toddleposter and Lady Ufferbub said, it was a bad plan from the start. You couldn't have known any better. That was our job. We should've taken more time to prepare, to teach you the spell, to discuss the details. Instead, we rushed into it, and we've paid the price...again." He scowled at Mardulo.

Mardulo switched from apologetic to exasperated in a heartbeat. "So this is all my fault, is it? The ruined plans. The failed spell. Lobster gone. Your missing arm. You blame me for all of it?"

"Yes." Bundersquash let the word drop like a weight. "I do."

Gilbert gulped. He'd only wanted to apologize. This wasn't supposed to happen.

"How could you even say that?!" sputtered Mardulo. "I tried my best, just like everyone else!"

"You ignored me at every turn." Bundersquash stood up, his face flushed with anger. He shoved what remained of his left arm toward Mardulo with a forceful stab. "This is your fault because *you* couldn't bother to slow down. Because *you* rushed us into that mess of a plan knowing full well we weren't ready. Because *you* were too impatient to do things properly."

"We made those decisions as a group!"

"No, we didn't. *You* made those decisions, and you wouldn't take no for an answer. I said taking Lobster was a mistake. I said we needed more time to prepare before leaving City Boratorus. I said we should have turned around after losing half of our supplies on Collywobbles Bridge. But you *never* listened to me. You just keep marching forward, blind to the danger, blind to the risks. You rushed into this plan like you rush into everything, and once again, it all went wrong."

"We had to rush!" Mardulo yelled. "Did you think Hobblebosh was just going to sit and wait for us?"

"We could have afforded a few more days, Mardulo! But no. In trying to cut corners, you've set us back months. I thought you'd have learned this by now."

Gilbert could see Mardulo shaking. "You dare to blame this on me? After everything I've done for you? You have no right. I've been laboring all morning trying to heal your arm, and you've been nothing but ungrateful!"

"You haven't been trying to heal my arm!" Bundersquash snarled. "You've been trying to ease your own conscience. You're only trying to fix my arm because you're the reason it's gone. You're running away from the consequences of your own poorly thought-out actions, like you've done so many times before. But this time it won't work, and you can't accept that." Bundersquash took a breath. "Don't act like you're doing this out of the goodness of your heart. You're just trying to make yourself feel better."

"Oh, for goodness' sake. You act as if you know everything I'm thinking, but you don't know the half of it."

"I know what runs through your head better than you do yourself, Mardulo."

Mardulo scoffed. "If you knew everything I was thinking, Bundersquash, you'd be a far better wizard than you are."

Emotions swept across Bundersquash's face in waves—confusion, disbelief, pain, and then, last and most prominently, fury. Something ignited behind his eyes.

"You have no idea how good a wizard I am," he growled. "You couldn't possibly know because you've been ignoring me for years. At best, I'm your personal secretary. At worst, I'm no more than a bloody pack mule. But you know what? Despite your blatant incompetence, I *have* managed to learn some things. I've seen what lies beneath that flimsy facade of modesty and vibrance you put on every day—an arrogant old man, gorging himself on the undeserved respect of others who know no better."

"Bundersquash! Mardulo! Enough!" Lady Ufferbub tried to get between them.

Mardulo stepped around her. "Is that what you think, Bundersquash? I taught you everything you know, and this is what I get in return? You think I don't treat you well enough? You think you deserve better?" He laughed bitterly. "And you call me arrogant...I've done more for this world than you ever will. I earned my place. I earned my position. I earned the respect people show me. When I was your age, I was busy changing the world with—"

"Oh, *shut up*!" Bundersquash flailed his arm. "So, you invented the sandwich generator. I know! Get over yourself. That was fifty years ago! What have you done since then?"

"What have you done *ever*, Bundersquash? If I hadn't taken you in, you'd still be stuck in Port Tup cleaning basements and serving clam chowder to tourists. You'd be nothing. You'd be nobody. Worse, you'd be boring. You've leeched a great deal off of my success, I'll give you that, but what else?"

Bundersquash clenched his fist, eyes reddening. "Maybe you're right, Mardulo. On my own, I haven't done much—but that's because I've been too busy serving as your resident pet! You won't *let* me do anything on my own! Thirteen years I've been your student. And what do I have to show for it? Coauthorship on a couple of dead-end papers written about whatever strange topic happened to strike your fancy? A few prototype devices that never made it down from floor twenty? If I'm a leech, I've attached myself to a pitiful host. Meanwhile, the projects I've started, the ones I actually care about, have been kicked to the side unfinished. I still haven't had time to complete my voice-to-illustration device, and it's been years!"

"Oh, please." Mardulo rolled his eyes. "I gave you my only myrian crystal for that pitiful project, and all you managed to create was a bunch of semivisible images! I've never seen such a waste in my life. But then, I suppose I shouldn't be surprised. Not with you."

Bundersquash shook his head. "You're just a sad old man with a single success among a sea of mistakes and disasters—and I've been foolish enough to stick by your side while the rest of the world has passed you by. Maybe it's time I did the same. Maybe it's time I moved on. I could be so much more without you."

"If that's what you think, then go," said Mardulo. "Get out of my sight. I have more important matters to deal with."

"You'll fall apart without me," said Bundersquash. "Just wait and see." Then he turned his back and stormed away, not even bothering with a second glance.

"Good riddance!" Mardulo shouted after him. He stayed standing for a time, glaring as Bundersquash trudged into the distance. Only when he sat back down did Gilbert notice the tear working its way down his cheek.

Gilbert was speechless. He'd only meant to apologize. How had things gotten so out of control? He should've just kept to himself. Ever since he'd entered this world, he'd been making things worse for everyone around him. It didn't matter what he did—whether he was trying to stop Hobble-bosh, or help heal Bundersquash's arm, or apologize for all his mistakes—it always went wrong, and he left things worse than he'd found them. Mardulo and Bundersquash had brought him into existence. They'd welcomed him into the Wizards' Tower. They'd taught him about the world, trained him in magic. They'd made a home for him.

In return, Gilbert had torn them apart.

He was surrounded by the aftermath of his own failures. He didn't belong here, and the longer he stayed, the worse he made things. He needed to leave, to get out of everyone's way. He would find some way back to Earth, instead. Back home. Lady Ufferbub had called it silly, but she was wrong. It was *right*. And it would be better for everyone.

He bit his lip. There wasn't time to think it over. There wasn't time to think better of it. The more he waited, the harder it would get, and the more damage he could do.

He stood up and looked at Mardulo, then Lady Ufferbub, then Toddle-poster, then into the distance, where Bundersquash was still walking away. A sudden, sorrowful pang seized his stomach. They were his friends...but this was the right thing to do.

He opened his mouth to speak, but the words caught in his throat. *Goodbye*, he might have said, or *Thank you*. But in the end, words fell short, and he left saying nothing at all.

The others didn't follow. They barely looked up. They were too busy with their own thoughts and worries. Gilbert supposed that was good. They needed to focus on Hobblebosh.

Lampellion was striking poses at himself in the water, immune to the troubles around him, clearly enjoying his new blue feathers.

"Hey, buddy," said Gilbert softly. "I think it's time for me to go." He glanced back at the others, still sitting mournfully in their circle. "I can't be here anymore."

Lampellion cocked his head and nuzzled Gilbert's shoulder. Gilbert hopped on, jostled the reins, and steadied himself. Lampellion started to walk, then trot, then canter, and then, just as the others realized what was happening, he entered a full gallop.

The group called after Gilbert, yelling for him to slow down, to come back, but Gilbert had made up his mind. He pressed his knees into Lampellion and leaned in. The two of them sped off together—away from the Splat, away from Town Forbik, away from the calls of his friends, away from everything.

For one blissful moment, the rush of wind and adrenaline was enough to smother his unceasing flow of sorrow and guilt.

Keep moving, he reminded himself. *Keep moving. Keep riding. Keep running.*

Interlude: Tree in the Aftermath

Tree and Lugbrush returned to Town Forbik with an entire battalion of eager trees. It had been a successful mission by every measure—nearly two hundred trees converted, all strong, able, and willing to fight. Now they marched toward the town gates filled with hope and enthusiasm...but no fanfare greeted them. No joyous welcome. Town Forbik was in complete disarray.

And everyone was blue.

Lugbrush had to threaten several guards just to get into town, and even then, most of the forest had to wait outside. The gatekeepers allowed Tree in, though, and Lugbrush negotiated for two additional trees to join as evidence of the mission's success—Old Oak and a young tree named Folia. Over a dozen identification checks later, they all stood in the palace courtyard, awaiting King Hobblebosh's arrival.

Hours passed. People—all blue—raced in and out of buildings, too busy to spare even a glance for Tree and their friends. When Lugbrush finally got a hold of someone willing to answer his questions, they learned there had been an attempt on King Hobblebosh's life, and it had almost succeeded...but in the end, of course, the king had prevailed, though the perpetrators were still at large.

And no one, under any circumstances, was to mention the new skin color, unless they wished to lose their tongue.

When King Hobblebosh arrived, Tree did their best to follow those instructions.

"I am happy to see you," said the king. "I'm told you succeeded. That is good. Our timelines have accelerated greatly. Lugbrush, your next assignment is prepared. Go see Iffrimae. Tree, come with me. We shall speak in the palace. These two may come as well." He signaled to Old Oak and Folia.

Tree bowed, then followed Hobblebosh through a massive pair of open doors, down a hall, and into an utterly disheveled, nearly destroyed throne room.

"I'm glad to speak with you, King Hobblebosh," said Tree. "I'm sure you have many questions. I have one of my own, as well."

Hobblebosh stopped just short of his throne, sections of which appeared to have melted. He turned to face Tree. "If you must ask something of me, ask quickly. We have much to discuss."

"It's only...for trees to receive the power of movement you so generously offered, Lugbrush required an oath of loyalty and service to you."

"Yes. What is the question?"

"We had spoken of freedom. Having to swear an oath, even to you, is not—"

"Tree, there will be no freedom for our kind until the humans have been annihilated. For that, we need fighters, not aimless wanderers. You should know this."

Embarrassment wormed through Tree like a snake. Suddenly, they wished Old Oak and Folia had not come.

Hobblebosh continued. "When you first came to me, Tree, you spoke of lumberjacks. You spoke of axes. Do you recall the horror you felt? The terror?"

"I do," said Tree, leaves wilting.

But the king shook his head. "No, I do not think so. I need you to *feel* it, Tree, to remember, and to understand."

He strode out of the throne room and returned a few moments later carrying a large sharpened axe.

Tree backed up instinctively. Old Oak and Folia did the same. An immediate tension seized the air.

Hobblebosh strode forward and held the blade to Tree's bark. "*This feeling, Tree. Do you remember it now? Remember the terror. Remember the pain. Remember the torture those humans put you through...yes, I think you begin to see. If that savagery is still possible anywhere in the world, if humans are still willing to do such things, will trees ever truly be free?*"

Tree was too shocked to respond. Old Oak and Folia stood back, filled with surprise and concern, but Tree's mind was elsewhere, in a tower far away, panicking as four lumberjacks hacked violently into their trunk. They could think of nothing else.

At last, Hobblebosh removed the axe and threw it across the room, where it clattered heavily into the opposite wall. The sound pulled Tree back.

"I am sorry to have to use such cruel reminders, Tree," the king continued more gently. "It hurts me as much as it hurts you, but we have limited supplies and even less time. I am forced to act quickly, even if it stings. When the war is won, perhaps we can help the rest of that forest, but for now, our priority must be fighting. Resources must only be used on those willing to help. Do you understand?"

"I do." Tree released one final tremor through their leaves, then bowed, as they had been taught. "I am sorry to have doubted you, my king."

"It is good you have come to your senses." King Hobblebosh gave Tree's trunk a reaffirming pat. "Now, let us put this ugly business behind us. I would like to learn more about the army you have brought me."

Tree fell into line beside Old Oak and Folia, and together, they recounted the journey in detail. Hobblebosh listened, interjecting occasionally to get clarity on certain points. Afterward, he questioned Old Oak and Folia much as he had done Tree, back when Tree had first arrived, to gauge their battle readiness.

When he was finished, the king sat in his damaged throne and thought to himself.

Eventually, he looked to Tree. "Very soon," he said, "I will march south, and I will bring the bulk of my strength with me. You will join us. It is vital that we travel quickly. The southern half of this continent has been left unattended for far too long, and they have festered. It has cost me much. Yesterday, it nearly cost me my life. But I shall not allow such disrespect to go unpunished!"

The king pounded a fist on the arm of his throne. His anger sent shocks through the very air of the room. His voice came thick with vengeance. Tree shrank away. They could feel the king's hatred seeping into everything around them.

"You see what they did to me?" Hobblebosh stood. "Of course you do. I am no fool. I have sensed your unease since I arrived. My precious lime skin, the final remnant of my former self, cruelly stripped away. Leave it to wizards to taint an entire town like this. It is why we must eliminate their magic and destroy them! We cannot afford to fail. I am counting on you, Tree. We are almost ready to strike."

"Almost?" asked Tree. "What more must be done?"

"Research." Hobblebosh paced in front of his throne. "Until now, no one has been able to perform magic inside the safe zone I have created. Yesterday, that changed. Someone's name was not on the Roster. I know not how, and it eats at me...but there is more. There was something in his mind, Tree. I saw it. I sought for the deeper layers of his person, to learn his true self before I crushed it out of him, but there was some disconnect. His mind was filled with...*other*. His past..." The king grasped for words but found none. He growled. "It made no sense. I was shocked, and in my surprise, he nearly overwhelmed me. He is a new threat, and a real one. Gigglebrit, he called himself. I cannot move south until I understand what happened and make sure it cannot happen again."

Tree hesitated. "This boy," they said to King Hobblebosh. "His name, Gigglebrit...I have heard it before. It was wrong, then, but perhaps he kept it anyway. His real name was Gilbert Betters."

Chapter 16

Departure

Part one of Gilbert's plan had been simple: Leave. Get away from everyone and everything before making anything worse.

Part two of the plan was going back to Earth, and Gilbert had absolutely no idea how to do that...

He was riding blindly through the meadows on the back of a hippalectryon. No food, no water, and no help. But images of Earth spiraled through his mind—his history, his friends, his family—pushing him forward. They'd been with him ever since his fight in Hobblebosh's throne room.

Do not be so silly, Lady Ufferbub had said.

But Earth wasn't silly. It was his home. He didn't care if it was fiction. He didn't care if it only existed in some book. If the others didn't support him returning, he'd find someone who did. Besides, it was better this way. They could get back to their work on Hobblebosh, free of Gilbert's destructive and distracting presence, and he could focus on finding his way back.

Somehow.

He didn't even know where he was going. This route led back to City Boratorus, but that meant constant reminders of his failed quest and, eventually, the return of Mardulo, Bundersquash, Lady Ufferbub, and Toddleposter. He didn't want that, but he needed to stay near the river. He had no bottles to store water in, nor any map to guide him to an alternate source, so he kept the river on the horizon and tried to stay out of the way in case the others came looking. The sooner they forgot about him, the better.

He and Lampellion kept a steady pace south, making only occasional excursions back to the river to drink. At the end of the day, Gilbert was sore and tired, but they'd traveled a good distance. He found a clearing among some tall meadow grasses and decided to stop for the evening.

He hadn't eaten anything all day, and after his stomach rumbled loud enough to startle a nearby bird, he set to finding food. He knew plants, and he'd gathered an absurd number of ingredients in these fields for Mardulo and Bundersquash. Surely he could find something to eat.

Mostly, he found berries. And a cluster of mushrooms he wasn't totally sure about. But at least it wasn't sandwiches.

He also needed fire. The night air was cold, and he could already feel a chill wind coming in from the north. This presented another problem. Gilbert knew how to make campfires on Earth, but he'd always had matches to work with. In this world, he had nothing. Mardulo and Bundersquash used a simple spell to do the job, but Gilbert hadn't learned the specifics.

He did remember how to heat tea, though.

Agethermon.

Mardulo had said it meant "bring heat."

Well, heat made fire. Not to be deterred this early in his bid for independence, he decided to give it a try. Heating water, heating dried shrubbery—how different could it really be?

He grabbed some wood, some dry grass and leaves, and a small rock. Then he made a ring of stones to contain the flame.

To heat tea, he'd placed the rock inside a filled teapot, then placed dry grass on either side of the pot. This time, he nestled the rock inside a bundle of kindling and leaves, hoping something would catch when the rock heated up.

He rubbed his palms together, focused on the rock, and brought to mind the heat from a fire.

"Agethermon."

The spoken word hovered in Gilbert's mind, a conduit, taking his thoughts of warmth and realizing them within the stone. His auric nebula faded into the kindling. The dry grass curled and blackened. Deep inside the pile of sticks and leaves, something fizzed. Then a small stream of smoke emerged. Shortly after, a flame took hold.

Heart fluttering, Gilbert shuffled some twigs closer to the heat, then gathered more dry grass and a few long stalks to keep things burning until the larger pieces caught.

It worked better than he'd dared to hope. The rock continued to pour out heat—enough, he soon realized, to light even the larger pieces of wood without much difficulty. Soon, he had a bright, crackling fire to keep him warm, so he released the spell and relaxed, soothing his muscles and munching thoughtfully on a motley assortment of berries with his back against Lampellion.

"Sorry I don't have any oats," he said as he fed the hippalectryon some blackberries. "Hopefully these will do."

Lampellion didn't seem to mind.

Having finally settled in, Gilbert took a moment to think.

Earth.

When he did get back, however it happened, he would live his life as he'd planned to live it before the wizards had brought him here. He would go to college, get a job, see his parents again. So what if it was fiction? It had been real enough the first time, and it was still his home. He was happy there. He could be happy there again.

The thought filled him with a gentle peace—with certainty, clarity, and purpose. It wouldn't be easy, but at least he had a goal, and for today, that was enough. He relaxed, gazing into the swirling flames of the fire, feeling like things might actually turn out okay.

Slowly, he drifted to sleep.

The sound of rustling grass woke him up. It was fully dark now. Clouds covered the stars. The fire was still burning, but low.

How long had he slept?

But that was the wrong question. Much more pressing—what was in the grass?

Frantically, Gilbert set to smothering the fire, but it was too late. He'd been spotted.

A woman emerged, riding a beautifully groomed hippalectryon.

"All right, let's cut to the chase," she said without preamble. "Do you know who I am?"

Gilbert stared at her, too confused to process what was happening. Then recognition dawned. He *had* seen her before. In Town Forbik. She was blue now, and the details were hard to see in the darkness, but he recognized the green of her eyes.

"Thorippela?" he said.

"Yes, very good. And?"

Gilbert hesitated. "You were in Town Forbik. A merchant. You gave me directions. And sold hippalectryons…"

"*And…?*" She looked at him, eyebrows raised.

"And…" Gilbert flushed. "I'm guessing my friends and I stole a few of those hippalectryons during our escape."

He had wondered if they were hers when he'd first seen them available by the palace, but he'd been hoping it wouldn't come up.

Thorippela scrutinized him for a moment. Then her face relaxed into a grin.

"Yes, you did." She dismounted and sat on the ground, making herself comfortable and signaling for Gilbert to do the same. "At least you own up to it. You're welcome, by the way. Those are my best. I'm sure they served you well."

"They did," said Gilbert, uncomfortable with the sudden shift in tone. He remained standing.

"And where are they now?" Thorippela asked. "That isn't one of mine." She pointed to Lampellion, a flash of envy in her eyes.

"They're with my friends. We...split up."

Thorippela pulled a sandwich generator out of her bag and grabbed a fried pickle on wheat. She looked up at Gilbert. "You split up?" she said, smirking. "What are you, a boy band?"

That caught Gilbert completely off guard. "What? No, I...what?" He re-collected himself. "I decided to go my own way."

"Well, obviously," she said, mouth half-full. "But why?"

"Because they're better off without me."

"Ooh, I see." Thorippela's eyes glimmered with amusement.

"I'm not joking!"

"I know, I know." She raised her hands—generator in one, half a sandwich in the other. "It's just, you looked so serious."

"It *is* serious. I really messed things up in Town Forbik. For everyone. You were there. You saw what happened. It was my fault. Everything Hobblebosh does from now on, all the suffering, all the pain—that's on me."

Thorippela raised her eyebrows. "Having a real pity party, aren't we?"

Gilbert's anger flared. "What are you even doing here? If you want your horses, go get them. They're north with Mardulo, Bundersquash, Lady Ufferbub, and Toddleposter. Two wizards and two librarians. You can't miss them." He pointed toward the Great Splat.

Thorippela shrugged. "I think I'll stick around, if it's all the same to you."

"It isn't."

"Why not?" asked Thorippela.

"Because I don't know you, and I don't trust you."

"Says the man who stole four of my best hippalectryons—and, if I'm not mistaken, just referred to them as *horses*."

Gilbert's retort stuck halfway up his throat. "I just...that was different, I—"

Thorippela cut him off. "I'm the reason you were able to escape Town Forbik alive. If I wanted you dead, I'd have kept the hippalectryons to myself."

"Great." Gilbert scowled. "You didn't let us die. Now you want me to trust you completely?"

"Pretty much, yeah."

When Gilbert didn't budge, Thorippela simply turned back to her meal.

"Trust me or not," she said. "That's up to you. Either way, I'm sticking around for a while."

"Why stick around if you aren't up to something? You must see how that makes you look suspicious..."

She wobbled her head, then took another bite of her sandwich.

Gilbert wanted to scream. He wished there was more he could do, but she already knew where he was, and he doubted he could outrun her, even if he tried. Besides, it was true—those hippalectryons *had* saved them in Town Forbik...

"Fine," he said. "Do what you want, but I don't have any food or water for you."

Thorippela held up her sandwich generator and a heavy leather canteen. "I have plenty of both." Then, eyeing the campsite, she added, "If you ask nicely, I might even share."

With one glance at the canteen, Gilbert became uncomfortably aware of the stickiness in his mouth and the dryness in his throat. He bit his lip while Thorippela took a long, deep drink of water...then gave in.

"I've had enough sandwiches for a lifetime," he said, sitting. "But I will take some water. Thanks."

The tension broke as she passed him the canteen. He drank, trying not to take too much too quickly.

"So, is your name really Giaborg?" she asked. "Or was that some kind of cover?"

"It's Gilbert."

"Gilbert?"

"Yes. Gilbert Betters. No stupid epithet. Not even a middle name. Just...Gilbert."

Thorippela looked at him. "Well, if you insist, *Gilbert*. Who am I to argue?"

"Thank you," said Gilbert, more relieved than he cared to admit.

For a few minutes, they simply sat there, listening to the soft sounds of a meadow at night—the grass swaying in the wind, the crickets chirping, the frogs croaking in the distance. But something about their earlier conversation was nagging at Gilbert.

"Do you really have boy bands here?"

"Of course we do," said Thorippela, as if it were the most obvious thing in the world. "The Ankersin Trio? Wizard in a Bottle? Six-Legged Mountain Troll? Rulfunder and the Gryphon Masters? Surely you've heard of Rulfunder and the Gryphon Masters."

"Not really, no." Gilbert scratched his neck. "Anyway. It's not important. I was just curious."

Thorippela blinked at him.

"What I want to know," she said, "is what really happened in Town Forbik. I didn't stay long after you left, but even so, I must've heard at least a dozen different rumors. I know for a fact the flying-rhinoceros one is true. I saw that creature with you when I was leaving the throne room. But there was another story about a one-armed kangaroo battling Hobblebosh all by itself? I don't believe that. And don't even get me started on all the different meanings people are attributing to the color blue...but you were actually there! What really happened?"

Gilbert tensed. This was the last thing he wanted to talk about. "I was supposed to stop Hobblebosh, but I failed and turned everyone blue. The whole town, apparently. That's it."

"That's it? Seriously?"

"Yes. What more do you want? There was a trapping spell, an automatic door that ruined everything, and I got distracted. I said the wrong words, and poof. Blue."

Thorippela squinted at him through the dark. "You're telling me you actually cast a spell in Hobblebosh's territory."

"No. I'm telling you I *messed up* a spell in Hobblebosh's territory."

"But you did magic. Proper magic. Auric nebula and all?"

"Yes, yes," said Gilbert irritably. "I can perform magic in Hobblebosh's restricted zone. If only I was good at it, I might actually be of some use! But I tried to help, and I only made things worse. It's a habit of mine, apparently. That's why I left. Now I'm just trying to get home."

This conversation needed to end. Gilbert turned away and shut his eyes, hunching his shoulders against the wind.

Thorippela sighed. "Well, if you're just going to sulk with your eyes closed, you may as well get some sleep. I'll take the first watch. And I'm putting out this fire. Hobblebosh sent out dozens of soldiers after what you did, and you're their priority target. You need to stay alert and stop advertising your location with a bloody great beacon of light."

"Fine." Gilbert clenched his jaw. "Do what you want. Good night."

He tried to tune Thorippela out as she extinguished the fire, but then she started scrubbing her arms and muttering about the blue on her skin, which was considerably harder to ignore. One more consequence of

Gilbert's screw-ups. One more person affected by his failure. The sooner he could get out of here, the better.

He didn't remember falling asleep, but the dreams came upon him vividly. He was back in the red mist, facing Hobblebosh, surrounded by the chaos of a burning Earth. His school, crumbling. His house, old and broken. People screaming. And his parents—always his parents—the last to go, cold disappointment clear upon their faces, flickering in the firelight as flames turned their bodies to ash.

He nearly jumped out of his skin when Thorippela woke him up. He was soaked in cold sweat.

"It's your turn to keep a lookout," she said, eyes narrow. "Are you okay?"

"Yeah, I'm fine." Gilbert tried to calm his breathing. He rose to his feet. "You just surprised me, is all. I've got this. Go rest."

Thorippela didn't wait to be asked twice. She was asleep in minutes. True to her word, she'd put out the fire. Gilbert supposed that was wise, though he couldn't help but shiver as he scanned the gloom. He listened, too, straining for any sign of footsteps, but none came.

In time, his thoughts turned to home once again. He wondered how, or if, he would tell his family about this adventure. Would the truth about Earth hurt them? Did they deserve to know, anyway? It probably didn't matter. They'd just dismiss the whole thing as some delusion. And if they didn't dismiss it...well, what would they think of him then? What would they say, knowing all the things he'd messed up and all the people he'd let down?

But there was plenty of time to figure that out. He had to get there first, and that would be hard enough. The only thing he knew for certain—he would need someone skilled in magic, someone able to make a spell that could insert him back into the story. There were tons of wizards in City Boratorus, but Gilbert suspected they all knew Mardulo and Bundersquash. Going that route was a surefire way to end up back in their custody, so he would have to look somewhere else. He could find a town nearby and ask around...or he could just ask Thorippela. She seemed knowledgeable enough.

When dawn rolled around, he did just that.

She gaped at him. "Seriously?! You want to know where to find some good wizards, after you just abandoned *Mardulo Vot Ponterous the Brilliant* and *Bundersquash Borum Balbagoose the Studious* in a meadow?!"

"I need someone else."

"If you want the best, it's them."

"It doesn't have to be the *best*, just someone good."

"Go back to City Boratorus and knock on a door. The odds are in your favor."

"I'm not going back there. Isn't there somewhere else?"

She stared, utterly exasperated. "There's a reason people call it the *Wizard's City*, Gigglebrit."

"It can't be the only place with wizards!"

"What do you have against it?"

"There are...memories there. And it's too close to Mardulo and Bundersquash. I don't want to be there when they get back."

She rolled her eyes. "Of course. How could I forget? Your melodrama."

"It's not *melodrama*. They wouldn't..." Gilbert stopped, exhaled. "I don't think they'd support my plans. Lady Ufferbub called them *silly*."

"I don't know what to tell you. Why do you need a wizard, anyway?"

"To send me back to Earth."

"Earth?" She paused. "You mean Evreth?"

"No!" Gilbert shouted. "Look, it's complicated, okay? I don't want to get into it."

"Then I can't help you."

"I just...there must be *somewhere* else I could find a person who can do magic."

Thorippela took a deep breath. "If you really don't want to go to City Boratorus—and let me remind you, they call it the *Wizard's City*—then you don't have a lot of options. There are the usual lunatics out in the wild, hidden up in the mountains or down in the forests and so on, but they tend to keep to themselves. They can be untrustworthy too. Town Lunkwargle isn't far, but that's mostly just gryphon-headed Luddites. There's one magic shop in the entire town, and it barely stays in business. That leaves you with Town Agol unless you're willing to travel all the way to a port city."

"Does Town Agol have wizards?"

"A few. Not many. I wouldn't go there if I could help it. They're not the friendliest bunch."

"But they have wizards?"

"Yes," she said grudgingly. "They have wizards."

"Town Agol it is then. Where is it?"

She looked at him, concerned. "On the shore of Lake Agolika. Narrowsplatter and splatterback from City Boratorus. From here…" She squinted at the surroundings, then pointed southwest. "That way. Toward the Green Mountains."

"You don't have a map by any chance, do you?" asked Gilbert.

Thorippela hesitated. "Maybe it's best if I just show you the way."

Gilbert wasn't sure how to take that. "How far is it?"

"A few days."

"What about your other hippalectryons? The ones we…uh…*took* in Town Forbik. Don't you want those back?"

"They'll turn up, I'm sure."

"It's a long way for you to go just to help me…"

"We've already had this conversation, Gilbert. I'm sticking around for a little while. Remember?"

"Yes. And frankly, I still think it's very suspicious of you."

"Well, tough. With Hobblebosh's soldiers invading from the north, I need to go splatterback. Agol is basically on the way. Besides, you clearly have no idea how to take care of that beautiful hippalectryon of yours, and I can't stand by while a crime like that is taking place."

Lampellion stood beside Gilbert proudly, but Gilbert had to admit, he probably had been mistreating the poor creature.

He took one tight breath. "Fine," he said. "Thank you."

Thorippela led the way. She seemed comfortable navigating the landscape and made continual adjustments to their course, though Gilbert couldn't help but notice they were still mostly following the path back to City Boratorus. He decided to hold his tongue—at least for now. City Boratorus was south. Town Agol was southwest. It made sense that the route would be similar, though he kept track, just in case.

An hour or two into the trip, Thorippela stopped. "I need to check something," she said. "You go ahead."

Gilbert eyed her dubiously. He moved ahead slightly but stopped and turned back to see what she was doing. Thorippela took no notice. She rummaged through her satchel and grabbed a lidded, coin-shaped container filled with cloudy water. A blade of grass floated feebly on its surface.

"Uck." She scowled, shaking it around in frustration. "Barely lasts an hour, these days," she grumbled to herself.

She dismounted, poured the container's contents onto the dirt, then replenished it using water from her canteen and a new blade of grass, freshly picked from the meadow. She added a pinch of purple dust from a packet inside her hippalectryon's saddle, then took note as the grass swung into position, pointing north, by Gilbert's guess. The water glowed faintly purple.

"So that's how you make a compass around here?" Gilbert asked, coming closer.

"What?" Thorippela looked up, startled. "Oh, um...yes. Sort of." She narrowed her eyes. "Anyway, come on, we'd best keep moving. We may want to walk for a bit. The hippalectryons need rest."

Reluctantly, Gilbert agreed. He didn't like to slow down, but Lampellion looked happy for the break. He seemed to be enjoying the company of Thorippela's hippalectryon. They pranced and frolicked together while Gilbert and Thorippela trudged along.

Their route grew more complex as they went. Turn after turn, they skirted hills and crossed over others; they cut through fields of flowers and maneuvered around swaths of tall grass. More than once, Gilbert lost sight of Thorippela as she hurried off in one direction or another, though she never went too far. She checked her compass regularly but rarely changed course because of it.

"Are you sure we're going the right way?" Gilbert asked as evening rolled in. "It still seems an awful lot like we're heading toward City Boratorus."

Thorippela scowled at him. "Do you want my help or not?"

"You're the one that insists on taking me there yourself. Maybe if you showed me a map, I would understand. I just want to know where we're going."

"We're going to Town Agol, like you asked."

"Sure, it's just..." Gilbert peered at the horizon, the sun setting in the west. He wanted to trust Thorippela, he really did, but they'd been walking south—directly south—almost all day. "I thought you said it was southwest."

"Look, if I had a map, I'd show you," said Thorippela impatiently. "But I don't. I've got what's in my head. If that's not good enough, you can find your own way there."

Gilbert took a deep breath. Like it or not, Thorippela was his best chance. She took his silence for the resigned acceptance that it was and resumed hiking—south, though with a begrudging glance back at Gilbert, she adjusted slightly to the west.

In the twilight, they stumbled upon what must have, at one point, been a small stone cottage, but only a ruin of chest-high walls remained alongside a vibrant ecosystem of weeds.

"We should rest," said Thorippela. "My legs are killing me."

Gilbert agreed. He cleared a space at the corner between two rundown walls while Thorippela tended to the hippalectryons.

"Do you think we can ride tomorrow?" asked Gilbert. On foot, they hadn't made as much progress as he'd have liked.

"Maybe," said Thorippela. "But hippalectryons can't run forever. Frankly, I'm impressed yours is still standing."

Lampellion nuzzled her as she handed him some oats from her bag.

"He's a good hippalectryon," said Gilbert. He stood up to stroke Lampellion's mane, then saw it—a glimpse of green and yellow on the northwest horizon, just visible through the fading light. His breath caught.

"Thorippela!" he whispered harshly, ducking behind one of the ruined walls. "Look!"

Thorippela turned, then dropped to the ground beside Gilbert.

"Are those Hobblebosh's soldiers?" asked Gilbert.

"Possibly," said Thorippela. "It looks like an encampment of some kind."

"Should we run?"

"No. We should see what they're up to."

Gilbert's stomach dropped. "You can't be serious? You said they were looking for me!"

"What if they've got prisoners?"

"Do you think that's likely?"

"No, but it's possible."

"I don't think—"

"Oh, *come on*. After all your talk about how you screwed everything up, why won't you actually help me fix some of it?! We should take them out."

"Take them out?" Gilbert gawked at her. "No! The last time I tried to fix things, I made them worse."

"Well, this time, don't."

"That's *obviously* easier said than done," Gilbert protested.

"Not really. Just do what I do."

"It's a bad idea."

"Shut up. It's a great idea. I'm doing it."

She crouched low and started toward the camp before Gilbert had a chance to respond. Grumbling, he followed.

"We check for prisoners," he said. "That's it."

They approached, hunched and uncomfortable, in the rapidly darkening night, then nestled themselves behind some bushes that weren't quite as tall as Gilbert wished.

"What can you see?" he asked.

"Not much," Thorippela whispered. "There's a tent—green and yellow, definitely Hobblebosh's colors. But there aren't many people. They're probably asleep."

"Is there a lookout?"

"I think...yes. On the other side. See?" She pointed at three armored figures huddled around a fire, deep in conversation. None of them had helmets on, Gilbert noticed. Their skin was blue.

"They're not looking at us," said Thorippela. "Quick, let's see what we can find."

Catlike, she approached the tent and put an ear to the fabric. "Just snoring."

"Good." Gilbert tried to tug her away. "And I don't see any prisoners, so let's go."

Thorippela checked her water compass again. She looked conflicted. "Don't you want to cause a little mayhem, first? Just a bit? The fewer Hobblebosh soldiers around, the better, right?"

"Not if it gets us killed."

"Yeah, well, it probably won't, so that's fine." She removed a packet of bright red and orange dust from her pocket.

Gilbert eyed it nervously. "You know, I though lorilell dust was hard to get."

"It can be," said Thorippela. "But not if you know the right people. Now stand back. I'm going to light their tent on fire."

"What?! Have you lost your mind?" Gilbert lurched for the packet, but Thorippela dodged out of his reach and tossed it directly toward the tent.

Gilbert suppressed a disbelieving shout as the packet flew through the air, tiny sparks scattering in its wake. On contact, the dust burst and popped, igniting the tent's fabric.

"There we are," said Thorippela, grinning wildly as flames licked the tent. "Now, run!"

Before Gilbert had time to process what was happening, they were dashing madly back to the ruined stone hut. He was completely out of breath when they arrived. He put his hands on his knees and tried to keep himself from fainting. Looking back at the camp, he saw a thick plume of smoke rising where the tent had been, silhouetted against a roaring orange flame. Shouts rang out all around.

"Are you insane?!" Gilbert grabbed Thorippela by the arm. "You are, aren't you? You're *actually* insane."

"I'm helping rid the world of Hobblebosh!" she said, shaking free of his grip. "People need to stand up to him. Isn't that what you and your friends have been doing all along? I'm just doing my part."

"That is not *doing your part*," Gilbert spat, pointing at the inferno on the horizon. "That's excessive, violent, and reckless."

Thorippela glared at him. "I don't understand you, Gilbert. All of last night and today, I've had to put up with your woe-is-me nonsense. You prattle on about how you failed to stop Hobblebosh and how everything he does from now on is your fault. But then an actual opportunity to help appears, and you want to run and hide! Then you get mad at *me* for doing what needs to be done!"

"I'm mad because this *didn't* need to be done. Mardulo and Bundersquash aren't setting people's camps on fire! They're trying to *reduce* the amount of pain in the world. You just added to it. Not everyone who works for Hobblebosh does so willingly, you know. Some of them might have been coerced. Some are just trying to avoid getting executed for treason."

"Well, I think those soldiers deserved it."

"I can't believe this." Gilbert turned away. "And I was just starting to warm up to you. But of course, that was another mistake. Everything I've done since I got here has been a mistake. I screwed up in Town Forbik. I ruined Mardulo and Bundersquash's relationship. I trusted you. Now look what's happened. More people suffering, *burning*, because I couldn't find my own way to Town Agol."

"Oh, get over yourself!" Thorippela snapped. "Always with the self-pity, always focused inward. '*My* mistakes. *My* screw-ups. *I'm* responsible for everything bad that's ever happened, and you should blame *me* for all of it.' You say Mardulo and Bundersquash are trying to reduce the amount of pain in the world? What about you? You don't care about anyone's actual suffering. You only care that you caused it!"

Gilbert gaped, furious. "You barely even know me!" he shouted. "You have no idea what I care about."

"Then why don't you try to *fix* the problems you claim to have caused instead of standing around bemoaning them?!"

"I am fixing them! I left Mardulo and Bundersquash so they could get on with their work. I removed myself from the equation. *That's* how I'm fixing things, and it's a hell of a lot better than your monstrous plan."

"That doesn't fix anything, Gilbert. That's just running away."

Gilbert balled his fists. "They had a good plan before I showed up. They'll get it done faster and better without me. Leaving is the right thing to do, so I'm doing it!"

"Really? Because it sounds like you're forcing them to clean up a mess *you* made while you run off back home! If you call that a success, it's a bloody selfish one."

Gilbert could hear his heart thumping. His face burned with anger. "You don't understand. You couldn't understand. Unless you've found yourself responsible for the suffering of thousands of people, I don't think—"

"Shut up." Thorippela raised a hand.

"No! I'm telling you—"

"Shut up!" Thorippela tackled him to the ground. "Someone is coming."

Dread descended on Gilbert like a shadow. They had been shouting, making so much noise...

"It came from over there," said a voice Gilbert didn't recognize.

"See anyone?" came a second voice. They were speaking quietly. Gilbert had to strain to hear them.

"Not yet, but the tracks lead this way."

Gilbert and Thorippela stared at one another in silence. The argument burned hot in his mind, but he forced himself to shelve it for the time being. There were more pressing matters at hand—like not dying. Their only hope was the darkness. Perhaps they could sneak away without being seen.

Slowly, with the utmost care to keep quiet, Thorippela reached inside her pocket and removed her water compass.

"Really? Now?" Gilbert hissed. "We need to leave."

"Yes, I know, but I have to check which way…"

Gilbert shuffled out from underneath her. "Anywhere!" he whispered. "Just away from here. Where are the hippalectryons?"

"I don't know," she said, tapping the side of her compass. She groaned. "I think it needs to be refreshed."

"Seriously, we do not have time for this." Gilbert peeked over the wall. A pair of Hobblebosh's soldiers combed the nearby grasses, their armor caked in ash.

"I think I see something over there," said one of them, just as Gilbert ducked out of sight. "Seems like a ruin of some kind. I'll take a look."

Gilbert jabbed Thorippela. She was still adding dust to her compass.

"We need to run," he said. "Your compass can wait."

Reluctantly, Thorippela stuffed it away. "Fine. How many are out there?"

"I saw two, but—"

"Someone's here!" shouted a soldier. "I see hippalectryons!"

Panic seized Gilbert. He had no weapons, no wizards to help him fight, and no plan. He was caught, defenseless, and the soldiers had just found Lampellion—his only chance at escape.

He stood up, too focused on finding Lampellion to worry about the risks. The hippalectryon was just a short distance away, already alert and aware of the danger.

Gilbert quickly whipped off his gloves, rubbed his palms together, and shouted, "BLURGLE FLURGLE BLAAGH!" hoping the nondeterministic behavior would cause something dramatic and distracting to happen.

His aura faded into a ruined wall. The stones shook, shattered, and turned into a muddy puddle.

But the shouting, if nothing else, had caught Lampellion's attention. The hippalectryon came running. Thorippela's kept pace behind him.

Unfortunately, the soldiers had also heard. One of them removed a horn from his belt and blew—the sound echoing across the meadows, boisterous and clear. Soon, more soldiers were on their way, emerging in groups from the night's mottled darkness.

Gilbert quickly donned his gloves again and tried to swing onto Lampellion's back without halting the hippalectryon's gallop—but he lost his grip and fell face-first into the muddy puddle he had just created. It was a lucky mistake. As he fell, an arrow whizzed through the air above his head, ruffling his hair. Thorippela helped him up, allowing just enough time to convey, with a glance, her disbelief at Gilbert's own stupidity. Then she hopped onto her own hippalectryon and took off. Gilbert recomposed himself at record speed, mounted, and followed close behind.

They raced through the grass and flowers, keeping as low as possible while arrows sliced the air. When Gilbert risked a look behind, he saw a dozen or more soldiers chasing them on hippalectryons. Thankfully, only a few had bows, and they didn't have many arrows. Still, one of those arrows came flying toward Gilbert, and though Lampellion shifted to the right, it wasn't enough. The arrow sliced through Gilbert's leg in a scarlet blur of pain.

Gilbert bit his lip to keep from crying out. The shock was worse than the actual damage. There was a red gash on the side of his calf, just above his ankle. His pants were torn, and the loose fabric clung to his skin, sticky with blood. Gilbert focused on his breathing. It could have been worse. This was just a scrape, a scratch. He'd been lucky.

He lowered himself against Lampellion and clung to the hippalectryon's neck, trying to keep the weight off his leg. It was all he could do to remain mounted.

Lampellion swerved with excellent unpredictability, loosely trailing Thorippela's hippalectryon as it zigged and zagged some distance ahead. The rush of grasses whipped at Gilbert's ankles, and the gash on his leg oozed, sending screeches of pain every time he shifted his weight. His face and hair were wet from the puddle he'd fallen into earlier.

Arrows zipped through the air, surrounding him on all sides, one mad flurry of terror—but slowly, dreadfully slowly, the guards ran out of ammunition, and the blood on Gilbert's leg dried, sticking to his skin. Soldiers' shouts rose and fell through the hours until they, too, dwindled. When Gilbert finally found the confidence to rise up from his hunched position and look around, the soldiers had given up pursuit entirely.

It was nearer morning than he'd expected. Dawn highlighted the eastern horizon as Lampellion charged west. Thorippela rode just ahead.

"Wait up!" Gilbert called. "I need to clean a cut on my leg."

He dismounted, mostly on purpose, and collapsed into the grass.

"I cannot believe," said Thorippela when she arrived, "that you would call *me* reckless, then go off and cast a nonsense spell like that! Not even a little direction to it. Literally anything could have happened. You ought to thank luck we're still alive!"

"Yes, okay," said Gilbert. "It was stupid. I learned my lesson. Now, can you please give me your water?"

Thorippela's face softened as she handed him the canteen. "Is it bad?"

"Just dirty...do you have any bandages?"

"Not really," said Thorippela. "Don't you have something to help with injuries like this? You didn't bring anything with you?"

"We lost all our supplies in Town Forbik."

Carefully, Gilbert unstuck the fabric from his cut, grimacing as it pulled at the wound. Then he rinsed it with water and looked for something to serve as a makeshift bandage. His clothes were filthy but ultimately the best he could think of. He tore his shirt—more than he would've liked—and tied it tight against his calf.

"You should rest," said Thorippela.

"I'm fine. I don't think it hit muscle or anything. I just need to make sure it doesn't get infected."

"Can you even walk? Can you ride?"

"I made it this far, didn't I?"

"Barely, from the look of you."

Gilbert sighed. "It doesn't matter. The soldiers could come back any minute. I had to clean the wound, but we can't stay for long."

"They turned back ages ago. I expect they won't stray too far from City Boratorus."

"We passed the city?"

"We came close, but we've been heading in the opposite direction for hours. You didn't see it?"

"I wasn't really looking..." Gilbert rubbed his temples. He'd barely felt time pass during their flight. "How far have we come?"

"I think we're mostly narrowsplatter of the city now, but splatterback too. We're well on our way to Town Agol." She shook her head. "You need to rest, and I won't take no for an answer. I have to fix this bloody wayfinder anyway."

From how she clenched the compass-like device, it seemed she'd rather shatter it than fix it, but she replenished the water anyway, then added more dust and waited for the grass needle to turn.

When she finished, she looked back at Gilbert.

"What?" she asked.

Gilbert eyed her doubtfully. "I still don't know if I should be traveling with you..."

"Look, I'm sorry about your leg, and I'm sorry I don't have anything to heal it, but I'm not sure what you want from me."

"Those soldiers only found us because *you* lit their camp on fire. It was cruel, and if you had just kept to yourself, this wouldn't have happened."

"Well, at least you're not blaming yourself anymore," said Thorippela dryly.

Gilbert frowned at her.

"Okay, fine," she said. "Maybe you're right. But come on, we just escaped a horde of angry soldiers on hippalectryon back, and we've inconvenienced more than a few of Hobblebosh's forces. That's got to count for something, right?"

"Not much."

Thorippela looked ready to argue but stopped herself. Her expression dropped. "I admit, I may have been too harsh, but honestly, I thought that was the kind of thing you were doing with Mardulo Vot Ponterous the Brilliant and Bundersquash Borum Balbagoose the Studious—taking risks, stopping Hobblebosh, mad flights from danger. I thought we could do some good, and I could help you get back on your feet in the process."

Gilbert pointed at his injured leg. "Didn't work so well, did it?"

"I meant figuratively," she said. "But yes, I get your point. I screwed up. I'm not as ready as I thought I was. But I can still help."

"Help me get to Town Agol or help stop Hobblebosh? Because I'm starting to think you didn't get the message."

"I told you, I think you should stop Hobblebosh."

"Was that before or after you called me selfish and cowardly?"

"I stand by what I said." Thorippela crossed her arms. "You *should* help, but so far, you've done nothing but run away from your problems."

"How many times do I have to tell you? I left because—"

"Because you think they'll be better off without you. I know. I heard it the first fifty times. But do they actually agree with you?"

"They're...too polite to admit it." Gilbert slouched. He didn't want to get into another shouting match. "I've caused them enough pain as it is," he said quietly, picking at the grass. "Bundersquash lost an arm in Town Forbik and a pet he loved, all because he trusted me and I failed. Mardulo and I tried to heal his arm, but that only made things worse. Now they're fighting, and there's nothing I can do. I just came into their lives and wrecked things..."

"So, you caused them pain." Thorippela waited until Gilbert looked up at her. "You caused them pain, and now you're just going to leave them with it?"

Gilbert looked away, eyes watering. His throat was dry. His arms were sore. His muscles burned all over. His leg throbbed with pain, and his head swam dizzily—half from blood loss, half from sleep deprivation. He couldn't think through the thickening fog of exhaustion.

Thorippela took a breath and continued more gently. "It's not too late to change your mind, Gilbert. You can still fix some of these problems. Maybe not Bundersquash's arm or his pet or whatever, but you can keep fighting Hobblebosh. He's the real reason these things are happening, not you."

"And what if I make it worse again?"

"Then at least you tried. It's better than doing nothing. If you want to reduce the amount of suffering in the world—that doesn't happen by running away from it. You have to act. You have to do something. Maybe I went too far burning down that encampment, but at least there are fewer soldiers harassing civilians, because of something we did. And if you fail, fine. Learn from it. Don't repeat the same mistake. Get better, then get back to it."

"Even if I wanted to, I'm useless here. I'm bad at magic. I can't fight. I don't even know how to navigate. I don't have *any* useful skills unless you need someone to throw biology facts or physics equations at him. I just don't belong here."

"No one *belongs* anywhere, Gilbert. You *are* here, right now, whether you want to be or not, and you have an opportunity to do some good. Seize it. I don't know what will be helpful, but I'm sure you can think of something. If throwing equations at Hobblebosh will do the trick, then by all means, throw them. If not, find something else. The point is, you'll be there, ready to do whatever is necessary, whenever it's necessary."

"And what about my home? I can't just abandon it. My family is there. My whole life is there. Everything I care about is *there*!"

"Clearly, that's not true. A lot of what you care about is there, sure, but not everything. I know for a fact you care about Mardulo Vot Ponterous the Brilliant and Bundersquash Borum Balbagoose the Studious, and those two librarians, and all those people in Town Forbik. Otherwise, you wouldn't go on about them so bloody much."

"It's not the same." Gilbert put his head in his hands. "Everything here is just...alien. I go to the *doctor* when I get an injury, I don't rinse it with water from a canteen then improvise a bandage from my shirt. I'm used to ordering pizzas, not generating sandwiches. I use cars, not hippalectryons; phones, not maps and compasses. I'm used to coming home after a long day at school, dropping my backpack in the hallway, sitting on the couch, and reading a book while my parents ramble on about work or music or travel...but here, I have none of that. I don't even have my old clothes. I threw them away when I arrived." He took a deep breath. "This whole place is completely different. The money doesn't make sense. Half the buildings are physically impossible. Mardulo and Bundersquash have a podium that makes animal noises, for god's sake, and a semisentient playset in their spare room. How could this ever be home for me?"

Thorippela blinked at him. "A semisentient playset?"

"Yes! Not to mention a plant that turned Bundersquash into a giant fancy rabbit and a man who crawled out of their mirror."

"Well, they're wizards. What did you expect? It doesn't sound much stranger than whatever a car or a phone is."

"It's strange *to me*. That's my point. I miss *my* world. My life. My home. I miss my family, and I want to be with them again. As nice as everyone is here, as exciting as it was to see it, it's not the same."

"I get that this is difficult for you, Gilbert, but you can always go home later. Is Hobblebosh even a threat there? Is your family in immediate danger?"

"I...I don't know. Probably not," Gilbert admitted.

"Well, there are people *here* who *are* in immediate danger, and you are in a position to help them. Your family will still be there when we're done."

Gilbert's stomach twisted. He could see where this conversation was going, closing around him like a trap.

"I can't just put them aside like that!" he said.

Thorippela suppressed her agitation with a breath. "Yes, Gilbert, you can. Picture this. You and your beloved family are on a vacation when Hobblebosh swoops in and occupies whatever town you happen to be visiting. Now, assuming you survive the initial invasion, you're suddenly at his mercy, watching every word you say, trying desperately not to draw attention to yourselves, hoping he doesn't execute you because you looked at him funny or said the wrong thing at the wrong time...those are the families you should be worried about, not your own."

With a pang, Gilbert thought of the Norwallises from Collywobbles Bridge. They'd been on their way to visit family. Instead, they were bruised, beaten, and carried away by thugs. Where were they now? Sold to Hobblebosh? Serving as slaves in the forest mines? How many more were out there, suffering like them?

His chest tightened. He didn't want Thorippela to be right, but the trap had closed. Because she *was* right. Earth would still be there when he was done. Right now, he was here, and people were suffering. Whether he liked it or not, he had a duty to help.

To his surprise, it made him angry. Angry at the situation. Angry at Mardulo and Bundersquash for summoning him here in the first place. Angry at Thorippela for pressing the issue. And angry at himself, because fighting Hobblebosh probably *was* the right thing to do, but he still didn't *want* to do it. He longed to see his family again, to let Mardulo and Bundersquash save the Norwallises of the world, and to leave it all behind. He didn't want to do the right thing. He wanted to go home.

Thorippela sat quietly, waiting.

"I just...I miss them," Gilbert managed eventually. "But I get it. I don't like it, but I get it. I'll help. Can I please just get some sleep first? My head hurts, and my leg is killing me. You said it yourself, I need rest."

Thorippela deflated but didn't push him. "All right," she said. "I'll keep watch. Just...take it easy."

Gilbert nodded and tried to clear his head as he lay down in the grass. He turned so Thorippela couldn't see his face, then allowed himself a few silent tears before forcing his eyes shut and steadying his breathing.

Red mist flared around him. Flames scorched the Earth. His parents stared—cold, detached, disappointed—at the disheveled mess that was Gilbert. Gilbert looked up at them, pleading.

Please. Please help. I don't know what to do. I want to go home. I...

But they burned away before he could finish.

Gilbert leaped in after them.

The world changed. The people and places looked different, unusual. The red mist turned blue. The fire flared hotter than ever. Thousands of people cried out, screaming horror into the streets. Arrows flew overhead. Somewhere in that mist, just for a moment, Gilbert thought he heard Mardulo and Bundersquash.

"Great bloody mess, isn't he?"

Gilbert clawed at the dirt behind him, scrabbling backward to safety.

"Who? What? Mardulo, you can't—" Slowly the world came back into focus. He'd been dreaming. He was still in the meadow. His pulse was racing. Thorippela was supposed to be keeping watch...

So why was Mardulo here?

"Good evening," Thorippela popped up from behind the elderly wizard. "Surprise!"

"Thorippela?" Gilbert rubbed his eyes. "How did...? How are...? They found us?"

Behind Mardulo, he could see Bundersquash, Toddleposter, and Lady Ufferbub staring.

"Hardly," said Mardulo. "Your new friend led us to you! We'd never have managed without her."

Gilbert couldn't think straight. "How long was I asleep?"

"Here, let me talk to him," said Thorippela.

"As you wish." Mardulo raised his hands and backed away.

"This doesn't make any sense," said Gilbert to Thorippela. "It can't have been *that* long."

"You said you wanted to help again, so why wait?" Thorippela grinned. "Honestly, I think it's in your best interest. Though I admit, they're not all *thrilled* that you left...but I'll let you sort that out."

Gilbert glanced at the others. None of them looked particularly pleased, but they were trying their best to hide it.

"A little warning would've been nice," said Gilbert. He felt embarrassed, though he didn't quite understand why. "How did you find them, anyway?"

"Oh, that was easy." Thorippela ruffled through her bag and grabbed the water compass. "I used this. It's not a compass, Gilbert. It's a wayfinder. I'm surprised you haven't seen one before. It points to whoever's essence is mixed into the solution. In this case, one of my hippalectryon's. I plucked a few of her feathers before I left her in Town Forbik, then ground those up, mixed them into dust, and that was all I needed—a guide directly to your friends, assuming they stayed with my hippalectryons. I only ever intended to *lend* them to you, I hope you realize."

Gilbert scowled at her. "You're telling me this whole time you said we were going to Town Agol, you were actually checking that thing to make sure we were heading toward Mardulo and Bundersquash?"

"Mostly, I was making sure we didn't stray too far away from them." She scratched her neck. "I was hoping, after giving you some room to breathe, I might convince you to join them again. They've been searching for you ever since you ran off, you know. Talk about being a distraction. At least now they can focus on important work."

Gilbert frowned. "I should've known," he muttered, then stood and limped painfully over to the wizards and librarians.

"You were supposed to go back to stopping Hobblebosh," he said.

"We could not simply leave you to die, Gigglebrit," said Lady Ufferbub.

"Gilbert. My name is Gilbert."

"Ah, yes. Thorippela mentioned that."

"She was surprisingly stubborn on the matter," added Mardulo.

"And yet, you refuse to listen." Thorippela walked to Gilbert's side.

"Gilbert. Gigglebrit. Does it really matter?" asked Mardulo.

"Yes!" said Gilbert. "It's my *name*. It's an Earthen name, and it's important to me. Honestly, the fact that you can't get it right is a little messed up."

"But you said it yourself," said Lady Ufferbub. "Gilbert is an Earthen name. Here, you are Gigglebrit."

Gilbert's anger flared. "Don't even get me started on you, Lady Ufferbub. You read *A World of Souls*. You *must* have known! Yet this whole time, you said nothing."

"I thought a new name would be good for you. Something to help you acclimate. We did it for Toddleposter."

"Well, I'm not Toddleposter."

"Clearly." Lady Ufferbub rolled her eyes. "He is much more sensible. Why do you insist on reverting?"

"It's not a reversion! It's who I am."

"You decide who you are, Gigglebrit. You are deciding to revert."

Toddleposter stepped between them. "I think we should listen to Gilbert. A new name helped me, yes, but that does not mean it will do the same for him. If he wishes to be Gilbert, that's his choice."

Mardulo shrugged. "You seemed perfectly content with Gigglebrit before," he said defensively.

"I know," Gilbert admitted. "But I was wrong."

Lady Ufferbub's scowl deepened. "If you wish to be called Gilbert, so be it. I shall call you Gilbert. But remember, Earth is *fictional*."

Thorippela raised her eyebrows.

"Fiction or not," said Gilbert, "it's my home."

"It *was* your home." Lady Ufferbub crossed her arms. "But none of this changes just how foolish it was for you to run off like that."

"I already told you. I didn't want to hold you back."

"Oh, you are the least of our worries," said Mardulo. "At least you weren't actively withholding vital information."

"What?" said Gilbert.

Bundersquash groaned. "For goodness' sake, Mardulo, I didn't *actively withhold* anything. You should be grateful I found a way forward! And it's far better than any of the plans you had."

"It *is* my plan, Bundersquash! You just adapted it, and now you want to take all the credit."

"It's not a question of credit. It's a matter of doing what needs to be done."

Gilbert turned to Toddleposter. "I take it they're still not getting on?" he asked.

Toddleposter looked weary. "Worse than ever. I suspect we'd have found you ages ago, if those two could agree on anything. But for every turn one of them took, the other argued for the opposite."

Gilbert sighed. "I'm sorry."

"Don't blame yourself. This fight has been building up for years. Our need to find you was about the only thing they could agree on."

"Only because they feel guilty about summoning me."

"Because they like you, Gilbert. You studied well with them. You always did your best, and you didn't complain, even after learning the truth about Earth. You saved Bundersquash's life on Collywobbles Bridge, and you did everything you could in Town Forbik, despite the odds. You were quick. You were brave. And most of all, you were kind."

"And then I ran away." The blood rose in Gilbert's cheeks.

Toddleposter smiled gently. "You're back now. That's what matters. It's good to see you. Will you help us finish what we started?"

"I'm not sure I can be much help. Evidently, I'm terrible at magic."

"So am I." Toddleposter laughed. "I haven't practiced since I was Bundersquash. But we can still help. It never hurts to have a spare pair of hands—especially now, with Bundersquash in his condition. At the very least, you can help me and Lady Ufferbub keep the peace." He looked at Mardulo and Bundersquash, still bickering in the background. "We could use you."

"What's the plan, anyway? Still going to summon the chosen one?"

"No, we've changed course." Toddleposter pulled Gilbert aside and lowered his voice. "When you cast the spell in Town Forbik, Bundersquash grabbed some of Hobblebosh's hair. Do you remember?"

"Yes."

"Apparently, he managed to pocket a few spare strands in the fight. Just a couple, but we think it might be enough...with Hobblebosh's essence in advance, we can use the same trapping technique as before, but simplify it dramatically. Mardulo thinks he could reduce the spell into something basic enough for lorilell dust, like your healing powder. We can prepare it in advance, then use that to trap him."

A flicker of hope sparked inside Gilbert. It was an actual plan, and it didn't sound totally impossible.

"It's just a theory," said Toddleposter. "We don't have the supplies to do it here. The meadows have served us well, but even they have their limits."

"So, back to City Boratorus?"

Toddleposter shifted uneasily. "That *was* the plan."

"Until a foolish young boy ran off, forcing us to stray too far narrows-platter and waste three days searching for him." Lady Ufferbub approached from behind.

A knot of frustration formed in Gilbert's stomach. "I didn't *force* you to do anything. You decided to come and get me."

"As if we had any choice in the matter. I told you, we could not leave you to die."

"I wouldn't have died."

She looked pointedly at his leg. "You were shot by an arrow."

"Scratched," said Gilbert, then looked down. The wound was already bleeding through his makeshift bandage.

Lady Ufferbub softened slightly. "Go see Mardulo. He will heal it for you in a heartbeat."

Sure enough, mere minutes after Gilbert had extracted Mardulo from his argument with Bundersquash, the elderly wizard cast a spell, and the cut on Gilbert's leg was fixed. Only a thin pale scar remained, the pain reduced to nothing more than a tingle.

Mardulo leaned in and spoke quietly, grinning. "Bundersquash will tell you the scar is unnecessary, but I think it looks good. What's the point of going on an adventure like this if you don't come away with—"

Then Bundersquash walked up. "Honestly, Mardulo. A scar?"

Gilbert laughed. "It's good to see you again, both of you." He rolled down the torn leg of his pants. "I hear you have a new plan?"

Mardulo scowled. "Yes. We would've had it sooner if Bundersquash had bothered to tell us about the hair *before* we split up."

Bundersquash turned to Gilbert. "I'm sorry I didn't mention it sooner. With my arm and then hitting my head when I fell from the hippalectryon, it all just—"

Gilbert raised a hand. "It's fine, Bundersquash. I understand."

"*You* might," said Mardulo, "but I don't. I mean, honestly? The all-important detail that guides our path forward? It's not the kind of thing you just *forget* because you received an injury or two."

"An injury or two?!" Bundersquash rounded on Mardulo. "I seem to recall you *lighting my arm on fire.*"

"I was trying to help!"

"Not this again," Toddleposter interrupted, looking haggard. "Quiet, both of you. Rattling through the same argument over and over isn't going to help anyone. Mardulo, give Gilbert some food. Bundersquash, see to the hippalectryons. Thorippela has agreed to let us borrow them for a while longer. We'll head out first thing tomorrow morning."

"But if we're not going to City Boratorus," asked Gilbert, "where are we going?"

"Town Agol," said Toddleposter, surprised Gilbert had to ask.

"But...I thought...you need to stop Hobblebosh."

"We *are* stopping Hobblebosh. Town Agol is just...the best place to do so."

"Toddleposter is putting it kindly," said Lady Ufferbub. "City Boratorus would have been undeniably preferable—three days ago." She peered at Gilbert over her spectacles. "But as it stands, more of Hobblebosh's forces are descending every day. If we had made it to City Boratorus *on time*, we may have had a chance to complete our work before they arrived, but now we have lost our head start, and the city is the first place they will look for us. So, we are pressed to go elsewhere until we can finish our preparations.

Town Agol is closest, now that we have come so far to find you, but they do not take kindly to strangers. Let us hope they look favorably upon our mission, or we really will be in trouble."

Interlude: Tree and the Seeds of Doubt

King Hobblebosh listened eagerly to all Tree knew about Gilbert, then immediately put plans into motion. For their loyalty, Tree was promoted. They now held command over all the trees they'd recruited.

But there was still work to be done in Town Forbik—failures that needed addressing, in light of the attempted assassination.

Two people under Hobblebosh's employ—a large one and a former wizard—had allowed Gilbert into Town Forbik, four guards had supplied him and his party with disguises, then another guard had let him through the palace gates. Several had failed to act with adequate forcefulness during the confrontation, and some had been unable to catch Gilbert as he fled.

They were traitors, all of them—disgraceful and dishonored. Justice demanded payment.

The king called a public gathering in the town center, determined to make an example of these failures. He insisted that Tree, in their new position, be present for the occasion.

Tree stood upon a stage among several other generals, not far from King Hobblebosh himself. Much to Tree's discomfort, a crowd of humans had gathered for the occasion, but Tree reminded themselves that these people knew to follow Hobblebosh's doctrine. As long as Tree stayed with the king, they were safe.

Across the way, the traitors came into view, their hands and feet bound with rope. Even from this distance, Tree could feel the shame emanating from them. That alone was enough to soften Tree's heart. But no, Tree reminded themselves, these were traitors. Humans that had betrayed their king. It was right that they should be punished.

The traitors marched solemnly through the jeering crowd while citizens bombarded them with rotten, stinking fruit—failed fruit for failed people, Hobblebosh had said—until at last, they climbed upon the stage and formed a line. The king announced each of their names in turn, and each of their families' also. They were stripped of their ranks and forced to beg for forgiveness.

Had that been the extent of their punishment, Tree could have looked the other way, trusting in King Hobblebosh's wisdom. It was harsh—cruel, even—but perhaps such displays were necessary if the king wished to maintain order.

But that was not the extent of the punishment.

Hobblebosh walked to one end of the line and bade the human there kneel. Despite her struggles and pleas, he forced her head upon a wooden block. Her hands and feet were bound. There was little she could do.

Tree sensed a tension in the air. Every human in attendance trembled, none more than the woman herself. In that moment, Tree felt her terror—a terror they recognized—sharp, cold, and deadly. A life in danger, with no hope of escape.

A man in black appeared carrying the same heavy axe Hobblebosh had placed upon Tree's bark the day before. Without so much as a pause, he raised it, then swung.

The crowd's gasp did little to mask the horrible noise of a living thing dying.

Tree recoiled. Here was their master, one they had sworn to follow, who had promised to stop the humans from hewing trees, doing exactly the same to others.

One by one, King Hobblebosh forced the traitors to kneel with their heads upon the block. But he did not kill them all. Some, he spared, seemingly at random, with a silent signal to the executioner that the stroke should miss its mark. Fifteen traitors entered the stage. Five walked away, disgraced and trembling but alive. The rest were carried, lifeless, to their families, that they might receive a burial.

Tree fled as soon as they could. They needed to get away, to think, to understand. But they didn't know where to go. Could Lugbrush help them? Probably not. The *yes* and *no* branches certainly wouldn't be sufficient. Tree needed someone they could talk to properly. Someone they could trust.

They needed a friend.

Their first thought was Dogwood the Wind-Dancer, but they were still rooted back in City Boratorus. Then Tree thought of Old Oak—the first in the forest to speak with them, the first to trust them, the first to embrace their freedom and change. Tree and Old Oak had spoken easily on the trip home, but always of lighter things—of the sun and the breeze, of critters and birds. This was different. Heavy. But Tree didn't have many other options, and they trusted Old Oak, so they rushed to the northern end of town, where the oak had planted themselves apart from the rest of the forest.

"Old Oak," Tree said desperately. "I need help. I don't know where else to go. King Hobblebosh has done something awful. The lime has become the lumberjack! I witnessed it firsthand!"

"Tree, my friend, slow down." A tremor ran through Old Oak's trunk and leaves. "I am happy to help, but there is too much panic in the air. I cannot make sense of your words."

The day's horrors buzzed around Tree like a nest of angry hornets, but they tried to collect themselves. "King Hobblebosh the Juicy," they said. "He executed almost all the traitor guards. It was horrible. Truly horrible.

In those poor souls, I saw the same fear that I once felt myself—the same dread of the axe, the same terrible, hopeless doom. How can I support a king if he puts into this world the very cruelties he claims to eradicate?"

"I am sorry you have had such a shock, Tree." Old Oak did their best to extend calmness into the ground and air, to weave the atmosphere with peace. "But you said it yourself: those humans were traitors. You are innocent, yet the humans tried to destroy you anyway. There is a difference, I think."

"Some difference, yes. They may deserve punishment, but this feels wrong—too much, too far. The humans, seeing this, could fight against Hobblebosh for the very reason we fight with him."

In so much as a tree can sigh, Old Oak sighed. "I have lived a long time, Tree, and I have learned a great many things. As a part of this forest, I have borne witness to wars before. I have heard what it means to fight as Hobblebosh must. I know how dark and dire these conflicts can become. But you, Tree...you have a kind soul. The forest sees it in you. It is one of the reasons so many of us responded to your plea. But it is important to understand that while a kind soul fares well in peace, in times of battle, a sterner hand may serve better, cruel though it seems. Your kindness is something to cherish, Tree, but we must trust in our king."

Tree faltered. "Perhaps you are right, Old Oak. But I do not understand. Why kill those traitors when they regret their failings? Why prescribe death if they are open to righting their wrongs?"

"That, I cannot say. You would have to ask the king. But mind your words, and remember, we swore an oath of loyalty."

Tree drooped. Old Oak was right to be cautious, but Tree could not simply stand by. They had to act. They had to do *something*.

"Thank you, my friend," said Tree. "I shall speak with the king and hope he understands."

Tree went to the throne room that very night and explained their concerns.

For a time, King Hobblebosh simply glared at them, eyes narrow, expression hard. Then: "Do you doubt my decision, Tree? Do you feel these traitors deserved anything better than death, after what they did to this town? After what they did to me?!" He gestured toward the melted throne, the damaged room, his skin.

"Perhaps, a little mercy…" Tree stammered.

"I did not kill them all. *That* was mercy. And more than they deserved."

"But is this not exactly the behavior you seek to end?"

"No, Tree, it is not. Humans are not the same as you and me. They are animals. They are lesser."

"I do not understand."

King Hobblebosh shook his head. "If you sympathize with them, then it is clear you do not understand them. I thought you would, given your background, but evidently, you failed to learn from that experience—a fact I shall keep in mind."

Tree leaned in, embarrassed and scared but determined. "If there is more for me to learn, my king, please, teach me."

King Hobblebosh paused, his anger mastered but not abated. "I do not speak of this often, Tree, nor do I speak of it lightly. But I shall confide in you, in the hopes that you will see reason."

He sat back on his throne and took a breath. "You may find it hard to believe, but when Corregal first cursed me with this human form, I was not the formidable, confident king you see today. I was weak and confused. It was difficult. I had grown accustomed to my life as a lime—the best of my crop, the pride of the farmers. I was luscious, ripe, and juicy. The other limes respected me. They honored and admired me, and I was sure of my place in the world. You see, fruit on a farm is raised to be eaten. That was always my destiny—to fill the mouth of some grasping, gluttonous human, to die horribly as they luxuriated in my succulent, antioxidant-infused flesh. The farmers whispered it to the trees. The trees whispered it to me. It was all I knew, and I was ready—I was *excited*—for this end. Such was the extent of my indoctrination.

"But along came Corregal Dorbus Forp. He is a wizard, and much as the accursed Mardulo Vot Ponterous brought you here, Corregal Dorbus Forp brought me into this form. When he did, everything I knew collapsed around me. My understanding of the world ruptured. Suddenly, I knew sight, scent, sound, touch, and taste, all as the humans know them. As a plant, you sense the world. You know what is there, understand it intuitively. You are connected to it, a deep and natural knowledge. But for humans, it is different. So, so different. Incomplete in many ways, but more vivid. Detached, but visceral. The senses distract more than they inform. They are obnoxious and utterly impossible to ignore. And my body...I had a heartbeat, Tree. I had lungs. I had a mouth and a nose. Saliva and snot. Ears and earwax. Blood. I could feel it all. Each intake of breath. Every drop of spit on my tongue."

Hobblebosh stopped and shuddered. "It does not do to dwell on such things. Suffice to say, I was displeased, and I did not know what I was, except that this was not what I was meant to be.

"Corregal tried to name me Subject L01. I told him I had a name already, that he should call me Obble Dor Hobblebosh, but the wizard refused. To him, I was a pet. He wished only to control me, to parade me as a trophy among his peers. I denied him that. Instead, I fled.

"But where was I to go? Even the need to ask such a question, let alone answer it, was new to me, so I followed the simplest path I could see. It led me to a town called Tobbelypop. There, I found more humans and told them of my plight—that I was a lime, that I was ripe and juicy, that it was my duty to be eaten, that everything had gone awry. And do you know what they did, Tree, in response to my pleas? *They laughed.*"

A glint of anger burned behind his eyes, an old fury, rekindled. Tree shrank back. They could feel the force of that anger from halfway across the room.

"There was no sympathy there," the king continued. "Only ridicule and shame to throw in the face of a lost, beaten fool. In a moment of desperation, I returned to Corregal's miserable hut. There, at least, I knew none would mock me or gawk at my form. Corregal tried to detain me, and for a time, I wondered if that was all that remained for my life. But as I stood in his home and saw his pathetic, sniveling form trying to salvage what was left of his ego, a defiance took root within me. How dare something as lowly as *he* try to command someone as kingly as *me*, Obble Dor Hobblebosh, the finest lime this world has ever seen! So, I grabbed him by the throat and threw him onto the street. I decided then and there to take my vengeance upon these bitter creatures, no matter the cost, and I gave the gibbering wizard a message.

"'You humans are maggoty little things,' I told him. 'I am better than you, superior to you all. I am a being of the lime, and that makes me more. I have come to save this world from the acrid horror of your humanity. So, flee, pathetic creature. Flee now and tell of my coming. King Hobblebosh, Master of the Lands. In my preeminence, I will rule. Warn them if you must. Say what you will, but know that you cannot stop me, and the world will be better for it. Your kind has had its day. Submit, learn your place, and perhaps I shall allow you to remain. But if you resist, you will die. The sun now rises for Obble Dor Hobblebosh. With it, a new era begins: The Age of the Lime Everlasting.'"

Tree shivered as Hobblebosh spoke. The air tingled with knifelike energy. There was magic in those words—and it wasn't the blasting, fire-wielding, flashy kind. It was something deeper, as if the words themselves held life enough to shape the world, fueled by King Hobblebosh's own conviction.

"And that was the beginning of everything," the king continued. "That is how I came to stand here today. I am a lime of my word, after all."

He took a breath. "As I said, Tree. I do not share this story lightly, and I trust that you will not share it either. I tell you only to illustrate the cruel indifference of these human creatures and their scornful nature. In the face of my suffering, they laughed and mocked. And the one who made me human? He sought only to box me up and put me on display, despite my own desires, just as those who summoned you tried to chop you from their tower. But beyond that, Tree, think also on the original lies the humans fed me. Born on a farm, raised to be consumed. I was grown among these falsehoods, trained to follow the human doctrine. I believed it.

"Yet despite Corregal's intentions, this form has expanded my understanding of the world, much as walking has expanded yours. It enabled independent exploration, and as I came to know life fully, I understood the treachery behind my former beliefs. The lies the humans bred into me, the cruelty of their deception. Would you ever hear such lies from a tree, or a fruit, or a plant of any kind? We are, by nature, different. What we do to humans is not the same as what they do to us because we are a better breed. In this war, we pay back old debts, and we will continue to do so until we wipe their stain clean from our world."

Hobblebosh spoke with a fierceness that brokered no argument. Tree could sense his certainty, near tangible, coursing through the atmosphere.

Tree faltered.

Earlier, they had been so sure that Hobblebosh was wrong to execute those traitors. Now conflict rose within them. It was true, a seed of cruelty lived inside the humans Tree had fought, and Tree had never witnessed such a thing in the plants and trees of the world. Did it justify everything Hobblebosh had done? Tree was not as sure as their king. But Hobblebosh had opened up to them, shown them his own vulnerability. The king had trusted Tree completely.

Perhaps, Tree thought, they should afford Hobblebosh that same trust.

"It is possible my reaction was too severe," they said at last. "I found the execution difficult to watch. It reminded me of my own struggles in the tower. But I should not have doubted you."

"Correct." Hobblebosh spoke sternly once more. "I am glad you have seen reason. But I am forced to remind you, Tree, that you are a general in my army, and you must act like one. I need to know that you will follow every command I give, no matter how you feel. Can I trust in that? Or shall I turn to another—someone with firmer will?"

Tree straightened. "You can trust me, my king. I shall not fail you again."

"Very good. Now I must prepare for our departure. Your information regarding this amateur assassin has proven useful, and we are almost ready to move south. Already, I have sent soldiers to scout ahead and prepare for our coming. But there is one final errand I must run before we can depart in full. I leave for City Mez tonight. I expect my armies ready when I return. Your forest is no exception."

"It shall be done," said Tree.

Chapter 17

Breaking and Entering

According to Mardulo, Town Agol was an isolated place, and wealthy. It sat on the edge of Lake Agolika, which boasted several unique species of fish, a plethora of otherwise rare underwater vegetation, and an abundance of valuable ore tucked deep inside its lakebed. What wasn't useful for food or crafting was certainly desirable for spellwork. The town was almost entirely self-sufficient, and on the rare occasion that something could not be obtained from the water or fields nearby, they could easily afford to import it.

Thorippela had agreed to travel with them at least as far as the town, but they made little use of her hippalectryons along the way. It was true, time was in short supply, but the soldiers had given up pursuit, seemingly disinclined to travel so far narrowsplatter, and everyone was sore from days upon days of near-continuous riding. Even Lampellion seemed in need of some well-earned rest.

So they walked, and the days passed, warm and slow. The hippalectryons moved leisurely beside the group, stopping occasionally to munch on the meadow grasses, which Thorippela and Toddleposter supplemented with a mixture of corn and oats.

Gilbert talked little during the journey, but he had come to a decision of sorts. He would help stop Obble Dor Hobblebosh, but afterward, he would ask to return to Earth. Surely, the others could not begrudge him that, even if they thought it was *silly*.

Still, he hadn't said anything yet. They needed to focus on Hobblebosh first.

One of the few conversations he did initiate came halfway through the first day of hiking. Something about Thorippela's story didn't sit right with him, and he was determined to get to the truth of it.

"I just don't understand how you got involved in the first place," he said. "You say you wanted me to rejoin the group, but how did you even know I'd left?"

She thought for a moment, swishing her feet through the grass as they walked. "I was already on my way south," she said, "and I was in a bit of a rush. After the mayhem in Town Forbik, I didn't want to stick around. I guess I just caught up with you. I saw Bundersquash walking by himself looking very upset. When I checked to see where the rest of you had gone, I found Lady Ufferbub, Mardulo, and Toddleposter panicking about how you'd just run off. I didn't introduce myself or anything. I just kept my distance and..." She fizzled out.

"Tracked me down yourself?" Gilbert finished for her.

"Yes. And since you made a bloody great fire in the middle of the night, it wasn't exactly difficult."

"But why do you even care?"

"Because I want to stop Hobblebosh as much as you do, and because you got closer than anyone's gotten in ages! It seemed like a waste to let a team like yours fall apart—especially now that you've made him angry. When Hobblebosh is upset, it's not just you who suffers. Everyone does."

Gilbert sighed. The rest of the group had warmed fairly quickly to Thorippela, but Gilbert still didn't fully trust her. Perhaps it was her too-convenient stories and suspiciously well-timed arrival, or perhaps it was the way she'd burned the camp or her lies about the wayfinder, but something didn't feel right. Unfortunately, it was difficult to get any more information when everyone kept cutting in with, "She led us to you, that's got to count for something," or "She's done nothing to hurt us, and she could've if she'd wanted to."

As far as Gilbert could tell, though, no one had told her the full story about Earth. She knew it was fiction, but everyone seemed to agree that the exact details of his creation were his business, and his decision when—or if—he wanted to share them. Right now, he didn't.

That said, everything else was fair game. Bundersquash and Toddleposter told her everything there was to know about the events in Town Forbik, and Mardulo divulged the entirety of their new plan. At the mention of lorilell dust, Thorippela gave Mardulo a strange look.

"Do you have much experience with it?" she asked.

"No," Mardulo admitted, "but I imagine I can figure something out."

"What about your contacts back in City Boratorus? I'm sure one of them would be happy to help."

"Perhaps," Mardulo hedged, "but we're pressed for time."

Thorippela closed her eyes, thinking for a moment. Under her breath, she muttered something about breaking personal rules, and then more loudly, "Let me know once you have the spell prepared. I...know some people. I may be able to help."

Mardulo raised his eyebrows. "Perhaps I will take you up on that offer."

Gilbert was less enthusiastic. Too many people knew about this plan already, and Mardulo looked all too willing to pull in even more. But he said nothing. He hadn't been involved in the post-Forbik planning, and it didn't feel like his place to interject.

The only person who may have held similar concerns was Lady Ufferbub, but Gilbert doubted he'd get any support from her. Ever since he'd run off, she seemed determined to ignore him entirely. For now, Gilbert simply let her be, though he hoped she might come around eventually.

Up ahead, a range of mountains rose against the horizon—not the craggy, snow-capped spires Gilbert might have imagined, but gentle, sloping, and green—almost hills, from this distance. The Green Mountains, they were called. Among them lay Lake Agolika.

The surroundings changed little as the group hiked. From tall meadow grasses to bright patches of flowers to tall meadow grasses again. All the while, weeds tangled around Gilbert's ankles and gnats buzzed past his ears. They had long since left the path, and the sun was out in full, burning the back of his neck.

It took two and a half days to reach the first sign of civilization—the remnants of an old forest, cut mostly to stumps. It looked ancient, but the trees had not grown back. The grasses grew differently there, lower to the ground among half-disintegrated logs and branches, covered in vines, moss, and clusters of mushrooms.

The group walked through that space in careful silence, and after a few hours, the echo of the forest faded away in favor of sprawling farmland.

The first field they passed had been growing corn, but most of the stalks were dead. Patches here and there had been eaten by wildlife, large swaths had snapped and fallen, and what little remained was saggy and brown. The second field was even worse. Some disease had taken hold and reduced the crops to nothing more than spotted black lumps. The group increased their pace just to get away from the smell. When they passed by the third field, also ruined, Bundersquash stopped the group.

"I don't understand," he said. "This time of year, these fields should be thriving. Farmers should be out and tending them." Bundersquash yanked a stalk of horseweed from the ground. "This is wrong."

"You're an expert in farming now, too, are you?" Mardulo sneered.

"Hush," said Lady Ufferbub. "It does not take an expert to know that Bundersquash is right."

"We have an evil dictator to deal with," said Mardulo. "We do not have time to investigate every failing crop we pass."

"If something has gone wrong, it would be good to know," said Bundersquash. "We are close to Town Agol. Whatever happened here could be a sign of trouble ahead."

Mardulo heaved a sigh. "Fine. Let's go knock on their door and see what they have to say, shall we?" He stomped through the field toward a large farmhouse atop a hill. "I'll tell them Bundersquash is about to call the homeowners' association."

Bundersquash grumbled something incoherent but certainly rude; then they all trudged up the hill after Mardulo. But when they reached the door, no one answered. After a good deal more hammering and shouting, they decided to check the next house, instead.

Three houses later, their luck had not improved. Gradually, Mardulo's tone shifted from annoyed frustration to genuine concern.

"I told you," said Bundersquash loftily. "Something is wrong."

"Now is not the time for gloating." Mardulo knocked on the fifth door. When no one answered, he clenched his fists and told everyone to stand back. He was going to force his way in.

"Mardulo!" Bundersquash gasped in horror. "That is immoral!"

"If they're dead, better we know sooner rather than later."

Gilbert had expected Mardulo to kick the door in or pick the lock somehow. Instead, he cast a spell using soil from the garden and a few ingredients from Thorippela's bag. The door swung open soundlessly, and everyone stepped inside.

It was a big house. Having entered without permission, they didn't want to stay long, so Mardulo suggested they split into pairs and search the place as quickly as possible.

"Toddleposter," he said, "you and Bundersquash search this floor. Thorippela and I can check the upper level. Lady Ufferbub, you and Giggle—sorry, *Gilbert*—see if there's a basement. Agreed?"

Lady Ufferbub took a deep breath, steeling herself. "I suppose," she said, then turned to Gilbert with a flat, expressionless face. "Shall we?"

They set about their duties. The house didn't look old, but dust had settled on the counters and windowsills, and the plants were dried and shriveled. What little food remained in the cabinets had been thoroughly nibbled by mice. The bread in the breadbox was growing more kinds of mold than Gilbert cared to count.

In the end, Thorippela located the staircase down to the basement. It was hiding behind a pale wooden door near the entrance to a study, looking as gloomy as can be.

"Have fun down there," she said, grinning. "If you die, make sure to scream really loudly so the rest of us know what's coming."

Gilbert shook his head, then walked down the steps.

It was pitch black at the bottom, and chilly. Gilbert could barely see his own hands, let alone the surroundings. Lady Ufferbub did not follow immediately, but just as Gilbert had decided she wasn't coming at all, she appeared with a small chamberstick and a lit candle. She eyed Gilbert disdainfully, then left to search the opposite side of the room, leaving him alone in the darkness.

Gilbert sulked back up the stairs, asked Toddleposter where Lady Ufferbub had gotten the candle, then grabbed one of his own and lit it using a tinderbox they'd found in the kitchen.

Back in the basement with Lady Ufferbub, he finally looked around. It was a bare place—just one room, with walls of uneven gray brick and a floor of pale stone. A single chair stood near the opposite wall beside a fireplace gone cold. There was a small table there, and some books atop it. Gilbert wandered over while Lady Ufferbub leafed through the books. An unlit sconce jutted from the wall.

Side-eyeing Lady Ufferbub with as much attitude as he could muster, Gilbert lit the sconce with his candle, then took a closer look at the few books Lady Ufferbub had not already put aside—one on swimming, one on boating, and one titled *Water Sports for the Everyday Man: A Beginners' Guide*. Gilbert flipped through the pages, found nothing of interest, and gave up.

"Well, at least there aren't any dead people," he said by way of conversation.

"There are no living people either." Lady Ufferbub walked to the opposite wall and started poking bricks.

"Look, Lady Ufferbub"—Gilbert trotted to her side—"I get that you're upset with me for leaving, but I actually wanted to talk to you about something. Or rather, someone. Thorippela."

Lady Ufferbub said nothing.

"I don't think she's being completely honest with us, and I think you sense it too. I've noticed you don't talk to her as much as the others do."

"Even at the best of times, I do not talk as much as the others do, Gilbert." Lady Ufferbub refused to turn her gaze from the bricks. She poked a few more, then moved to the adjacent wall.

"But still, I think you've noticed something's off."

"The magical world is at war with a lime. Things have been *off* for some time."

"You know what I mean."

"Of course I know what you mean, Gilbert." Finally, Lady Ufferbub faced him. She spoke quietly, but her eyes burned with steely anger. "I have chosen to ignore you. Just because you feel like you belong to some bleak fictional world, it does not mean the rest of us have to mistrust every person we meet. Thorippela has helped us. You most of all. Why not show some gratitude, for once?"

She shook her head and walked back to the room's exit. "There is nothing down here," she said. "We are wasting valuable time." Then she disappeared up the stairs.

Gilbert stood motionless for several seconds. He'd known Lady Ufferbub was upset with him for leaving, but that seemed harsh, nor did he feel he deserved it. Gilbert *knew* Lady Ufferbub didn't trust Thorippela. Her body language, her speech, the way she handled their interactions—it was clear. She could act aloof and superior, but at the end of the day, Gilbert was right, and she knew it.

He stormed back toward the table bristling with frustration, determined to find something Lady Ufferbub had missed. He flipped through the books again, then checked under the chair. He pulled at the sconce. He kicked the fireplace.

Nothing.

Then he noticed a small paper tucked beneath one of the old, ashy logs. It was charred but intact. Gilbert wiggled it free.

To Our Neighbor(s) at Whelmur Manor, 107 Street Shale, Town Agol

An urgent and mandatory evacuation is ordered for all residents in your district. Town Agol's outskirts have been deemed "At Risk," and residents are asked to relocate downtown. Enclosed, please find a packing list and map containing your designated zone of assembly. Further instructions await upon your prompt arrival.

Yours truly,

Kalyra Moritel Trillien the Enchanted

Head Representative, Town Agol Board of Representatives

Gilbert grinned. This was it. There was some kind of diagram lower down, but it had been lost to the embers of the fire. He brushed the ash off the paper, then tucked it into his pocket.

The group reconvened in the entryway. Toddleposter had found a small vial in the kitchen, which they could use to store Hobblebosh's hair. Mardulo and Bundersquash squabbled briefly over who would carry it before Mardulo simply snatched it off the table and stuffed it into a pocket, putting an end to the discussion. Bundersquash rolled his eyes, then dropped some coins on the counter by way of compensation.

In all other respects, their search had proved fruitless, which made Gilbert all the more pleased to shared his own findings, though Lady Ufferbub refused to acknowledge his smug grin.

"Well," said Mardulo, "I suppose that explains it."

Lady Ufferbub stared out the window, looking glum. "To send them into town...I wonder at the wisdom of such a move. Town Agol is not well guarded at the best of times. Now they will be overcrowded and short on food. Tensions run high in such an environment. How does this keep them safe?"

No one could answer that. With a sigh, Lady Ufferbub stepped outside. The others followed.

They rejoined the hippalectryons on the road, then continued east toward the lake, making no more stops along the way. They saw no people, and when they spoke, they did so in whispers. Only the rising wind and the rhythmic, faraway lapping of waves upon the shore broke through the heavy silence.

At last, they reached their destination, but where they had expected to find a lively, bustling metropolis, they found, instead, a crater.

Chapter 18

A Warm Welcome

It was a big crater, almost as deep as it was wide, attached to the lake like a bloated tick. Water had pooled in its basin. Almost no trace of Town Agol remained.

"Well, I can't say I'll miss them," said Thorippela casually.

Everyone else was at a loss for words. Disbelief and shock mingled together, filling the silence. Gilbert's stomach churned as he thought of all those townsfolk. Had they gathered together in the hope of safety, only to fall victim to some kind of bomb? Had Hobblebosh already sent soldiers this way? When had it happened? And why Town Agol?

Then Bundersquash pointed at something in the lake. "That's new," he said.

It was a landmass—large, but a long way from shore. Gilbert would have called it an island, except it bobbed with the waves and wind, as if it wasn't fully attached to the ground below but anchored in place like a massive floating platform. Upon closer inspection, a pale pathway ran along the shore, dotted on one side with houses. And perhaps it was Gilbert's imagination, but when he focused, he thought he could hear a faint rustle of liveliness—of hippalectryons and pedestrians, mingling among the streets.

"What is Town Agol doing in the middle of a lake?" Mardulo asked, astonished.

"It was quite firmly in the ground the last time I was here," said Lady Ufferbub.

"Clearly, they've uprooted themselves." Toddleposter leaned over the edge of the crater, inspecting the scene. "Perhaps they thought, this way, more lakefront property."

Gilbert's relief was short lived. In its place, frustration took root. Why were things never simple? And would it have killed them to put up a sign? A plain *Don't Worry. Not Destroyed in Some Horrible Disaster, Just Relocated* could have saved a lot of stress.

Bundersquash turned to Mardulo and spoke in as businesslike a tone as he could muster. "A third-tier monodirectional voice-amplification charm should be sufficient. I would do it myself, but..." He waved what remained of his left arm.

"I was just about to cast one." Mardulo grabbed a bundle of something from his pocket, mixed in some water from the lake, then cast a spell. The auric nebula faded into his throat.

"Hello!" he cried, and his voice carried out like the wind across the water, causing ripples in its wake. When there was no response, he called louder. "Hello? Town Agol?"

After a minute or two, a voice came soaring back toward them. "Who goes there?" it demanded. "Are you agents of the Hobblebosh regime?"

"No, we bloody well are not!" Mardulo shouted back. "Why is Town Agol in the middle of a lake?"

"We are protecting ourselves against the threat of Obble Dor Hobble-bosh."

"And you think a lake will stop him?"

"Well, it certainly won't speed him up, will it?" answered the voice.

"I would be surprised if it made any difference. It seems a bit—"

Lady Ufferbub tapped Mardulo on the shoulder and gestured impatiently.

"Right. Sorry." Mardulo reset himself. "What I meant to say was, we humbly request permission to...er...board your town, please."

There was no response, so Mardulo added, "We are seeking asylum. We have a plan to stop Obble Dor Hobblebosh, but we need somewhere safe to work."

"How do we know that you are not spies?" the voice returned.

"Do I look like a bloody spy to you?!" Mardulo flailed his arms. Lady Ufferbub smacked him across the back of the head.

"You do not, but that is the point."

"We are not spying," Mardulo replied moodily. "If we were, I would not have used a voice-amplification charm to announce myself."

When that didn't do the trick, Bundersquash whispered, "Why don't you just introduce us?"

Mardulo frowned. "My name is Mardulo Vot Ponterous the Brilliant. My...*associate* here is Bundersquash Borum Balbagoose the Studious. I also have Lady Normishdae Relidor Ufferbub the Triumphant, Toddle-poster Hunderrum Balbagoose the Second, Gigglebrit Maistowne—er, Gilbert...Betters?" He looked questioningly at Gilbert, who nodded. "And Thorippela Luggude Swedgett the Crisp," he finished. "Our home is City Boratorus, though we come most directly from Town Forbik and are flee-ing Hobblebosh's soldiers. We need your assistance."

The voice took some time to respond. "Your reputations are known to us," it said eventually. "We shall send a boat, but if you are not who you claim to be, beware. Your deception shall be known, and Town Agol does not take kindly to liars."

Something left the island and slowly approached the shore. As it came nearer, it took shape—an empty rowboat, oars moving by themselves. A pale sheen of light rose up around the boat's perimeter. When it finally arrived at a nearby wooden dock, it produced a strange, disembodied voice.

"Mardulo Vot Ponterous the Brilliant. Enter."

Mardulo did as he was told. The light around the boat shone brightly as he passed through, unharmed.

"What happens if the wrong person enters?" Gilbert asked.

Toddleposter shrugged. "Nothing good, I imagine."

"Bundersquash Borum Balbagoose the Studious. Enter." Bundersquash stepped aboard. Lady Ufferbub went next, then Toddleposter.

"Gilbert Betters. Enter."

Gilbert took a breath. After all this business with his name, he had no idea what would happen. But there was nothing for it. He stepped up, fingers crossed...and though a chill shock danced across his skin as he passed through the light, it let him through unharmed. He sighed with relief and sat down on one of the three benches.

"Thorippela Luggude Swedgett the Crisp. Enter."

Thorippela wavered. "I think I'll stay here, actually. I've never liked Town Agol much, and someone needs to look after the hippalectryons."

Lady Ufferbub looked at her strangely. "I'm sure the hippalectryons can fend for themselves."

"Certainly," said Thorippela, "but they're mine, and they've been through a lot. They deserve some looking after."

"Thorippela Luggude Swedgett the Crisp. Enter," the boat repeated.

Mardulo looked dismayed. "But what about our plan? How will you help with the lorilell dust?"

"I'll help you when you get back. We can't do anything until you've simplified the spell, anyway."

"Thorippela Luggude Swedgett the Crisp. Enter," the boat repeated once more.

Thorippela stepped away from the dock. "It was nice to meet you all. May luck travel with you on your way!"

Bundersquash leaned closer to the edge of the boat. "It was nice to meet you, too, Thorippela!"

Gilbert waved. Despite his misgivings, he felt a pang of sorrow at leaving her behind. "See you soon," he said.

Thorippela winked. "I should hope so. I'll wait for your return. Until then, farewell."

At that moment, the boat gave up waiting and took off for Town Agol.

Moments later, the border light shimmered upward and away, and the disembodied voice returned. "Welcome to Town Agol. This newly created, soon-to-be-historic autonomous ferry ride is brought to you by the Agolian Board of Representatives. Please keep your arms and legs inside the boat at all times."

Gilbert tucked in his elbows.

"Please be advised, all visitors entering Town Agol may be subject to search. Food, beverages, animal products, incendiaries, toxins, explosives, and seeds are strictly prohibited. If you have visited a farm or pasture in the past thirty days, you may be subject to additional screening. We appreciate your cooperation in these efforts."

A wave jostled the boat, and the magical sound system struck up a fanfare. A different, cheerier voice spoke out.

"Town Agol, where innovation meets opportunity, and every neighbor is a friend you can count on. The Agolian Board of Representatives is delighted to welcome you to our new island locale. Did you know, for the past three years, our Agolika beaches have ranked among the top ten luxury vacation destinations for young couples? We're a dream come true! Our distinctive architecture has won over a dozen awards..."

The boat rowed on, trundling through an assortment of prerecorded "fun" facts about the town and its citizens. Gilbert gazed into the lake, trying to turn off his ears. The water was clear, almost invisible but for the glisten of the sun along its ripples. Beneath, dozens of fish poured through their rainbow kingdom of coral and stone, slipping out of sight as the boat followed its course. For a moment, Gilbert almost forgot his guilt, his sorrow, and the horrors he had failed to stop. It was enough to marvel at the scenery and lose himself in the gentle rocking of the boat.

"—did you know, this boat has carried a total of *thirty-one* people from shore to shore? Combined, it has traveled almost *fifteen* miles—"

"Not the most impressive statistics..." Mardulo muttered under his breath.

"They've only just moved," said Bundersquash testily. "I'd like to see you do better."

"I'm just saying, this whole thing is ridiculous. And all this nonsense about searching and screening—is that really necessary?"

"Hobblebosh has them scared. Can you blame them?"

"Yes, I can."

"Quiet," said Lady Ufferbub. "Now is not the time for bickering."

So they approached in silence. A group of guards awaited them at the dock, outfitted in matching gray mail and red cloaks.

"Please allow us to accompany you to the town hall," said one of them, holding a sword to indicate that such an allowance was entirely nonnegotiable.

"After you," said Toddleposter, bowing slightly in a clear effort to appease.

The dock led to a wide path of pale wood, which stood on stilts about an inch above the ground, not unlike a boardwalk—but this path moved well beyond the shoreline. It connected everything, twisting between buildings, expanding to form entire courts and plazas. As far as Gilbert could tell, no one in Town Agol ever needed to touch the ground. The path would take them everywhere. Meanwhile, the ground itself had been left to grow a blanket of lush green grass. The tangy scent of docks and wet wood soon faded, replaced by fresh air and the smell of trees and flowers.

Gilbert drank it in, impressed by the sheer effort this place must have taken. The buildings, too, were a marvel. Whomever had designed them was particularly corner averse. No sharp angle existed where a smooth curve could suffice. Everything was made of the same pale wood as the pathway, polished and shining, and most houses boasted prominent glass windows, which often consumed entire walls or ceilings. Trees sprang up between the path and the houses, manicured to fit into the townscape alongside carefully pruned bushes and evenly spaced benches.

It was busy, if not crowded. Citizens hurried from one place to another, barely sparing a glance for any of the town's architectural spectacle, though they certainly stopped to ogle Mardulo, Bundersquash, Lady Ufferbub, Toddleposter, Gilbert, and their armored escort.

They reached the town hall in a matter of minutes. It was a massive building, curved and shining like the others, but made of a darker wood with flourishing designs carved into the beams around its windows and doors. Farther back, a paneled glass dome rose high into the air, reflecting the bright summer sunlight like a beacon.

They entered through an arched doorway into a wide hall, then followed the leader through a maze of corridors lit by nothing but daylight. At long last, they came upon a spacious atrium—the glass dome Gilbert had noticed outside—brimming with vegetation. Whole trees, grown tall and busy, towered above the wooden floor, dappling the room in shade. Pots lined every other surface, overflowing with flowers and vines.

A wide tiered staircase rose before them, draped on either side with vibrant wisteria, bordered by thin streams of water that trickled along carved pathways from the highest tier of the stairs and down to ground level, where it disappeared underneath the floorboards. The steps led up to a moat of sorts, and beyond that, on an elevated stage, stood five robed people.

"Hello," said the woman in the center. "For those who do not know me already, my name is Kalyra Moritel Trillien the Enchanted, head representative of the Town Agol Board of Representatives."

"Nice to meet you. I am Mardulo Vot—"

"—Vot Ponterous the Brilliant, yes," said Kalyra. "I know. And I know of you, too, Bundersquash Borum Balbagoose the Studious. And of course, Normishdae, hello again." She nodded stiffly toward Lady Ufferbub. "I have even heard tell of Toddleposter Hunderrum Balbagoose the Second, Normishdae's new assistant, as I understand it. Which leaves you." She looked suddenly at Gilbert. "I presume you are either Gilbert Betters or Thorippela Luggude Swedgett the Crisp."

"Gilbert," said Gilbert.

"And what sort of name is that?" Her eyes narrowed.

"Mine." Gilbert met Kalyra's stare.

"Very well," she said, then turned to the guards. "And where is Thorippela? You were supposed to collect six of them."

"Thorippela stayed behind," said Bundersquash.

Kalyra clamped her jaw. "To business, then. You made quite the scene at Town Forbik. The birds have been busy. We've heard many reports."

"Ah, good," said Mardulo happily. "In that case, you know why we're here."

"I am not impressed."

The smile slipped from Mardulo's face like melted ice.

"Gilbert." Kalyra turned on him. "We had not heard of you. At least, not until news of this most recent fiasco came to our doorstep. Now, it appears, you are everywhere. Do not think we missed Mardulo's blunder upon our shores. Gilbert, Gigglebrit, you cannot hide. We know who you are, and we know you turned an entire town blue. Even Normishdae, it would seem, did not escape your foolishness." She gestured to Lady Ufferbub.

"I know," said Gilbert. "I'm sorry."

One of the other representatives let forth a snort of laughter. Kalyra eyed him, irritated.

"Please excuse my fellow representatives," she said flatly. "It would appear they find much humor in your disastrous failure."

Gilbert's throat tightened.

"Your actions in Town Forbik are inexcusable," Kalyra went on. "To have an opportunity like that and squander it? I am not surprised you changed your name, when such shame hangs upon the old one."

"Says the woman who hides in a lake!" Toddleposter shot back fiercely. "Gilbert fought for this world. What have you done?"

Gilbert turned to Toddleposter with a sudden gratitude equaled only by his surprise that Toddleposter could speak with such venom in his voice.

"Gilbert did his best," Bundersquash added more softly. "We all did."

Kalyra was not moved. "Nonetheless," she said, "it was wasted. Consider the cost of that failure."

"I have done nothing but consider that cost since it happened," said Gilbert, emboldened by his friends' confidence. "We're here because we're trying to fix it. Please, don't be another obstacle for us to overcome. Help us."

"We have a plan." Mardulo jumped in. "We just need a place to sort out the details. And we could use some ingredients."

Kalyra frowned at him. "Your plans have not gone well as of late, Mardulo. Why should this be any different?"

"Because we have something new. Hobblebosh's essence."

Kalyra hesitated. Her eyes glimmered. "And this essence—is this how you were able to use magic in his restricted zone? Did it allow you to bypass his restraints?"

"What? Um...no," said Mardulo awkwardly. "That doesn't make any sense. It's not—" Lady Ufferbub nudged him with an elbow. Mardulo cleared his throat. "It has nothing to do with that. Rather, the essence is useful because it will allow us to craft a vastly simpler trapping spell, one that may be reduceable to lorilell dust."

Kalyra scoffed. "Trapping spell? Lorilell dust? No, Mardulo! Capture is insufficient. Lorilell dust is imprecise. Why use such indirect means when you have figured out how to cast magic in his presence?"

Mardulo cocked his head in confusion. "You misunderstand. Only Gilbert has that ability."

Slowly, Kalyra's animated expression fell into stonelike frustration. "If Gigglebrit can do it, why not others?"

"Ah, well. That is a long story." Mardulo took a deep breath. "It started with a prophecy, one about one Pottleswee Plugg Thudigarde the Brave. Bundersquash and I were trying to—"

"The short version, if you please," Kalyra interrupted.

Bundersquash answered. "Gilbert could do it because his name is not on the Roster."

Not to be outdone, Mardulo added, "But I expect Hobblebosh has long since remedied that particular vulnerability, at least as it pertains to Gilbert. We cannot rely upon it again."

Kalyra closed her eyes, frowning. "So, you are telling me," she said, "that this *imbecile* was the only one who could do it, he failed, and now we're back where we started?"

"Gilbert is no imbecile." Mardulo glowered at her. "And we are not back where we started. As I said, we have the hair!"

Kalyra ignored him. "Meanwhile," she said, "here we were, hoping City Boratorus was braced for battle with an entire battalion of wizards at the ready. At the very least, we thought you might *weaken* Hobblebosh before he got here. Alas, it seems we must fall back on our contingency plan."

"What in the world are you talking about?" asked Lady Ufferbub.

Kalyra shook her head. "Another time. The board must convene."

She waved her hand at one of the guards, who escorted Gilbert and the others into a small side room.

Gilbert turned to Toddleposter, Bundersquash, and Mardulo. "Thank you for the support," he said.

"Not to worry, lad," said Mardulo. "Let's just hope they agree to help us."

They waited several minutes before Kalyra strode in, followed by a slender wisp of a man.

"The board needs more time to discuss these matters," Kalyra said. "We will have an answer for you tomorrow. Until then, I have arranged your lodging. We are short on space, but my fellow representative Ormish Korbur Lunkus the Sighted has agreed to house you for the night." She signaled to the man who had followed her in.

"Nice to meet you," said Ormish, extending a hand to everyone. "It may be a little tight, but we'll make it work."

"You have our gratitude," said Lady Ufferbub. "Kalyra, what time should we expect you tomorrow?"

"I will come when we have decided."

Mardulo frowned. "Just know, the longer we wait, the closer Hobblebosh gets to City Boratorus, and it is not far from there to here."

"I am very much aware, Mardulo." Kalyra turned on her heels and strode to the exit. "Good night to you all," she said, and left.

Ormish clapped his hands. "Right then! Follow me. I will show you to your home for the evening. It's always a pleasure to entertain guests!"

It was nearing nightfall as he led them out of the town hall and along the wooded path to a massive, warmly lit home. The front entrance connected directly to the main path, with a gate to delineate the property. The entrance hall led into a round living room with a fluffy beige carpet, a sofa, two armchairs, and a coffee table. Straight ahead was another door, which opened to a large backyard. There, for the first time since arriving on the island, Gilbert saw no wooden path to stand on—only soft, thick grass and a sandy beach against the lake.

Gilbert stepped out into the yard while Ormish showed the others to their rooms. The town streets had been bustling, but now, he found himself alone amid half an acre of open space. He stared across the grass to the beach beyond, enjoying the sudden calm, the feel of soft dirt beneath his feet.

He was considering taking off his shoes when Ormish appeared behind him.

"There you are!" he said.

"I was just admiring the yard," said Gilbert. "Is this all yours?"

"It is indeed," said Ormish. "It's not much—nothing like what you'd see in the really nice parts of town, anyway—but I get by."

"I like it," said Gilbert.

Ormish smiled. "It is not uncommon by Town Agol's standards, I assure you. Now come. Please leave your shoes on the mat, if you don't mind, and I will show you to your room."

Gilbert did as he was told, suddenly embarrassed by a sizable hole in his sock. He followed Ormish up a staircase to an interior balcony overlooking the living room, then through a hall to a door near the back.

"This is you." Ormish showed Gilbert inside. It was cozy. The ceiling curved and lowered toward the back of the room, with a spacious window gazing up at the stars. Directly beneath the window was a bed, and a nightstand next to that. A tall cupboard stood near the door.

"Now," said Ormish. "You must be starving. I have ordered dinner. It should arrive in an hour. In the meantime, there is a bath down the hall to the left and a second downstairs, if the one up here is taken. Please, help yourself, and take your time. I will bring some fresh clothes to your room."

"Thanks." Gilbert bit his lip. First his socks, now his smell. He was quickly becoming aware of how unsightly he must appear. Ormish showed himself out, and though Gilbert was eager to wash, both bathrooms had already been taken by Lady Ufferbub and Mardulo. He went to find Bundersquash and Toddleposter while he waited.

They were in the backyard, sitting in the sand at the edge of the lake. Gilbert joined them.

"Obviously a myrian powder palm infusion isn't an option," said Bundersquash, "but I wonder if I could use one palm and some other part of my body. Maybe even what's left of my upper arm."

Toddleposter waffled. "It's been a while since that class you took on myrian powder infusions, but if I recall correctly, isn't it calibrated specifically for the properties of a human palm?"

"In some ways. Rubbing the palms together initiates a reaction that activates the imbued myrian powder," said Bundersquash. "Then the activated powder reacts with the blood inside your hands, and you get an auric nebula. The activation sequence involves some calibration for the palm's properties—heat, blood flow, and the like—but that can be adjusted as long as the activated powder still mixes with the blood. We would need a different composite, and I'm sure I would have to change the imbuing process, but I think it's doable."

"It sounds risky."

"It may be," said Bundersquash, "but how can I expect to fight Hobblebosh if I'm paying a tax on every spell I cast? It's not practical to hope for some external source to materialize for my auric nebula every time I need to cast a spell."

"You can help in other ways."

"I've been training to be a wizard over half my life. This is what I want to do."

Toddleposter sighed. "If you're sure, perhaps you could consult with Madame Martoonisplau once we get back to City Boratorus."

"That's a good idea," said Bundersquash. He turned to Gilbert. "Do you remember her from the Wizarding Consortium? She did your palms. Maybe she'll do mine, too—or my arm, I suppose."

"I remember." Gilbert clapped Bundersquash on the back. "I'm sure you'll find some way to make it work. With or without a palm infusion, you're a great wizard. Don't doubt it."

"Many thanks." Bundersquash smiled, then rose to his feet. "I'm going to head in and start thinking up some plans. The sooner I get started, the better!"

As he left, Lady Ufferbub emerged.

"Good evening, Toddleposter," she said. "Gilbert."

"Ah, you're done!" said Toddleposter. "That means it's my turn." He hopped to his feet and looked meaningfully at Lady Ufferbub, then Gilbert. "You two seem disconnected lately. Perhaps now is a good time to start a dialogue?"

Then he bounded off.

Gilbert sat awkwardly in the silence, hoping Lady Ufferbub would say something first. When she didn't, he took the initiative.

"So, it sounds like you and Kalyra know each other?" he asked.

Lady Ufferbub looked at him. "We were friends once."

"I'm sorry to hear that," said Gilbert. "Er, not that she's...well, what I mean to say is—"

"I expect Mardulo is about to finish his bath," Lady Ufferbub cut in. "Perhaps you should go get ready."

Gilbert took the excuse, got up, and left Lady Ufferbub to her thoughts.

Mardulo had, in fact, finished, and was inside talking to Bundersquash through the increasingly irritated medium of Toddleposter, who had yet to reach the bathroom.

"You tell Mardulo I wouldn't ask for his referral, even if he wanted to give me one!" Bundersquash growled.

"And you tell Bundersquash that without my referral, he may as well head back to Port Tup. I'm the only thing that gives his name weight in City Boratorus. Madame Martoonisplau may act like she—"

Gilbert swept past them and headed for the second-floor bathroom, but he could still hear the argument downstairs. In an attempt to tune it out, he focused on the water. It was warm—cozy, but not scalding—and pristinely clean. He supposed some magic kept it that way. The flakes of dirt and dried blood that fell from his skin turned to nothing in the water. Slowly, his muscles relaxed. He soaked and detangled his hair, then scrubbed himself all over.

Comfortable and content, he remained in the bath until the angry voices below had calmed. Then he changed into a set of clothes Ormish had provided and went downstairs feeling like a new man. There, he waited excitedly for his first hot meal in days.

"I hope you like trout and potatoes!" said Ormish as he emerged from his study. "I asked the town hall chefs to prepare something special. They do wonders back there, let me tell you. Affordable, too! The citizens like to treat their representatives well, here in Town Agol. It's a real honor to serve them, even if they do get a bit *rambunctious* at times." He laughed lightly and stepped outside before reappearing with several boxes of food. He led everyone into a dining room and quickly dished out six plates.

Gilbert tucked in. Warm, flaky fish glazed with white sauce on a bed of soft potato slices, seasoned with several herbs he didn't even recognize. It was, perhaps, the best food he'd ever eaten. He devoured it.

The others were more measured, if only slightly, and the first few minutes of their dinner passed in silence.

Eventually, Lady Ufferbub slowed enough to speak. "On our way into town," she said to Ormish, "we learned that the people on the outskirts, farmers and the like, had been evacuated and directed here."

Ormish nearly choked on his fish. "Did you? They were supposed to keep that information secret."

"An abandoned, decaying farm is hard to conceal," said Lady Ufferbub. "And yet, now that we are here, I see very little evidence of those people. Where are they?"

Ormish's expression tightened. "They are around, spread out, filling in all the nice nooks and crannies that used to give Town Agol its charm. We've lost three of our best parks to their encampments and two of our nicest hotels. Honestly, I don't know why we ordered them to come here."

"Presumably to keep them safe," said Lady Ufferbub, an edge to her voice.

"Perhaps. But it's a real burden, and they've never really been members of the Agolian community." Ormish shook his head. "Certainly, they fall under our jurisdiction, but they don't *engage* in the same way our real citizens do. I say, if they want to keep their distance when times are good, let them keep it also when times are bad. I don't see any reason we should let them turn around and crawl back just because things got a little rocky on their end. Not at the expense of our more contributing citizens, anyway. You understand, I'm sure, being such generous contributors to City Boratorus."

"But surely, they do contribute." Lady Ufferbub's disdain cut across the table. "Where did these potatoes come from, if not them?"

Ormish rolled his eyes. "Certainly, they send food, and as Kalyra is fond of reminding us, they pay taxes, but for all that, they remain an arms-length away. You'd never see them at a community gathering, building a playset for the local school, or volunteering to help on picnic day. There's contributing, and there's *contributing*—that's all I mean to say." He sighed. "Alas, it does not make for very enjoyable dinner conversation. Let's speak of cheerier things. Mardulo, Bundersquash, how fares your research in City Boratorus? I recall having to approve an order from your university not long ago—a rather a large quantity of Agol's finest mesozan ore, I believe."

Bundersquash frowned into his plate. "They were using that on floor fourteen, making wings for their jumping rhinoceros. They did it, too. But the rhino died in Town Forbik—one of several remarkable creatures."

"I am sorry to hear that," said Ormish. "It sounds as though Town Forbik was an unpleasant experience for all involved. Perhaps tomorrow, you will find Agol's solution more agreeable."

"And what is Agol's solution?" asked Mardulo. "Kalyra mentioned some kind of contingency plan?"

Ormish held up his finger. "Ah, ah. I am not at liberty to disclose that information—not yet. Suffice to say, I believe it will be effective. Obble Dor Hobblebosh is a dire threat. Great Port Opperwob, Town Tarley, and City Mez have all fallen under his accursed rule, and it seems City Boratorus is next. We had been hoping your city would stop him before he became our concern, but that sounds less and less likely, given your reports. Nonetheless, I can assure you, we Agolians are prepared to do whatever it takes to keep our town safe, should it come to that."

"It has *already* come to that," said Mardulo darkly. "It came to that long ago, when Hobblebosh's horrors first started to spread."

"It is none of Agol's concern if the other provinces cannot be bothered to put up a real fight. But as I said, we will put up ours when the time comes, and Hobblebosh will feel the full wrath of Town Agol."

Gilbert and his friends looked at one another uneasily.

"It is hard to comment, with so few specifics," said Mardulo at last. "I'll reserve judgment until tomorrow."

"And rightly so." Ormish smiled. "Now, how about dessert?"

The rest of their dinner passed through idle conversations about the weather, the food, and the curiosities of island living. Before long, Ormish had to excuse himself and return to the town hall, where the board of representatives still had much to discuss.

Gilbert and the others were free to rest, and for once, there was no need to set a watch. With a full-to-aching stomach, Gilbert waddled upstairs and fell asleep before he even had a chance to delight in having a soft mattress once again.

The same dream plagued him. Hobblebosh standing, swirled in red, Earth taking shape all around him. Slowly, the mist became flame, and Hobblebosh vanished, laughing as Gilbert's home burned away—nothing but red fire and black shadows flickering mercilessly through a ruined land. Ahead, his parents stood, silent and unmoving, silhouettes against the flame. They gazed solemnly in his direction.

Gilbert cried out, stumbling as he rushed toward them. But no matter how quickly he ran, he never got there in time, and his parents burned away. Usually, Gilbert wound up in the fire himself and turned to ash at their side.

Perhaps that was the best he could hope for.

He woke to a knock on the door. It took a moment to remember where he was. His back was sore after sleeping on the feather mattress, and his stomach ached from dinner the night before. His head pounded against the inside of his skull, dreams still fogging his thoughts.

He would see his parents soon, he told himself. He just had to help stop Hobblebosh first.

The knock sounded again.

"Coming." Gilbert forced himself to stand and open the door.

Bundersquash stood at the entrance. "Sorry to bother you, Gilbert. It's just, I didn't want you to miss breakfast. Also, Kalyra showed up a few minutes ago to speak with everyone, but..." He fiddled with his glasses. "Well, I think it might be a little while before we really get down to business." He leaned in close and whispered. "If I can offer a suggestion, don't get involved. Kalyra and Lady Ufferbub...it's a sensitive subject."

Gilbert nodded, dressed, then hurried downstairs to meet the others. He heard voices as he approached—Lady Ufferbub and Kalyra. They were talking casually, but tension filled the air, sourced primarily from the uncomfortable expressions of those sitting nearby. Toddleposter was uncharacteristically interested in the fireplace's stonework. Bundersquash was tracing lines on the wood of the coffee table. Mardulo was reading a newspaper, never turning the page. Ormish hurried this way and that, paying very little attention to anyone.

"No, Kalyra," said Lady Ufferbub quietly. "I stopped monitoring your activities after I heard about the hundreds of disfigured bundletup corpses that washed up on the shores of Town Sugwater a week after your visit. I could bear no more of your *antics*."

Kalyra scoffed. "Bundletups? Really, Normishdae? That is where you draw the line? They are vermin, barely more than fish—except in their capacity for deadliness and greed. Sugwater needed them eradicated, and I did the job. Only you would find that problematic."

"I expect if you asked the bundletups, they would disagree."

"If bundletups had the ability to understand anything beyond 'How shiny?' and 'How pointy?' perhaps I would have asked them. But they do not."

Gilbert had no idea what a bundletup was, and at the moment, he was fairly certain he didn't want to know.

Lady Ufferbub crossed her arms and leaned back in her chair.

"Well, I can't say I'm disappointed," Kalyra continued, carelessly inspecting a fingernail. "I barely spared you and your precious library a second thought after leaving City Boratorus. It's good you can finally do the same for me."

"And yet, after all your talk about unbounded adventure and worldly travels, you end up here in Town Agol, comfortably settled."

"That is true," Kalyra conceded. "But I did travel. I covered the main continent twice. I visited six of the archipelago islands. I did good work. Except more often than not, when I returned to the places I'd helped, I found them reverted—back as they had been before. Even your dear bundletups managed to regain a foothold along Sugwater's coast." Kalyra shook her head. "You were right about one thing, Normishdae. To withstand the storm, a tree needs roots. I planted mine here."

"But why Town Agol, of all places? Why not come back to the library?"

"Your library stifles and quells. Town Agol brims with potential, though it was not at its best when I arrived. As it turns out, if you give everyone money for a few generations, they suddenly forget how to do anything except horde it. But I saw the possibilities. To everyone here, innovation meant bigger beachfront villas, automated pathway cleaners, and fiat money. But I knew better. With these kinds of resources, there was nothing I couldn't do. I could finally make my mark on history. It was the perfect place. So yes, Normishdae, I settled, I made it my home. And then I got to work. I am proud of what I have done here, and I am proud of what this town has become under my watch."

Kalyra took a deep breath, then stretched and spoke more loudly. "Which is why we must deal with Hobblebosh quickly and permanently. I will not let him destroy what I have worked so hard to build."

"But first, breakfast!" said Ormish suddenly. "I've already put in the order—seven omelets on the way."

They ate quickly. Gilbert had little more than the side of toast they provided. Kalyra hardly spoke during the meal, and she ignored Gilbert entirely. Afterward, she led everyone to a stretch of mud on the eastern edge of the island, where the other representatives waited beside a small band of guards and a wooden boat. It was much bigger than the boat Gilbert and the others had taken to Town Agol. This one had an entirely enclosed lower deck, an aft cabin, and enough space on the upper level to fit all those present and then some.

They boarded, and the boat set off at once.

"Now that we're all here," said Kalyra, "we can finally begin our business in earnest. Mardulo, Bundersquash, Normishdae, Toddleposter—the board has given it much thought, and we will not help you with your plan."

Mardulo and Lady Ufferbub raised immediate objections but cut themselves short at a stern look from Kalyra.

"We will not help you with your plan," she repeated curtly, "but we will accept your help with ours."

"And what is this mysterious plan of yours?" asked Mardulo, eyeing the boat suspiciously.

"Quite simply, we eradicate Hobblebosh and all who support him."

Mardulo actually laughed. "Right. As simple as that. It's a wonder we didn't think of it."

"It is possible," said Kalyra. "That is why we have brought you here this morning. A demonstration."

She signaled to one of the representatives, who brought forward a strange device about the size of a dinner plate. Two engraved silver disks made up the top and the bottom, connected by a rim of glass about an inch tall. A turquoise gas ebbed and swirled within it. One of the guards pulled a catch on the top disk and a strip of metal slid away, revealing a small white button on the surface.

"At first glance," said Kalyra, "this appears to be a common wood-harvesting device—"

"Invented right here in Town Agol!" interrupted one of the representatives, who was mostly moustache. "No matter what those blighters in Town Lunkwargle say."

"Many thanks, Lorfus." Kalyra smiled patiently. "As I was saying, it *appears* to be a common wood-harvesting device, but the keen eyed among you may have noticed a few modifications. Most obviously, the gas inside is different—heavier, with higher concentrations of ozone and argon. But the inscriptions, too, are different. I could not comment on the specifics, but our in-house wizards have been working tirelessly. No doubt, Mardulo and Bundersquash, you can see some of what has been modified. Perhaps you can guess what it does?"

"It is not my area of expertise, but…" Mardulo leaned in to examine the device. "I recognize a few markings here. One would typically attribute those to a teleportation-stamp inscription, but they are incomplete." He frowned. "Shoddy work."

Bundersquash stepped in next. "I see the harvest's targeting parameters over in the corner—markings for organic material, but the filtering mechanism doesn't look right for trees. And this…" He pointed to one of the many squiggles. "This is dangerous. Very unstable."

They both looked at Kalyra uneasily.

"What have you done?" said Mardulo.

"You shall see soon enough."

The boat moved through the lake in silence, plotting a course toward a relatively flat valley among the otherwise steep cluster of mountains on the eastern edge of the lake. Gilbert noticed a number of figures waiting on the shore, but this was opposite where they had left Thorippela. His first thought was Hobblebosh's soldiers, and a stark prevalence of green and yellow seemed to confirm his theory…except none of them were moving. In time, it became clear that they were not people at all, but life-size models.

The boat docked, and everyone disembarked. Only then could Gilbert examine the full extent of the diorama. The dummies were roughly human shaped, made of some strange squishy material he didn't recognize. Each was dressed in real clothing, which had been dyed in a mockery of Hobblebosh's green-and-gold uniforms. Some of the figures carried rusted spears or toy swords. A few were marked with crudely drawn faces, all making hideous expressions.

There were hundreds of them spread across several acres of flat land. Of the valley itself, there was not much to say except that no grass grew there, and a river ran swiftly through its center, feeding Lake Agolika. The grimacing effigies littered both halves of the plane.

Kalyra poked one of them. It jiggled. "Sandermik's Simulated Organic Matter," she said. "It took us weeks to obtain a sufficient quantity, but we have enough now for a few more trials. This will be our third. Bonguth, the disk, if you please." She gestured at a small rock near the river, where Bonguth placed the device, white button pointing up.

"Now, Ormish, the trigger mechanism."

Ormish stepped down from the boat carrying an unusual lever. Both ends held pointed glass weights, like the upper halves of hourglasses. The lighter of the two was half-filled with sand. The heavier was filled to the brim. Gilbert didn't understand what he was looking at until Ormish carefully positioned the raised, lighter point over of the modified wood-harvesting device, then opened a small latch on the bottom of the heavier end. A trickle of sand poured onto the grass. As the heavier side lost weight, the lighter lowered toward the device's button like a seesaw.

"Right then," said Kalyra. "That should give us about half an hour. Everyone back on the boat. Quickly please."

An urgency possessed the group as they shuffled onboard. The boat carried them well into the lake and stopped about a mile away from the dummy soldiers, still visible in the daylight. Everyone watched as the minutes ticked by. Gilbert picked nervously at the dirt under his nails.

The device erupted silently. A bright flash of teal skittered across the field like lightning, then blue slime rose up around each of the dummies and coated them. Moments later, everything vanished in a puff of silver particles. Just like that, not a single figure remained.

"There you have it," said Kalyra. "Be mindful, this was just a taste of the actual device's capabilities. To ensure complete annihilation of Hobblebosh's forces, we are working to increase its area of effect tenfold, if not more."

"Please tell me they rematerialize, whole, in some jail cell somewhere," said Lady Ufferbub quietly.

"Of course not." Kalyra waved her hand dismissively.

"An intentionally incomplete teleportation, coupled with an energy matrix that would destabilize just about any living thing it touched." Mardulo's face darkened. "This is barbaric."

Kalyra crossed her arms. "Just be glad we took out the enchantments responsible for chopping the wood."

"Kalyra." Lady Ufferbub's voice remained low and stern. Only a slight quiver betrayed the full extent of her anger. "You are proposing the murder of hundreds—thousands—of people, and you expect us to be pleased about the lack of a mess to clean up afterward?"

Kalyra shrugged. "And why not? It would be a beastly mess, I assure you. I have seen the aftermath of Hobblebosh's battles. This is better, and will cost us less—in time, money, and lives."

"How do you filter the device's targeting so that it only affects those loyal to Hobblebosh?" Mardulo asked. "True loyalty discernment has long been considered impossible in spellwork."

"The disk is indiscriminate," said Kalyra. "To limit its effects, we must ensure we only activate it around Hobblebosh's soldiers."

"And what of the soldiers who have been placed under some enchantment?" said Lady Ufferbub. "What of those being coerced?"

"They still serve Hobblebosh. They are guilty."

"Hobblebosh could have their families, their children, their loved ones!" said Lady Ufferbub. "What choice do they have?"

"The choice to resist! How many families have they ruined, trying to protect their own? It is no excuse."

Lady Ufferbub clenched her jaw. "Truly, spoken as someone who has never had a family to protect."

"That, coming from you, Normishdae? Quaint." Kalyra rolled her eyes. "I understand they have been put in a difficult situation, that they are scared and suffering, and I can empathize, but I can also empathize with those they have harmed—people who have died or had their lives ruined because of these soldiers. Coerced or not, they have exposed others to extreme cruelty in a misguided attempt to curtail their own troubles. They are guilty."

"They do not deserve death!" Mardulo strode forward. "You go too far."

Kalyra rounded on him. "What is the alternative? A battle? A war? If you win, the result is the same. They die, but at a higher cost of *truly* innocent lives. And if you lose—which, by all accounts, you will—what then?"

"My alternative is a trapping spell using the essence we obtained in Town Forbik!" Mardulo growled. "With that, no one need die. Why not help us?"

"It is too likely to fail. You stretch farther and farther for some kind of merciful solution, and your plans become less and less realistic. We cannot afford the luxury of optimism when Hobblebosh is only a few days' march from our shores."

Mardulo shook his head. "You honestly believed we would help you with this?"

Kalyra took a short breath and lifted her chin. "I expect you to, yes."

"I will not," said Mardulo.

"Let me put it differently, then," said Kalyra calmly. "We have the device. As you have seen, it works. But it has flaws, and you can help us solve those. Not flaws in effectiveness. Flaws in mercy. It takes longer than it needs to, and it will be painful. Additionally, we need a proper remote-activation mechanism. Our current timer system will not work inside an enemy encampment. Without that, one of our own must sacrifice themselves for the greater good. Lastly, we expect the next time Hobblebosh gathers in sufficient numbers will be when he attacks City Boratorus. We do not know how close he will be to the city, but we are willing to accept a certain threshold of collateral damage should it become necessary. Obviously, a dynamic perimeter would be preferable, but we would need your help to create one. You claim to care so much about reducing pain and suffering, so help us reduce it here, with this device. Because it will be used, Mardulo, with or without your help. The only difference is how kind its effects will be."

Kalyra looked at them all, never breaking her composure. "If it makes you feel any better," she added, "I will even throw in funding to refine the device so it only affects those who are genuinely loyal to Hobblebosh—if such a thing can be done. We can punish the rest of his soldiers more leniently over time. Though as you said, magic to detect one's true loyalties has long been considered impossible."

Everyone on the boat stared at Kalyra. Gilbert was completely at a loss for words.

Mardulo stammered. "That is the most ridiculous thing I have ever heard! To even begin work on loyalty detection would take months! You speak as if we would save lives by helping you finish this device, but those lives are only at risk because of your insistence upon this awful plan. I would save more lives if I simply sank this boat here and now!"

"I admit, the disk necessitates sacrifice, but it is still our best option. I was hoping you would see the reason in this, Mardulo. It is a decisive and effective plan—and far more likely to succeed than your own."

Lady Ufferbub took a step forward. "You are as bad as Hobblebosh himself. You attempt to force us into cooperation with your cruel schemes, holding innocent lives hostage."

"It is obscene!" Mardulo puffed his chest and marched to Lady Ufferbub's side. "We will not let you do it! I will stop you myself if I must."

Gilbert stepped into line beside them. "Yeah!" he added emphatically.

Kalyra raised her eyebrows. "And what about you, Bundersquash?"

Bundersquash was huddled a few steps away, whispering hurriedly with Toddleposter. He stood up straight when he heard his name. Toddleposter shot a troubled glance at Lady Ufferbub, but nothing more.

"Will you help us?" asked Kalyra.

Bundersquash gulped. He looked nervous, conflicted, but when he saw Mardulo, his face hardened into a scowl.

"I will help," he said defiantly. "I do not like this plan of yours, Kalyra. I detest that you deal with lives as if they are nothing more than bait, and I feel as though I am saving them from you as much as I am saving them from Hobblebosh. But Mardulo's methodology has proven ineffective, that much is clear. Again and again, it has led to failure and loss. First Burrid, then the Norwallis family, Lobster, the other animals in Town Forbik, all those we have failed to save..." He took a deep breath. "I do not know how to do all you have suggested, but if that is what it takes to finally put an end to Hobblebosh, I shall do what I can. So yes, I will help you, because you give me no other choice." He looked directly at Mardulo. "Standing by and doing nothing—that is no choice at all."

Toddleposter stuttered uncomfortably. "I will help as well," he mumbled, staring at his feet.

Mardulo opened and closed his mouth, wordless and utterly shocked.

"Very well," said Kalyra. "Then I suppose we should get to work. As for the rest of you..."

Someone shoved a bag over Gilbert's head.

Muffled cries sprang up all around. Gilbert struggled to pull free from his captors, but it had no effect. Two hands seized his wrists and wrenched them behind his back; then he was dragged several paces toward the back of the boat, where another pair of hands sent him stumbling down the stairs to the lower level. It sounded as though Mardulo and Lady Ufferbub were receiving similar treatment.

"Be careful with them!" Bundersquash cried out, but his voice fell away among the raucous clatter of guards, chain mail, and struggle.

Upsettingly quickly, Gilbert had been bruised into submission and forced to sit still on the musty wooden floor of the lower deck, hands bound behind his back, listening to the slow creaks and cracks of the boat. He could feel Mardulo and Lady Ufferbub pressed to either side of him, but whenever he tried to speak, he was silenced, forcefully reminded that he was not in control of this situation.

Eventually, they docked back in Town Agol, and the guards escorted Gilbert off the boat. His head was still bagged, but he could feel the slippery mud of the beach, then the solid wood of Agol's pathway as they made their way back into town.

Gilbert tried to keep track of their route, counting the turns and steps so he could find his way back if he ever managed to escape. Off the beach and onto the wooden path, then a left turn, then one, two, three, four, five steps forward, then a right turn, then another right, then straight for, um, thirty-four-ish steps, then a slight bend to the left and straight for...a while. Then left again...

He gave up.

With no better ideas, he resigned himself to the solemn march, stubbornly shuffling his feet as slowly as the guards would allow. The bag's coarse fibers scraped against his skin. When he inhaled, stale fabric clogged his nose. Exhaling left him swimming in his own hot air. He heard a few startled gasps from pedestrians as he lurched along, but mostly, his ears filled with the constant drumbeat of footsteps on wood. *Thud, thud, thud* hammering all around him.

A change in the echoes signaled they had walked indoors. A few minutes later, his escort jostled him carelessly down several flights of steps. The air cooled noticeably as he descended. A smell of dirt and moss clung to it. The floor changed from smooth wood to rough stone, and what little light pierced the bag's fibers weakened and paled. Gilbert had no idea where in Town Agol he was, but he supposed it made no difference. A dungeon was a dungeon.

They turned so many corners in that damp stone hall they must have been walking in circles. No single building could be that big. But at last, they pulled to a stop, and Gilbert heard stone scrape against stone—a heavy door, opening—followed by a flurry of rustling, then a string of rude remarks as Mardulo and Lady Ufferbub were pushed inside. A rough hand shoved Gilbert in after them, and the door slammed shut.

All fell silent.

Interlude: Tree and the Journey South

King Hobblebosh drove his forces toward the Great Splat at a grueling speed. It was easier for the trees than the soldiers, but everyone kept pace, and they reached their destination after a single day's travel. They had intentionally veered narrowsplatter, away from Collywobbles Bridge, to avoid any defenses or alarms the wizards may have created. They wouldn't need the bridge anyway. The king had something else in mind.

That evening, the army pitched their camp a mere mile from the bottomless chasm.

Trees did not sleep, but they did need rest, and they got very little that night. The sharp fizz of magic in the atmosphere made them uneasy, and no one really knew what awaited them the next day. King Hobblebosh had been sparse with the details.

He had not been the same since the attempted assassination. A new determination had taken root within him. He moved more quickly, with more force, and he was increasingly hard to predict.

At last, as dawn traced the horizon and light flittered through the swirling veil of the Splat, their king summoned everyone to the edge.

"Today," he cried to them all, "I show you true power. It is something often claimed by the wizards of this world, but I tell you now—they are charlatans. They do not understand magic. They *cannot*, for they lack the connection to those deeper parts of the universe, and so must experiment blindly, crafting clumsy theorems, guidelines, rules, and procedures with no actual knowledge behind them. But I am no mere wizard. I am of the lime! I have forged those connections with the universe, and I understand—truly understand—magic. I can make full use of its potential."

He gestured to his side. "Behold the Great Splat. Until this day, there has been but one passage connecting the two halves of this world. Decades, it took, and the labor of hundreds, including many a wizard. But today, single-handedly, I shall create a new path, and we will cross this chasm faster than any have crossed since its creation! Watch, all of you, and witness the might of your king, the venerable Obble Dor Hobblebosh the Juicy, the all-powerful savior of this land!"

The listeners launched into applause as King Hobblebosh rubbed his palms together and created an auric nebula. He raised his arms, cast his voice out over the Splat, and spoke using a language Tree did not recognize.

"Khazerri vormik'tel nor delvarish. Soldeur congramma rizilde magik intermerrin! Trek ondri, kai versei encom'al khazerri..."

On the ground before him, a strange device flickered to life, its wide top glowing with energy. Tree could sense its insides working—shifting, warping, grasping the intangible world in a way they could never have imagined. The very light of the sun seemed to funnel through that device and into King Hobblebosh. The world fell into twilight. The ground shook violently, the land itself bending around him.

Then it passed, but even as sunlight returned to the world, the shimmers of the Great Splat clustered before the king. The silken, lilac veil wove within itself, twisting, spiraling, joining. Then the king thrust his arms forward, and a streak of solidified energy drove out to form one shimmering, translucent bridge, maybe fifty feet wide, made of the very magic that poured from the Splat.

The device glowed for a moment, then burst into a cloud of silken swirls that merged with the newly created bridge.

Tree could still sense the Splat's fog churning within the bridge, but the structure itself was solid, if hollow. Hobblebosh stepped onto it, out over the abyss, confident and unafraid. He commanded his troops do the same.

Tree's leaves shook anxiously. The other trees were absolutely terrified. Hobblebosh, in stepping out, had shown them it was safe for a human-size creature, but what of a tree? They were something else entirely—heaver, taller, with roots instead of feet, designed to tunnel into the ground, not slither precariously over a smooth magical surface. But this was the way the king had provided. There was no other choice. They had to cross.

And Tree was their general. With that role came duty.

They focused on the forest. "I understand many of you fear this crossing. I myself am nervous. But do not forget, we have already done the impossible! We are trees, yet we wander. We have walked through meadow and field. We have shown this world that we are more than fodder for humans and their axes, and we have done all that through the might of Our Grand Master, King Hobblebosh the Juicy. Why doubt him now, after all he has done in our favor? He is one of us, and he knows us. I trust him, so let us use the gift he has given us and walk bravely into the unknown. We do this for trees around the world, and for our master, King Hobblebosh. Advance!"

It was not bad, Tree thought, for a first attempt at inspiring speechcraft. A little rough around the edges, but it worked—at least enough to get everyone onto the bridge.

Then Hobblebosh cast another spell, and the bridge's surface started to *move*. It rolled underneath the army, steadily pulling everyone forward as if the bridge itself walked on their behalf. But that alone was not enough, and Hobblebosh bade them march as well, their speed doubled by the bridge's own movement.

The other troops whooped and hollered, exhilarated by the boost, but the trees hated it. Even before the bridge had moved, their sense of its existence was fuzzy. It was a hollow thing, filled with swirling magic, as weightless as the air around it. Now, with it rolling underneath their roots, the trees felt as though they were walking on nothing but an icy wind.

"This is madness," said a tall pine, Coniferon the Tranquil. "I cannot tell where the bridge ends and the abyss begins! We shall fall, surely!"

A murmur of agreement echoed through the forest.

"I know it is difficult," said Tree. "The king asks much of us, but I have crossed this chasm once before, and I shall help you every step of the way."

Tree pressed on, acting far braver than they felt. A few followed, but not everyone. Already, the forest was falling behind Hobblebosh's long line of troops.

Old Oak came to Tree's side. "How may I help, Tree? I refuse to fear a bridge, and I refuse to fear a fall—not when half the world lies ahead, waiting to be explored. We joined so that we might roam this world and live in freedom. This crossing is a challenge, but one we shall overcome. I am with you."

"I am heartened by your words, Old Oak. Please, lead those who are willing and able. Go forth together and tell the king we are coming. I am sure he will understand. I shall stay with the others and guide them."

Old Oak bent their trunk, then gathered the faster trees and advanced into the distance.

Tree turned to the rest—fifty trees, maybe more. "Come, my friends. It is a long journey, but together, we shall pass."

"I wish I could follow, Tree, but I cannot see the way." The young tree named Folia trembled. "This is no place for a tree."

Tree came to their side. "You are right, Folia. Nonetheless, we are here. Think how far we have come. It is a hard road, but ahead lies a world of adventure."

"At times I wonder if this adventure will ever come. We risk so much to see it."

Tree reached out a branch and guided Folia forward. "This crossing, this war...it is scary and difficult, but one day, it will be nothing more than an echo in the past. Our king fights so we can live in freedom—free from worry, free from axes, free from fear. It is a future we must work for, but it shall be our present soon enough. I trust him. I trust that we will win this war, and when it is done, we can have our adventure."

Step by step, Tree coaxed everyone along, offering words encouragement, guiding them by their branches when needed, herding them away from the edge. With time, some gained confidence and helped, Folia first among them. Tree themselves nearly tumbled off the edge while helping a willow named Amenta, but Folia extended a root and pulled them back into balance.

For a time, Tree kept pace with a young ash named Seedspring, one of the first to enlist. They had joined against the wishes of those nearest them and now wondered if the others had been right to resist. Tree stayed by Seedspring's side as they walked carefully down the center of the bridge, taking slow, deliberate steps. They told tales to each other, taking their minds off the danger.

When Thistlefel the Nimble and Poppy the Elder, two lifelong friends, helped a tree named Asper avoid the edge, a sudden burst of energy rose from the Splat. All three of them froze in fear. Tree came to their side and patiently eased their minds. Tree had never met them personally but found the words to comfort them, then guided them back to the main group.

In their caution, the forest moved slowly. Hobblebosh's other soldiers had long since disappeared into the distance, but Tree kept moving, pushing everyone forward. They established a perimeter, rotating the trees that marched in front, and kept the surer footed to either side. An hour passed, then two. The sun moved steadily across the sky. On and on they went.

Unexpectedly, Old Oak returned.

"Hello," said Tree. "Where are those that went with you? Have they finished the crossing already?"

"Yes, Tree, but the king is furious." Old Oak's anxiety was almost tangible, even in the Splat's magical haze. "He has ordered you to double your pace and warned that if we do not finish the crossing by sundown, the bridge shall be destroyed, whether we remain upon it or not. I told him it was a cruel ultimatum, that we needed more time, but I was unable to persuade him. He has been so long in his human form, I fear he has forgotten what it is like to sense as a tree. He...removed one of my branches as punishment for my insolence."

Tree nearly tripped over their own roots. "The king has drawn arms against his own kind?"

"I am afraid so."

Extending a branch, Tree could feel Old Oak's pain. The shreds of the missing branch burned like fire through their wood and bark. Tree had felt that pain before.

"The king has gone too far," said Tree. "Thank you, Old Oak, for your warning. You have shown great valor today, and I stand by you. On this bridge, we are at his mercy, but I shall speak with him the moment we reach land, for this affront cannot be ignored! I do not care if he is king. He shall not harm anyone under my command!"

Old Oak bowed. "You have my gratitude, dear Tree."

Together, they both did their best to shepherd the others along. The sun was already setting. Tree had never been so tense. The bridge moved beneath their roots, pulling like a swift river current, but it tripped them as often as it helped. At last, just as the sun touched the western horizon, Tree caught sight of land ahead. They turned to Old Oak.

"We are almost there. Please, help the others finish. I will go speak with Hobblebosh, to buy us time and end this awful madness."

Old Oak agreed, and Tree rushed ahead.

"King Hobblebosh the Juicy!" Tree called, hurling themselves onto solid land. They lurched at the sudden stillness of the world. "Old Oak tells me you threatened to destroy this bridge, even if trees remain upon it. And they say you cut off one of their branches. Is this true?"

"Yes, Tree," said Hobblebosh. "Because of your battalion's constant dithering, we are behind schedule. We were supposed to finish this crossing in half a day. The cowardice of your troops has cost us dearly, and I have already shown more patience than you deserve. As for Old Oak's branch—I will no longer be questioned by my subordinates. You had best learn from that example, Tree, or I will chop more than a branch from you."

Tree trembled. "You go too far, Hobblebosh. I cannot—"

"*King* Hobblebosh!" Hobblebosh bellowed. "Do not disrespect me, Tree! Say one more word and I shall remove the bridge this instant! I do not care who remains upon it. I have had enough of your impudence and ineptitude. I remove you from your position as general. I shall find another to command." He signaled to one of his men. "You, find Lugbrush and tell him he has just been promoted. Then have him bring me an axe. Tree, you have questioned my wisdom three times, now—the oath, the executions, now this. For that, I shall take three branches."

Tree waited while the axe was fetched, their anxiety rising—but not because of the impending punishment. Their thoughts remained with Old Oak, with the other trees on the bridge, and with the steadily lowering sun. If this punishment bought them time, it would be worthwhile. The forest was close now. Some of the trees were already dismounting. Folia and Amenta leaped to solid ground together.

When Lugbrush arrived, axe in hand, then sun had set completely. Most of the trees had finished their crossing, but nearly a dozen still remained upon the bridge. Old Oak was with them, pushing them forward. Tree could feel their panic.

"Alas, your time is up," said Obble Dor Hobblebosh. He walked to the edge and prepared a spell.

"No, wait!" cried Tree. "Take my branches first. Please. Three, you said. I will give you six, twelve, whatever you need, but take them before you remove this bridge. If time is your only concern, the order of events makes no difference. Take my branches first, and more trees shall remain to strengthen your forces. They may not be fast on this magical bridge, but on land, their strength is unmatched. You know this, my king. Please. Take my branches first."

Even now, some of the stragglers drew near. A stone's throw. Maybe two.

Hobblebosh looked at Tree. "Six branches I shall take," he said. "Three for your earlier transgressions, and three for questioning me once again...but I shall take them afterward, Tree, for this, too, is a lesson. A lesson in how your king receives failure."

Tree cried out in horror, but it was no use. Hobblebosh had already created his nebula, and the spell was short. With a blinding flash, the bridge vanished, and Tree stared as their friends, Old Oak among them, lurched, scrambled, and fell.

Panicked and terrified, they disappeared into the abyss below.

"Thus, the weak fall, and the strong remain," said Hobblebosh. "Our army is better for it."

Tree barely listened. Their mind was blank—a static hum of fury and disbelief. How could Hobblebosh do this? Why had Tree trusted such a ruthless figure in the first place?

Down in the depths, their friends' lives winked out, one spark at a time.

Hobblebosh shrugged, turned away, and took the axe from Lugbrush.

"Six branches," he said to Tree. "Say any more against me, and I shall make it twelve. Or perhaps I will find a torch and destroy you altogether."

He rolled his shoulders, hefted the axe, and swung.

Chapter 19

Life Inside

"I cannot believe the nerve of this bloody town!" Lady Ufferbub fumed. It was rare for her to raise her voice. Earlier, with Kalyra, it had never grown beyond an angry simmer. Now she paced up and down, fists clenched, frustration boiling over. Even Mardulo looked surprised.

They were in a rectangular cell. The walls were gray stone. The floor was gray stone. The door was gray stone, concealed within the wall so that, closed, it looked invisible. There were two adjoining rooms, one with two stone beds, and one with a toilet and a wooden cupboard. Shortly after everyone had been thrown inside, a guard had come to remove the bags that covered their heads, then left without a single word. They'd been alone ever since.

"A mass murder device?" Lady Ufferbub put her ear to the wall, then kicked the stone. "And then they imprison us! Us! We are their best chance at stopping Hobblebosh, and they shove us in here to...what? To rot?"

Mardulo glanced at Gilbert. Gilbert glanced back. Neither said a word.

Suddenly, the door opened with a low rumble, and a heavily decorated guard walked in. He had finely combed hair and several important-looking badges adorning his half shoulder cape. He wore rust-red cloth gloves.

"Good evening, friends!" he said, shaking everyone's hand. "My name is Neothud Rud Inklebee the Adventurer. Master Jailer. It's such a pleasure to make your acquaintance!"

"Um," said Mardulo.

"I hope the living quarters are to your liking. Truth be told, we're fortunate this room was available! It's our last original-condition deluxe suite. Many of our other cells—particularly the larger ones—have been refurbished to serve as housing for the refugees. But not to worry. Here, you can rest assured you're getting the full prison experience! Some might even say you're living in a real heritage site!"

"Um," said Gilbert.

"Of course, there are a few other cells still around, nondeluxe, filled with the usual rabble. But this is something special." Neothud stroked the wall.

"Excuse me," said Lady Ufferbub. "Is there any actual purpose to your visit?"

"Ah! A woman of action. I appreciate that." Neothud bowed. "Primarily, I am here to introduce myself and to get to know you a little. I consider it my personal responsibility to ensure that all of our guests here in the Town Agol dungeons feel comfortable and appreciated. Secondarily, we shall be having dinner soon, and I must ask if you have any dietary restrictions I should be made aware of."

"I would like to leave," said Lady Ufferbub. "When will we be released?"

"Ah, well, you do ask the difficult questions, don't you, Normishdae?" Neothud leaned in with a conspiratorial chuckle but straightened up when Lady Ufferbub made no sign of reciprocation. "I am afraid I cannot say for sure," he continued more formally. "Once we have eradicated Hobblebosh, I expect. Though of course, it is my personal hope that during your stay, you will reconsider your decision to abandon your loved ones to a life of desolate servitude under the tyrant Obble Dor Hobblebosh—in which case, we may release you sooner to aid in our ongoing efforts."

"Now, that's hardly fair!" Mardulo shouted. "We had a plan of our own!"

"I have heard about it," said Neothud, "but please understand, it is our firm belief here in Town Agol that the time for such half measures has long since passed. We must all strive for definitive action. But enough about that. I'm not here to talk politics. Is there anything more I can get for you? Elsewise, I must circle back to my earlier inquiry about the dietary restrictions."

"I have none," said Mardulo.

"Er, me either," said Gilbert.

"And you, Normishdae?"

"You may call me Lady Ufferbub," she said. "And no."

"Very good. Dinner will be delivered to your room at seven thirty this evening. Breakfast is at seven o'clock tomorrow morning, and lunch is at noon. But of course, if you wish to personalize any aspect of your schedule, please do not hesitate to ask. In the meantime, I am here to serve you, however I may. Please, take some time to relax, unwind, and enjoy your stay in our dungeons."

With that, he left.

Mardulo walked to the edge of the room and sat with his back against the wall, head in his hands. "What a mess..." he said softly. "Do you think Bundersquash is really going to help with that device? I knew he was upset, but I never thought...is this what I've made of him?" Mardulo's voice quivered.

Lady Ufferbub looked at him but said nothing.

"We don't know what Bundersquash and Toddleposter are up to," said Gilbert. "But right now, we're on our own. Do you know any spells to break us out?"

"I expect everything is warded." Mardulo waved a hand at the door without even looking.

Gilbert took a slow, calming breath. Lady Ufferbub looked ready to explode. Mardulo looked ready to cry. Gilbert felt like he could go either way, but none of that would help them escape. If everyone could just reenergize and refocus, Gilbert was sure Mardulo and Lady Ufferbub could think of something. They needed some positivity. Some hope.

Gilbert put on a smile. "Well," he said, "at least Neothud seems willing to make us comfortable. Perhaps we can get some mattresses for the beds in the other room. Then we can rest and revisit our options in the morning."

Silence.

"If you'd like, I can ask for some pillows too. Maybe a few sheets and some blankets. There's no point in—"

"Be quiet, Gilbert." Lady Ufferbub looked ready to say more, then stopped herself.

Gilbert's already-false smile dropped to a scowl. His willpower might have held longer, but he was utterly done with the constant passive aggression Lady Ufferbub had been serving him the past few days.

"If you have something to say, you may as well say it," he said. "It's not like we're pressed for time."

For a moment, Lady Ufferbub seemed to debate whether to take him up on the offer. Then she looked him squarely in the eye and said, "Only that we would not be here, if not for your irresponsible, angst-ridden escapade into the wilderness. When we left Town Forbik, we had just enough time to get to City Boratorus and complete our task before Hobblebosh's soldiers arrived. But we wasted all of that time searching for you."

"Oh, for goodness' sake! We've been over this!" Gilbert stepped toward her, meeting her stare with his own. "I didn't ask you to search for me! I told you to go back to City Boratorus, but you didn't listen. That was your choice. Not mine. Don't blame me."

"You know, there was a time when such ungrateful immaturity would have surprised me from you, Gilbert," Lady Ufferbub's voice lowered, and it was far worse than any amount of shouting would have been. "But no longer. You have proven to be one of the most thoughtless and unappreciative people I have ever met."

Gilbert roiled. "Where is this coming from?"

"Where do you think?" said Lady Ufferbub. "Everything you have done since Town Forbik. You abandoned us, just when Toddleposter and I could have used your help with Mardulo and Bundersquash. You mistrusted Thorippela and spoke badly of her behind her back after everything she did to help you. And even now, you act as if you wish to help, but in secret, you plot to return to Earth at your earliest convenience. I thought you meant it as a punishment when you proposed the idea in the meadows. Now I learn you actually *want* to return! And not only that, but you expect us to assist you too—despite all that we have done to help you integrate into this world."

"That…I never…" Gilbert took a step back. He hadn't told anyone about that. Anyone, except…"Thorippela told you?"

"She said you wished to return to your homeland and even had the *gall* to claim we owed it to you to help."

"Gilbert, is that true?" asked Mardulo, now more upset than ever.

"You see?" said Lady Ufferbub. "Mardulo and Bundersquash took you in. They clothed you, they fed you, they taught you. They helped you adapt in every way. And after all that, you would ask them to send you back into oblivion?"

"Not oblivion!" A sudden defiance took root inside Gilbert. "Earth! My home! And it's my choice if I want to go back."

"Earth is fiction, Gilbert! It does not exist! There is no Earth for you to go back to."

Gilbert hesitated. "You don't know that for sure."

"Neither do you," said Lady Ufferbub. "We've worked hard to give you a place in this world. Now you think nothing of what it might mean, asking us to send you back, to undo your very existence. Imagine if Toddleposter had—" She cut herself off. With a few shallow breaths, she recomposed herself. "As I said, thoughtless and ungrateful."

"And what about you, Lady Ufferbub? You're the ones who pulled me here in the first place! Was that thoughtful? Should I be grateful that you tore me away from everything and everyone I ever loved, just to subject me to...*this*?!" He flung his arms around.

Lady Ufferbub's expression wavered. "It was an accident."

"Sure, like that makes it all okay," said Gilbert bitterly. "And now you tell me Earth isn't real, that there's nowhere to send me back to, but you have no evidence to support that. You've made an assumption because you can't be bothered to figure out the truth! But tell me this. If Earth isn't real, why did I have to disappear from the book in order to appear in this world?"

A flicker of uncertainty crossed Lady Ufferbub's face. "The spell simply pulled you out at the end of your part in the story."

"Then why did it pick me," said Gilbert, "the person who just *happened* to disappear unexpectedly? You haven't even considered it, have you? And you call me thoughtless...don't you think it's worth investigating, at least?"

But before anyone could answer, a loud scraping came from the wall that held the door. Alternating columns of stone slid into the floor, transforming the entire wall into the bars of a prison cell. Kalyra stood on the other side, staring.

"Having a little squabble, are we?" she said.

"If you are here to try and convince us to join your cause," said Lady Ufferbub, "you can leave. We are not interested in your savagery."

Kalyra glared at her. "It is not savagery."

"Clearly you have been too long away from the library. Release me, and I shall fetch you a dictionary."

"Enough." Kalyra closed her eyes, mustering patience. "Did you know, Normishdae, that I was visiting Town Tarley when Hobblebosh first began his expansion? I was there on an errand from the board of representatives to discuss a potential trade agreement. I watched as their famous Town Tarley Militia marched off in glory to fight the lime at the River Ikk. I saw hundreds upon hundreds of soldiers leave those gates, trailed by the cheers of their loved ones. And I saw all twelve who returned."

Lady Ufferbub scowled. "A horrible story, I expect, but I, too, have seen my fair share of Hobblebosh's cruelty, and it does not excuse the murder of innocent people."

"Normishdae, if you still believe Hobblebosh's followers to be innocent, then you really do not understand. The battle at River Ikk was not just deadly. To this day, it remains the deadliest of Hobblebosh's time. Hobblebosh had not blocked magic yet. It was a bloodbath on both sides. Hobblebosh's numbers were halved, at least. Town Tarley lost nearly everyone. The assistance from City Mez never even saw the river. If you ask Town Tarley's citizens now, they will say you could hear the screams from inside the town. Nonsense, of course. But I do remember the moans and retches of those twelve who returned.

"Hobblebosh himself had force-fed them saproweed seeds. Have you ever witnessed its effects, Normishdae? And I don't mean some hyperanalytical encyclopedia description. I mean the terrible, visceral reality. Once swallowed, the seed plants itself in the stomach and starts to grow. The victims were bedridden in a matter of days. I am sure you can imagine it was not a pleasant experience for any of them, nor their loved ones. But it was not the constant pain that took them—not the cramps, not the vomit, not the bleeding. No. Saproweed is not so kind as that. It fills the stomach but offers no sustenance in return, nor does it leave room for anything else. All twelve of those brave, noble soldiers, after weeks of horrid suffering, died slowly of starvation.

"So, look me in the eye, Normishdae, and tell me that any soldier—coerced or otherwise—who can stand by and watch while Hobblebosh does that is innocent."

Gilbert swallowed.

"As I thought," said Kalyra. "I tried to help in the aftermath of that battle, but there was little I could do, so I returned to Town Agol as soon as possible and immediately got to work. I was determined. Hobblebosh would never do to us what he did to Town Tarley, should he make it this far south. And here we are. He is almost upon us and stronger than ever. His power has quadrupled since he conquered City Mez. He has money and resources. His restricted zone has already spread below the Great Splat, and every day, it continues to expand. There is even talk of moving trees serving at his beck and call.

"Don't you see? Our plan is not barbaric, Normishdae. It is not savage. It is necessary—a desperate last resort, yes, but we have no other choice. We cannot afford to risk everything on some half-baked trapping-spell-in-lo-rilell-dust plot conjured up by a band of misfits who have otherwise failed at every turn. We must act, and we must do so now."

After a pause, Lady Ufferbub spoke. "Hobblebosh goes too far," she said softly. "That is no surprise to any of us. He is cruel beyond measure. You need not remind us of that." Her tone shifted, took an edge. "But perhaps, if Town Agol had bothered to lift a finger before Hobblebosh reached its own doorstep, we could have avoided these 'desperate last resorts' entirely. Perhaps, we could have worked together and stopped him months ago. But you stayed your hand, and you waited, and others fought and died while you watched from a distance, hoping you would not be next. But Agol's time has come at last, and you find yourself backed into a corner. So now you wish to meet Hobblebosh's excessive cruelty with an excess of your own, but doing so drains what little remains of your already dwindling integrity. You waited too long to lend your aid, and no choice that remains is a good one. Yet still, you have chosen the worst."

Kalyra glanced at Lady Ufferbub, almost pitying. "Your refusal to act decisively will be the end of you, Normishdae. I do not think I shall miss you."

This had very little effect on Lady Ufferbub. "You will not listen, Kalyra, and you have nothing I wish to hear. Leave or waste your breath, but I am done with this conversation."

"Just as well," said Kalyra. "I did not come to argue ethics with a librarian. I came to speak with Mardulo."

"Me?" Mardulo lifted his head, still sitting on the floor. He looked tired—more tired than Gilbert had ever seen him.

"Bundersquash tells me you are still in possession of Hobblebosh's essence. He needs it. He thinks it might be useful for the remote targeting and activation of the device."

"Then he is wrong," said Mardulo, "and I will not give it to you."

"You are not in a position to negotiate, Mardulo. We will get it, one way or another. Do not make me fetch the jailer."

Mardulo's face showed nothing but age and weariness. "Do what you must," he said.

"I will." Kalyra sighed. "Why will the two of you not see reason?"

When she received no answer, she huffed impatiently and gestured for one of the guards to reseal the cell.

"Wait!" Gilbert cried out. "Before you go..."

Kalyra looked at him, eyebrows raised. "Yes, Gigglebrit?"

Gilbert continued, hesitantly. "I understand that something has to be done about Hobblebosh, but why risk everything on a single plan? You said it yourself: we can't afford to mess this up, and we're on the same side. You can work on your disk if you must, but why not allow us to work on this trapping spell too? Where's the harm?"

"That is simple," said Kalyra. "Mardulo and Lady Ufferbub—and even you, if you recall—wished to destroy our device. Mardulo even threatened to stop us himself. You have become a threat to our mission, and thus a threat to our town. And we prefer to keep such threats down here, in the dungeons, where they cannot do us harm."

Gilbert thought back to his words on the boat and suddenly wished he had been less enthusiastic.

Kalyra left. The guard pulled a lever, and the stone strips rose back up from the floor. The wall was solid gray once more.

"A valiant effort, Gilbert." Mardulo heaved onto his feet. "She's right, though. I would have destroyed that murder disk the first moment I could." He reached into his pocket and pulled out the vial containing Hobblebosh's hair. "Best you hang on to it. I expect they'll search me quite thoroughly."

"Why give it to me?" said Gilbert, eyebrows raised. "Why not Lady Ufferbub?"

"Because Kalyra would expect me to give it to Lady Ufferbub." Mardulo smiled, if weakly. "It might buy you some time to find a good hiding spot, though perhaps not more than a few minutes. And do be careful. Essence is delicate—at least, in an incorporeal sense. Try not to expose it to anything too...*magic-y* if you can." He looked as if speaking that sentence may have physically harmed him, but he pressed on. "If we lose the hair before we can extract a signature from it, we really will be back at square one."

Gilbert took the vial. "I'll do my best."

"And Gilbert ..." Mardulo had a nervous look on his face. He glanced toward Lady Ufferbub, then lowered his voice. "It's just, while I have your attention, I thought...about Earth. You returning there, I mean. To be honest, lad, I don't know what's possible, but if you want to go back...well, that's your decision, and I'll do what I can. I consider you a good friend, and I will help you, if you wish it." He took a breath and straightened. "But don't blame Lady Ufferbub. She is concerned for you and under great stress. We all are. But it was Bundersquash and I who pulled you here, not her, and I was the instructor. That makes this my responsibility, and mine alone. I am sorry for the pain it has caused you."

Gilbert looked at the wizard in front of him—his hooked nose, his long, straggling beard. Mardulo seemed older than ever, the usual mischievous grin wiped clean from his face.

"It's all right, Mardulo. But thanks. I hope they're not too rough, searching for the hair."

Mardulo scoffed, and just like that, the grin was back. "I'll manage."

He shook his arms, rolled his neck, and kicked his legs a few times. Then he stood by the wall and waited for the jailer to tackle him.

And he waited.

And he waited.

In the meantime, Gilbert hid the essence inside the bathroom cabinet. The bedroom had a simple arched entrance connected to the main cell, but the bathroom had an actual door. It wasn't exactly secret, but at least it was private.

When Gilbert reemerged, Mardulo was still waiting, eyebrows furrowed. He tapped his feet anxiously.

The jailer never came.

At least, not until dinner, when Neothud returned with three meticulously plated meals.

"I thought you were going to search me!" Mardulo almost sounded disappointed.

Neothud looked at him. "Apparently Bundersquash has decided there are better ways to get what he needs. And believe me, I am relieved to hear it. I would never wish to subject you to such indecent discomfort."

He handed each of them a plate of food. Mardulo took his with some skepticism but seemed disinclined to press the matter, and Gilbert certainly wasn't going to argue. Soon enough, Neothud bowed his exit and left them to their meal.

They sat on the floor to eat. It was better than Gilbert had expected. Warm bread with apple butter, a thin wedge of cheese, and some water. The plain food sat more easily in his stomach than the rich fish and potatoes he'd eaten the night before. Afterward, Neothud came to collect their dishes and wished them all good night.

There was a subdued air to the cell that evening. Lady Ufferbub and Gilbert barely acknowledged one another, and Mardulo had entered a thoughtful kind of melancholy. Not long after dinner, Gilbert went to sleep.

In his dreams, he chased his parents once again. They watched him from the fire. When Gilbert reached them, the flames blistered his skin, but he held their hands all the same. He and his parents burned away together, burned with the Earth, and vanished.

The next morning, he awoke scared and tense; every muscle was sore. He had taken one of the two beds, though the floor may have been more comfortable. The bed was little more than a slightly different shade of equally cold, equally hard stone, with the added risk of rolling off.

Gilbert stood, stretched, and walked into the main chamber of the prison cell. There, he found Lady Ufferbub humming to herself, and Mardulo tapping his fingers listlessly in the back corner of the room.

"Good morning," said Gilbert. "I think it's morning, anyway."

"Yes," said Lady Ufferbub. "You missed breakfast. Neothud brought us some tea and crumpets. I saved you a crumpet."

She held it out, still plated. It was buttered, cold, and slightly soggy.

"Thanks," said Gilbert. He took a bite.

"Listen." Lady Ufferbub spoke once Gilbert's mouth was full. "About our disagreement yesterday...I was too harsh. You are grieving the loss of your family and home, and I am sure the reality you face every day is far beyond anything I could imagine. Nonetheless, I want what is best for you, and I feel I must express my concerns. I leave it to you whether you heed them. There are many unknowns in this situation."

It sounded rehearsed, but Gilbert didn't mind. She was making an effort. He took another bite of his soggy crumpet and signaled for her to continue.

"I was wrong to suggest that you change your name," she began. "And I was wrong to imply that Earth should be forgotten entirely. It is a part of you—an important part—and one worth keeping. But the world itself...the world is fiction. I know the author personally. Podish Gubber Tuggerbug the Stumped. I have seen him create and destroy and change Earth in a hundred different ways, often on a whim, shaping it to suit his needs. There need not be logic to it, nor reason, nor any kind of backing beyond the will of the author and the needs of the story. With a quick flourish of a quill, an entire city moves, simply because it suits the narrative. With a scratch and a scribble, a character disappears entirely, and no one ever knows to miss them. You were born of a draft, Gilbert, one with many revisions pending.

"Had I sent my notes to Podish a week earlier and received a different draft in return, you may have been created with an entirely different set of memories. Your family would have camped less, for example, but taken a trip to Rome, and you would be several years younger. You would not be *you*, in other words, simply because Podish had wished it or because I had suggested it. Perhaps it is true we do not fully understand what a fictional world entails nor whether one can enter it as you desire, but it is still fiction. Even if you did return and did not simply disappear, what then? What meaning would your life have, truly, if you lived in a fiction and knew it?"

Gilbert had finished his crumpet. He sat quietly for a moment, biting his lip, consciously containing his frustration, and forced himself to remember what Mardulo had said the day before. Lady Ufferbub only wanted to help. He tried to appreciate her willingness to offer advice, however intrusive, and to think through all she had said.

"Maybe you're right," he replied at last. "But they're my family. The chance to see them again, the time I could spend with them if I returned—that gives my life meaning enough."

"I understand that you miss them, but please think carefully. Is it truly worth sacrificing your chance to live in the real world? Is that what your parents would want? It is difficult to move on, but at least you have the opportunity to do so. And you have the book and your memories. In those, your family remains. But *you* can do more than linger in word and recollection. *You* can shape the real world, through real action, and live a real life—if only you choose to stay."

"I'm choosing to go back to the ones I love!" Gilbert's bottled anger threatened to break loose. "You keep saying they aren't real, but they are. They're real to me. I'm here, I'm real, and I have those memories. Real memories, even if they're from an imagined place and a fictional time. I can't just dismiss them." He paced the room, and suddenly, an idea occurred to him. He marveled that he hadn't thought of it sooner.

"What if we summoned them here?" he asked. "My parents, I mean. From the book, just like you summoned me. Then you don't have to send me back. We can all live here, in the real world, together."

Lady Ufferbub looked at him for a moment. "I am not sure that is possible. Remember, you were summoned here by accident, through the semiguided nondeterministic behavior of a spell gone wrong. If I recall correctly, it also summoned a tree. To replicate that..."

"I get that it might be difficult," said Gilbert, excitement building, "but we could still try. We have the book and everything! It's just sitting on my bookshelf in the Wizards' Tower." He looked eagerly at Mardulo. "You're the best wizard in the world! If anyone could do it, surely you could!"

Mardulo shifted uneasily. "I'm...not sure, Gilbert."

Gilbert's enthusiasm froze on his face. It was rare to see Mardulo admit so openly that something might not be possible. His spirits plummeted. "Why not?"

"It's difficult to explain," said Mardulo. "It may be possible to bring them here. It may not. I couldn't say for sure without further investigation. Certainly, it would be hard work, potentially years of research, but when has that ever stopped me? No, that is not the issue. It's this town. It's Kalyra and her mass murder device. It's Hobblebosh, his very existence, and even you, Gilbert, pulled into this world, all you've been forced to go through. It's gotten me thinking. We see it in history too. Just look at the fall of Great Port Sugwater, or the use of a magic-infused plant like saproweed seed, or the creation of the Great Splat and the history behind it. There is a common thread. If you just take a step back and ask yourself *why...*"

Mardulo looked at his hands. He seemed to shrink into himself as he spoke. "So many of the problems we find ourselves facing today—they're all tied to magic. Unheeded, unbounded, unchecked magic. Magic created Hobblebosh. He uses it daily to terrorize his subjects. Magic enabled the creation of Town Agol's murder device too. And magic created you, Gilbert, and tore you away from so much. All because I—as Bundersquash would say it—rushed into my plan to summon Pottleswee Plugg Thudigarde the Brave with hardly a thought to the consequences."

Lady Ufferbub looked awestruck. "Of all the people in this world to caution us against the use of magic," she said, "I would never, in all my life, have guessed it would be you, Mardulo."

"It's not all bad." Mardulo grinned at her. "For every Great Splat, there's a sandwich generator. Bundersquash lost his arm because of Hobblebosh's magic, but lorilell dust saved his life on Collywobbles Bridge. All I mean to say is, we have been reckless. We need to consider the ramifications, intended or otherwise, of what we do and what we create. And Gilbert, I am worried about the ramifications of pulling more people out of fiction."

Gilbert blinked at him. His chest tightened. "Can you please explain? Because as far as I can tell, the main ramification is me seeing my family again."

Mardulo nodded. To Gilbert's surprise, the elderly wizard's eyes brimmed with tears. "I understand. I do. But I have been to a wizards' university. Do you think we are the first to wish for fiction made real? Worlds and creatures that do not exist, suddenly there at our fingertips. Who wouldn't want to have their favorite storybook character sitting beside them as a friend? And how many adolescent wizards, do you think, have obtained a copy of *Veribelle's Message* and conjured up certain ideas about Merrywhill the Lush or Bandoo the Strong?"

Lady Ufferbub raised her eyebrows.

"If we pull your parents out of fiction, Gilbert," Mardulo continued, "then we prove that it can be done intentionally. And from there, it is only a matter of time. Imagine how many more people would have to suffer through what you are experiencing now if we open that door—and not all of them will be able to bring their families with them."

Gilbert wavered. "Couldn't we just keep it secret?"

"As I said, it would take years of research, and who knows how many resources. It would be difficult to gather those without raising suspicion." Mardulo smiled sadly. "As it stands, we can explain you away as an anomaly—nondeterminism at work, anything can happen, and ideally, not *too* many people will ask. But if you suddenly had a family too...it would be tricky, Gilbert, to do all that and keep it a secret."

Gilbert closed his eyes. A hollowness grew in his chest.

Mardulo spoke again, hesitantly. "With that said, tricky does not mean impossible. There is no need to jump to conclusions. Not yet. Let us take some time to think on it, shall we? We have many pressing issues at hand, and I expect we will not be able to do anything regarding Earth until we put an end to Hobblebosh."

"You're right." Gilbert sighed, letting the weight of the conversation fall away. "Hobblebosh first. Earth later. Until then, maybe we can let the matter rest?"

"I think that would be wise," said Lady Ufferbub.

"In that case, has anyone figured out how to escape?"

"Alas, not I," said Lady Ufferbub.

"Nor I." Mardulo shook his head. "I expect our best course of action may be to win over a guard or simply make a break for it when someone opens the door. If this place was not so devoid of useful ingredients, perhaps I could cook something up. But as it stands, I'm rather at a loss."

"What about the essence?" said Gilbert. "Yesterday, you mentioned extracting a signature from it?"

"Yes. Generally, if you have essence that risks deteriorating before you can use it, you extract a signature. You can calibrate spells based on that signature instead of the essence itself. It's trickier to do but better than nothing. The trouble is, extracting a signature is costly. Ascorbic acid, murex mucus, transferrable fluorescence, salt, clay, calcined bone dust, the list goes on...I was hoping Town Agol would have what we needed. Alas, that did not go well."

Gilbert took a deep breath. "Perhaps making a break for it isn't the worst idea after all..." But he doubted their chances. It seemed unlikely their cell would be left so unguarded as to allow for that kind of thing.

Lunch came a few hours later. Gilbert and the others had decided not to attempt an escape just yet. They would only get one chance, and they needed to gather as much information as they could, first. Every interaction with the guards was an opportunity to do just that.

"Oh, Neothud!" Lady Ufferbub caught him before he left. "I know that we are your prisoners here, and, well, normally I would not ask, but you made such an impression earlier—speaking so kindly, ensuring our comfort, taking personal responsibility for the enjoyment of our stay. I thought, perhaps, you would be understanding. It is just…I find I am rather at a loss for things to do in this cell. Is there any chance you might bring me a book or two, just to help me pass the time?"

Neothud glowed. "My dear Lady Ufferbub, it would be a perfect pleasure! I live to serve, after all. Have you any requests? What is your genre of choice?"

"Perhaps a history of Town Agol if you can find one. I hear it has an exceptionally vibrant past, and I find myself woefully unknowledgeable on the subject. Hardly a state to be in, if I am to stay long term."

"Of course! It shall be done." Neothud bowed, then skipped out of the cell, closing the door behind him.

"Well, that was easy." Lady Ufferbub smiled. The hope was, a history book would shed some light on where the town kept their jail cells. And who knew what else they might find in the process?

"Maybe we can ask him for some mattresses and pillows next." Gilbert's shoulders were still sore from the night before.

"A mattress or pillow wouldn't be a bad place to hide the essence, actually," said Mardulo thoughtfully.

"As long as no one rolls on it…" said Gilbert, then started on his lunch. Clam chowder, some bread, and a large jug of orange juice. Gilbert tried the chowder first—and almost gagged.

"That is…really salty," he said, grimacing.

Mardulo tried his next. "Goodness gracious me." He spit the soup back out.

"It cannot be that bad," said Lady Ufferbub, who quickly learned that, actually, it could.

"Well, so much for that." Gilbert shoved his bowl away. "At least the rolls are warm."

He was halfway through his bread when he took a sip of orange juice, and a thought occurred to him. "Mardulo, you mentioned needing ascorbic acid and salt to extract the essence's signature. Doesn't orange juice have ascorbic acid? And the salt in the soup...do you think that could work?"

Mardulo stroked his beard, looking at the food. "We could certainly use the juice for ascorbic acid. But I would have to extract the salt, and that would usually require..." His voice trailed off. Suddenly, he lunged for Lady Ufferbub's roll, having finished his own, and tore it in half. "This might work!" He removed one of the clam chunks from his soup, juggled it briefly while it cooled, then squeezed it between two fingers. "Yes!"

He sprang from his position on the floor, charged into the bathroom, and blocked the sink's drain with his sock. Then he dumped everyone's chowder into the basin, pulled out several chunks of the roll's soft center, and added those to the mix.

"Quick, guard the door," Mardulo said to Lady Ufferbub and Gilbert. "We don't want Neothud walking in on this."

They did as he asked, and a few minutes later, Mardulo came back into the main cell, shirt dripping wet, with several tablespoons of salt in hand.

"I'm not sure where to put it." His eyes swept the room. He looked excited, a little of his old mischief returned.

Then the door opened.

Mardulo yelped and scrambled back into the bathroom, still holding the salt. Gilbert and Lady Ufferbub tried to look natural.

"Lady Ufferbub!" Neothud walked in. "I have brought you Boric's *History of Town Agol*. A real humdinger of a historian, Boric. Agolian native, did you know?"

"I did not," said Lady Ufferbub. She grabbed the book and led Neothud back to the cell door before he could notice the missing dishes—or the missing wizard. "I very much look forward to reading it."

"Please, do let me know once you finish. I would be happy to bring you another. And you, Gilbert, if there's anything I can get you, please do not hesitate to ask. And Mardulo...where is Mardulo?"

"I'm in here!" Mardulo shouted from behind the door. "If I may put in a request, perhaps some playing cards."

Gilbert and Lady Ufferbub looked at one another. Lady Ufferbub shrugged.

Gilbert decided to go with it. "More fun than books, if you ask me," he lied.

"Of course!" said Neothud. "It is a common enough request. We have a dozen decks in the guard room. I shall bring you one shortly. Have a good day, all of you!"

When he left, Mardulo reemerged. "Sorry. I just thought, cards tend to come in boxes, and we may need one or two."

"I see," said Lady Ufferbub.

Gilbert scratched his head. "You know, in hindsight, we probably could have just asked for some salt."

"That...is true." Mardulo wrung his shirt dry. "Oh well."

"What more do you need to extract the signature?" Gilbert asked.

"Quite a lot, but I suppose this is a start. The more we can get here, the less we'll have to scavenge if we do somehow escape."

"Certainly," said Lady Ufferbub. "But we should be wary of our requests from Neothud. We cannot afford his suspicion. Besides, if we remain in his good graces, he may relax our guard, and that could prove even more valuable than the ingredients."

That night, Gilbert slept on the floor of the cell. He rolled and writhed in his sleep, dreaming again of Earth in flames, of his parents staring, even as they burned. Gilbert ran as quickly as he could, ready to jump into the inferno, to be with them once again. It had happened so many times before. But this time, just as he neared the fire...he hesitated.

He awoke panting, shivering, beaded in sweat, and resigned himself to a sleepless night.

From then on, the days passed strangely. Kalyra never came to see them again, but Neothud visited frequently—at least three times a day to deliver their meals, and occasionally more often for friendly check-ins.

Over time, Gilbert, Lady Ufferbub, and Mardulo managed to obtain three sleeping pads, two pillows, a small table for eating, several chairs to place throughout their cell, a wall tapestry, and a veritable library of books.

Some of these were necessary, either to plan their escape or to extract the signature. Some were simply nice to have.

Not every meal was helpful, but enough were—in often strange and specific ways—that they began to suspect an ally in the kitchens. Whether it was Bundersquash, Toddleposter, or some magically literate cook, none could say, but they were grateful all the same.

From nettle soup, Mardulo extracted formic acid. From a green, leafy oil that came with one of their salads, he mixed together a vaguely fluorescent elixir. One day, their meal came on intricate porcelain dishes, which Mardulo used to obtain calcined bone dust. While Neothud was not pleased to hear of the shattered plate, he never noticed the missing chips.

Their attempts to map the jail proved less fruitful. From Lady Ufferbub's history books, they learned that Agol's prison was maintained as a complex labyrinth of stone tunnels several stories underneath the town hall, but they found nothing of its specific layout. Lady Ufferbub did deduce, however, that they were probably below the surface of the lake at this depth, so they had best be mindful of blowing any holes in the wall.

They tried three times to convince Neothud to let them out so they could scout the surrounding area—Lady Ufferbub asked to go to the library, Gilbert requested to see a doctor, and Mardulo simply asked to go on a walk—but Neothud rejected them at every turn, though he did send a doctor to see Gilbert.

Day after day, Mardulo scurried off to the privacy of the bathroom and wrangled together supplies for the signature extraction. Meanwhile,

Gilbert and Lady Ufferbub developed a system for keeping watch without looking too suspicious. They got to know the schedules of the guards and became familiar with Neothud's routine. Soon, they had the entire operation running smoothly and were quite comfortable besides.

But progress came gradually, days became weeks, and the outside world kept moving.

Interlude: Tree and the Spark of Rebellion

It was no secret that Hobblebosh had allowed a dozen trees to fall to their deaths—nearly a tenth of the forest, gone. Most of the soldiers thought it was a reasonable punishment for the delay the trees had caused, but for the surviving trees, morale had never been lower. Whispers of doubt and unrest seeped into their muted conversations.

Tree kept to themselves. They had asked Old Oak, their best friend, to stay behind with the others. Now Old Oak was dead, lost to the abyss, and it was Tree's fault. That wound hurt far worse than the six shredded stubs Hobblebosh had left behind from the savage removal of Tree's branches. The lime had not spoken to Tree since.

Luckily, Lugbrush was more understanding. In his new command, he did not exile Tree. Instead, after shaming them briefly, he allowed Tree to rejoin the forest as a regular soldier, though he refused to slacken the pace to account for Tree's injuries. Tree mastered the pain and pushed on, silent.

The army wasn't far from City Boratorus, now—a day or two's march, at most—yet with each step, a dread grew within Tree. Hobblebosh's forces left nothing but destruction in their wake. They littered every campsite with garbage and waste. They ransacked the huts of harmless farmers. They burned and salted the fields. It was clear to Tree now. Hobblebosh was no savior for plantkind. He was not here to free them from the bonds of humanity or teach humans the wrongs of their ways. He was a conqueror, bitter and vengeful, greedy for dominance. That was all.

The plants, the trees, the flowers, the forests—they deserved better from the humans, but Hobblebosh's actions did more harm than good. There had to be another way. A better way. The humans did not need to be "demolished for their insolence," as Hobblebosh had led so many to believe. They needed to understand.

It was Lugbrush, of all people, who had shown Tree that.

"You know," the general said one evening, "if you'd asked me five years ago where I'd be today, I'd never've guessed this. I mean, look at me, leading an army of trees. Hah!" He slapped his knee and took a swig from his flask. "Didn't even know you lot could think for yourselves." Then he glanced uneasily at a dandelion nearby and gave it an affectionate pat. "S'pose I'll have to find something else to collect for Belindel, eh? Bit morbid, once you start thinking about bouquets and the like..."

It was a passing thought, but with it, a string of scattered ideas clicked into place in Tree's mind. The humans—most of them, at least—were not malicious. There was no spite in their felling of trees. They simply did not understand the full scope of their actions, nor the severity of the ramifications. But if they could see that, if they could understand the value of this different form of life, perhaps they would make space for it.

Hobblebosh, on the other hand...Hobblebosh *knew* the consequences of his deeds. But still, he torched the fields. Still, he chopped down trees. Still, he killed his followers. To him, everything was expendable—human, plant, or tree, it made no matter. They were tools in his quest for dominance, useful when controlled, but disposable.

That night, when most of the army slept in their tents, Tree crept deep into the midst of the forest. The trees rested uneasily, away from the main encampment.

"My friends," Tree began, rousing them all from their slumber. "I come bearing dangerous words. Perhaps, I come bearing death. But wrongs have been done, many of them mine, and I cannot leave them unaddressed. I did not realize it back in Northern Tillman's End, but I deceived you. I told you Hobblebosh fought for good, that his war was noble and right. I told you he was a virtuous king. But I know now he is not. He is cruel and callous, and this war is wrong."

Tree paused. Every tree in the forest was listening intently. In some, Tree could tell, a fierce anger had taken root. Tree hoped it was directed at Hobblebosh but could not tell for sure.

"We have all seen what Hobblebosh is capable of," Tree continued. "I can stand for it no longer. He is no king of mine, and I must do what I can to stop the damage he wreaks. I know I swore an oath, and I know that what I do now—to break that oath entirely—is a stain upon my character. But better a stain of disloyalty to an unjust king than the stain of blood from those he slaughters. I do not order you to stand with me. I do not expect your support. I come only to tell you, so that those who already wish to fight may know this—you do not fight alone."

A surge of exhilaration coursed through the forest like electricity in the wind. A contagious energy took hold of them all. The message was clear.

Stand for our fallen. Stand for our kind. Stand together with Tree.

The force of the forest's determination swept through Tree's surroundings. Leaves shook, branches swayed, roots stomped and hammered. The air shimmered with their zeal.

"Your support gives me hope," Tree called out. "Together, we stand a chance. Hobblebosh is a formidable foe. He does not trust us, and he is ever alert. But we are trees! We are bold. We are confident. We break stone and weather storms. We are no simple horde to bend and sway at the mercy of this wrongful ruler. Together, as one, we are mighty—a forest, and a family. Win or lose, at least we fought!"

The forest roared with approval, and Tree very nearly started the battle then and there, but they needed a plan. They could not simply storm

Hobblebosh's tent, not with so many soldiers around. Even if they did succeed, the losses would be devastating.

So, all night, they prepared. The forest's web of shared consciousness buzzed with tactics and strategy. Come dawn, the plan was ready. The first phase would begin the following evening. Anxiety and anticipation filled the atmosphere.

But all did not go as planned.

That day, the forest marched behind the rest of Hobblebosh's troops and crested a hill around noon. From its apex, Tree could see City Boratorus once again—the first time since they'd left weeks ago—a staggered sprawl upon the horizon, ringed within a high stone wall. Buildings poked the sky, their branches and offshoots sprouting to and fro. It was not unlike a forest itself, and Tree wondered briefly if the humans felt as connected there as the trees felt in their own forests. How did it compare to that expansive, interconnected life Tree had observed in Northern Tillman's End?

Suddenly, Lugbrush halted their march. "Orders from the king," he said. "The moment City Boratorus comes into view, we stop and await further instruction."

Lugbrush shrugged, then sat in the grass until Hobblebosh came. Several dozen soldiers accompanied the lime. They all carried burning torches.

"Lugbrush, I'm glad you're here," said Hobblebosh. "Your command of these trees has proven utterly inept. I hereby remove you of your command and sentence you to death."

"What? My king, I have—"

"You have allowed treason to flourish within your ranks. Death is a just punishment, and a merciful one. It is better than the trees shall have."

A soldier struck Lugbrush down before he had any opportunity to protest. Hobblebosh stepped to one side, distancing himself from the mess, and turned his attention to the forest.

"Do you think me deaf? Did you think I would not sense your plots and schemes as you deliberated a mere mile from my tent? All night I listened to your raucous treachery, pondering how best to deal with you. I could leave you behind or send you back and force you into the Splat. I could chop you down. I could burn you alive. But as I lay there, listening, I realized there was only one punishment suited to repay such childish, arrogant egotism. I must show you your own insignificance.

"You think yourselves strong. You think yourselves brave. But you have forgotten—you are nothing without my magic. Were it not for me, you would have grown and died in that pitiful forest, motionless, steeped in dirt and decay, knowing nothing beyond your unchanging horizon. Yet here you stand, plotting treason against your savior, thinking yourselves superior! Never before have I seen such naïve audacity, and you shall pay for it. The punishment is simple. All that I have given, I take away. You will stand and watch as I finish my work, knowing that no amount of your self-proclaimed strength can stop it—because without my magic, you are nothing."

Hobblebosh began a spell. Several of the trees charged at him, but the soldiers, brandishing flame, kept them all at bay. Then the spell was done.

A silver mist rose from the cluster of trees, silent as sunlight, and disappeared into the sky. With it, the forest's movement, granted by Hobblebosh, vanished.

Tree stood in horror as everyone around them struggled, trying desperately to move. The trees tortured themselves, straining every fiber of their beings, but nary a leaf rustled, and the forest's wild, motionless panic soon dwindled into a disheartened whimper, then silence.

Defeat.

It broke Tree's heart.

But Tree themselves did not try to move.

In fact, they tried very hard to stay still. They tensed—rigid, unyielding—and they focused, keeping silent.

"Watch the trees," said Hobblebosh to a pair of his guards. "If you see anything unusual, burn the whole forest down."

Then the lime turned his back and strode confidently toward City Boratorus.

Hours passed, and Tree waited, hardly daring to think.

All was silent. All was still.

Then, finally, when the tyrant had moved well beyond any possible range of hearing and the guards had long since lost interest, Tree readied themselves.

It was true, Hobblebosh's magic had allowed the forest to move, but Tree had discovered that skill themselves. They had earned their freedom under the threat of axes atop a tower in City Boratorus. It was theirs and theirs alone. Hobblebosh could not take it away.

Slowly, Tree stretched their branches. Quietly, they tested their roots.

The rest was a matter of care, caution, and planning. There was much to do, and Tree was the only one left to do it, so they kept themselves hidden, made a plan, and waited for the moment to strike.

In the distance, Hobblebosh advanced on City Boratorus.

Chapter 20

Jailbreak

It was a Thursday, according to Neothud. Lady Ufferbub was sitting in her armchair drinking tea and reading a book on lakeside ecosystems. Gilbert and Mardulo were both lying on the carpet, musing over a game of merchantillia. The previous evening, Mardulo had made use of a dyed purple napkin to extract something related to sea snails. Gilbert couldn't quite remember the name.

Neothud walked in with lunch—hot beef sandwiches and dipping gravy, plus a plate of strawberries and cream.

"Here we are!" he said. "Fresh from the kitchen. I brought you some more of those strawberries, Gilbert, after seeing how much you liked them during breakfast. And Lady Ufferbub, how is the book treating you? I admit I read a passage myself before passing it along. I never knew reeds could be so...*teeming*." He looked mildly disgusted. "But I hope it's keeping you engaged! And of course, Mardulo. Having fun with merchantillia, I see? It's one of my favorites."

"All is well, all is well." Lady Ufferbub rose from her seat and helped set the table for lunch. "How are things outside?"

Neothud looked at her with a now-familiar look of mock disapproval. "You know I cannot talk about such things, my dear Lady Ufferbub. Suffice to say, I am still here, so you may assume Town Agol is still standing, safe and sound."

"Well, I suppose that is something."

"Thanks for the strawberries," said Gilbert, already helping himself.

Neothud bowed. "My pleasure, as always. I'll be back for the dishes later on. Please, try not to break anything this time."

When the door sealed shut, Mardulo leaped to his feet. "Quick, give me the beef from your sandwiches. I think this might be it!"

"It?"

"The last ingredient!" He scurried into the bathroom, followed by Lady Ufferbub and Gilbert, who were much too excited to worry about their watch-keeping protocol.

Mardulo opened the cabinet, now filled with a rainbow of oddities salvaged from various meals. He grabbed a small clay jar that had originally held honey and, from it, retrieved a damp purple powder.

He dropped the meat in the sink, lathered on the powder, spit into the mixture, plucked some wood from the cabinet's splintered interior, then ran the water.

"What are you two doing in here?" Mardulo turned on them suddenly. "Go keep watch! Do you want to spoil this whole operation on the final step?"

Shamefaced, Gilbert and Lady Ufferbub walked back to the main cell. Several long minutes passed before Mardulo returned. "I'll need some paper and something to write with," he said. Gilbert tore a sheet from one of Lady Ufferbub's books, then handed Mardulo a pen they had obtained a few days previously.

"Lovely," said Mardulo. "Now make sure the bathroom door stays shut—no matter what. I will need time to read the sequence, and the room must remain completely dark while I do so. I can cancel their lighting charms, but if the door opens halfway through, it's over. There's only enough for one spell."

Gilbert and Lady Ufferbub both nodded. Mardulo went back inside.

A silence fell over the cell—tense and expectant. Gilbert's heart hammered nervously against his ribs. Weeks of preparation, all leading to this moment. Extracting the essence was the start. Once that was done, they had no more reason to delay their escape. They had already obtained as much information as they were going to from Neothud and the books. They were ready. Or at least, they weren't going to get any readier.

Neothud opened the door.

"Just came in to see if you needed any more gravy," he said, entering. "One of the other prisoners said she ran out halfway through her sandwich."

Gilbert was eating some of his sandwich's bread. "Oh, I'm all right," he said, still chewing. Neothud hated it when people spoke with their mouths full. Gilbert hoped to disgust him into leaving more quickly.

It almost worked. Neothud grimaced and turned his gaze to Lady Ufferbub. "And how about you?"

"I am quite satisfied," she said gently, "but I appreciate your concern."

"Ah. Well. Just thought I should make sure." Neothud glanced around the room. "Mardulo's in the bathroom again?" he asked casually, picking a fleck of dust from one of his gloves.

"Sure is," said Gilbert, chewing as horribly as he could manage. "Stomach troubles. Thanks for stopping by, Neothud. We'll let you know if we need anything."

"Of course. My pleasure…" Neothud stood in the entryway for a moment, hesitated, then left.

The cell door sealed. Lady Ufferbub and Gilbert breathed a sigh of relief, though neither truly relaxed until Mardulo reemerged, brimming with excitement.

"Take that, Obble!" he said, waving a handful of paper scraps. "I've written it down in triplicate. We should each have one, just in case."

Gilbert took his from Mardulo. There were five rows of symbols on it, each several dozen characters long.

"Only the bottom two rows are legitimate," said Mardulo. "The rest are there to confuse prying eyes. Understood?"

"Understood." Gilbert folded the paper and put it in his pocket. "So, when do we make our big escape?"

Lady Ufferbub looked anxiously at the door. "It is an awfully risky plan," she said. "Are we sure there is not something more...*robust* we could attempt? No more spells we could scrap together?"

"Not without more ingredients," said Mardulo. "We've done all we can, given the situation."

"Unless you think whoever's been sneaking us ingredients will send along an invisibility potion next," said Gilbert.

There was a quick pause while they weighed the chances of such an event, which didn't seem entirely unlikely given how helpful the food had been. But still...

"I suppose we shouldn't count on it," said Gilbert.

"Tonight, then?" asked Mardulo.

"Dinner," said Lady Ufferbub. "When he comes to collect the dishes."

The cell's guard changed around that time—the evening shift swapped with the first round of night guards, two of whom had a tendency to panic when presented with trouble. The third, Comber, was a relative unknown, having joined just four days ago, but he had replaced Entoola, who had proven particularly astute.

"Dinner," Mardulo confirmed. "May luck stand with us."

"We shall need it," said Lady Ufferbub, shaking her head.

They spent the rest of the day anxiously waiting until, finally, the moment arrived. They ate little of their meal, and the moment Neothud entered to collect the dishes, Mardulo jumped into action.

"At last, you're here!" he said. "Quick, something's happened to the bathroom. There's water everywhere!"

This was true. Mardulo had shoved a spare shirt down the drain and left the tap running.

Neothud went to look. Then several things happened at once.

Lady Ufferbub wedged her foot in the cell door to prevent it from closing properly, Gilbert edged nearer the bedroom, and Mardulo held the bathroom door open for Neothud.

Gilbert held his breath.

Neothud entered the bathroom.

And Mardulo slammed the door shut, trapping Neothud inside.

Gilbert had to act quickly. While Mardulo held the door fast against Neothud's pushing, Gilbert grabbed the chest of drawers from their bedroom. They'd moved it onto a fluffy upside-down rug, so it slid smoothly when pulled. As he neared the bathroom, he tipped the chest sideways off the rug and blocked the door with its bulk.

Already, Neothud was cursing and shouting behind the door. Mardulo had done his best to cast a silencing charm using a few byproducts of the signature extraction, but it was weak and wouldn't hold long.

Lady Ufferbub was next. She stepped into the hallway and cried, "Help! Help!"

Mardulo and Gilbert followed her out, putting on panicked expressions.

The two impulsive guards, Runkus and Ohillian, nearly knocked over their dice table as they dashed toward Lady Ufferbub. Comber came quickly on their heels.

"What is the meaning of this?!" Ohillian brandished his club. "Back into your room, now!"

"It's Neothud!" Gilbert wailed, pointing inside the cell. "He's in trouble!"

Comber looked at Gilbert skeptically. "I'll take a look. You two wait here." He gestured to the other guards.

He went in, turned to face the bathroom, and said, "Oh, bollocks."

Which worried Runkus and Ohillian, who immediately followed him inside.

The moment all three guards had entered, Lady Ufferbub pulled the door shut.

She, Mardulo, and Gilbert stood in the hallway, speechless and alone.

"I can't believe that worked," said Gilbert. "I mean, it's almost sad..."

Mardulo grinned. "Now we'd best get moving."

But even as they started their flight down the hall, two more guards raced around the corner. Lady Ufferbub about-faced and cursed. Another three were closing in from that direction.

Gilbert cracked his knuckles. "Run!"

He charged at the first set of guards, who were not as surprised as he'd hoped they would be. One of them knocked him back, and he stumbled into Lady Ufferbub. Mardulo threw a shoe, which missed.

Four more guards rounded the corner, and the three behind soon caught up. In moments, Lady Ufferbub, Mardulo, and Gilbert were surrounded and outnumbered three to one.

Gilbert drooped. Their one shot, and they'd barely even made it out the door.

The guards freed Neothud immediately. The master jailer brushed himself off and stormed toward Gilbert and the others, his face rigid with anger.

"After all I have done to make you comfortable," he said, "after all my care and service, you would lock me in a bathroom and attempt to escape?! The sheer insolence of it! I have never, in all my life, felt so blatantly abused."

"If you would just hear us out—" Gilbert tried.

Neothud cut him off at once. "No. I will hear no more from you. I will hear no more from *any* of you." He paced circles around them. "I received an alert this afternoon that your bathroom lighting charm had been disabled. I thought, *That seems suspicious*, but I gave you the benefit of the doubt and allowed you your privacy. Thankfully, I also took the appropriate precautions and called in a few extra guards. But after what I just saw in that bathroom—the vials, the bottles, the boxes—I am beginning to think I should have called for more!"

He took off one of his gloves, and for a moment, Gilbert thought the jailer might cast a spell. But instead, Neothud turned to Mardulo, who happened to be closest, and struck him across the face.

"That is for hiding from me and for lying to me!" He glared at Lady Ufferbub and Gilbert, considering whether to strike them as well, but after a sidelong look at the surrounding guards, he seemed to think better of it. He put his glove back on and mastered the fury on his face.

"All this time," he continued, "you have been plotting to betray me. You took advantage of my hospitality. You took advantage of Town Agol's goodwill. And you took advantage of *me*. I guarantee you—all three of you—that you will come to regret this."

He looked them each in the eye, then turned away and barked a string of orders at the guards.

Mardulo, Lady Ufferbub, and Gilbert were soon placed in three separate cells. Where the original cell had been a three-room suite, these were barely ten square feet in size, carved roughly into the stone wall and sealed off with metal bars.

From his own cell, Gilbert couldn't see the others. His only companions were the two guards posted by his door, and they weren't the talkative sort.

He sat on the floor with his back against the wall, surrounded once again with cold gray stone, completely at a loss. In time, he fell asleep.

A worried shout woke him. He sprang to his feet and pressed his face against the bars. One of the guards was missing.

"What happened?" asked Gilbert.

"Silence." The remaining guard planted the butt of his spear on the floor. His expression betrayed no emotion.

Then Toddleposter came careening down the hallway and threw a vial of purple gas at the guard's chest. It struck its mark and shattered, releasing the gas. In moments, the guard was asleep.

Gilbert scrambled back, holding his breath, trying to get away from the fumes. "Toddleposter?!"

"Hello, Gilbert!" Toddleposter waved away the last of the purple air, then leaned over the guard's sleeping figure, found the keys, and opened the door. "It's great to see you. It's been such a long time."

Gilbert exited his cell and gave the clone a hug. "It's good to see you too. And thanks. Is Bundersquash around?"

"He's helping Lady Ufferbub. You had two guards on your cell. She has six..."

Gilbert wondered at the implications there, then decided they weren't important. "Let's go help," he said.

"Yes, good idea," said Toddleposter excitedly. "You know, I've never done a jailbreak before. It's very exciting!"

Gilbert looked at him. "Let's hope this one goes better than my first."

Toddleposter removed a napkin from his pocket and checked a hastily scribbled map.

"This way," he said, and together, they ran through a number of identical stone tunnels.

The sound of footsteps cut them short. Then Bundersquash appeared and ran full speed into Toddleposter.

"Oh! Hello. Got him already, did you?" said Bundersquash.

"Yes! Only two guards. Piece of cake."

Gilbert coughed.

"Hello, Gilbert." Bundersquash smiled and held out a hand. Gilbert hugged him.

Lady Ufferbub walked up slowly, inspecting a red gash on her forearm. "What a pleasure it is to see you all intact."

"Mardulo next?" asked Bundersquash.

Toddleposter checked his napkin map. "He should be close. Block F, cell number two seven three."

They took off running. Gilbert's legs already burned from the effort. Weeks of lounging around a jail cell hadn't done much for his athleticism. Luckily, it wasn't long before Toddleposter slowed to a halt.

"It's just around this corner." He tilted his head, listening.

Gilbert peeked. Four guards stood about the cell, chatting amicably with Mardulo.

"Seems like they're getting on well," said Gilbert.

"I expect he's trying to ingratiate his way to freedom," said Lady Ufferbub. "Before Bundersquash came, I thought I might have to do the same."

Gilbert considered how he himself had simply given up hope and gone to sleep. He said nothing.

"Best to go in prepared, regardless," said Bundersquash as he reached into his cloak and grabbed another purple vial, similar to the one Toddleposter had used. He shoved the others out of sight, then walked calmly into the open.

Unable to see what was happening, Gilbert listened—a clash of breaking glass, four heavy thuds, and it was done.

"Bundersquash? You're here!" Mardulo's voice filled the hall as Lady Ufferbub, Toddleposter, and Gilbert approached.

Bundersquash grabbed the keys from an unconscious guard and opened the door. "Of course I'm here. You needed help."

Mardulo stepped out and dusted himself off. "Was it you sending us those ingredients in our meals?"

"Toddleposter, mostly. Once you refused to give Kalyra the hair, we decided to send you supplies so you could extract the signature yourselves. Toddleposter befriended the cook and started working in the kitchens."

Lady Ufferbub bowed. "Many thanks, Toddleposter."

"But why did you try to escape?" asked Bundersquash. "We were only a few days away from sending you everything!"

"We had what we needed." Mardulo showed Bundersquash his scrap of paper. "I extracted the signature this afternoon."

Bundersquash looked it over in disbelief. "How did you do it without lorian fragments?"

"Swapped them out for wood and saliva. It meant we needed more salt, but we had plenty."

Bundersquash's expression lifted. "Of course! Well, we're not as badly off as I feared, then." He smiled up at the elderly wizard. "I'm glad you're okay, Mardulo."

"I'm glad you're okay, too, Bundersquash."

"As lovely as this reunion is," said Lady Ufferbub, "we really must be going."

"Right." Toddleposter pulled out his map again. "This way!"

Bundersquash spoke as they ran. "We thought we'd have a few more days to plan the escape, but when we heard you'd tried to break out, we got worried. Decided to come early. We weren't sure what they'd do to you, but there was a lot of talk about air-suppression spells and indelible cognitive recalibration."

"Still, almost everything is prepared for our departure," said Toddleposter. "We just need to stop by the lab and pick up some supplies."

"And we should destroy what remains of that murderous disk while we're there," added Bundersquash.

"Yes, I'd been meaning to ask about that." Mardulo stopped to catch his breath. "Why did you offer to help Kalyra?"

"I never intended to help," said Bundersquash. "I just thought, if I wished to stop it, I would be in a better position to do so from inside their lab, not a prison cell. Kalyra seemed upset after you refused to help, so Toddleposter and I pretended to be useful instead. But we tried to hinder the project as much as we could behind the scenes."

"That was...very sensible of you."

"I know." Bundersquash raised his eyebrows. "But I understand why you did what you did. I'm just glad you were able to extract the signature. Now, let's be off before someone finds us."

He used a key to open a secret passage in one of the halls, where four unconscious guards lay at the base of a staircase. As Gilbert and the others ascended, panting and sweaty, the floor changed from stone to wood. The air warmed and freshened.

Then, for the first time in weeks, Gilbert saw sunlight.

They emerged into a wooden hallway with glass windows all around, daylight streaming through. Gilbert could feel his mind clearing in the fresh air.

"The lab is this way," said Toddleposter. "Quickly!"

They raced through the corridors of what Gilbert quickly came to recognize as the town hall. After a few minutes, an alarm sounded, whirring across the building like a siren. The noise gave Gilbert a headache and no small amount of anxiety, but mostly, it encouraged him to push through his cramps and move faster.

Three soldiers guarded the lab door. Bundersquash dealt with them as he had done the others.

"Only one sleeping vial left," he said, putting it back in his chest pocket.

Inside the lab, they found themselves face to face with a wizard. He had a freckled face and thin strands of silver hair that floated like cobwebs. His eyes seemed twice as large as they should have been.

"Hello, Ulkertund," said Bundersquash. "I'm afraid we've come to destroy just about everything in here. It would be of great assistance to us if you left."

Ulkertund blinked once, twice, then looked at the unconscious guards outside, put his head down, and shuffled away without a word.

"Let's get to work!" Bundersquash ran to a cupboard and removed two large bags, one at a time. "This is everything we need for the trapping spell, plus a few extras. The rest of this lab exists for that annihilation disk, as they call it. Best if we clobber the lot."

And just like that, Gilbert found himself thrown into a strange and unexpected realm of wish fulfillment. He hadn't minded chemistry in school, but given the opportunity to rampage through a laboratory stocked full of beakers, vials, and bubbling solutions of who-knew-what, he discovered that he had, in fact, been harboring a deep reservoir of suppressed aggression toward the subject.

Gilbert thought of pop quizzes and trick questions, then picked up a beaker and threw it against the wall. He thought of busywork and homework, then swiped his arm across a workstation, knocking everything to the marble floor. He thought of stressful tests and impossibly long labs squeezed into a single hour, then yanked a thick pipe from a large whirring appliance, and the whole thing fell to pieces.

Pipe in hand, he really got going. Before long, shattered glass covered the floor, several cauldrons lay upturned, and a sinister orange liquid had melted through the floor and fizzled out about ten feet underground.

The others did their part too. Toddleposter cracked open several globes containing weedy, knotted plants, which grew rapidly in the open air and tore into the surrounding architecture. A burst of purple smoke signaled the end of some planetary-motion simulator, a credit to Lady Ufferbub's skill with a hammer. Then Mardulo cast a spell using some ingredients from the floor, and the entire room's gravity reversed. In a moment of sheer panic, everyone and everything fell upward, then crashed back down with a terrible clamor. The lights flickered.

"Sorry," said Mardulo. "Got a bit carried away."

"Well, I should say that is sufficient." Lady Ufferbub straightened her robe.

"Just one more thing." Bundersquash opened a drawer in a now-sideways desk and pulled out a much larger version of the disk Kalyra had shown them before. He dropped it into a puddle of sputtering liquid, where it dissolved almost instantly. Gilbert gave the puddle a wide berth as he followed the others to the exit.

The door opened before they could reach it. Kalyra stood in the entryway beside a meek, huddled Ulkertund.

"You five," she said, bleeding hatred. "Our guards have been looking everywhere. They assumed you would flee—yet poor, defenseless Ulkertund finds you rampaging through the town hall causing all manner of havoc. Right in the middle of everything. I should have guessed. It always was your way, Normishdae. Ulkertund, fetch the guards. I will keep watch over these delinquents until they arrive."

Ulkertund nodded anxiously and disappeared down the hallway. Kalyra stepped into the lab, then closed the door behind her. Her face wavered between frustration and despair as she processed the full extent of the damage.

"You have brought ruin upon us all," she said. "I regret that I did not leave you to die as you begged for entry upon our doorstep."

"This annihilation disk is not the solution, Kalyra," said Bundersquash.

"Silence, traitor!" she spat. "Hundreds of thousands of tille we put into this project, and you have thrown it all away. For what? I thought you wanted to *stop* Obble Dor Hobblebosh. Now you have allowed him to run free. And you three—Normishdae, Mardulo, Gigglebrit—after all your talk about being on the same side, you have finally shown your true colors. This is spite, plain and simple. We would not support your plan, so you destroy ours in turn. You have chosen revenge over the well-being of my town."

Lady Ufferbub advanced. "You crossed a line, Kalyra. My friends and I understand the suffering Hobblebosh causes, and we work to stop him because we long for a kinder, better place to live. Because we care about the *people* in this world. But you? You wish to stop him simply because he is a threat to your legacy. You do not care about bettering this world, only making your mark upon it—a mark that Hobblebosh threatens to erase. And in such a blind struggle to preserve your own influence, you have become as much of a problem as the lime himself, so we have had to stop you too."

"Preach all you wish, Normishdae. I stopped listening to your effusive rambling years ago. Just know that when Town Agol lies in ruin, there will be no one to blame but yourselves."

Lady Ufferbub turned to Bundersquash. She walked up and hugged him, saying, "Bundersquash, I am so proud of you."

Gilbert thought this was an exceptionally strange time for Lady Ufferbub to express her affections—until the librarian turned around and threw the final vial of sleeping gas directly into Kalyra's face. The glass shattered, the fumes spread, and Kalyra collapsed to the floor, asleep with a frightful new cut across her cheek and eye.

"We had better get moving before Ulkertund returns." Lady Ufferbub shouldered one of the ingredient bags and made for the exit.

The others roused from their startled trances and followed her. Gilbert took the second bag from Bundersquash, freeing the young wizard to gather ingredients along the way, which he stuffed into his robe's pockets. Mardulo grabbed some too.

They didn't make it far before a troop of guards spotted them, and so, with half a dozen hunters on their tail, they burst from the town hall.

A massive crowd had gathered near the entrance. Some held signs. Others chanted. "*You* tore us away, so where do we stay?" "Justice for the farmers!" "You moved us here, now move us in!"

Across the street a separate crowd had formed, jeering and pointing at the first. "You don't belong here!" "Go home to your farms and cousins!" "Hobblebosh can take the lot of you!"

Gilbert could barely think. There was too much happening, too many people, too many things at once.

"Tensions have been high," said Bundersquash. "From what I've heard, this is happening almost every day now."

"Jolly good," said Mardulo. "Maybe they'll distract the guards. Now, which way to the nearest boat?"

"At a guess, that way." Bundersquash pointed.

"At a guess? You didn't check?"

"They never let us leave the town hall!"

Toddleposter tugged them both. "Come on. We came from this street when we first arrived. It's the best we've got!"

They shoved their way through the crowd and broke into another run. Gilbert had been out of breath even before leaving the lab. Now he had a stitch in his side and his lungs burned, but he forced himself to keep moving. Pedestrians and protestors leaped left and right to avoid the party's charge. A growing horde of guards followed, their footsteps thundering down the pathway. Gilbert tried not to think about it too much. They rounded turn after turn, one mad dash for the shore.

The dock had just come into view when someone finally cut them off—a guard, quickly joined by three others. They barred the exit as more guards barreled down the street behind.

"Think real-time synchronous consumption," said Bundersquash to Mardulo, fumbling through his collection of spare ingredients.

Evidently, this meant something to Mardulo, who quickly threw his gloves into his pocket and created an auric nebula. Bundersquash tossed three ingredients into it, each consumed in the silver mist. Then Mardulo said a word in the ancient tongue, and a burst of white light shot toward the guards ahead, paralyzing them.

Gilbert and the others took off before the paralyzed bodies even hit the wooden path. Mardulo made another nebula as they ran, doing something fancy with his fingers to make it follow him, and then he and Bundersquash repeated the same spell several times over, now targeting the guards behind them. When Bundersquash ran out of spare ingredients, he started picking flowers from gardens and leaves from the surrounding trees, always adding them directly to Mardulo's nebula. The spells shifted with the ingredients, but Bundersquash never needed to tell Mardulo what he was planning. The elder wizard just seemed to know—he knew what to do with his hands, what to do with the nebula, what to say, and when to say it, all in the moment, just by looking at the ingredients Bundersquash added.

In the mayhem of their spells, wooden planks disintegrated, some guards started levitating a few inches in the air—unable to run when they couldn't touch the ground—and several others' boots transformed into skis.

Gilbert found himself in the lead. The ingredient bag jostled awkwardly at his side, but he refused to let it slow him down. He sprinted toward the only boat in the dock, the same one they had used coming into town. A familiar white sheen rose around its perimeter as they approached—a barrier to prevent unwanted occupants from boarding.

"We've prepared for this." Toddleposter rifled through his pockets and pulled out a thin, receipt-like list of everyone's names. He poked around the outside of the boat until he found a small slot in the side, then inserted the list just as Mardulo and Bundersquash fired off another spell—this one, a dazzling firework of red that startled more than anything else.

"Gilbert Betters. Enter."

Gilbert leaped inside, clutching his ingredient bag. The boat lurched with his weight.

"Lady Normishdae Relidor Ufferbub the Triumphant. Enter."

Gilbert guided her in as she stepped backward onto the boat, keeping her eyes on the opposition.

By now, Bundersquash had truly run out of ingredients. He was scavenging through the grass for scraps—anything that might prove useful. Three guards still stood, preparing to attack. A crowd of townsfolk and protestors had gathered to watch the spectacle, though none dared interfere.

"Toddleposter Hunderrum Balbagoose the Second. Enter."

Toddleposter pulled Bundersquash up from the grass. "We're almost free. Leave it!"

Bundersquash nearly pushed Toddleposter into the boat. "Go! I'm right behind you."

Toddleposter fell sideways onto Gilbert. Lady Ufferbub steadied them both as the boat rocked sickeningly beneath their feet.

"Mardulo Vot Ponterous the Brilliant. Enter."

But Mardulo was busy holding off the guards using little more than a threatening stare.

"Don't you come near me!" he shouted at them, stumbling back toward the boat. "I'm a wizard! The real thing! I won't hesitate to turn you all into toadstools! Just you watch!"

It didn't work. Two of the guards seized him. The third grabbed Bundersquash.

Then someone else pushed through the crowd.

Neothud.

Gilbert was almost relieved, but there was a visceral look in the jailer's eye that spoke of hatred and vengeance.

"Mardulo Vot Ponterous the Brilliant. Enter," the boat repeated. Mardulo struggled against the guards holding his arms.

"Just let us leave, Neothud," said Lady Ufferbub.

"No." Neothud removed his gloves. "This town put its trust in you, Bundersquash and Toddleposter, and you betrayed us. I don't know how such things work in City Boratorus, but here, that comes with a price. As for you—Mardulo, Lady Ufferbub, Gilbert—I told you that you would regret ever trying to escape my hospitality. That time has come."

He rubbed his palms together, forming a faint yellow nebula, then cast a spell using some dust from his pocket. Smoky chains sprang from the wooden dock and wrapped around Mardulo. In an instant, they'd bound him flat on his stomach, the chains tightening around his body, squeezing him against the dock. Gilbert could hear the wood creaking under the pressure.

Bundersquash roared. He wrenched free of the guard holding his shoulders, then barreled headfirst into Neothud. There was a struggle. Neothud kept trying—and failing—to create another nebula, but Bundersquash was content to use his fist and feet. It didn't take long. Bundersquash wrenched the master jailer's arm back with a horrible pop, then threw him into the water. The three guards, now furious, nearly tripped over each other as they charged for Bundersquash. Bundersquash merely shifted his position and sent them floundering into Neothud's wake.

But even with all four adversaries bobbing helplessly in the lake, the binding spell held. Mardulo groaned as a board cracked under the pressure.

"Mardulo Vot Ponterous the Brilliant. Enter," said the boat.

Bundersquash turned to Gilbert. "Give me the bag, quickly!"

Gilbert tossed it to Bundersquash without hesitation. From it, the young wizard retrieved a palm-size diamond of glass with shimmering rainbow powder floating through its interior.

Gilbert recognized it. He'd seen one before, in Bundersquash's voice-to-illustration device. A myrian crystal, filled with activated myrian powder.

Mardulo protested feebly, unable to move his limbs, but Bundersquash ignored him. In one definitive motion, he closed his fist around the crystal and squeezed. The glass shattered. Several shards sliced into his palm.

The crowed stared in horrified fascination as the rainbow dust from inside the diamond mixed with Bundersquash's blood, and a lilac nebula burst into existence.

With a breath, Bundersquash mastered his pain and cast a spell to break Mardulo's binding charm. He took his time helping Mardulo up, then carefully guided him to the boat.

After Mardulo had entered, the boat spoke again: "Bundersquash Borum Balbagoose the Studious. Enter."

Bundersquash rolled his shoulders and looked back at the dumbstruck crowd. Without a word to any of them, he grabbed the ingredient bag from the cracked wooden pathway and stepped onto the boat. The instant he'd boarded, they departed for the opposite shore.

Relief rushed over Gilbert like a wave. He could still feel his heart pounding, his hands shaking. For several seconds, he sat in complete silence with the others.

At last, Lady Ufferbub spoke. "Bundersquash, Toddleposter, you have our deepest gratitude." Still sitting, she bowed her head to each of them. "With your plan, you showed far more cunning than Mardulo, Gilbert, and I—and more courage too."

Bundersquash and Toddleposter blushed with identical expressions of embarrassed pride.

"And Bundersquash," Mardulo added softly, "I'm sorry. I said many hurtful things to you after Town Forbik. I was upset, and I was angry, and I did not want to lose my best pupil. Nonetheless, I should not have lashed out so cruelly. All good students outgrow their professors, but that is a burden for me to bear, not you. You are a competent, independent wizard, and I am sorry that I led you to believe otherwise."

"It's all right, Mardulo. I was bad to you as well, frustrated after our failures, but they are no more your fault than mine. We are a team, and I could not have done what we did today, nor anything Toddleposter and I have done over the past few weeks, without the help and guidance you have given me over the years."

For a moment, they simply looked at each other, then they shook hands, and then, after a pause, they hugged.

Gilbert, Lady Ufferbub, and Toddleposter breathed one collective sigh of relief.

"As a curiosity," Mardulo asked hesitantly, once the sentimentality had faded, "did we need that myrian crystal?"

Bundersquash looked at his injured palm. The powder had stanched most of the bleeding, but not all of it.

"We did," said Bundersquash. "But there's still the one in my voice-to-illustration device. We should be able to repurpose it. We can head to the Wizards' Tower, get the crystal, finish the lorilell dust, and hopefully have everything ready before Hobblebosh can take the city."

"That is good to hear," said Mardulo, "though I am sorry you will have to break your device to get it."

"I can always make another when all of this is done."

The boat trundled leisurely through the lake. Gilbert kept a close eye on Town Agol's shore, watching for anyone following them, but no one came.

Eventually, he relaxed. Muscles he hadn't even realized were tense gradually loosened. The headache he'd grown used to during his time in prison finally subsided. Fresh air filled his lungs. The gentle waves of the lake soothed him. At last, he closed his eyes, and though he kept himself from sleep, he rested far better than he had done in weeks.

When they reached the shore and disembarked, Mardulo looked around. "I suppose it would be too much to hope Thorippela waited this long for us to return."

There was no sign of her.

"The hippalectryons are still here, though!" Toddleposter rushed to greet them. They had grazed half the grass in sight but looked well for it. Toddleposter took a quick count. "Five," he said. "Thorippela must've left with one of hers."

Bundersquash took a deep breath. "Back to City Boratorus, then?"

"I think that would be best," said Lady Ufferbub. "As far as I can tell, Town Agol sent no one after us, but that does not mean they will let us linger long."

Gilbert walked to Lampellion and placed a hand on his nose. Lampellion nuzzled him affectionately in return. As the others picked their own mounts, Gilbert swung onto his back and settled in for the trip back.

His muscles soon found their riding rhythm again, and time passed smoothly. A few hours after sundown, Toddleposter pulled everyone to a halt so they could eat, sleep, and rest the hippalectryons.

Gilbert lit the fire using one of the few spells he could actually cast reliably: *Agethermon*.

"You ought to be careful with that, lad," said Mardulo, noticeably surprised by Gilbert's display of magical autonomy. "While I admire the ingenuity, it's usually used to heat tea, not start fires. It could be a bit hard to control if things get too hot too quickly."

Gilbert shrugged awkwardly. "Sorry. It's the only one I could use when I was alone."

"Not to worry. It's good to see you doing magic again, and I'm glad not everything Bundersquash and I taught you has gone to waste."

Before long, they were sitting in a circle, eating from a sandwich generator Bundersquash had packed for the escape. Gilbert had to suffer through a peanut butter, jelly, and salmon paste baguette, and ruminated briefly on how he might actually miss prison food.

That night, he took the first watch. He focused on the air, the sounds of the meadow, and the stars shining brightly above. The moon was waning, almost new. There was no Milky Way in this world, no constellations he recognized, but the sky held a vivid beauty that needed no chart. He simply lay on his back and lost himself in the gentle, flickering canvas.

His parents would like it here.

In the jail cell, Gilbert, Lady Ufferbub, and Mardulo had never solidified their plan to extract his parents from the book, but Gilbert was confident they could find a way. After a few peaceful hours, he woke Lady Ufferbub for the second watch and went to bed himself.

He woke to a shimmering dawn. Mardulo and Bundersquash spoke softly nearby. Gilbert turned toward them but didn't get up.

Bundersquash was smiling, wiping a tear of laughter from his eye. "It never even occurred to me to check her outfit! I almost never wear purple. It just wasn't something I'd considered..."

Mardulo chuckled. "I thought she was going to run away then and there," he said. "I still remember the look on her face—total surprise."

"Well, it's not every day your clothes pop off and start exorcising shadow demons, is it?"

Mardulo laughed so hard Gilbert was surprised he didn't wake the others. "You know the first thing she said to me once it all died down? I was just standing there, trying to look away, thinking about how mortified the poor woman must feel, and she looks me right in the eye, face straight as a board, and says, 'I should've worn my purple socks. We might have set a record.'"

They laughed for a good while at that, but when it settled, Bundersquash's smile slipped away. He picked at the grass in front of him. "Oh, Burrid. She had flair. That's for sure."

Gilbert turned back to his sleeping position in silence, feeling suddenly guilty for eavesdropping—but it wasn't long before Mardulo and Bundersquash made the rounds to wake everyone up for another day of riding.

They traveled almost directly widesplatter, trying not to overwork their hippalectryons, but if anything, the hippalectryons seemed to want to go faster.

"I don't know what Thorippela did to get them to stay in one place for so long," said Bundersquash when they stopped for lunch, "but they're certainly excited to be moving again."

So they rode toward City Boratorus and that very evening glimpsed its crooked towers rising above the horizon. But a smell of smoke filled the air, and as they neared, they saw upon the city walls four giant flags of green and yellow.

Chapter 21

A Covert Operation

Mardulo dropped to his knees. The sight of Hobblebosh's flags flying over City Boratorus was too much to bear. He rubbed his hands together, but his auric nebula refused to form. Gilbert did the same and found that his magic, too, was blocked. That loophole really had been closed, then. All they had now was the signature from Hobblebosh's essence.

"We should head back to where we can still do magic." Lady Ufferbub tried to rally everyone. "It cannot be that far. We can prepare the spell, package it into lorilell dust, then return to win back our home."

"We need the myrian crystal." Bundersquash's voice came out hollow. "It's in there, in the Wizards' Tower."

"Could you summon it out?" asked Toddleposter.

"Mardulo might be able to," said Bundersquash. "I didn't save any activated myrian powder from the previous crystal, so I couldn't even if we *weren't* inside the restricted zone."

"It's worth a try," said Mardulo.

They galloped away from the city. Lady Ufferbub had been right. It wasn't far before they could cast magic again, but when Mardulo tried to summon the crystal, he got nothing but a few scraps of paper and a splintered piece of wood.

"Maybe it's been moved," he said. "I hope Hobblebosh hasn't gotten a hold of it."

Bundersquash sighed. "I'm probably just misremembering where I put it."

"Can we make the trapping spell without it?" asked Gilbert. "Is there a workaround?"

Mardulo and Bundersquash shook their heads.

"Then I guess we'll have to sneak in and get it." Gilbert fully expected this idea to be dismissed as too dangerous, but to his surprise, the others offered little resistance.

"It may be our best option," said Lady Ufferbub. "Besides, I would like to see the damage for myself."

"And we have friends in the Wizards' Tower," said Bundersquash. "I hope Bellgiggle is all right."

"And Ulden." Mardulo tugged nervously at his beard. "Gurming, too. We'll have to sneak in anyway once the lorilell dust is ready, if only to reach Hobblebosh. We may as well get some practice."

"It's settled, then," said Toddleposter. "Let's hope the crystal is still there."

Mardulo remounted his hippalectryon. "I have an idea for how to get in. Hobblebosh may have captured this city, but it's still my home. I know more secret passages than he could ever discover."

As they neared the city again, an inky night fell across the land. The moon was new, and clouds covered the stars, sinking the world into near-complete darkness. Gilbert was grateful for it. "We really couldn't have asked for better sneaking weather."

"Nonetheless, I suggest we leave the hippalectryons here." Lady Ufferbub pulled to a stop. They were less than a mile from the walls, near a sheltered hillside where the hippalectryons could stay hidden. "We must approach quietly, with caution. We cannot ride up like Aan Andro Maskervik the Clamorous and expect to go unhindered."

After some deliberation, they decided to leave the bulk of their supplies behind as well to keep their hands free for the mission. They needed to move quickly. The fewer burdens, the better.

Keeping low and silent, Mardulo led them to a section of the city's wall covered in a thick blanket of ivy. Pulling the ivy aside revealed a crude gash, just large enough for one person to squeeze through at a time.

"Accidently made this when I was a student practicing my tangible luminosity charms. I planted the ivy too." He glanced sidelong at his friends. "Don't tell the city council."

They crept in one after the other, Gilbert first, bent slightly to avoid hitting his head on the stone. When he'd made it through, he scanned the street. The lamps cast a flickering orange light over the cobbled way, but there were no guards or soldiers in sight. Gilbert tiptoed as quickly as he could to the nearest shaded alcove, then hid himself while the others trickled in.

Once together, Mardulo took the lead, and they started slowly down a bare, shadowed alleyway, hardly daring to breathe.

The city was in absolute shambles. The air smelled of ash, smoke, and dust. Entire buildings had collapsed or caved in. The few that remained standing did so only barely, and the dull thunk of falling bricks sounded every few moments. Street lanterns lay uprooted, scattered across the road or crushed by falling debris. Shop windows hung cracked and shattered. Even the streets themselves were broken, a jumble of uneven stones where once they had been smooth and solid.

"It's because of the blocked magic," Mardulo whispered. "Most of this city depends on architectural enchantments to keep things together. If no one maintains those, they fade, then everything returns to its natural order...in City Boratorus, that usually means they collapse."

Gilbert remembered all the twisted, impossible buildings he had seen when he'd first arrived in this world. "Will the Wizards' Tower be okay?"

"The enchantments there are strong. They should hold for more than a few weeks." Mardulo sounded uncertain, as if he was trying to reassure himself.

"We shall see soon enough," said Lady Ufferbub. "Now hush. This is not the time for idle chatter."

A burned and fallen building blocked their way along Street Hillmar and forced them to hurry down a separate string of paths, all of which were more brightly lit than Gilbert would have liked. They hid from everyone, guards or otherwise. Twice, they had to stop while people passed by, until at last, Mardulo ducked into a partially destroyed café and guided everyone down a staircase near the back. From there, they followed a lengthy underground tunnel and resurfaced near the partial ruin of a shop Gilbert recognized: Ravens' Thread Outfitters.

Mardulo seemed anxious but was sure in his route. Before long, they were scurrying through a chain of unnamed alleys, each narrower and stranger than the last. The darkness wavered between barely lit gloom and total shadow, making shapes in the corners of Gilbert's eyes. Where there were lamps, their timid light bounced across the walls and windows in a hundred different ways, echoing through the streets like phantoms.

With little to no warning, a building collapsed to their left in a blast of dust and smoke. But for Gilbert's own startled cry, no shouts or alarms were raised. The explosive clamor of collapsing stone fell dead against the silence of the city.

They soon found themselves sidling, single file, through a narrow gap between two buildings, barely large enough for a cat to crawl through, let alone five humans.

"We're almost there," said Mardulo.

"I can see it!" Bundersquash was first in line and had the best view. "It's still standing."

"That's a relief," said Mardulo. "Now, this last stretch may be tricky. Avenue Tanglewater doesn't have many lights, but it's wide and well traveled, nonetheless. Even at this hour, we should stay to one side and keep our heads down. We must remain completely silent. Understand?"

"AHH!" Bundersquash screamed.

"What did I *just* say?!" hissed Mardulo.

"I'm sorry. A strange man just appeared!"

"Did he see you?!"

"He certainly heard you." The man blocked the alleyway's exit, a silhouette against the light. "What do we have here? Hooligans up to some mischief, no doubt."

"What? Me?" Bundersquash stammered. "No. Certainly not. No mischief here. I'm just a law-abiding citizen out for a stroll in the nighttime."

"You are sneaking through a dark alley whilst speaking to your friends in a poorly hushed voice."

"Friends? I don't have any friends. Just me. Talking to myself. Everyone does it." Bundersquash tried to signal for the others to run, but they were too transfixed by this trainwreck of a conversation. No one budged.

"Then why did you shout when you saw me?"

"Oh, that?" Bundersquash wheezed a pitiful laugh. "That was just a good old-fashioned surprise, nothing more. And a good one, too, I might add. Gets the blood pumping and no mistake! Many thanks for your time. Now, if you'll excuse me, I must be on my way."

He tried to shuffle farther back into the alleyway, but the stranger reached in and grabbed his arm.

"If you're such an honest and upstanding citizen," the stranger said, "then let's have a good look at you, shall we?"

He pulled Bundersquash forcefully into the light. With no better options at his disposal, the young wizard straightened his rumpled shirt and looked headlong at the man in front of him. Gilbert tensed in the shadows.

"Oh!" The stranger staggered back. "Bundersquash?"

"Nope. Definitely not Bundersquash. What's a Bundersquash? Not me, that's for sure."

"Nonsense. I'd recognize you anywhere. I'm a friend of Mardulo's!" The man stuck his head into the alleyway. "Mardulo? Are you there? How about Gigglebrit?"

Mardulo launched himself out of the alley. "Leepog?!"

"Leepog?" Gilbert followed. Sure enough, there he was—the man who had tried to sell him lorilell dust, who had given him the healing packet that had saved Bundersquash's life. Gilbert could hardly believe it.

"Hello, Mardulo! And you too, Gigglebrit! I never forget a face, and it's a real pleasure to see yours again, let me tell you! I thought you were a couple of kids up to something nefarious, sneaking about like that. I've never been happier to be wrong."

Mardulo looked giddy. "It's lovely to see you again, Leepog. Evidently, you've already met Gigglebrit—he goes by Gilbert now—and you just met Bundersquash. This is Lady Ufferbub and Toddleposter." He waved them both out of the alley. "Come, meet Leepog! He's the one who sold me those glamours we used in Town Forbik! One of the best craftsmen around."

Leepog bowed before them. "Mr. Leepog Guddlegap Tutswither the Vast, proud salesman, honorable merchant, and *discreet* dealer in unlikely goods, at your service!"

The others seemed to relax, but Gilbert was less than enthusiastic. This man looked just as he had done before—bold green hair, visible even in the starless night; orange pants; a turquoise coat; and a carefully calibrated grin. But one thing had changed—one very notable thing.

His skin was blue.

It was hard to tell in the near-complete darkness of night, but Gilbert was sure of it.

"You were in Town Forbik," he blurted.

The conversation screeched to a halt. "Come again?" said Leepog.

"Your skin. It's blue. You must have been in Town Forbik when I messed up the spell."

Leepog gasped. "That was you?! There were so many rumors flying around I could barely keep my head on straight. It's true, I was there. But surely, that is no surprise to you, Gilbert. You must know I haven't made a living selling goods in just one city. Any clever businessman knows you have to spread things out. You don't want to saturate the market."

Mardulo, Gilbert, and the others took a step back.

"You were selling to Hobblebosh?" Gilbert asked.

"Hobblebosh? No! Of course not! Don't you remember what I sell?" He leaned in closely and whispered. "*Lorilell dust.* And right now, with Hobblebosh's spell blocking, where do you think that sells best?"

"Where people cannot do their own magic," said Mardulo.

"Precisely. I sneak into his territory, then do what I can for those poor souls Hobblebosh has oppressed...for a fee, of course."

"Listen, Leepog." Mardulo pulled the salesman into the shade and glanced along the alley, checking for eavesdroppers. "I think you might be able to help us."

"No!" Gilbert stomped on Mardulo's foot. "We can't trust him."

"Do you still have that healing dust I gave you, Gilbert?" Leepog asked, mocking innocence. "Remember? It was free. A gift."

"I...used it." Gilbert glanced at Bundersquash.

"I gave you that dust out of the goodness of my own heart. Is that not enough for you to trust me? Go on, Mardulo. Tell me what you need. If you are fighting against the tyrant, I am happy to help. It is frustrating, having to leave this city every time I wish to create more product. I would be glad to get rid of him."

Mardulo looked at Gilbert, Bundersquash, Lady Ufferbub, and Toddle-poster. "The glamours worked," he said. "The healing dust too. I think we can trust him."

Gilbert wasn't comfortable with it, but he felt bound to the aid Leepog had provided before. It had saved Bundersquash's life, after all.

"Let us find somewhere more sheltered, at least," said Lady Ufferbub begrudgingly.

"Certainly, my lady." Leepog ushered them into a small, unassuming building that had fared reasonably well against the lack of magic. "The owner was executed three days ago," he said, by way of justifying their forced entry. "Now, what do you need?"

"We have a spell—a trapping spell, mildly complex, but simplified with the presence of an essence signature. We need to convert it into lorilell dust. Is that possible?"

Leepog stroked his chin. "Perhaps. It's hard to say without the spell itself. Do you have words prepared? The ingredients?"

"Not yet." Mardulo wrung his hands. "We were...confined for some time, and I had to focus on extracting the signature. Bundersquash got us most of the way, though. We just have to iron out a few details, then pick up one more ingredient."

Leepog took a deep breath. "Well, I cannot say anything definitive without more information, but let me give you this." He reached into his trench coat and pulled out a small square of paper.

Mardulo took it carefully. "A teleport stamp?"

"It's linked to a farm near Town Lunkwargle. One of my suppliers lives there. The magic blocking has not spread that far yet, and it should buy you some time. Just leave the restricted zone, teleport through the stamp, and tell my supplier Leepog sent you. I will meet you there and help with the conversion once you're ready. I assume you know the spell to activate the stamp?"

"Yes, many thanks." Mardulo pocketed the paper. "How much do I owe you?"

"Mardulo, if you put an end to Hobblebosh, that is payment enough."

"Then we will do everything we can," said Mardulo. "But first, we need to get into the Wizards' Tower."

Leepog paled. "The Wizards' Tower?"

"Yes," said Bundersquash. "There is a myrian crystal on floor twenty. We need it for the trapping spell."

"Is there no other way? That tower is heavily guarded, day and night."

"Myrian crystals are hard to come by at the best of times. Perhaps the Wizarding Consortium…"

"You will find nothing there, I'm afraid," said Leepog. "Hobblebosh robbed it clean."

"Then the tower is our best option. Heavily guarded, you say? How heavily?"

Leepog's expression told them everything they needed to know.

"If it is the only way, then so lies our course, difficult or not," said Lady Ufferbub.

"We will manage," said Mardulo. He patted his pocket with the teleport stamp. "Many thanks for your help, Leepog. We can take it from here. I look forward to seeing you in Town Lunkwargle."

Leepog bowed. "Until then, my friends, may luck travel with you. I shall go and make preparations." He took a moment to look at them all, then smiled. "It is good to see that you have rejoined the fight. Hope rides swiftly on your heels!"

With that, he left out a window into darkness.

"I hope we did not just give ourselves away," said Lady Ufferbub, grimacing.

"If we did, it's too late to worry." Toddleposter sighed. "We can decide whether to use that stamp once we escape to somewhere we can use it. For now, let's focus on getting into the tower and getting that crystal."

"Agreed," said Lady Ufferbub. "If it is as heavily guarded as Leepog says, we need a plan."

"Perhaps, though we can't do much without seeing it first," said Toddleposter, "and our plans have a troubling way of dissolving halfway through."

Somewhat forlornly, the others admitted this was true, then snuck back onto Avenue Tanglewater and crept through the shadows toward the Wizards' Tower. Leepog had not exaggerated. The area crawled with guards.

Fluorescent orbs floated through the air, filling the surrounding park with a light even brighter than day. Hobblebosh had chopped down the trees, too, so there were no convenient hiding places. At the center, the tower rose as crooked as always, but there was an unsteadiness to it now. The roof had lost half its shingles, the curved brickwork creaked and wobbled in the wind, and several of the windows had vanished altogether. Two guards stood watch by the door. A dozen more patrolled the park.

Gilbert and his friends had but one advantage. The guards' vision had adjusted to the area's brightness, and they were unable to see much beyond it. Lady Ufferbub led everyone to a refuge in the shadowed darkness along the outskirts of the park.

"There's nothing for it." Mardulo shook his head dismally. "We'll just have to run in and hope for the best."

"Do not be absurd," said Lady Ufferbub. "We would not make it a dozen paces before they caught us."

"I am open to alternatives..."

Toddleposter fidgeted. "Well," he said. "I have one idea. It's a gamble, and I doubt any of you will like it...but I can run out, cause a distraction, and try to draw them away. I'll lead them narrowsplatter down Street Filberg—as many as I can, for as long as I can, but I'll focus on the two near the door. While they're busy chasing me, you run in, grab the voice-to-illustration device, then leave. You may need another distraction on the way out, but if that tower has retained even a tenth of its usual oddities, I am sure you can find something."

"No," said Lady Ufferbub. "They would capture you, Toddleposter. Surely."

"All we need is a distraction. If they're anything like Hobblebosh's other soldiers, they won't be properly trained. Just civilians in armor they barely know how to put on."

"Even so, there are too many. You cannot outrun them all."

"I know, but I can give them a good chase. Hopefully, that'll be enough to get you four through the door."

"There must be another way." Bundersquash peered into the brightness, shielding his eyes. "Perhaps we can find a gap in their patrols or wait until they change shifts."

"We cannot wait. In the daylight, this will only get more difficult." Toddleposter stood straight. "We do not have time to argue. This is the best solution given our constraints, and I am ready. Bundersquash, Mardulo, Gilbert, Lady Ufferbub, it has been a pleasure. If luck is with us, perhaps I shall see you again. If not...well, we gave it our best, didn't we?"

The clone winked, took a deep breath, and turned to face the park.

"No!" Lady Ufferbub grabbed his arm. "I will not let you go—"

"Lady Ufferbub." Toddleposter turned on her. "While I have the utmost respect for you, we cannot stand here all night and debate. Kalyra was right about one thing. We must act decisively. I am willing to do this. Please, let me."

"You did not allow me finish," said Lady Ufferbub gently. "I will not let you go—alone."

Toddleposter's expression softened. His eyes flickered with a moment's hesitation, but ultimately, he nodded. "Together, then."

Gilbert wanted to call out, to grab them and pull them back, but when he opened his mouth to speak—throat dry, mind racing—he could think of no alternative, and the words never made it past his lips. So, in dreadful silence, he, Mardulo, and Bundersquash watched them go.

The guards noticed them both immediately. A tension took hold across the park. The brazen nonchalance of Lady Ufferbub and Toddleposter's entrance seemed to put them off balance, and in their uncertainty, the guards froze.

"Hello!" Toddleposter waved. "Lovely evening, wouldn't you say?" He walked directly toward the tower's entrance, focused on the two guards at the door. "You there," he said to one of them. "I've got something to say to you."

The guard straightened up. "This is a restricted area. By order of His Magnificence, the Grand King, our Savior, and Triumphant Lord of Masters, Obble Dor Hobblebosh the Juicy, I demand you leave at once."

"No." Toddleposter wrinkled his nose. "I hate limes."

All around the park, the guards tensed. They moved closer, forming a ring about the librarians. The guard who had spoken moved his hand to the hilt of his sword. "I must have misheard you," he said. "Surely, you did not speak treason?"

"Treason?" Toddleposter raised his eyebrows in mock surprise. "Is it treasonous to dislike limes? I mean, give me a lemon any day, but a lime? Blech!"

"Of course it's treason!" The guard frowned at Toddleposter. "Speak no more of this, or I shall place you under arrest."

"Bah!" Lady Ufferbub raised a fist. "They taste like rubbish, and they smell like rubbish!"

The guards stared, stupefied by this blatant blasphemy.

"But I must admit to some confusion on this matter," Lady Ufferbub continued, "for if *I* were a lime, I would not want people eating my kind. It is not as if I go around arresting people, simply because they refuse to eat my fellow humans. Why would dear old Obble the Nob consider it treasonous, then, to dislike the taste of limes?"

"A just and poignant question!" said Toddleposter. "Of course, nowadays, the real issue may not be limes at all. I hear he's rather more of a blueberry."

"Honestly, I suspect the difference is negligible," said Lady Ufferbub casually. "A useless idiot is a useless idiot, and our king is certainly that."

At last, this knocked the guards out of their horrified trance, and Toddleposter and Lady Ufferbub found themselves the focus of a sudden uproar. Guards from all directions charged at them—some with their weapons drawn, some simply waving their fists.

The librarians ran as quickly and as madly as they could. They tripped several guards along the way. Toddleposter rammed himself into one, and Lady Ufferbub managed to grab a sword from another's sheath. She made good use of it. A flurry of mayhem followed them as they put distance between themselves and the Wizards' Tower.

Gilbert's heart hammered. This was it. This was their opportunity. Both of the door guards had left, and the few others who hadn't joined the fray were utterly bewitched by its spectacle. He tapped Mardulo and Bundersquash on the shoulder, then gestured to the tower.

They sprinted into the light. In the rush, Gilbert's world shrank to the thumping of his feet on the grass and his ragged pulls of breath. Everything else fell away. He was alone, in a muted haze of panic, a bubble against the chaos of Lady Ufferbub and Toddleposter's distraction.

He almost careened headfirst into the door, stopping just in time. He pulled the handle and threw himself inside. Bundersquash charged in afterward, then Mardulo, who crashed directly into Gilbert. The door slammed shut behind them.

Gilbert hunched, hands on knees, panting. He tried not to think about Lady Ufferbub or Toddleposter and how miniscule their chances of escape really were. At least the guards seemed inclined to capture, not kill.

He looked up at the wizards. The harsh sound of heavy breathing pressed against the silence of the room. It was empty, if disheveled. What had once been a pristine marble lobby was now smeared with dirt, grime, and splinters of wood. A sharp crack ran across the center of the marble floor.

Bundersquash tugged at Gilbert's sleeve. "This way," he said quietly. "We cannot linger."

Gilbert straightened and followed the wizards upstairs. Each floor was as devastated as the last, and all were devoid of wizards. Mardulo and Bundersquash grew increasingly anxious with every step.

"It's more ruin than home now." Mardulo's voice quivered. They had reached floor eight. A film of dust darkened its white carpet and lightened its pitch-black walls. The table was tipped to one side. Bundersquash muttered something about a friend who had lived on this level.

Then a guard emerged from one of the bedrooms. He stared at Gilbert, Mardulo, and Bundersquash for a few torturous seconds, then shouted at the top of his lungs. Two more guards came to see what the fuss was about.

Gilbert didn't hesitate. He launched into a sprint up the stairs, Mardulo and Bundersquash with him, hoping to reach floor twenty and hide before the guards caught up. He felt as though he were falling upward, barely landing each footfall before lifting the next, leaning so far forward he could place his hands on the steps ahead.

Floor nine, floor ten, floor eleven. All a blur.

When they reached floor twelve—with its forest-like walls, and rows upon rows of magical plants, now mostly toppled—they ran headlong into another patrol. Three more guards, and Gilbert could hear the others coming up from downstairs.

"Blast," said Mardulo. They swerved off the staircase and backed into the room, tripping over tables as they went. The patrol from downstairs burst through the doorway in a fury.

"Six on three," said Gilbert. "Any ideas?"

"Nothing yet." Bundersquash's gaze darted through the room for inspiration. "Mardulo?"

"Short of tackling them? No."

"We really aren't very good at this," said Gilbert.

"Yes, well, neither are they," said Mardulo. "At least, that's what I'm hoping."

The guards encroached slowly and deliberately. They had spent long enough in this tower to understand the need for caution.

Gilbert backed up and accidently knocked a plant off a table. He grabbed it as it fell—a clay pot holding a red flower with long, closely bundled petals.

His heart almost stopped.

"I've seen this before," he said. It was the very same plant Bundersquash had sniffed before turning into a giant tuxedo-wearing rabbit.

"Ah, yes, Bellgiggle's work." Bundersquash smiled as if six guards weren't actively advancing toward him. "I wonder if they've sorted that out yet."

"I hope not," said Gilbert, and attacked.

He held the pot an arm's length away and shoved the petals into the nearest guard's face. The guard raised his weapon, but not in time. He gasped, then choked on the fumes and floundered back, hands to his throat. His hair receded into his skull. His skin turned green and warty. His legs scrunched. His arms shrank. His face squished horribly. Before long, the guard had transformed into a blinking, human-size toad. A white suit materialized around his new body, tailored perfectly to fit his wrinkled figure.

But Gilbert didn't stay to watch. By the time the first guard had sprouted warts, Gilbert was well on his way to the others. He converted four—the initial toad, a dapper toucan, an exceptionally sophisticated dormouse, and a black bear, complete with monocle and artificial moustache.

But fancy or not, a bear was a bear, and Gilbert decided against any further use of the plant. He turned back to the wizards, who had used the distraction well and were now sheltered behind a makeshift barricade of tables and chairs with a hoard of heavy objects to throw.

Gilbert dashed in their direction, swerved to dodge the swift stroke of a sword, and stumbled sideways over a table. The blade rang as it struck the floor beside him. In a rush of alarm, he abandoned the plant and crawled on his stomach to the wizards' improvised shelter.

Mardulo picked up a potted cactus, tested the weight in his hand, then lobbed it at one of the two still-human guards. It hit with an unnatural gunshot bang. The guard flew back, crashed through the wall, and descended gracefully to the ground among a slow-motion shower of bricks. The mouse, the toucan, and the frog fled down the stairs in a panic. The wall around the hole started to crumble.

Now only one human guard remained, and she was busy defending herself against the bear. Gilbert looked past her. If he, Mardulo, and Bundersquash could edge along the wall, they might be able to sneak by and reach the stairs without drawing too much attention...

The bear reared and struck the guard down. She smashed face-first into the plant Gilbert had dropped, shattering the pot with her chin. The monocled bear stood victorious upon her back.

But the guard was not defeated.

She screamed. Her eyes bulged. Her throat gurgled and warped. The bear backed away reflexively, as did Gilbert and the wizards.

The guard tried to rise—but couldn't. She gripped her stomach as two leathery golden wings burst from her back. Her limbs jittered uncontrollably against the floor. Her nose lengthened into a scaled, lizard-like snout, and when she opened her mouth to scream, her teeth sharpened to lethal points. Jagged spines sprouted along the top of her head and ran down her back. A tail grew. Her armored boots shattered as her hands and feet transformed into angular, clawed talons.

With a faint pop, a top hat fell into existence upon her head, and a bow tie fastened itself around her neck. And then, with the transformation finally complete, she opened her mouth and let forth a deep, guttural roar.

Gilbert stood dumbstruck alongside everyone else in the room, bear included, at a newly minted dragon.

The dragon took a deep breath. Red heat glistened against the scales at the back of her throat, and for one dreadful moment, there was silence. The air itself seemed to rush out of the room...

Then she breathed fire.

Gilbert would have been burned alive if Bundersquash hadn't tackled him to the ground. Mardulo leaped in the opposite direction. The dragon flapped her wings, breaking several tables in the process, and rose into the air, scanning the room from above. The bear stood on its hind legs as it growled a fierce challenge.

Gilbert said, "Nope," and then he, Mardulo, and Bundersquash made a break for it. The wall sagged dangerously as they passed the hole from Mardulo's projectile cactus, but Gilbert's adrenaline was more than enough to compensate for the concern it caused him. They rushed up the stairs, leaving the monocled bear and the top-hatted dragon to wrestle each other, embers smoldering among the plant life.

From thirteen to seventeen, Gilbert stopped only once—in response to a terrible crash from below. He doubted much remained of floor twelve. Then they all pressed onto floor eighteen, where they ran headlong into an elderly wizard brandishing a sharpened broom handle in their direction.

"Gurming!" Mardulo threw his hands into the air. "You're alive! What a relief!"

Gurming dropped his broom and beamed. "Mardulo! Bundersquash! I should have known it was you! No mangy old lime can keep you down!"

"It's good to see you, old friend," said Mardulo.

"And you." Gurming turned to Gilbert. "I remember you. Gigglebrit, wasn't it?"

"Gilbert," said Gilbert uneasily. "Sorry, we're in a bit of a rush."

"And you had best leave if you can, Gurming," added Bundersquash. "I don't think the Wizards' Tower is long for this world. A dragon and a bear are fighting downstairs, and there's a great big hole in the wall."

"Yes, well, it was only a matter of time," said Gurming gravely. "The architectural enchantments have been wearing off all over the city. But if we're about to find ourselves underneath a pile of rubble, why are you lot running up, not down?"

"We need to fetch something from floor twenty." Mardulo glanced anxiously at the door. "The myrian crystal in Bundersquash's voice-to-illustration device. I hope it's still there..."

"It is!" Gurming grinned. "The moment I heard Hobblebosh was coming, I hid as much as I could. I'm not letting some rotten lime lay his grubby hands on our good work! No, sir! I moved everything I could in floor twenty. You've got some real goodies up there!"

Mardulo clapped his hands. "That's wonderful news, Gurming! Wonderful! Where is it? And can we get to it quickly?"

"I hid it inside a mirror world!" He winked conspiratorially. "Still on floor twenty, but not the kitchen this time. It's in the bathroom of room two. Pardon the violation of privacy, but those bathrooms are the best-hidden rooms we have nowadays, and they have mirrors. I've been staying in one myself, if you'll believe it. You should be able to see the boxes through the mirror. Just dive in, get what you need, then dive back out again."

"And are you still using those switches to trigger the entrance?" Gilbert winced as another crash sounded downstairs.

"Yes indeed! Never did get around to adding that Roster filtering, unfortunately. But I did fix the exit. The mirror-entrance should remain open as long as anyone is inside, so you can run right out the way you came in." He jogged over to a drawer and pulled out a thin silver plate. "Now, you'd best hurry. It looks like more guards are coming up from the ground level."

Gurming showed them the plate. Inside was a bird's-eye view of the Wizards' Tower, with half a dozen guards marching in the door like ants.

"Will you be able to get out before the place collapses?" asked Mardulo.

Gurming looked around the room thoughtfully. "A dragon and a bear, you said? I'm sure I can think of something. But don't worry about me. I'm two hundred and seventy-three! I've lasted this long. I'm sure I'll last a bit longer. What about you? Do you have an escape plan?"

"From the tower?" Mardulo grimaced. "Run like blazes, mostly. If we can get out of the restricted zone, we have a teleport stamp. Do you know Leepog?"

"The lorilell dust fella? I've met him once or twice, though I hear more about him than I see these days. Hobblebosh's soldiers complain about him endlessly. Has a habit of popping up with one kind of lorilell dust or another and ruining everyone's day, then disappearing before anyone can catch him. They're mighty peeved."

"Jolly good," said Mardulo. "He gave us the stamp. Apparently, it goes to Town Lunkwargle. If all goes well, he'll meet us there and help with the final stages of our plan."

"Then I'll do what I can to buy you time," said Gurming, "though I doubt it will be very much. Now, off with you!"

He shoved them up the stairs onto floor nineteen.

"Many thanks!" Bundersquash called back as the door shut behind them. Without so much as a pause for breath, they climbed, at last, to floor twenty.

The room was in absolute shambles. Their table had been flipped. The animal-noise podium was little more than a pile of ash. Books and papers were everywhere. The ceiling had a number of concerning cracks along its length, and the paint on the walls, while still doing its best to mimic the outside world, was chipped and faded.

"Gurming said the bathroom in room two." Mardulo rushed toward the door, knocked twice, then opened it. They entered the bathroom just as the dragon let forth a terrible, ear-splitting roar from below. The whole building shook in response.

"Where's the mirror?" Gilbert's voice rose a few octaves.

"Here." Mardulo shut the door. It was hanging on the back. Sure enough, there were boxes everywhere in the reflected image—in the bathtub, in the sink, on the floor—but none of them existed in the real world.

And there was something else, too, tucked away near the back. Gilbert leaned in, hand on the glass, squinting—

"Aha!" Bundersquash flipped a switch on the edge of the frame.

Gilbert immediately toppled headfirst into the chilly air of the mirror world. He regained his footing, then turned back to the wizards, heart pounding heavily in his chest.

"I'll grab the voice-to-illustration device!" he said. He remembered what it looked like from Bundersquash's demonstration, back when he had first arrived in this world. But there was one more thing he needed to pick up. He was sure of it now. Sitting on a box at the back of the room: *A World of Souls: Volume 362.*

Home.

He waded toward the book, frantically shoving boxes to either side, his eyes locked on the plain brown cover, the loosely bound pages. He reached out and grabbed it. A wave of relief washed over him.

He had it.

Only then did he turn back and look for the voice-to-illustration device. It wasn't in the sink, nor did he see it among the items strewn across the bathtub. At random, he opened one of the boxes on the floor. Loose papers. The next held an assortment of rose-petal trinkets. The third carried jars of colorful slime. He tried another, then another, then another.

A heavy thud sounded from the outside world; then Bundersquash jumped in to join him. "The guards are almost here," he said. "I guess they got past the bear, the dragon, and Gurming. They're trying to knock down the entrance to floor twenty. Mardulo has a plan, but we need to hurry. Oh..." He noticed the book under Gilbert's arm. "Mardulo told me you wanted to return—"

"Another time!" Gilbert waved his free hand at the boxes littering the floor. "I need your help. I can't find it. There's too much stuff!"

Bundersquash's expression hardened. "I'll start here. You check that side of the room."

Together, they rummaged through box after box, growing increasingly frustrated that Gurming hadn't bothered with labels. At last, in the twelfth box Gilbert opened, he found it—a silver orb punctured with evenly spaced holes.

Bundersquash ran over and took the device. "So much for this project," he said, quickly tearing off the top half and tossing it aside. The myrian crystal was there—smaller than the one from Town Agol, but with the same rainbow dust floating restlessly inside. Bundersquash wrapped it in a sock from one of the other boxes and tucked it neatly into his robe's inner chest pocket.

He smiled at Gilbert. "Now all we have to do is escape!"

Gilbert grinned half-heartedly. Together, he and Bundersquash raced out of the mirror. Mardulo was in the bathroom waiting for them.

"Did you get it?" he asked.

"We did," said Bundersquash, patting his pocket.

"This too." Gilbert held up *A World of Souls*.

Mardulo looked at him—a mix of pity, concern, and understanding. "All right then," he said. "The door is still locked, but the guards will break through any minute. I've opened the door to room five. I'd say the playset looks sufficiently angry."

Gilbert remembered his first night in this world—the loud thumping he'd heard while trying to sleep, a semisentient playset with a temper.

"I'm hoping it will be a sufficient distraction to let us sneak past undisturbed," Mardulo explained.

With no window in the bathroom door, they had to listen. A violent shattering signaled the guards breaking in, then a brief scurry of feet, then several cries that suggested they'd found the playset.

"Probably as good a time as any," said Bundersquash.

They opened the door and entered a warzone. Four guards had made it up, and the playset had clambered into the common area. It had two swings, a slide, and a small wooden hut, reachable only by ladder.

It had used one of its swings to grip a guard by the ankle and was now throwing him about the room gleefully. A second guard had somehow managed to enter the wooden hut but now lacked the space required to swing her sword. A third had fallen unconscious, and the playset, flapping its slide, bounced him up and down like a paddleball. The fourth and final guard sat huddled in the corner, shouting encouragement to the others.

Mardulo, Bundersquash, and Gilbert ran directly for the exit.

Then Gilbert saw it.

On the wall, in the fading rendition of the outside world, a terrible streak of gold flew toward them. Mere seconds before it made contact, a flare of red, yellow, and white burst across the scene, illuminating the room with a blaze of light.

Then the wall exploded, and the dragon burst through, laced in flame and fury.

The force knocked Gilbert back into the middle of the common area. He gawked up at the creature standing over him—human sized but with enough presence to fill the room. Heat shimmered off its scales. It still wore its well-fitted top hat but now had a monocle to match. Gilbert dared not consider what had happened to the bear.

He covered his head uselessly as the dragon unleashed its fiery breath once more—but the flames were not directed at him. The entire back of the room came alight. Gilbert pulled himself together and crawled away, sweating, still clutching *A World of Souls* beneath his arm. Everywhere filled with smoke and haze. He had to find Mardulo and Bundersquash. Somewhere, a guard was screaming.

Gilbert reached the stairs and stood up to look around. Behind him, where the wall had been, was nothing but the cold open air and a horrible, twenty-story drop. Bricks fell left and right. The entire roof sagged. The fire ate at everything.

But even through the flames and smoke, there was no mistaking the playset's hulking, burning figure as it launched itself bodily into the dragon. The dragon screeched on impact, viciously tearing the playset's wood and rope with her talons. The guard inside the hut dove for safety, rolled onto the floor, and ran right past Gilbert down the stairs.

Gilbert coughed, squinted through the smoky air, and scoured the scene for Mardulo and Bundersquash. They had to be there somewhere.

A movement caught his attention, just in the corner of his eye. Mardulo, trapped under a pile of rubble. Gilbert dove toward him. Carefully, he placed *A World of Souls* where it was least likely to catch fire, then shoved as much debris as he could off Mardulo. His lungs seared in the heat as he struggled. His eyes watered terribly. He wheezed and choked, but brick by brick, beam by beam, he cleared the rubble away. At last, he helped Mardulo to his feet, then grabbed *A World of Souls* and extinguished a small flame that had caught on its cover.

"Where is Bundersquash?" Mardulo asked.

"I'm here!"

Gilbert turned just in time to see Bundersquash dive underneath the playset's raised slide moments before it crashed down upon the dragon's sturdy skull. The slide shattered. The dragon staggered back. The entire Wizards' Tower rumbled, then slumped. Gilbert nearly lost his footing as the floor shifted beneath him and settled back at an angle.

"Impressive tumbling, Bundersquash," said Mardulo. "Now we really must be off. Do you still have the crystal?"

Bundersquash checked his pocket. "I do."

"In one piece?"

"Yup."

"Right then. Run for it!"

Gilbert took the lead, sprinting down the steps two, three, four at a time. Stone, wood, and burning embers rained around him. The tower shifted constantly. Floor eleven had collapsed completely into floor ten. Twice, Gilbert tripped on broken steps, then one of them shattered completely underneath him, and he fell into a common room. He didn't even know which floor it was. He landed heavily on his shoulder, checked the book was still intact, then got up and ran again, too panicked to feel the pain.

They reached the marble lobby, and Gilbert nearly threw the door off its hinges as they launched themselves outside. When they reached the grass, they collapsed to their knees. There were no guards left. They had all either fled or perished in the tower.

Still catching their breath, they turned back to look at the conflagration. Ash and smoke caked the air. The entire top half of the tower was aflame.

The lower half was crumbling in horrible slow motion—the last of the architectural enchantments stretched beyond their limits. High above, the roar of the dragon could still be heard among the occasional whomp of the playset. Then the whole structure finally gave way and collapsed into a formless heap of rubble and flame.

"Now, isn't this a surprise."

Gilbert's stomach dropped. He knew that voice.

"I had always assumed I would be the one to destroy that miserable tower, but you have done it for me."

Mardulo, Bundersquash, and Gilbert turned slowly, dreading what they would see, but there was no avoiding it. With their backs to the inferno, they stood face to face with Obble Dor Hobblebosh. He glared at them, robed in black, wreathed in the shadow-filled firelight. He was as blue as the day Gilbert had fled Town Forbik, but the quiet confidence in his eyes had taken on a manic glint.

Already, the lime had created his auric nebula. *"Teveret Bomvakat!"*

A force like an explosion launched Mardulo, Bundersquash, and Gilbert away from each other. Mardulo and Bundersquash went the farthest, landing halfway across the park in either direction. Gilbert flew forward—closer to Hobblebosh.

He twisted in the air and landed heavily on his back. His entire spine felt bruised and warped, but he got his feet underneath him and rose, panting. He was only a few feet away from the tyrant.

Gilbert braced himself. If this was how it had to be, he would at least put up a fight. He raised his fists and stared Hobblebosh in the eye.

But a curious look came over the lime. He cast a second spell, and his auric nebula glowed silver and blue, then split into five floating orbs that surrounded him in a ring, pulsing white with electricity.

Gilbert tensed and prepared for a scuffle, but Hobblebosh walked right past him.

Startled, Gilbert turned to attack anyway—then realized what Hobble-bosh was walking toward. A terrible pang seized his stomach. There it lay, open in the grass by the burning remnants of the tower: *A World of Souls.* He must have dropped it when Hobblebosh cast the first spell.

Hobblebosh leaned down to grab it.

Gilbert ran, screaming, his mind lost in panic—but one of Hobble-bosh's orbs launched toward him and hit his chest like a lightning bolt.

Gilbert flew back and crashed into the ground, his limbs convulsing. Pain seared through his muscles. But he had to get up.

He had to.

Slowly, he regained control. Painfully, he stood. Hobblebosh was hold-ing the book in his hands, flipping through the pages. He grinned at Gilbert, his eyes alight with malice.

"I have been researching you, Gigglebrit Maistowne Nebraska the Fic-tional," he said, "or should I call you Gilbert Betters?"

Gilbert froze.

"You look surprised." Hobblebosh laughed. "It appears you have under-estimated me once again. I admit you almost got the better of me in Town Forbik. Almost. But after an incident like that, did you honestly believe I would not investigate and take the necessary precautions to prevent a repeat occurrence? Surely you have realized you can no longer do magic in my territory. And that is just the start. I know about this book too. I know about Earth. And I know about you—Gilbert Betters—what little of you there is."

Gilbert wanted to throw back a retort, an insult, some snide remark, anything to gain the upper hand, but the words never came. Dread and despair filled his mind.

Hobblebosh had the book.

Gilbert stared helplessly at the tyrant's grip on his home, his life, his past. Somewhere in the corner of his eye, he saw Mardulo rise to his feet. Bundersquash was still facedown in the grass.

"Did you ever meet Podish Gubber Tuggerbug the Stumped?" Hobblebosh asked. "He was the author, you know. He lived in City Mez. I paid him a visit just the other day, and we had the most enlightening chat. He had three other drafts of this story, though I hear it was still unfinished. That does not surprise me, looking at you. I destroyed them all, of course, then torched the house for good measure. Poor old Podish. He never saw it coming. I left with his head and his writing hand, and a great deal of information on you."

Mardulo had heard enough. He charged fiercely at Hobblebosh, but one of the electrical orbs intercepted him and sent him flying back, much as it had done Gilbert.

"My point is this, Gilbert," Hobblebosh continued, undisturbed. "I know everything about you. I know your parents were named Sarah and Francis Betters. I know they married at the age of thirty-one, though you were born two years earlier. I know that when you were a child, they used to read to you every night before you fell asleep. I know your first dog was named Kal, short for Kal-El, but your friend Brian insisted on Cal Ripken Jr. I know your favorite song is 'Dancing Queen,' by ABBA—"

"That's enough!" Gilbert finally found his voice. "So what? You know a bunch of facts about my life. That's trivia. You know *about* me. You don't know me."

Hobblebosh smirked. "I know enough. This book, for example. It must be very important to you." He held it an arm's length away, then took two steps back toward the fiery rubble and dangled it over the flames.

Anger boiled in Gilbert's chest. All reason left him. He charged at Hobblebosh in a red haze of fury, even knowing what would happen. His eyes never left the book. One of Hobblebosh's electric orbs struck him, but he was ready for it. He braced against the shock and pressed on. Then a second orb struck. Heat seared his chest, and he smelled his own skin burning, but still, he continued, one shaky step after another. Then a third orb struck, and finally, he fell. The orbs returned to their master.

Gilbert lay on his side, his muscles jerking uncontrollably. His heart beat an irregular rhythm in his chest, and spit bubbled at his lips. He lurched onto his stomach, vomited, then trembled to his knees. It was all he could manage.

"Yes, very good, Gilbert." Hobblebosh looked down upon him, his features silhouetted against the flame. "I want you to witness this. I want you to understand the totality of your failure—how you have failed this world, and how you have failed your dear little Earth. If you had not moved against me, I would have no reason to destroy this book. But you did, Gilbert. You did move against me. And now your world must pay the price. It is your fault. Remember that well, when your head rests upon my chopping block, and perhaps you shall accept your fate more willingly."

Gilbert lunged, trying to take the book from Hobblebosh, but succeeded only in stumbling forward and collapsing dangerously close to the fire, all strength lost. His home, his life, his family—they hung mere inches from total destruction, and Gilbert was powerless to save them.

"Please..." he pleaded, tears in his eyes. "Please, don't." He didn't know what else to do.

Hobblebosh only grinned. Torturously slowly, he lowered the book toward the fire. The pages singed and curled as they neared the heat.

"You came all this way to get your precious home back," he said, "and in doing so, merely surrendered it to me."

"Please!" Gilbert sobbed despite himself. "It wasn't even why we—" Even as he spoke, Gilbert realized the risk of those words. He nearly choked trying to stop himself from saying more.

But Hobblebosh had heard enough. His eyes narrowed, and he raised the book. A small flame danced along the spine. Hobblebosh put it out with a finger.

"It wasn't even why you *what*, Gilbert?"

Gilbert blanched. The book hung above the fire, nothing but Hobblebosh's grip keeping it safe from destruction. He turned to the wizards—now both conscious and standing, staring at Gilbert with wide, fearful eyes. Neither offered any hint of guidance.

"Why you *what*?" Hobblebosh repeated angrily. "Why you came into my city? If there is some other reason, Gilbert, tell me now or I shall be sure that your death is as painful as any I have ever devised and that it comes only after you have witnessed the end of all else you hold dear. This book will be the first...however"—he stood up straighter—"if you tell me now, perhaps you shall find me more *forgiving*."

Again, he lifted the book—ever so slightly—farther from the flames.

Gilbert couldn't pull his eyes away. Even knowing that Hobblebosh would never keep his word, it felt like a chance, more than he'd had mere moments ago. And it tortured him. Because he knew what he had to do.

His chest burned, his eyes stung with tears, and his body almost didn't obey—but he did it. He forced himself to stand, to turn around, and to run in the opposite direction. He ran past Mardulo and Bundersquash, knowing they would follow, then fled into the shadows of the nearest street, leaving Earth behind.

He glanced back only once. The book was already burning among the rubble, its pages turned to ash. Hobblebosh wasn't chasing them. He glared, cast a spell, and calmly walked away.

"I believe he just alerted the guards," Bundersquash panted.

"Perhaps they'll panic," said Mardulo hopefully. "If luck is with us, they may scramble and leave their posts."

Gilbert couldn't find it in himself to care. He put every ounce of his energy into running. Tears streaked his dusty face, his chest screamed with pain, and his legs shook under the pressure of his steps. But still he ran, driven by a maddening fury.

"I am sorry about the book," said Mardulo, struggling to keep up.

Gilbert clenched his jaw. "Left or right?"

"What?"

"Ahead. Do we turn left or right?"

Mardulo looked. "Left."

They ran through street after street, around dozens of turns and bends, sticking to the shadows as much as possible, though they focused mostly on speed. They reached Mardulo's wall opening in a matter of minutes—but a blue soldier stood guard beside it.

Gilbert didn't even stop to think. He grabbed a stone from a collapsed building nearby and rushed in with a strangled shout. The guard drew his sword.

Gilbert threw himself fully into the fight. The soldier's first swing missed, but scraped the outside of Gilbert's arm. Gilbert didn't even feel it. He struck the guard's unhelmeted head with the stone, and the guard staggered back, eyes wide. Gilbert closed the distance and half pushed, half threw the guard against the wall. Then he struck once again with the stone.

The guard collapsed. Gilbert held him down with one knee. Using both hands, he lifted the stone above his head and brought it down on the guard's chest. It jolted against armor with a metallic clunk. Once more, Gilbert raised the rock, eyeing the guard's bleeding nose, but this time, Bundersquash caught his hands.

Gilbert didn't resist. He slumped onto the cold stone of the street, gasping for air. He wanted to shout. He wanted to cry. He wanted to curl into the shadows and disappear. He wanted to rage through the city, screaming.

He wanted everything in this world to burn alongside the Wizards' Tower, and he would happily burn himself with it.

Mardulo pulled him to his feet. "This way, lad," he said softly. "We're almost out."

He tugged Gilbert's arm and guided him through the wall, into the meadows beyond. Gilbert followed wordlessly. It was the simplest thing to do.

It wasn't long before a guard spotted them from the battlements. She raised the alarm, and Gilbert, Mardulo, and Bundersquash soon found themselves the quarry of a ruthless hunt. They rushed toward the hippalectryons, grabbed their supplies, and rode off as quickly as the creatures would carry them.

The moment they'd escaped Hobblebosh's restricted zone, Mardulo dismounted. He shot a quick glance over his shoulder, then rummaged through his pocket for the teleportation stamp.

"Whether Leepog is trustworthy or not, I think this is our best option," he said. "There's no way we can outrun that many soldiers. Bundersquash, you know what to do. Gilbert, grab onto me."

They could already hear the thundering advance of soldiers on their trail. Bundersquash offered the hippalectryons a quick but earnest thanks, then wished them all goodbye. Lampellion neighed appreciatively and galloped away with the others, off into the distance.

Mardulo rubbed his palms together, held the stamp inside his auric nebula, and babbled an incantation. Gilbert grabbed the elderly wizard's shoulder just in time. The world collapsed into nothingness around him.

Chapter 22

Identity

Gilbert awoke on his back in the middle of a field. The first light of morning had just rolled in, and with it, a gentle fog. The sky was one solid blanket of gray.

Bundersquash leaned into view. "You're awake! How are you feeling?"

"Horrible." Gilbert curled into a sitting position. "My chest is on fire, and my head feels like...death."

"I'm sorry to hear that." Bundersquash helped Gilbert to his feet. "Your headache is probably from the teleportation. As for your chest, we could try a few healing spells, but we don't have much by way of ingredients..."

"It's all right. Where are we?"

"We're not sure. The stamp was supposed to send us to Town Lunkwargle, but we don't know much beyond that. I'd guess we're somewhere on the outskirts. Mardulo has gone to find the supplier Leepog mentioned. He should be back any minute."

Gilbert nodded. Memories from the previous night were returning to him, each as unwelcome as the last. The fall of the Wizards' Tower, Hobblebosh's malicious grin as he threatened *A World of Souls*, the book turning to ash in the flames. He wished he could shove it away and pretend it didn't matter, lock it deep in the back of his mind, repress it, and move on. Focus on the present.

But he knew that wouldn't work. There was too much Earth in him to let it go so easily.

His heart sank. With the book gone, with Podish gone…His friends and family existed in his memories, and his alone. He didn't even have someone to reminisce with.

"I need a minute." Gilbert turned away from Bundersquash and sat on a fallen log, head in his hands. This was too much. After all that had happened. Just when he thought there might be a chance…

He felt as though he ought to cry, but he couldn't. His whole body was just…numb.

His shirt was in tatters, singed and sweaty. The skin beneath it, blistered. Dried blood caked his arm. He didn't even remember getting cut.

Mardulo's voice chirped from the horizon. "There's a house over here!" he called. "I'm going to take a look. Want to come?"

Gilbert rolled his shoulders and took a breath. "Better than doing nothing, I suppose."

He and Bundersquash grabbed the ingredient bags from Town Agol, then joined Mardulo near the house. It was moderately sized, with walls of stone and a roof of tiled slate.

"I'm not sure if we can trust whoever is in here," said Mardulo. "I like Leepog, but I don't know anything about this supplier—or even if this house belongs to them."

"We keep it simple, then," said Bundersquash. "Vague."

"Precisely." Mardulo turned to the front door and knocked.

A few seconds passed before a meek voice sounded from the other side. Whoever it was didn't open the door. "Hello?"

"Hello!" said Mardulo loudly. "We're a little lost, but we're looking for someone. I was wondering if you could point us in the right direction."

A moment of silence, then, "Who's asking?"

Mardulo turned to the others, who shrugged. Gilbert tried to peer into the nearest window to see who was there, but the angle wasn't right.

"This would be simpler if you opened the door," suggested Bundersquash.

"Simple?" came the voice. "No. Nothing is simple. Simplicity is an illusion. Life is complex—every event the result of an unimaginable network of interrelated actions and consequences. To fully grasp the mesmerizing infinity of our reality, one must never strive for simplicity, but for a more profound level of deeper understanding."

Mardulo, Bundersquash, and Gilbert looked at one another.

"Leepog Guddlegap Tutswither the Vast sent us," said Gilbert.

"Oh." The door opened, revealing a middle-aged man with green eyes, salt-and-pepper hair, and a pair of leather overalls.

His skin was blue.

"I'm Thoegg Dulepatters Wilpudge the Calm."

"You're blue," said Gilbert.

"Yes. I was with Leepog in Town Forbik when it happened. Please come in. You look like you could use a bath...and a change of clothes."

Gilbert looked him up and down, then cautiously entered the house. They passed through a small entryway into a larger, cozier room. It had a wooden floor, a small fireplace, a few soft armchairs with fluff poking out of the seams, and a large oak table holding a bowl of not-quite-fresh fruit. There was a set of shelves on one wall, all filled with wooden toys. Gilbert examined everything, then peered around the backs of the shelves, scanning for signs of danger.

"You are Mardulo, Bundersquash, and Gilbert, yes?" Thoegg asked after a time. He handed Gilbert a wet rag to wipe the blood from his arm. "Where are the other two?"

Mardulo looked at the floor. "We lost them in City Boratorus. If any luck is with them, they're only imprisoned."

"I am sorry to hear that."

Gilbert eyed Thoegg carefully. "Have you met them before?"

"Who? Lady Ufferbub and Toddleposter? No, I'm afraid I haven't. Leepog just said—"

"Then how did you know they're the ones who are missing?"

"Come again?"

"How did you know that we were Gilbert, Mardulo, and Bundersquash, and that Lady Ufferbub and Toddleposter were missing?"

"Oh...just a guess, I suppose. Half the people on this continent would recognize Mardulo, of course, and at least a quarter would recognize Bundersquash. As for you, Gilbert...well, you have the gloves of a wizard, and I understand the others are librarians."

Thoroughly unconvinced, Gilbert peered into an adjoining room—a kitchen, by the look of it. "I'm just going to wash my hands," he said and walked in for a better look.

There was nothing obviously amiss. Empty counters. Cupboards filled with food and dishes. A small hearth stood unlit at the back of the room. A stone basin had been filled with water.

Then Gilbert looked to the floors, and his eye caught something strange in the trash can. He fished it out—a glass bottle with Leepog's distinctive L. G. T. branding and a trace of sparkling pink liquid inside.

"What's this?" Gilbert marched back into the living room. "This is from Leepog."

"Oh. That?" Thoegg chuckled. "That's just a little something—"

"It looks like the remnants of a glamour," said Gilbert. "Exactly like the ones we used in Town Forbik. Mardulo? Bundersquash?"

Mardulo tipped a drop of the remaining liquid onto his finger, licked it, then spit it back out. "It *is* a glamour! Who are you really, Thoegg?"

"I'm Thoegg!"

"Grab him!" said Mardulo. "He must work for Hobblebosh."

"I don't! I don't!" Thoegg squirmed as Bundersquash and Gilbert seized his arms.

"Then tell us who you really are!" Fire burned behind Mardulo's eyes.

"I told you! I am Thoegg Dulepatters Wilpudge the Calm!"

Gilbert tightened his grip, ignoring the bolt of pain that shot up his arm. "We're not falling for it. You may as well come clean."

"I'm telling the truth! I really am Thoegg Dulepatters Wilpudge the Calm!" But even as he said it, his face fell. "...or at least, that's this one's name."

Mardulo raised an eyebrow. "Excuse me?"

"Thoegg. He's a farmer. Smarter than he looks but wholly without luck as far as crops go. Never liked the dirt, but it's the family trade, so he sticks with it. His proudest moment was when his kids decided to move on, get past this filthy business and into something fresh—oceanographers, the three of them."

Gilbert could have sworn a tear glistened in Thoegg's eye. He loosened his grip. Bundersquash let go entirely.

"What in the world are you on about?" asked Mardulo.

"It's a role. I play roles." The person sighed, then flopped onto an armchair. A clump of fluff puffed into the air. "Given my recent behavior, I suppose it was only a matter of time before you found out. But these roles have been my life for...oh, at least a decade or two, by now. Thoegg is one of them, one of my first. Leepog is another—the sneaky, charismatic salesman, deeply embedded in the criminal underbelly of a big city, for which he holds a stalwart loyalty and fondness—in no small part because it lets him get away with so much. But of course, you know me best as Thorippela Luggude Swedgett the Crisp."

Gilbert's eyes widened. "*You're* Thorippela?"

"Sometimes, yes. Honestly, Gilbert, I thought you'd found me out in Town Forbik. I sold Mardulo enough glamours to disguise all five of you twice, but what do I see when I go to Town Forbik? You, wandering about with your plain face on! Then you came right up and asked me for directions! I was so flustered I almost gave myself away. Still, when I found you later, you only seemed to care about having stolen my—or her—hippalectryons, so I let the matter rest."

"This is ridiculous." Gilbert threw up his hands.

"It would've been a lot more convincing if this bloody blue ever came off. I don't know what you did, Gilbert, but I'm sure you've put the Department of Magical Espionage on alert. Not even my best glamours can break through it."

"So, you're with the Department of Magical Espionage?" said Bundersquash.

"No, of course not! I just meant...look, I already told you. I play roles. That's it."

"Then why have you been following us?" asked Mardulo. "First, you befriended me and sold me glamours in City Boratorus—"

"And you snuck up on me and tried to sell me lorilell dust!" Gilbert cut in.

"Then you followed us in secret to Town Forbik," said Mardulo.

"And then you teamed up with me afterward as Thorippela!"

"And somehow you found us again in City Boratorus!" Bundersquash finished.

"Well, yes. When you put it like that...but Mardulo, Leepog has been your go-to lorilell dust salesman for years now. It's how I first got to know you—your character, I mean—and I admired you. So, when it came time to create a *new* role, I thought you would be a worthy case study. With all you'd done for the world, you seemed a good fit, a sort of template for the character to come. And my conviction only solidified once this trouble with Hobblebosh started. You, Bundersquash, and Burrid working tirelessly. Strong characters all around...it was such useful material! I kept my distance, of course. I didn't want to interfere. But just as I was finalizing my plans, just as I thought this new character might finally be ready to go, everything changed!"

Thoegg—or whoever they were—stood up from their armchair and started to pace.

"The Wizarding Consortium had just been attacked. It gave me the perfect opportunity to bring out Whirga Sludgepoge Tudlepett the Stationed. She's a useful character to have on hand—struggled with gambling in her past but found purpose in the city guard. With her, I could pose as your door guard and get a closer look at your day-to-day lives, but the very first time I saw you in that role, what did I find? Well, firstly, Mardulo, you clearly have a thing against door guards. But more to the point, you suddenly had a new member!"

He pointed, somewhat accusingly, at Gilbert.

"Naturally, I needed to learn more. There was obviously something big brewing. Mardulo bought *ten* glamours from Leepog the very next day, and as for Gilbert...well, you spoke to me about buying new clothes but refused to reveal much beyond that, so I popped off to intercept you as Leepog and learn more that way. And my word, how clueless you were! You barely knew Street Undoora from Street Onduura, and you'd clearly never heard of lorilell dust. You seemed so...bewildered. To be perfectly honest, I was worried about you, so I did what I could and gave you that healing dust." He turned to Bundersquash. "You're welcome, by the way."

Bundersquash opened his mouth, as if wondering whether to say thanks, then closed it with a disconcerted frown.

"Anyway, I came to Town Forbik as a curiosity more than anything, to keep an eye on you and see how things developed. I thought I might be able to help too—just in the background, so to speak. I really do want Hobblebosh gone, you know. So I donned the role of Thorippela. She's been up that way before for her hippalectryon business, and it seemed as good a cover as any. I snuck into town using a fake name—a real person's fake name, mind you, belonging to one of my contacts back in Port Opperwob—then I left those hippalectryons for your escape, thinking you might need a quick getaway regardless of how things went. And I was right. You're welcome, again.

"As for the rest of my time as Thorippela...well, I was distraught when I saw you'd all gotten upset with each other, and I wanted to help. The team I'd grown so fond of, the team I'd based so much of my new character on, was falling apart! I couldn't have that, so I broke one of my principal rules and intervened directly...more than I had done already, that is. And I succeeded, too, I might add. You're all back together again. You. Are. Welcome."

Mardulo furrowed his eyebrows. "But why didn't you come with us into Town Agol? If you're also Leepog, you could've helped us package the trapping spell into lorilell dust!"

"I offered to help! But for obvious reasons, I couldn't get into that silly name-checking boat, could I? And I'm no wizard. I can turn an existing spell into lorilell dust, sure, but I can't make a spell from scratch. That was up to you and Bundersquash. I did wait for you—days and days, I stayed in that field—but you never returned. In the end, I assumed the worst and went to help City Boratorus by myself. I cooked up as much lorilell dust as I could before Hobblebosh arrived, supplies for the resistance once his magic blocking took effect, but I stayed near the Wizards' Tower whenever I had the chance, thinking that's where you'd go if you ever returned—and lo and behold, I was right once again! And lo and behold, you needed another escape plan. And lo and behold, I was there to assist with a teleport stamp. You're welcome."

Gilbert shook his head. "I get that you've been helpful, but...all this? You've been stalking us, stalking Mardulo and Bundersquash, all in the name of making some new character? It makes no sense!"

Thoegg's face flattened. "It was necessary research! A good case study is essential when crafting a new persona. I'm an actor. Life is my play; the world, my stage; these roles, my art. But every artist needs a muse. One cannot act from nothing. It's the details that make all the difference, and for those—research. But I was also there to help, and I did so at almost every turn. As I said, I want Hobblebosh gone just as much as you do."

"But why not simply introduce yourself?" asked Bundersquash. "We could have *told* you about our lives and saved you the trouble of sneaking around."

"And let you know you were being observed? Certainly not. I needed your true selves—not you as you see yourselves, and definitely not you as you describe yourselves. You as you are. Authentic."

Everyone looked at him uneasily.

"And which of these roles is *actually* you?" asked Gilbert.

"I am all of them. All of them are me."

"Originally, I mean. Which one is real?"

"I do not answer that question, Gilbert. They are all a part of me, each as real as the next."

Gilbert groaned.

"I genuinely don't know what to say." Bundersquash looked around, then sighed. "I suppose you *have* done rather a lot to help...perhaps that is reason enough to trust you."

Thoegg bowed his head. "Many thanks."

"But can you help us now?" asked Mardulo. "With the lorilell dust?"

"I can. Is the spell prepared?"

"Almost. We need a place to finalize the details and run tests. Ideally somewhere hidden but with plenty of space. Is there anywhere on your farm that might work?"

"I can do you one better," said Thoegg. "Or, rather, Wilestre can. Wilestre Pugglepodd Thaegut the Quick Winged. He owns several gryphon warehouses down near town. One of those should suit you nicely. You can find him over at Thaegut's General Store and Rentals—out the door, down the hill, turn left when you hit the road. It's just past the Tawny Barn." He hesitated a moment. "I'm sorry you didn't get to spend more time with Thoegg. I really thought you'd get along well together. I was preparing some tea for the occasion. Still, duty calls...and I'm sorry to hear about Lady Ufferbub and Toddleposter too."

"With any luck, we can stop Hobblebosh before anything unspeakable happens to them," said Mardulo. "But I doubt we have long. Come, time is of the essence."

Thoegg gave Gilbert a change of clothes but stayed behind when everyone else left for the store. Mardulo, Bundersquash, and Gilbert walked along the road in silence, passing by thatched cottages and wattle-and-daub homes. The road varied between dusty dirt and well-trodden, compact dirt but never progressed to stone.

Gilbert's mind wavered, unease and uncertainty clouding his thoughts. Thorippela had made a fool of him. He'd known *something* was off—but this? They'd spent so much time together. They'd bonded, become friends. And yet, that whole time, she was actually Leepog the sleazy salesmen, who was actually Thoegg the middle-aged farmer, who was actually...well, who knew? But he had to admit, she—he?—had done a lot to help.

Mardulo and Bundersquash were taking it in stride. The news that they'd been stalked for several months, maybe even years, didn't seem to bother them much.

"People follow me all the time," said Mardulo. "Honestly, I'm impressed he managed to avoid my notice. That doesn't make it okay, of course, but—well, saving our lives several times? That helps."

"I wonder what character he's been working on," said Bundersquash wistfully.

"With us as his muse?" Mardulo grinned. "Clearly a handsome, inspirational wizard, the likes of which the world has never seen."

Bundersquash rolled his eyes, in a friendly sort of way.

As they rounded a corner, a tall stone tower came into view, its roof a thick cone of straw. It had no decorations, except a rim of windows that lined its uppermost level.

Mardulo gasped. "So that's where we are!"

"Where?" said Gilbert.

"That tower—it's Town Lunkwargle's warrior gryphon stable. I'd recognize it anywhere. I didn't realize we were so near the town center. We must be getting close to the general store. This place isn't very big…"

He was right. The Tawny Barn—a pub, as it turned out—was only a few minutes away, and as Thoegg had said, they found Thaegut's General Store and Rentals just beyond. The door said closed, but they walked in anyway.

It was a small corner shop with three aisles of shoulder-height shelves, each carrying ornaments, trinkets, snacks, and drinks. Near the back, a magically cooled barrel held three different flavors of ice cream. On the walls, a number of plaques hung for sale, with sayings like "Home Is Where the Gryphon Is," "My Other Wagon Is a Gryphon," and "I Take My Eggs Hatched, Not Scrambled."

A number of framed drawings hung behind the checkout counter, but those were not for sale. Most looked to be the ambitious scribbles of children, with stick-figure people, rectangular houses, and a number of rotund birds. A few did look professionally done, though. One in particular stood out among the rest. Two young men—one, with black hair and a grizzly beard, the other, red hair and a full smile. They looked content, sitting arm in arm at a picnic on a hill.

With a pang, Gilbert thought of Earth and the hill beside Berrywood Lane. He couldn't have been more than ten the first time he'd rushed up those grassy slopes for a picnic of his own. He'd carried the food using a homemade bindle—his dad's sweater and a stick. All gone, now. The lane. The hill. Everything. Nothing left but memory.

Thoegg rushed in from the back room, breathing hard. "Goodness me, you move quickly! Just a moment." He uncorked a bottle of dark-red liquid and guzzled it without so much as a grimace. Then he transformed, and Gilbert recognized him instantly as the burly, black-haired man from the photo, though his hair had grayed, and his once-full beard was now little more than stubble.

Gilbert frowned. "Really?"

"Wilestre, I take it?" asked Mardulo.

"Indeed! Wilestre Pugglepodd Thaegut the Quick Winged. Having retired after several long and arduous years in the ranks of the gryphon war riders, I chose to start this modest shop. Mostly, it's a way to stay busy and feel useful. The ornaments are a delight to tourists, and the ice cream brings smiles to the children's faces. It's simple, but in little ways, it matters."

"That's very good of you," said Bundersquash.

"And who's the other guy in that picture?" Gilbert pointed to the image on the wall.

Wilestre's face fell. "Aliber Morfin Dalwik the Favored. My late partner."

"You look very happy together," said Mardulo. "I am sorry for your loss."

"He was a great man, and one of the best war riders Town Lunkwargle has ever known. Losing him was...I do not like to speak of it." He forced a smile. "But come, you are in a rush."

He reached for a rack of numbered keys and gave one to Bundersquash. "Gryphon Warehouse Six. Medium sized, but vacant. We use it to train the overly rambunctious young'uns. I expect it will be more than sufficient for your purposes. And if you find yourselves short on anything, it's not too far from a magical supply shop. They don't have much these days, but it's better than nothing in a pinch."

"Do you own that too?" Gilbert raised an eyebrow.

Wilestre laughed. "No. That would be our dear Moribella Tormin Norvika the Splendid. To get to the warehouse, just head widesplatter along Path Wulf. You'll see it on the edge of town. You really can't miss it. When you're ready for the lorilell dust conversion, fetch me here. I'll set things up while you work. Try to keep the spell down to two lines if you can. Ancient tongue, of course."

"Two lines, one line, whatever you need," said Mardulo. "Many thanks, Wilestre."

"Many thanks to you as well. May luck travel with you all."

As the wizards left the store, Gilbert paused. His eye caught something on the nearest shelf—a small notebook with a horrible red-barn pattern.

An idea struck him.

"Can I, um, buy this?" he asked, even knowing he didn't have any money. "And a pencil? I can pay you back later, probably..."

Wilestre looked at him curiously. "That's been sitting there for years," he said. "It's yours. As for the pencil..." he reached under the counter and removed a quill. "Will this serve? It's self-inking."

"That would be great. Thanks." Somewhat embarrassed by Wilestre's generosity, Gilbert grabbed the book, took the quill, and thanked him again. Then he rushed to catch up with the wizards.

The warehouse was absolutely massive. It rose at least three stories into the air and easily ran the length of a football field. The walls were made of simple, unpainted wood panels. Thick block letters had been affixed near the top of one side: "Gryphon Warehouse Six." Each letter must have been at least six feet tall.

They entered through a metal door on one side of the building. Indoors, it was a single enormous room with bales of hay lining the perimeter and a floor of compact dirt. A littering of straw had been spread throughout, and a small ring stood in the center holding several items Gilbert could only assume were gryphon toys—a large feather on a stick, a bouncy ball, and some miniature wind-up critters, many of which looked like they could fly.

Mardulo and Bundersquash hurried to one corner and unloaded their bags, which took several minutes and left Gilbert wondering if the bags were somehow bigger on the inside. But he didn't go over to investigate. A spell of this caliber was well beyond his understanding. He had no help to offer the wizards in this.

Instead, he glanced at the notebook Wilestre had given him. His stomach tied into knots. He'd picked it up on an impulse. Now he wasn't sure he wanted it.

He sat down on a bale of hay, opened to the first page...

Then stopped.

Perhaps Mardulo and Bundersquash could use his help after all.

He put the notebook to one side and wandered toward them. They were looking over the notes Bundersquash had made in Town Agol. Gilbert picked up snippets of their conversation.

"I struggled with the quasilength conversions." Bundersquash handed Mardulo a piece of parchment. "And this material deconstruction here. I wouldn't mind if you could give that a once-over. In the meantime, I'll prepare the testing platform."

Mardulo stroked his beard, mouthing equations as he examined the page. The whole sheet was covered in symbols Gilbert didn't recognize, organized in a format Gilbert had never seen before.

Having confirmed what he already knew, he moved back to the bale of hay, sat down, and picked up the notebook and quill again. His stomach dropped even as he did so, but he was determined to give this a try.

He adjusted his position, making his face less visible to the wizards, then braced himself...and started to write.

It was like a dam broke in his mind. The words poured out, a wave, a flood.

A dozen pages later, Mardulo came to check on him.

"Bundersquash and I were going to get some food. Proper food, not sandwiches. Would you like—are you okay?"

"Oh, uh. Yeah." Gilbert sniffed and wiped his face. He hadn't seen Mardulo coming.

"What's the matter?"

"I was just...remembering." Weakly, he held up the notebook. "Writing down things about Earth. My friends. My family. Stories. That kind of thing."

Mardulo looked at him, enough sympathy in his eyes to make Gilbert turn away.

"I understand," said the elderly wizard, "but Gilbert, I have to tell you—even with the actual book, it would have been a stretch to extract your parents. It's very unlikely we'll be able to do it with just a notebook of your own making, no matter how good your memory is."

"I know," said Gilbert. "It's not for that. It's just...for me. To remember."

Mardulo's face softened. He put a hand on Gilbert's shoulder. "Of course," he said. "In that case, I will leave you to it and fetch you some food from the nearest shop I can find. Don't give it another thought. I'll bring you whatever sounds good."

"No, it's all right." Gilbert stood. "You and Bundersquash should focus on the spell. I'll grab food. It's the least I can do."

Mardulo hesitated. "Well, if you're sure, take this." He handed Gilbert a bag of coins.

"What're they worth?" asked Gilbert, looking into the bag.

"The brown ones are each one penna. The silver, one tille. The gold, one hundred tille."

"And a typical meal should cost..."

"Ten, maybe fifteen tille."

Gilbert nodded. "I'll see what I can find."

"And Gilbert, if you ever need to talk, I'm here."

"I know, Mardulo. Thanks." He smiled at the elderly wizard, then stepped outside.

The warehouse sat on the outskirts of the main town, removed from most of the shops. Gilbert walked along the street they had arrived on, hoping to find some kind of takeaway restaurant closer to the town center. Did takeaway restaurants exist in this world?

The first place he stopped was Lermop's Meats, but everything they sold was raw. He glanced through the windows of the Happy Haberdasher, but passed, fairly certain haberdashers had something to do with sewing. The Tawny Barn was closed. Was Lunkwargle's Psaltery and Dulcimer Emporium a food store?

A sudden rush of wind sounded overhead. Gilbert looked up and caught a glimpse of gryphons soaring through the air. They flew in a V formation, each carrying a rider, following the leader through a series of twirling acrobatics. They rushed past with staggering speed, and in a matter of seconds, they were gone.

Gilbert's gaze lingered on the empty sky, his head a mess of emotion. Gryphons and wizards, haberdashers and butchers, penna and tille. This was his world now. It had felt so temporary before. Even when he'd had no plans to return, when he was out on his mission to Town Forbik, to learn magic and save the world, he'd always viewed it as something with an end. An adventure. There and back again.

But the thought of living here for the rest of his life put everything into a new perspective. Every unusual shop, every weird item, every strange new event was something to get used to. The idea that, years from now, he might walk down a street like this with a handful of penna and tille, understand what he was looking at, hear a herd of gryphon riders overhead, and barely think twice about any of it...it was daunting. Terrifying, even.

But he wasn't alone. He had friends here, and he was lucky to have them. Mardulo and Bundersquash, of course, and Lady Ufferbub and Toddleposter...if they survived. He hoped they were okay. With everything that had happened, he'd had almost no time to process it. He supposed there was little to be done now except hurry to get this spell prepared. But for that, he was dependent upon Mardulo and Bundersquash, and for now, Mardulo and Bundersquash were dependent upon him for food.

Lunkwargle's Psaltery and Dulcimer Emporium, Gilbert soon found, sold musical instruments.

With a sigh, he picked another street at random.

Half an hour later, he'd passed by two sandwich shops, decided against a clam chowder dispensary, and finally found an open tavern, where he bought three apple pastries and a midsize pork pie.

When he returned to the warehouse, Mardulo was adjusting the stance of a small figurine. Bundersquash stood at his side, inspecting several sheets of parchment through the thick layer of his glasses.

"This little figure is made of Sandermik's Simulated Organic Matter," said Mardulo as Gilbert approached. "We've calibrated it using the essence signature. Amazing what you can do with a strand of hair, isn't it? The spell should react to it as it would to Hobblebosh. Care to watch our first trial?"

"Sure!" Gilbert placed the food to one side and waited as the wizards made their final arrangements. Mardulo added an assortment of petals, salts, and creams to a bowl of muddy goop, then angled the myrian crystal so it caught the light. A reflection hit the bowl and seemed to react to the mixture, remaining even once Mardulo put the crystal away. Then he surrounded the Hobblebosh figurine with five gryphon toys, cracked his knuckles, and stood back.

"*Humei'pente skeuae,*" he began, "*sullégete enerheiás humoun...*"

The incantation differed somewhat from the one Gilbert had learned for Town Forbik. This one was shorter, but it contained a level of complexity beyond the words. Mardulo's rhythm, volume, tone, and gestures all seemed to play a role.

He finished the spell with practiced delicacy. When it was done, the toys started to glow a faint, silvery blue. The bowl rose into the air, then dropped and vanished in a heartbeat. At the same time, the miniature Hobblebosh figurine lifted off the ground, just an inch, and cobalt beams of energy struck out from the five gryphon toys, each one connected to all the others, forming one great web of light underneath the figurine. Slowly, the toys rose and moved toward each other. The web became a cage.

But the cage fell away. The figurine jolted. The light flickered and died. Then one of the toys caught fire.

"Ack!" Bundersquash grabbed a heavy blanket from the ingredient bag and snuffed out the flames.

Mardulo stared, forlorn, at the untrapped figurine. "Blast," he said. "We were so close."

"Did you see the wobble at the end?" asked Bundersquash. "That, combined with the fizzling anchor objects and the toy bursting into flames...I'd say the essence simplifications didn't overlap well with the anchor-object-generalization interface."

"Sorry, Bundersquash," said Mardulo. "That realignment was my suggestion."

"It was worth a try. Besides, we'll need to do something, given the complexity of the signature..." He took a deep breath. "Come, let's eat. Perhaps afterward we'll be able to think more clearly."

Gilbert's offerings were well received, and they shared a quick lunch in the fresh air outside the warehouse. When they'd finished, the wizards returned to their work, and Gilbert went back to writing—though he sat nearer his friends than he had done before, to be there in case they required assistance.

The writing was easier this time, though still not easy. He'd been worried his real memories from Earth would get replaced with the vivid horrors of his nightmares, but as he wrote, he found they came easily, often faster than he could get them down.

He wrote of his school, with its strange stains on the tiled ceilings, with the lunch trays that always seemed wet, and with the much sought-after though ever-disappointing rectangular pizza slices. He wrote about his friends, of Brian's fondness for baseball equaled only by Cindy's fondness for Star Wars or Angel and Malia's insistence on playing Dungeons and Dragons. Gilbert had never actually gotten around to doing that with them. He even found himself dipping into lessons from class, jotting down physics equations he thought might prove useful and one or two notes from biology.

But it was the memories of his family, his parents, that hit the hardest, and to those he kept returning. The process of remembering was painful, but on the other side of that pain lived a quiet kind of peace. At times, it felt impossibly far away, blurred behind a fog of longing and uncertainty...but every now and again, it shone clearly—just a glimpse, a brief settling of the mind, an exhalation. It was enough to keep him going.

And when it was all too much and the longing got the better of him, he forced himself to take a break. He paced the warehouse or went outside and walked around the building.

The day passed in a hazy blur. The sun set. The stars came out. Dinner—leftover pie—was eaten under a pale sliver of moon; then the wizards went back to work. Gilbert tried to stay awake in case they needed him but found himself dozing where he sat.

Hour after hour, they toiled, until a second failed attempt threw Mardulo to the floor.

The elderly wizard sat up and dropped his head. "We need rest," he said. They had not slept properly since before sneaking into City Boratorus.

"I cannot think in this state, and we'll be no good to Lady Ufferbub and Toddleposter if we waste the last of our ingredients on failed trials. How many more can we afford?"

Bundersquash looked through the ingredients bag. "If we continue to ration out the nesic oil, and if we fetch a few more cobwebs from the warehouse walls...perhaps three more attempts—meaning two trials, then the real spell."

Mardulo nodded. "Then an hour or two's sleep may be wise. Best to approach this with fresh minds."

"I agree," said Bundersquash.

"Should I keep watch?" asked Gilbert.

"I don't think that's necessary." Mardulo was already seeking out a place to lay down. "The door is locked, and I trust Leepog. Rest. We shall all feel better for it."

With a grateful nod, Gilbert made himself a bed of straw and lay with his notebook in hand, wondering uneasily at their chances. But neither those worries nor the pain in his chest could keep his eyes open long.

He woke to a frantic knocking on the warehouse door.

Chapter 23

Being Fiction

Bang! Bang! Bang!

The hammering grew louder and more aggressive. A voice called from the other side. "Mardulo! Bundersquash! Gilbert! Open up! It's me!"

Gilbert crawled from his makeshift bed, flinching as his shirt grazed the burns on his chest, then went to see what was happening.

"Leepog?" he said, opening the door. It was still dark outside.

"Hello. Where are Mardulo and Bundersquash?"

"Sleeping." Gilbert tried to pull himself together. "What's going on?"

"You were *asleep*?!"

"Yeah. We're exhausted. We haven't slept in days."

Leepog shook his head. "Can you fetch them? We need to talk." He sounded out of breath.

"Sure," said Gilbert. He jogged to the other side of the warehouse and shook the wizards awake.

"I've just received word from Gurming," said Leepog. "He's with Madame Martoonisplau and a few others in City Boratorus. They're doing what they can by way of resistance, and they have news—some good, some bad..." He wavered. "Well, mostly bad when you get right down to it, but Lady Ufferbub and Toddleposter are alive!"

Mardulo, Bundersquash, and Gilbert drew their breath.

"Are they with Gurming?" asked Bundersquash. "Did they escape?!"

"I'm afraid not," said Leepog anxiously. "Hobblebosh has them, and they're being put to death. Today. At dawn. A big spectacle. Making a point. That kind of thing."

Gilbert clenched his fists. "We have to go now. The trapping spell isn't ready, but maybe we could just—"

"We can get it ready." Mardulo stepped forward. "What time is it? Two, maybe three in the morning?"

"Closer to three." Leepog looked at the wizards anxiously. "How 'not ready' are we talking?"

"We have one puzzle left to solve," said Mardulo. "Bundersquash, come. We can do this."

"Right." Bundersquash rolled his shoulders. "For Lady Ufferbub and Toddleposter."

Together, the wizards hurried to their corner and started throwing ideas at one another.

"Listen, Gilbert," Leepog whispered in his ear. "I'm going to get my supplies. If they don't have the spell ready when I get back...well, they'd better have it ready. Let's leave it at that."

"Understood," said Gilbert, and Leepog rushed into the night.

Mardulo and Bundersquash didn't even notice. Their discussion was heating up, each suggestion refuted as quickly as the next one came. Gilbert soon grew concerned. He recognized several of the ideas, things they had already dismissed the day before, revisited now out of sheer desperation.

"What if we only used a partial signature from the essence?" said Mardulo. "How likely is it that someone in the same vicinity will actually share over two-thirds of Hobblebosh's incorporeal structure?"

"I don't know," said Bundersquash. "He's a lime. That could affect things in any number of ways, or not at all. At a guess, one in ten? It depends if there's a crowd. What if, instead, we rescoped our anchor-object abstraction layer? We may not be able to fully generalize them, but by building upon a few assumptions—Hobblebosh will be standing on cobblestones or something—we could restructure that aspect of the spell."

"And if he's standing on pavement? Or wood? Or grass? We just don't know enough about the environment we'll encounter him in."

"Well, we have to sacrifice something! The perfect solution is too involved for lorilell dust! Two lines, Leepog said. We'd need luck just to get it under four."

"How about selecting anchor objects via a fifth-dimensional rewrap into predefined constant material elements?"

"That would take days to prepare...but if we infiltrated an existing ethereal interface, we might be able to preempt its defined procedures and repurpose those known components as our anchors."

"And risk being rebuffed by an actuarial entity? I don't think so."

Bundersquash threw up his right hand and what remained of his left arm. "I knew I should have brought more books. There has to be something we can do..."

Mardulo took a deep breath.

Then Gilbert stepped in. "The problem is with the anchor objects?" he asked hesitantly. "Something about generalizing them?"

"Yes," said Bundersquash. "The spell requires the selection of five anchor objects that surround Hobblebosh. Since we don't know where we'll be when we encounter him, we have to make it flexible enough to handle whatever objects happen to be available at the time."

"Meanwhile," said Mardulo, "to incorporate the essence's signature while keeping the spell under two lines, we've had to overlay a set of simplifications that aren't mixing well with the generalization."

Gilbert looked at the two wizards. "I mean...could we just bring some anchor objects with us? Then you don't have to generalize them at all. You'll know exactly what they are. We'd have to place them around Hobblebosh before casting the spell—or releasing the lorilell dust or whatever—but if that's the only way to get it to work, I'd say it's better than nothing."

Mardulo and Bundersquash blinked at him—once, twice...

"You're a bloody genius, you are," said Mardulo. "Any ideas what to use? Plenty of hay around. But that's too risky, too light. Might blow away. Gryphon toys could work, but they're a bit obvious."

"What about rocks?" Gilbert had seen plenty outside the warehouse.

"Rocks could work," said Bundersquash.

"Quickly!" Mardulo pushed Gilbert out the door. "Go! Fetch five! Bundersquash and I will get everything else prepared."

Gilbert scoured the nearby grass and found several nicely weighted, palm-size stones, then dashed back into the warehouse.

"Lovely," said Mardulo. "With rocks of that size..." he scribbled something on a sheet of parchment. "That should do it!"

Gilbert placed the five stones in a circle around their miniature Hobblebosh figurine. Bundersquash had already prepared a new bowl of ingredients. Mardulo cast the spell.

Instantly, a glowing vein of cobalt energy pulsed through the rocks. The figurine rose into the air, the blue web formed, then the rocks lifted, curling the web upward to form a cage. When they came together at the peak of their arcs, the cage solidified into a hazy azure bubble...and remained.

Mardulo, Bundersquash, and Gilbert stepped back with a collective sigh of relief.

"We've done it!" said Mardulo. "That bubble will isolate Hobblebosh entirely. No sound can escape. Even light is distorted. Any magical links he's created—say, perhaps, forcing his soldiers to obey him—should break. If we can capture Hobblebosh in this, he's done."

Gilbert marveled at the cage. The figurine was still visible but looked strange, almost blurred. It hovered peacefully in the center.

"How do we turn it off?" he asked.

"There is a spell to cancel it, should we need to, but more importantly, there is a spell to move it, so we can transport Hobblebosh without having to free him."

"Now we just have to wait for Leepog," said Bundersquash. "I hope it's not too late…"

They had barely finished setting aside their new batch of ingredients when the salesman reappeared. He was breathing heavily, pushing a rickety cart of beakers and bottles.

"This should be everything," said Leepog. "Is the spell ready?"

"Yes." Gilbert held the door open as Leepog jostled the cart inside.

"Do you think we can make the lorilell dust in time?" asked Mardulo, handing his notes to Leepog.

Leepog looked them over. "I'll work as quickly as I can. I've prepared almost everything in advance. I just have to make a few adjustments…"

He peered into two vials held within a wooden rack. Each contained clear, slowly bubbling liquid. Leepog tipped a little of the left vial's contents into the right, then grabbed a bag of orange flakes and added a pinch to the right vial.

"The ingredients, if you please." He held out one hand, keeping his eyes on the vials. The one with flakes had turned milky white.

Bundersquash carefully balanced the entire ingredient bowl on Leepog's outstretched hand. Leepog raised his eyebrows at it, then placed it on his cart, grabbed the left vial, and poured it in. Immediately, the liquid expanded to fill the bowl, right to the brim. Some of the ingredients floated. Others sank to the bottom.

"Mardulo, when I add the catalyst, please create your auric nebula and cast the spell."

Mardulo nodded, and Leepog dropped a small bead of purple slime into the bowl. On contact, silver steam puffed from the mixture. Mardulo made his nebula, which instantly mingled with the steam. Then he said the words. As he did so, the steam siphoned into the full vial on the right side of the rack, bringing Mardulo's nebula with it. The stones, sitting in a pile on the floor, jostled slightly but did not activate.

The last of the steam funneled into the vial just as Mardulo spoke the final words of the incantation. The ingredient bowl was completely empty. Meanwhile, the vial's contents had thickened and taken on a sapphire sheen.

"Right, then." Leepog brushed his hands. "That will take a few minutes to process."

Gilbert pointed to a separate beaker that sat at the back of the cart. This one was made of tarnished gray metal. "What's that? Do we need it?"

"I'm glad you asked!" said Leepog. "That one's for me. It's a glamour—nice and fresh. I put it together last night."

"Which character is it?"

"My newest creation! It's the one I've been researching all this time—with you three, and Lady Ufferbub and Toddleposter, and even Burrid, as my inspiration. I think it's finally time. She is a noble hero who grew up in the remote hills of Land Turmentarp, but her humble village was burned and pillaged, utterly destroyed by raiders. After years of training and struggle, she took her justice and has since dedicated her life to the protection of the innocent and helpless, and to the betterment of this difficult world."

Leepog took the vial, uncorked it, and drank the contents in a single swig. His whole body stretched. His arms and legs lengthened, then thickened with muscles. His skin remained blue, but his hair blossomed—lengthening as it turned from green to shining silver. It formed a thick braid at his back. Even his clothing changed—from Leepog's turquoise trench coat and orange pants to plated, polished silver armor, engraved with an emblem of a gryphon. On his back—or rather, her back—there hung a deep-red cloak. She stood well over six feet tall.

"Mardulo, Bundersquash, Gilbert." The new character spoke with a clear, resonant voice. "I am excited to introduce you to Pottleswee Plugg Thudigarde the Brave."

Bundersquash jolted. "I...that...brilliant!"

"How delightful!" said Mardulo, eyes alight. Then he paused for a moment. "I'd assumed you'd be a man. Talk about unconscious bias..." He stroked his beard thoughtfully.

"You know," Bundersquash added, "that probably wreaked havoc on our summoning spell, even aside from the wodowood tree mix-up."

Gilbert gaped at Pottleswee. "You're the chosen one."

"What?" said Pottleswee, frowning. "What's gotten into you three?"

"You're Pottleswee Plugg Thudigarde the Brave!" said Mardulo. "Your arrival was foretold in a prophecy!"

"Was it really?" Pottleswee raised an eyebrow. "Fancy that."

"The prophecy also mentioned a flaming sword?" Mardulo tried to avoid looking too expectant.

"Ah. About that...I had *planned* to use a flaming sword, but when I was Thorippela, Gilbert gave me quite the talking-to regarding my potentially excessive use of fire as a problem-solving device, so I changed course...but I did bring this!"

She opened the bottom drawer of Leepog's mobile chemistry set and grabbed a long bundle of fabric. Inside was a plain sword with a slightly rusted blade. It definitely wasn't flaming.

"I've had it for a while," she said. "Technically, it's ceremonial. Blunt as anything, but good for a few solid whacks. I'll do my best not to maim anyone."

Mardulo shrugged. "Well, that's prophecies for you. Never trust 'em, that's what I say. We've still got a decent chance!"

"Is the lorilell dust ready?" Bundersquash peered into the vial. There was nothing left but shimmering blue powder.

Pottleswee swirled it gently, wafted the smell toward her nose, then grinned. "Looks like it!" She grabbed a cork from the countertop and sealed the container shut. "Now, we had best be off. Lady Ufferbub and Toddleposter are counting on us!"

"I'll grab the rocks!" Mardulo raced to pick them up. "Remember, we have to place them around Hobblebosh before we use the lorilell dust."

Gilbert emptied one of the ingredient bags and held it open for Mardulo to place the stones inside. Then he added his journal, buttoned the bag shut, and slung it over his shoulder.

"Please tell me you have another teleport stamp," he said to Pottleswee.

"I'm afraid not. I didn't have time to set one up before coming to meet you, and they have to be prepared at the destination. With magic blocked in City Boratorus, that's not really an option. But I have something almost as good." She fumbled around yet another drawer, shoving aside crucibles, flasks, droppers, and tongs, and pulled out a single copper key. "A remnant from Wilestre's war-rider days. This'll get us into the warrior gryphon stable."

Mardulo's eyes widened. "That's...an interesting plan."

"Plan?" Pottleswee shook her head. "Please understand, I am making this up as I go along. Another trick I learned from you."

"For better or worse," muttered Mardulo.

Gilbert raised his hand. "Um. Are you saying we have to ride gryphons to City Boratorus? Because I don't know how to do that." His mind raced back to the looping, twirling maneuvers he had seen the gryphon riders perform the day before.

"Don't worry. We'll keep it simple. Just hold on tight and trust the gryphon. I will lead. Now hurry!"

The four of them burst from the warehouse and sprinted down the deserted street, Pottleswee in the lead. Gilbert tried his best to keep pace, but with the bag of stones jostling at his side and the pain lingering in his chest, it was a struggle. He was grateful when Bundersquash pulled them to a halt.

"A public execution, you said?"

"Yes." Pottleswee looked at him irritably. "At dawn!"

"That means a crowd. And since we'll be flying in on gryphons, subtlety is out of the question. We need a distraction while we surround Hobblebosh with the stones—enough to keep him busy, but nothing that could harm the bystanders." He looked at the building to his left—the magic shop Wilestre had told them about before. Splendid Spellcraft.

"I'll be right back." Bundersquash tried the door, which was locked, then kicked it down. He and Mardulo raced inside to collect all manner of dusts and powder. When they'd gathered just about all they could carry, Bundersquash tossed an entire bag of gold coins on the counter.

"We can't cast spells while we're there," he said, "but many of these can make quite the show on their own. Silvermist, scintillating colorweb, propagating pseudosparks...they should be enough to stir up a commotion and buy us time." Bundersquash stuffed them into his pockets. "Now, let's be off!"

Adrenaline, more than anything, kept Gilbert moving at pace with Pottleswee. His lungs felt near to bursting. His legs were trembling. But his mind focused on one thing—saving Lady Ufferbub and Toddleposter. He was covered in sweat by the time they reached the tall stone tower of the warrior gryphon stable.

Pottleswee opened the door with her key. Two leather-clad people—gryphon war riders, Gilbert guessed—were playing merchantillia at a table in the center of the room. They looked up, startled.

"Sorry, lads. It's an emergency," said Pottleswee. "We need your four fastest gryphons!"

"Who are you?" The war riders stood and approached her.

"I am Pottleswee Plugg Thudigarde the Brave. As I said, this is an emergency."

"Never heard of you," said the war rider.

"Really? Because apparently, I'm the chosen one." Then she lifted her blunt sword and struck them both on the head. They fell to the floor, unconscious.

She shrugged. "What? We're in a rush. Come, the stairs are this way."

They ran up, spiraling clockwise around the edge of the tower. There were only two levels—the ground level, then the upper level some three hundred feet above. Gilbert staggered his way to the top, clutching his side, barely breathing.

When they arrived, the air hit him like a wall, thick with the barn-like scent of wood and straw. There were windows here, but the view only reinforced how many stairs he'd just climbed. A dozen or so gryphons were sleeping in their nests along the perimeter. A few looked up as the group entered.

"Quickly, pick one that likes you," said Pottleswee, already heading toward one herself.

Gilbert looked around, wondering how to tell if a gryphon liked him. They were large creatures, easily the size of a fully grown horse, and covered in sleek golden feathers. They had pale beaks, massive wings, and sharp, lethal claws.

One of them tilted its head.

Good enough, Gilbert told himself. He held out his hand, and the bird rose to face him. Its legs were strong and steady. Slowly, Gilbert leaned in and stroked the gryphon behind the ears. The gryphon seemed to enjoy it.

"Ready?" asked Pottleswee, once Mardulo and Bundersquash had done much the same as Gilbert. She went around and saddled each of the selected gryphons. Thankfully, the saddle had handles and a sealed pouch. Gilbert placed the stones in the pouch, added his journal, then fastened it shut.

"Not so fast, Gilbert," said Pottleswee. "You'll need this." She handed him the vial of lorilell dust.

"Me?" Gilbert took a step back.

"Yes, you. Mardulo and Bundersquash will be coordinating the distraction with all those things they just stole from Splendid Spellcraft."

"You should do it. You're the chosen one."

"Oh, I'll help." Pottleswee grinned. "I'll be keeping Hobblebosh's guards away from you. Besides, I've already saved your life half a dozen times. I think that's enough chosen-one-ing for me. You know the spell better. You know Hobblebosh better. And you already have the stones in your bag."

Gilbert gulped.

"You can do this," said Pottleswee. "Really."

Nerves twisted in Gilbert's stomach, but there was no time to argue. He clenched his jaw, took the vial, and placed it inside the saddlebag. "All right."

Pottleswee nodded, then dashed toward a metal contraption attached to the wall.

"Oh, dear," she said.

"What is it?" asked Mardulo.

"We need a key to open the roof for takeoff. It's usually left in the lock, but I don't see it...one of the guards downstairs must have it."

Gilbert tensed. They didn't have time for this. He scanned the floor and found what he was looking for—a small pebble and plenty of dried straw.

He arranged them, then rubbed his hands together. The walls were stone, he assured himself. They probably wouldn't burn...

"*Agethermon!*"

As soon as he said the word, he grabbed the stone, already scorching hot, and threw it up at the thatch roof.

"What in the—Gilbert?!" Mardulo nearly tackled him.

"Look!" Gilbert pointed. The stone had hit its mark, and the thatch was already burning, revealing the night sky behind.

Pottleswee frowned at him. "I knew I should've kept that flaming sword..."

But as the flames strengthened, the gryphons got uneasy. One—an unsaddled one, thankfully—stood up and flew the coop. Several others looked ready to follow.

Pottleswee hopped onto hers and called out. "Best be quick! Mount up!"

Gilbert swung himself onto the saddle and got his feet into the stirrups. Ash rained down around him, singeing the sleeves of his shirt. When Pottleswee's gryphon took flight, Gilbert's followed suit. He lurched, holding on for dear life as they burst through flame and smoke into the fresh, open air beyond.

Trust the gryphon, he told himself. That's what Pottleswee had said. Trust the gryphon. He didn't really have a choice.

Soon, after a few nervous exclamations from the wizards, they all fell into line behind Pottleswee. Gilbert didn't know where Town Lunkwargle stood relative to City Boratorus, but they were heading mostly narrowsplatter and moving at a staggering pace. The wind whipped his face and pulled at his hair and clothes. Even squinting, his eyes watered terribly. The air rushed past with a clamorous roar, a constant strain on his ears, and to top it all off, he was freezing. He hunkered down in the saddle and tried, with limited success, to use the gryphon's head as a windshield.

He knew better than to look down.

Up ahead, Pottleswee yelled something inaudible over the rushing wind, then swerved splatterbound. Gilbert's gryphon followed.

They rode on.

Gilbert kept his eyes on the horizon. The shimmer of the Great Splat did little to dim the stars. On any other night, it would have been beautiful, but Gilbert's mind focused solely on the dawn. It hadn't come yet, but it couldn't be far off, and with it came the execution.

A discordant tangle of worries thrashed through his mind. He yearned to arrive as soon as possible, to save Lady Ufferbub and Toddleposter. At the same time, a slow-burning dread gathered in his chest as he thought of the upcoming confrontation. His own reluctance to face Hobblebosh again, and the small vial of lorilell dust sitting in his saddlebag, weighed heavily on his mind.

Yet even as these worries pulled at his attention, they battled against the terrifying onslaught of physical sensation that was flying on the back of a gryphon, hundreds of feet in the air. Gilbert's mind simply couldn't process all of it, and time passed in a strange web of panic and noise.

Dawn arrived.

At first, it was nothing more than a lighter sheen against the darkness on the eastern horizon, but the stars soon faded into a shadowed navy blanket as the sun's rays reached upward at merciless speed. In a matter of minutes, the horizon was alive with near-blinding light. The sky above glowed all shades of pink, purple, and blue.

"I see the city!" Mardulo cried.

Gilbert turned to look—and there it was, just visible along the splatterbound horizon, the sprawling metropolis of City Boratorus. Pottleswee leaned in. The gryphons swooped lower. With the city as a point of reference, the full extent of their speed became horrifyingly clear to Gilbert, and they arrived mere minutes after Mardulo's first sighting—but they didn't land. Instead, Pottleswee drew them down, much closer to the ground, lower even than some of the still-standing structures, and they skimmed above the city walls, heedless of the guards that shouted after them. From there, they raced between buildings, twisting with the turns of the streets below. Gilbert resisted the urge to close his eyes.

Trust the gryphon. Trust the gryphon. Trust the gryphon.

He barely had time to register what was happening before they burst into the open courtyard in front of Lady Ufferbub's library. It was there Hobblebosh had called his assembly, and there he stood on a tall stage among a crowd of hundreds. Lady Ufferbub and Toddleposter knelt at his side, bound mouth, hand, and foot. Hobblebosh was delivering some kind of speech.

A terrible screech sounded behind Gilbert. He turned to see another flying creature bearing down on his location. It wasn't a gryphon. It had black leather skin, bat-like wings, and teeth the size of kitchen knives. Its rider wore Hobblebosh's green and yellow. Even before Gilbert had fully registered the danger, his gryphon swerved to the side to avoid the creature's bite.

Mardulo and Bundersquash let loose a battle cry and, reaching into their saddlebags, threw pouch after pouch of magical powder, raining chaos over the crowd.

Gilbert's world dissolved into mayhem. Clouds of rainbow smoke shot through the air, filled with glowing confetti. Cold sparks of light poured from the sky and multiplied with every point of contact. Tendrils of heavy steam rose up from the ground, clinging to feet and legs. Before long, the very air of the courtyard was opaque with color and dust. The crowd was screaming, yelling. No one knew what was happening.

Then the horrible screech sounded again, and another bat-like creature swooped down at Gilbert—but a golden blur of feathers sped upward in front of him and intercepted it.

Pottleswee.

She gave Gilbert a quick nod, then engaged Hobblebosh's bat rider, sword against sword, pulling the fight away.

Gilbert took a deep breath. He had a job to do. The air was filled with shimmering fluorescent smoke, but somewhere down there was the stage—and Hobblebosh. The lime had gone disconcertingly quiet. Gilbert pushed his gryphon lower, peering through the mist, and dismounted in the middle of the crowd.

He grabbed the lorilell dust and stones from his saddle as he scanned the area. He'd never felt so disoriented. Smoke and steam filled his lungs. His eyes burned from the dust. But a quick gap in the haze showed him what he needed—the stage. Without wasting a moment, he charged, wrestling the crowd to either side.

The platform rose to shoulder height. Gilbert pocketed the lorilell dust, carefully placed the bag of stones on the wooden platform, and hauled himself up.

He took a breath. He could do this.

Except he could barely see his own two hands, let alone Hobblebosh. How was he supposed to place the stones in a ring around a person he couldn't see?

And why was Hobblebosh so quiet?

Blindly, Gilbert stumbled forward...and nearly tripped over Lady Ufferbub.

The librarian's eyes widened. Her glasses were askew. She was still bound, but she'd fallen to one side. Gilbert shushed her and tried to untie her ropes. She jostled him away. Her eyes said it all. *Focus on Hobblebosh.*

Gilbert nodded. She was right. If he captured Hobblebosh, there would be plenty of time to untie Lady Ufferbub and Toddleposter later.

He thought for a moment. If Lady Ufferbub was here, then—judging from what he'd seen before the chaos started—Hobblebosh should be just ahead and a little to the right.

And there he was, a shadow in the fog. He looked like he was kneeling, pulling something out of a trapdoor in the stage.

Ingredients, perhaps?

Gilbert didn't wait to find out. He had what he needed. He placed the first stone, then ran and placed the second. After a few more paces, keeping the circle tight, he placed the third.

Only two to go.

Then, at last, Hobblebosh spoke. The tyrant's voice boomed across the courtyard, silencing the crowd in an instant. *"Alvekerin tolmoria talkiternam—"*

Gilbert didn't have time to think about it. He kept running. Fourth stone, dropped. A few more paces. Finish the circle.

Fifth stone.

Dropped.

He fumbled inside his pocket for the lorilell dust. His hands wouldn't stop shaking. He grabbed it. He pulled it out. He removed the cork...

"—lannderikal verikin makoria!"

Hobblebosh finished his spell. With a resounding rush of air, the smoke, fog, and dust drained away from the courtyard. Somewhere behind Gilbert, Bundersquash screamed. The crowd cried out, but a heartbeat later, all noise strangled to a halt. Everything was clear. Everyone was still. The entire courtyard was frozen in place.

Gilbert couldn't move.

The uncorked vial of lorilell dust was still in his hand, tipped at an angle, barely a degree away from spilling—but unspilt, nonetheless.

His heart sank. He had been so close.

Hobblebosh looked directly at him, his lime-green eyes filled with rage, malice, and the sinister glint of victory.

"Gilbert Betters, we meet again." The tyrant took a deep breath, savoring the moment, then turned toward the immobile crowd. "All of you here," he said, "take note. This boy has tried, time and time again, to rob me of my throne. He has tried, time and time again, to end my rule. And time and time again, he has failed."

Gilbert paid no attention. The stones were still in place. The lorilell dust was *this close* to spilling. If he could just move his hand, just an inch, maybe less, it would all be over. He put every ounce of his energy into it.

Hobblebosh continued his monologue. "But his failure is not surprising. He is small. He is insignificant. He is barely even real. A paper boy, fiction gone too far. It is time I made him understand that." Hobblebosh turned back to Gilbert, grinning. "You play at being real, Gilbert. You act as if you have value. But here, in reality, you are empty. Even your hollow shell of a home I have destroyed. Tell them how it feels, Gilbert. Tell them how it feels, being fiction, knowing there is nothing left to your name. Not even a story."

Just tilt your hand! Gilbert scolded himself. *Just...move!*

"Tell them!" Hobblebosh's voice boomed.

Gilbert clenched his jaw, then realized with a start, he had really clenched his jaw. His mouth had moved. It was the only part of him that could. Hobblebosh actually wanted him to speak.

Fine. Every moment Hobblebosh wasn't casting a spell was another chance for Gilbert to break free. He could stall if he had to.

"It feels..." Gilbert said, his jaw working for every word. "It feels..."

"Louder, Gilbert. For the audience." Hobblebosh beamed a mocking smile in his direction.

"It feels," said Gilbert, with volume, "like you're an asshole."

That took Hobblebosh by surprise. For one frantic moment, Gilbert felt as though he could move again. Almost. But as quickly as it came, it went, and Gilbert was stuck once more.

"You dare speak treason to my face?!" Hobblebosh roared. "So be it. I have already destroyed everything you hold dear. Now I shall—"

"No." Gilbert interrupted him. He didn't have a plan, but he needed time, and Hobblebosh looked dangerously close to wrapping things up. If his mouth was the only thing he could use, he would use it. "You haven't destroyed everything I hold dear. Maybe I am just some kid from Nebraska. And yes, you destroyed that world. But I have friends here too. I have—" and he might have said more, but something wholly unexpected hijacked his attention.

A tree.

A moving tree.

A *charging* tree, in fact.

A Tree, careening down the street in an absolute fury of twigs, leaves, and branches.

Something of Gilbert's surprise must have shown on his otherwise paralyzed face, because Hobblebosh turned just in time to witness the storm of branches bearing down upon him with clear intent to pulverize.

The lime acted quickly, instinctively. He threw up his arms and shouted a few magic words. The tree froze midswing—but with Hobblebosh's attention turned away, Gilbert found his own magical bindings suddenly loosened. His arm, once completely still, now shook with the effort he was exerting.

Progress.

He focused.

Hobblebosh sensed the threat. He turned back to Gilbert, extending one hand while leaving the other pointed at Tree. Gilbert's bonds tightened once again, though they were still weaker than before. Gilbert pressed against them, put everything he had into the effort, and slowly, his hand started to tip.

Tree rammed closer, their branches inches above the lime's head. Hobblebosh backed away, tried to reinforce his spell...and spread himself too thin.

All at once, Gilbert's bonds snapped. His hand didn't just tilt—it lurched forward, and he threw the vial of lorilell dust toward Hobblebosh.

The glass shattered as it struck the stage, then the five stones started to glow, shining cobalt blue.

Hobblebosh growled. Ignoring Tree entirely, he charged at Gilbert, but even as he did so, the trapping spell lifted him off his feet. A blue web of energy formed beneath him, and the stones rose into the air. Hobblebosh's eyes flared. He rubbed his hands together to cast another spell, but the cage formed before he could finish, and his auric nebula fizzled into nothing.

For a few moments, Hobblebosh raged inside the bubble, his shouts silenced by the boundary, but he soon realized his own powerlessness and resolved to a calm, simmering quiet. His eyes spoke threats. Gilbert ignored them.

Hobblebosh had been defeated.

The whole courtyard could move again. Suddenly remembering Bundersquash's scream from earlier, Gilbert turned to see what had happened and was relieved to find the young wizard dangling from his gryphon, one foot tangled in a stirrup, using his good arm to hold an exceptionally grateful Mardulo, who had fallen clean off his own gryphon and nearly dropped to his death. Gradually, Bundersquash's gryphon lowered them both to the ground.

Bundersquash untangled himself, then got up and brushed the dust from his robe. Looking toward the stage, he smiled at Gilbert. Mardulo gave an eager thumbs-up.

Pottleswee hopped onto the platform and untied Lady Ufferbub and Toddleposter. Then, after a few confused glances, began the somewhat lengthy explanation of her existence.

In the courtyard, the crowd slowly figured out how to behave. Some had cheered the moment they were free, but others were cautiously eyeing Hobblebosh's guards—many of whom had lain down their weapons, confused and disoriented. Others were trying their best to appear inconspicuous. Gilbert suspected several had already run away.

Then there was the matter of the tree. Gilbert felt he ought to thank it, but when he turned to do so, it had already gone. He scratched his head. It was strange, but somehow, that tree had looked familiar...

He shrugged. It had been a long day. He probably wasn't thinking straight.

He lay down on the stage and listened as the crowd's muddled confusion morphed into a cautious celebration. A wave of relief and exhaustion lifted the weight from his chest.

Somehow, they'd succeeded. There were a thousand ways it could have gone wrong, a thousand ways it *should* have gone wrong, but it hadn't. The possibilities no longer mattered.

They'd won.

Gilbert lay there, staring at the sky, listening to the cheers of the crowd, and breathed.

Interlude: Tree and the Gift of Freedom

Shuffling and unsteady, Tree left City Boratorus. They'd lost track of the days since they'd entered.

It had been easy to eliminate the guards Hobblebosh had posted near the forest on the hill outside the city—a matter of timing and decisive action. Sneaking into the city had been harder, but staying hidden once inside had been the greatest challenge. The parks and gardens were largely destroyed. Little more than grass remained.

Dogwood the Wind-Dancer was dead.

To stay hidden, Tree had needed to keep moving, always forced to remain among the shadows despite their constant longing for the sun's nourishment. Each day was more difficult than the last—dark and lonely, the hardest Tree had ever faced, but they'd faced them. Day after day, they had watched the tyrant, waiting for a moment to strike, but Hobblebosh was careful. He almost never let his guard down.

Then, as Tree stood on the outskirts of the library's plaza, dreading yet another public execution, it had finally happened.

The young boy, Gilbert, had come again and caught Hobblebosh by surprise. Sudden flares of smoke and color blazed through the plaza. In an attempt to regain control of the situation, the tyrant overextended himself, and Tree knew there would be no better chance—so they attacked.

And now it was finished. Hobblebosh was captured.

There was only one thing left to do.

Tree limped through the meadows to the north of the city. Several of their roots had been damaged, and Tree doubted they would ever truly heal, but slowly, slowly, they climbed the hill where the other trees stood, as motionless they'd been when Tree had left them.

"My friends," Tree said to them all, "it is done."

The trees roused, as if from a long sleep. "Tree? You have returned? You succeeded?!" Word picked up slowly but gathered momentum as more trees heard the news.

"Yes," said Tree, trying to keep their own exhaustion from polluting the forest's excitement. "Hobblebosh has been defeated."

"This is the best news we've had in many days!" said Folia. "We are happy for you. And now you are free, as you have always wished, to move and explore the world. We regret only that we cannot join you on the journey."

"That is the problem," said Tree, branches wilting. "This would be no victory if I left you all stranded on this hill. It is my fault you came here in the first place. It is my fault you left your home, your forest. And it is my duty to set things right."

"None of us blames you, Tree. You did what you could. There is nothing more to be done. Without Hobblebosh's magic, we have no choice but to remain. We were still once. In time, we shall find peace with it again."

"I do not accept that," said Tree. "The magic that unlocked your move-ment—Hobblebosh used me to craft it, my own bark. It was his spell, but my essence, that allowed you to move, and though I do not have his magic, I am still me. Perhaps there is a way...at the very least, I must try, though I know not if it will work."

The forest stood, silent and unsure, as Tree wove toward the center. This was it. Tree paused, feeling the sun's light on their leaves, the softness of the soil around their roots, reflecting. Here they were once again, a tree atop a hill, not unlike how they'd started. But they belonged to a family now. A family that needed them. Tree would give everything to this forest. Hopefully, it would be enough.

Because no matter how familiar it felt, this was not the start. It was the end.

Tree plunged their roots deep into the soil, spread their leaves and branches wide, then sought out the forest's web of awareness—that same beautiful, life-filled force they'd felt back in Northern Tillman's End, uniting every tree and plant and creature there. Now Tree felt it again, connecting everyone here.

Tree released themselves to it. Everything that made them Tree, they funneled into that interconnected life force. Every thought. Every wish. Every dream. Tree gave themselves to it completely.

They could feel the other trees with them, each reacting in their own unique way. Surprise and shock. Acceptance. Rejection. Confusion, uncertainty, understanding. A hundred trees, a hundred voices, a hundred thoughts at once, and Tree was with them all. The very world shimmered into a weave of thought and feeling as Tree's essence dispersed among that shared, connected consciousness.

And with their essence scattered, Tree's own sense of self dwindled. Their trunk settled in place. Their roots slackened, deep underground. Their branches drooped, softly, silently. Gradually, the shell of their body emptied, and what little remained of Tree said goodbye to the world around them—to the sun, to the soil, to their forest of friends, and last of all, to themselves.

But then, something changed.

Just as Tree's final sliver of self faded into the forest, the forest pushed something back. A little energy. A little life. A spark of Tree's individuality returned.

"You give much to the forest." Folia's voice echoed through Tree's hollow mind. "The forest gives back, in turn. Accept it, Tree. You need not surrender everything. As you said once before—together, as one, we are mighty. One forest, many voices. One of those voices is yours."

Tree became aware of a new life filling their limbs. They knew themselves again, but knew more of the others too. They were Tree, but where once they had been little more than an observer, they were now a full part of this forest, this family. They floated upon that shared support, knowing each of the trees better than one would know even their closest friends, and each of them knowing Tree as fully.

Eventually, Tree's awareness regrounded and returned to their own bark, their own roots, their own leaves.

They were Tree again.

"Thank you...all of you," Tree said after a time. "I do not know what to say."

"You need not say anything," Folia assured them. "We are happy to have you with us, Tree the Dreamer. And it may please you to know, your gambit appears to have worked."

Suddenly, to Tree's utmost delight and surprise, the whole forest rippled like the wind. Leaves shook on swaying branches. Roots lifted and twirled. Not knowing what would happen, Tree moved a root of their own and found that it lifted with ease. The forest danced around them.

"At last, we are free." Folia moved to Tree's side. "The world is open. Where would you like to go?"

Tree looked to the horizon, to the Great Splat and beyond. Their mind raced with possibilities.

"With so many wonders to see, how could I possibly choose?" Tree thought once again of mountains and oceans, of rivers and fields, of forests and islands and waterfalls, then they turned to their friends and said, "We'll just have to visit them all."

Chapter 24

Looking Forward

While the city celebrated and the citizens transitioned from the war against the lime to a more amenable war against their livers and eardrums, Mardulo, Bundersquash, Lady Ufferbub, Toddleposter, Pottleswee, and Gilbert all retreated to the relative peace of the library. Hobblebosh had never managed to break in, apparently, much to Lady Ufferbub's pleasure.

"This library has more than a few tricks up her sleeve," she said with a grin. "It seems they never even made it past the outer shielding."

She led everyone to a comfortable community room, and there, they enjoyed a celebration of their own, with tea, biscuits, and stories.

Privately, Gilbert flipped through his journal, wondering what his friends on Earth would've thought about all this and if his parents would have been proud.

Lady Ufferbub sat beside him. "Mardulo told me what happened to *A World of Souls*," she said. "I am sorry. I cannot even imagine how you must feel."

Gilbert bit his lip. "I'll miss them," he said quietly, "but I have my memories. My family, my past—real or fiction, they've shaped me, and they're a part of me. I won't forget them. But I think it's time for me to make a home in this world too."

"I am glad to hear that." Lady Ufferbub put a hand on his shoulder. "I am here to help, however I can. We all are."

"I know. Thanks."

"And for what it is worth," she added, "I read a fair amount of that book. I am happy to serve as a reference if you ever need help with your journal."

"That'd be great," said Gilbert, and he meant it.

The day passed easily. They joked, relaxed, and enjoyed their tea and biscuits. Pottleswee spoke of her adventures as various characters around the world. Then Toddleposter produced a collection of games. Mardulo beat everyone at merchantillia. Lady Ufferbub beat everyone at chess.

It was well into the evening when a messenger came knocking. Lady Ufferbub let him into the library. He was only a child, maybe nine or ten years old, and he stared up at everyone, equal parts excited and nervous.

"I've been sent by the City Boratorus Council of Five," he said. "They are eager to meet with those who saved our city and have requested your presence at their chamber."

"Not those buffoons again," said Mardulo. He sighed, ignoring the messenger's shocked expression. "I suppose we'd best get it over with."

"They will be ready as soon as you arrive," said the boy, still trying to sound cheerful.

Mardulo thanked him, tipped him, and shooed him out the door. After fetching a few of their belongings, everyone left together.

"What do you think they'll do with Hobblebosh?" Gilbert asked as they walked. The streets were quiet. Most of the parades had moved to other areas of the city.

"Oh, there'll be a big to-do," said Mardulo. "He'll be tried before the High Order of Deciders. They will assess the evidence and presumably find him guilty. From there...well, that's for the Deciders to decide. I expect it'll be something unpleasant. Politicians do not like being usurped."

"More than likely, they will turn him back into a lime and have done with it," said Lady Ufferbub. "Pretend the whole thing never happened."

"I'm inclined to agree," said Bundersquash. "They'll want to get past all this, onto the Next Big Thing. I hear Great Port Opperwob has had an unusually high volume of spirit whale sightings this year."

"And apparently a new forest has just appeared splatterbound of the city," said Toddleposter. "That'll warrant some looking into, I expect."

Mardulo stroked his beard thoughtfully. "Vegetation these days…"

"So, everyone moves on," said Gilbert. "I suppose it's the best we could hope for."

At the council chambers, a City Boratorus guard ushered everyone inside. The building was clean, but Hobblebosh had clearly redecorated. Pale-green pendants hung from the ceiling, the curtains alternated green and yellow, and the paintings had all been replaced with portraits of Obble Dor Hobblebosh. A green carpet guided the group to a formal conference room, where they seated themselves and waited.

The council members appeared moments later.

"We are so grateful you could make it," said the first. "I am Chief Executive Councilman Sunkyburger. These are my associates, Executive Councilman Pup, Councilman Belligorm, Acting People's Representative Hildinverk, and Commander Ospoggle. To those of you we have not met, it is a pleasure to make your acquaintance. To Mardulo and Lady Ufferbub, your company is ever valued."

When everyone had settled in, Acting People's Representative Hildinverk took over. "We know you are busy," she said, "so we shall keep this quick. It has been agreed that you deserve our respect."

There was a pause, and because Gilbert felt uncomfortable, he said, "Thanks."

"You are welcome," said Hildinverk. "We have also decided that, given the significant global ramifications of these events, it is time to usher in a new age. As of today, the Age of the Empty Box has ended, and it is with extreme excitement that I welcome you all to the Age of the Soggy Banana."

Pottleswee coughed. Lady Ufferbub raised her eyebrows. Bundersquash and Toddleposter looked at one another. Mardulo rolled his eyes.

"Thanks," said Gilbert again.

"You are welcome," said Hildinverk. "It may also interest you to know that Town Lunkwargle has been in contact regarding the burning of a certain gryphon stable rooftop. They are not thrilled at the damage but, given the circumstances and the fact that no humans or gryphons were hurt, they have kindly agreed to waive all charges. They do ask, however, that we ensure there will be no repeat occurrences."

"Er, yeah," said Gilbert. "Sorry. It won't happen again..."

"Many thanks." Hildinverk nodded at Gilbert. "Now, we have one final matter to address. As you may know, Hobblebosh seized this very building to serve as his personal palace. Many of his treasures remain in our halls. One in particular we thought might interest you."

On Hildinverk's signal, a guard entered the room carrying a golden cage. Inside, a vibrant blue butterfly looked out at them.

"Lobster!" Bundersquash leaped from his seat, hugged the guard, then hugged the cage. "You're alive!" he said, opening the hatch. Lobster fluttered out, twirled through the air, and landed atop his shoulder.

"She was among Hobblebosh's personal effects. From what we've heard, the lime was quite fond of her, though she gave him a hard time more often than not."

"Of course she did. She's a good girl!" Bundersquash faced her, a tear rolling down his cheek. "The very best."

He sniffed loudly. Lobster fetched him a tissue.

"And that's just about all we have," said Hildinverk. "Many thanks for your service. We are honored to call you our citizens. Goodbye."

The councilmembers shook everyone's hands, then led Gilbert and the others outside.

"So...what now?" asked Gilbert. They stood in a ring by the building's exit.

"I'd best be off," said Pottleswee. "There's still a lot to do, and I'm eager to spend time as Pottleswee Plugg Thudigarde the Brave. We captured Hobblebosh, but some people will remain loyal to his cause. Rounding them up, I think, shall be my next calling."

"Do you need help?" asked Toddleposter.

"Certainly, I will. But for now, City Boratorus needs you more than I do. There's a lot of rebuilding ahead, and though Pottleswee may not have much stake in it, I'm sure Leepog would be glad to know that you five are here to facilitate."

"We will do all we can," said Lady Ufferbub. "And it will be a comfort to know that you are out there, watching over those who need it."

"If I may," said Toddleposter, "you might consider a visit to Forest Plawg. Hobblebosh had some mines out there. We've heard they're using forced labor. Perhaps you could ensure those operations cease?"

"I shall make it a priority." Pottleswee took a deep breath. "I hope our paths cross again, and soon. But I expect to be in this form for quite some time. If anyone asks about my other characters, please tell them whatever you like. Just make it a good story."

She winked and, after one final glance at her friends, strode confidently into the city.

"On that note," said Lady Ufferbub, "I suppose Toddleposter and I should return to the library."

"Indeed!" Toddleposter grinned. "While imprisoned, we worked out a new system for organizing large-scale book collections. It's based on Tikkerton's Theory of Sorted Pairs. I'm looking forward to trying it."

"I hope it goes well," said Mardulo. "Will we see you tomorrow?"

"I certainly expect so," said Lady Ufferbub, mocking sternness. "You are behind schedule on your other areas of research. We shall put a few books aside for you."

"Many thanks," said Mardulo. The others waved goodbye as the two librarians left side by side.

Mardulo turned to face Gilbert and Bundersquash. "I propose dinner," he said. "Perhaps a picnic, back in the old Wizards' Tower park?"

"What a wonderful idea," said Bundersquash.

The Wizards' Tower was little more than a blackened pile of rubble now, but the park was pleasant enough. The three of them sat together in the soft grass while Lobster helped herself to some nearby flowers. Mardulo passed around the sandwich generator, and for several minutes, they sat in silence, breathing the fresh air and enjoying the peace.

Eventually, Mardulo spoke.

"Bundersquash," he said softly, hesitantly. "I know there is a lot of rebuilding to do, and I'm sure we'll all be busy, but once it's done...well, I would be honored if you would join me back at the university. Not as a pupil. As a colleague. An equal."

Bundersquash looked back at the rubble of the Wizards' Tower and the sky where it used to rise. For a time, he said nothing. Then: "It's a kind offer, Mardulo. I am grateful, truly. But I think it's time for me to move on. I'd like to try something new. Madame Martoonisplau was always asking me to join the Wizarding Consortium. Perhaps I will give that a try. I find myself suddenly motivated to examine alternate methods of auric nebula creation."

Mardulo looked at him, smiling despite the tear in his eye. "I understand. And I have no doubt you will do well." He took a heavy breath. "With that in mind, I would like to say, quite simply, that it has been a privilege to serve as your professor. You are the best student I have ever taught, and I am proud of you."

He extended a hand. Bundersquash took it, then closed the gap and hugged him. When the two let go, Bundersquash sniffed. "I'll be sure to drop by often, and I'm always happy to join you in the library for research."

"I'm counting on it," said Mardulo. "Meanwhile"—he turned to Gilbert—"it would appear a spot has just opened up. What do you say, Gilbert? Want to learn magic—properly, this time?"

Gilbert raised his eyebrows. "You're willing to have me? After everything in Town Forbik?"

"Of course! You seemed eager enough before, and now we'll have an actual classroom to work with! And more than a week to do it!"

A bubble of excitement rose in Gilbert's chest. "It sounds great. It really does." Then he grinned. "Maybe I can teach you some science in return. We never did finish that conversation on electricity."

Mardulo laughed. "I'm always happy to learn."

"It's settled, then," said Gilbert. "Many thanks, Mardulo," and again, because that didn't feel like enough, "Thank you."

They finished their dinner in the park that evening and stayed well into the night. For the first time in a long while, Gilbert felt at home. He stared at the stars and the clouds, dreaming of days to come—of learning and teaching, of spending time with his friends, of making a life in the real world. There was a lot to do, and he was looking forward to it.

He would tell his own story now.

The End

Acknowledgements

Writing a book, it turns out, is very difficult. By myself, I wouldn't have gotten far. However, a huge part of the joy in this project has been working alongside the many wonderful people who have helped shape it into something I could never have accomplished on my own. Any attempt to list them all and portray the full extent of their contributions would be futile, but that won't stop me from trying.

First and foremost, a big thank you to my family—such a positive and stalwart net of support. Several of you suffered through the entirety of this book in its initial draft, and that was no small feat. Your feedback and kindness during that time is what kept me eager, motivated, and determined to stick with writing. Without you, I'm quite certain this story would still be sitting as an unfinished Word doc tucked away on some old computer, totally lost to time. Special callouts are due to Rebecca, for the beautiful map at the front of this book, and to Jenny, for all of your help with my digital artwork and design.

A huge thanks also to Nicole. I could not have asked for a kinder, sweeter, more generous person to have by my side as I wrote the bulk of this book. You read the story early on and provided clear, considerate, and thoughtful feedback throughout. You supported me through countless long and tiresome hours of revisions and re-writes, and you continued to believe in me and this story, even when I couldn't find it in myself to do the same. I will always be grateful for your unwavering patience and support throughout the many years it took to pull this novel together.

Next up, Nick. If there's one other person whose name should be listed on the cover, it's you. There was a time when I tried to keep track of all the ways your detailed, engaged, and honest feedback shaped the story—but at some point, I simply gave up. You've influenced almost every aspect of this book. You were one of my very first readers, well before I'd even finished the first draft. I still remember sitting in a college dorm cringing at my own words as you read them aloud—but you laughed when I'd hoped you would, and that kept me going. Then years later, through our numerous hours-long video calls, you helped me solidify character arcs and story ideas, fill in plot holes, and iron out many (*many*) pacing issues. You helped me navigate all sorts of narrative conundrums that I couldn't wrap my head around, and you pointed out several more I wouldn't have noticed myself. But most of all, you stuck with it from beginning to end. Your feedback helped me improve as a writer and a storyteller, and I'm forever grateful for your support.

My Writers' Group also deserves a great deal of thanks: Katy, Daniel, Steve, and Homer. I have no idea how you made any sense of this story told in piecemeal increments every-other-ish week as the story shifted constantly underneath your feet. It took literal years, but you did it, and the insight and wisdom in your feedback cannot be overstated. You've helped me think more deeply and critically about my own writing, and I've learned so much from every one of you.

Tracy also deserves a shoutout. Your patience and honesty as you read through the story, as well as your thoughtful discussions afterwards, helped me see the book from a new perspective. Your feedback saved me from publishing more than a few blunders, and your support and curiosity were always encouraging.

Thank you also to Pauline Harris. You were one of the first strangers I ever trusted with this story, and your honest critique was rich with knowledge and thought. The skill with which you can simultaneously offer critical advice and friendly encouragement is truly mind-boggling.

Now to Hannah VanVels Ausbury and Stephanie Chou, my two amazing editors. I could never thank you enough. If you're an author reading these acknowledgements in the hopes of finding people to work with, consider this my official recommendation. Not only are they wonderful human beings, they are also phenomenal editors. All of the flaws in this book are mine, not theirs.

Hannah, you took a book I'd been struggling with for over seven years and, through your feedback, made me feel enthusiastic again. You saw beyond the rambling, overwritten text I sent you and helped me transform it into a story to be proud of. I cannot thank you enough.

Stephanie, you made the proofreading process an absolute joy. Through your detailed feedback, impressively thorough knowledge, and tremendous support, you polished this book well beyond my own capabilities. I am so grateful for your patience and kindness as you guided me through a process that I had no idea how to navigate on my own.

To the artists over at Ebook Launch, thank you for this beautiful cover. I expect I was a real pain to work with, but you managed it nonetheless, and I'm incredibly pleased with what you created. Thank you!

And of course, to my cats: Ludwig, Arwen, and Belle. They didn't really help with this book, but I'd be remiss if I didn't mention them anyway. That's life with cats, for you.

And to all the others I've forgotten to mention, and to those who have opted to remain unnamed, just know that I appreciate you all the same. This book has been such a massive part of my life...every person who has supported it has supported me, and vice versa. I'm so lucky to be surrounded by this incredible community of patient, kind, and compassionate people.

Thank you, all of you!